I0658502

'86 Love Affair

80s Love Affairs, Volume 2

Joshua Fields

Published by Joshua Fields, 2023.

'86 LOVE AFFAIR

First edition. August 1, 2023.

Copyright © 2023 Joshua Fields.

ISBN: 979-8986504032

Written by Joshua Fields.

Table of Contents

These Dreams

Elliott Warden sat on the bar stool reserved for him by his sister, Emma Hastings, the proprietor of Johnny Dubs. The bar-turned-club once again hosted its most famous band, Morning Cloak, a country quartet led by singer and guitarist Toni Cullen.

"What the hell is she wearing?" Elliott asked aloud. The tall, leggy Toni, with her brown, boyishly short hair, wore an uncharacteristically ostentatious country outfit. Its white blouse had a plunging neckline and was ribbed with gold chains of shiny fabric while its tight, sparkling pants were solid gold in color and possessed matching tassels running down their hems. She also wore gold, four-inch heels. Suddenly cognizant that Toni lingered in a bizarre trance, Elliott said, "Something's wrong."

Elliott noticed that Toni's makeup was far too brazen for the downhome girl next door. Her lipstick and eyeshadow were gold and glittery.

"Toni!" Elliott beckoned. She sat on a wooden stool and remained motionless. Toni did not have her guitar but instead held a microphone that rested atop her right thigh. Sliding off the bar stool, Elliott attempted to approach her and repeatedly called, "Toni!"

Toni did not move or acknowledge Elliott. Maneuvering through tables and chairs, he eventually arrived on the dance floor. A stream of unending patrons flowed past him and, despite his desperate efforts, hindered his progress towards Toni. After what seemed an eternity, Elliott arrived in front of her, he on the dance floor and she above him on the stage.

"Toni!" Elliott shouted. She started and looked to Elliott in puzzlement. An initial glimmer of recognition exploded into a vibrant smile.

"*Elliott,*" Toni greeted him melodically.

"You never told me why you call it Morning Cloak," Elliott said to Toni. He surprised himself with the inquiry as he had never once pondered the origin of the band's name.

"Call what Morning Cloak?" queried Toni as if genuinely ignorant of her band's name.

"*Your band,*" Elliott replied. The glimmer of recognition returned followed again by the beaming grin.

"Do you really wanna know?" asked Toni coyly.

"*Yeah*," Elliott replied emphatically.

A stage light flashed in Elliott's eyes and he averted them. When he returned his gaze to the stool, Toni was gone. The light blinded him again and, when he recovered his sight, it was now her fiancée Bobby sitting on the stool. He launched himself from it with a horrid scowl and hurled a fist at Elliott's face.

. . . .

THE DISTANT "POP" OF a gunshot jolted Elliott from sleep. He attempted to rise from his bed but realized someone clung to him and prevented him from escape. Glancing down, Elliott saw that Nora held him tightly despite being ensconced in slumber.

"Oh, yeah," Elliott thought, "this happened."

Two more "pops" echoed in the distance. A frustrated Elliott sighed.

"Damn Taylor-tuckians," Elliott whispered in complaint, "always shootin' their damn guns on New Year's Eve."

Elliott relaxed his body and laid back down. All he remembered of his dream was Toni's presence in it. His guilt burgeoned and he felt as if he was unfaithful to both Toni and Nora. He repressed it.

"She was never yours," Elliott reasoned as he saw Toni in his mind. Surrendering her with considerable angst, he looked on Nora's comely face and said, "And she wasn't yours until now."

Elliott's pain eased when he wrapped an affectionate arm around Nora's shoulders. The twenty-three-year-old stirred slightly, readjusted her grip on him and cuddled into his body.

Remembrances trickled into Elliott's mind: Nora's adorable face peeking out from behind the white shower curtain, the endless moment in time before their naked bodies pressed into one another and the way she began gently lathering his chest. She meticulously and lovingly washed away the grime and odor from his body and his spirit. Elliott shivered.

"Helluva way to start 1986," Elliott said to himself as the fresh memories of their tryst percolated in his head. Though not a virgin, Nora was deferential and her lovemaking was timid. Elliott recognized her inexperience and, while leading their sexual dance, he remained tender and gentle. Disentangling from his regenerating libido, he admonished himself, "Just let 'er sleep."

Elliott remembered the moment Nora began disrobing. *Sans* clothing, she led him upstairs to his bedroom but, to his surprise, he could not look at her nakedness. Elliott instead stood in the bedroom doorway as Nora proceeded to the telephone, sat on the bed facing away from him and dialed a number.

"Luke, it's Nora," Nora said bluntly. She glanced over her shoulder at Elliott and then instructed Luke firmly, "Get Emma."

From his vantage point in the doorway, Elliott could only see Nora's bare, slender back as she spoke on the telephone. Her body sank low enough on the mattress that the messy covers concealed her buttocks. Elliott heard Emma's voice as if she stood in the room.

"Is he okay?" blurted Emma. The commotion of New Year's Eve preparations at Johnny Dubs traveled on the heels of her words.

"He's in pretty rough shape," Nora said gravely. She glanced at Elliott again and gave him a muted grin, declaring with burgeoning hope, "But he's gonna be just fine."

"I'm coming over there," insisted Emma.

"I got it, Em," Nora replied confidently. Heartened by her rally to his aid, Elliott smiled as she asserted, "I'm gonna stay with him tonight."

"Nora, I-," began Emma with skepticism.

"I'm gonna stay with him as long as he needs me to," Nora interrupted her. Emma paused.

"Are you sure that's a good idea?" asked Emma in a hushed tone.

"Do you have a better one?" Nora countered astutely. Emma paused again.

"Take care of my big brother," pleaded Emma with a disjointed inhale that signaled her worry. Elliott, as sleep overcame him, heard Nora's final words in his head.

"I will," Nora confirmed. She added resolutely, "Remember, *I'm one of you now.*"

• • • •

PASSING LIKE THE PROVERBIAL ships in the night, Elliott drifted into sleep while Nora emerged from it. Her head lay on his chest; she lifted it briefly, confirmed that Elliott slept and again rested it on him. Nora heard each beat of his heart and felt his warm breath tussling her hair. The rhythm nudged her back to sleep and into a dream.

"Where am I?" Nora asked as her consciousness faded and the dream became her reality. She found herself on Bart's parents' boat with the motor burbling in the water and the watercraft slowly moving forward. The sun rose in the East but struggled to penetrate the heavy fog.

"Bart?" Nora said when she glanced to her right. Her former boyfriend sat emotionless in the passenger seat while she stood in front of the captain's chair and steered the boat. Nora panicked and implored him, "Bart! Help me!"

Bart ignored her, the young man seemingly in a trance. She maintained her grip on the wheel despite her trembling hands.

"Bart! *Please!* Help me!" Nora yelled. She scanned the fog with her eyes but could discern nothing, begging, "I can't see anything out here. What do I do?!"

Bart remained inert and mute. Nora looked anxiously around her and, noticing the shifting levers, she attempted to pull back on the throttle. The motor idled but the boat continued to move forward. Nora shifted it into full reverse but nothing happened.

"You have to go forward," droned Bart as the boat continued in that direction and sliced through the fog.

"What?" Nora asked. Anxiety-ridden, she demanded, "Why, Bart? Why do I have to go forward?"

Bart did not answer. Arising in the distance, a rumbling sound washed over the boat. Moments later, with the rumbling intensifying, a shadowy bridge appeared in the fog and seemed to pass over the waterway on which they travelled.

"Bart! Bart, look," Nora pleaded as she motioned towards the looming bridge. The rumbling noise became louder and clearer and Nora recognized it as an approaching train. Its whistle abruptly screeched through muggy air.

Nora's dream ended.

. . . .

"WHAT THE HELL WAS THAT?!" Elliott asked after he and Nora jumped into sitting positions on his bed. An air horn again sounded several parking lots away and was followed by excited shouts. Elliott flopped back onto the mattress and griped, "Idiots."

"They're just having fun," replied a sleepy Nora as the memory of her dream and the distress she felt within it evaporated. She snuggled into Elliott, the warmth of his body and the touch of his skin calming her, and said through a yawn, "It *is* New Year's Eve."

Elliott reached to the bedside table and turned the digital clock towards them. It read "3:30 am".

"Not anymore," Elliott countered.

"Oh, wow," commented Nora. The couple's amorous encounter ended before midnight and they slept through the arrival of 1986. She shivered as she considered the early morning temperature and said, "They've gotta be freezing. Isn't it, like, in the teens tonight?"

"Yep, but I doubt they're feelin' it," Elliott muttered as he readjusted the covers to engulf both he and Nora and pulled her closer. She slid her knee up Elliott's thigh and, continuing upward, inadvertently nudged his erection. The contact paralyzed them both; their first dalliance was an emotional surrender but now they faced a less desperate decision. Nora forced herself to speak.

"Do you, like, wanna?" queried Nora sheepishly. The comfort and safety she felt with Elliott disappeared when the prospect of sex arose. She bit her lip.

"Yeah, I, like, wanna," Elliott answered with a smirk. Nora playfully smacked his arm. Swiftly maneuvering from underneath her, he engulfed her with his body. She screamed and laughed.

"Hey!" objected Nora. Elliott went nose-to-nose with her and his countenance became serious.

"But the real question is: do *you* wanna?" Elliott queried. Nora blushed and wilted under his attention.

"You're so weird," said Nora with a grin. She paused when he did not smile in return, pondered her words and then added, "I didn't mean that. You're just . . . *different* than most guys."

Nora's assertion tweaked Elliott's ego and he studied her face. She ran a hand through his hair and looked on him with doe-like eyes.

"Different than most guys, huh?" Elliott said. He caressed Nora's cheek with the backs of his fingers and inquired, "How's that?"

"Most guys don't usually worry too much about what girls want," replied Nora.

"Yeah, I guess so," Elliott conceded. He dropped his gaze and became lost in his thoughts. Nora allowed him to find his own way back and, looking at her once again, he declared earnestly, "But it's a whole helluva lot nicer when you're into it, too."

"Elliott, I wanna," Nora said as her body tingled with both nervousness and sexual desire. The lovers leaned into one another and kissed. Ignoring the airhorn as it sounded several more times, their bodies entwined and the world outside the apartment window faded away.

· · · ·

ELLIOTT SNAPPED OUT of his slumber to the smell of smoke. He instantly panicked but soon relaxed when Nora's moans of disappointment pierced the air. He could hear her cooking breakfast in the kitchen.

"Hopefully she didn't burn the coffee," Elliott said with a muted grin. He felt like a new man, the sudden, unexpected infusion of Nora into this life lifting his spirits. Elliott chuckled and said aloud, "Eh, who cares if she did."

After a quick stop at the bathroom, Elliott descended the stairs to the sizzling of burnt eggs. He stopped on the landing and watched Nora scoop them onto a plate.

"Darn it," sighed Nora. She wore one of Elliott's t-shirts and her underwear, the t-shirt riding up on her right hip and revealing her panty-clad buttocks.

"That's the cutest dupa I've ever seen," Elliott said to himself. He approached Nora from behind, slid his hands under her shirt, ran them over the smooth skin of her stomach and then embraced her. Elliott planted several soft kisses on her neck.

"Mornin'," Elliott greeted Nora. She squirmed.

"I burnt the eggs," pouted Nora as she scooped the last of them onto a plate. Her frustration surged and she griped, "This is why I just *serve* food."

"Looks fine to me," Elliott replied despite his reservations about the meal. He released her, grabbed a fork and sampled the blackish scrambled eggs. He stifled a grimace but still consumed them for Nora's sake, contending, "See, still passable."

"Liar," replied Nora. She set down the frying pan, turned off the burner and rotated to face Elliott. Setting her forehead on his chest, Nora exhaled dramatically and said, "I guess we're having cereal."

"Right now, I just need coffee," Elliott replied. Nora lifted her head, dutifully prepared Elliott a cup of coffee and offered it to him.

"I can at least do that," said Nora. She poured herself a half cup, heaped sugar into it and then filled it with milk. Elliott chuckled.

"Kinda defeats the purpose, doesn't it?" Elliott asked.

"What?" said Nora without taking his meaning.

"Let's sit," Elliott answered with a nod to the living room.

"Okay," Nora agreed with a shrug. Elliott seated himself on the right side of the couch next to the end table while Nora sat on its middle cushion facing Elliott. She folded her legs beneath her and held her coffee mug loosely in both hands.

"So, what're we gonna do about Em?" Elliott inquired.

"Do about Em?" asked Nora with a puzzled expression. She reasoned, "She's the one who sent me over here."

Elliott gave her a skeptical look. Nora paused to contemplate the accuracy of her statement.

"Well, I guess I, like, offered to go first," admitted Nora. Elliott sipped his coffee while she argued, "But she agreed to it."

"Yeah, out of desperation," Elliott remarked.

"She said I'm one of you guys now," declared Nora proudly in contravention of Elliott's doubt.

"Oh, boy," Elliott said with widening eyes. He set his mug on the end table, stretched his legs and arms and exhaled, "Bet she wishes she had that one back."

"Hey!" whined Nora in response to Elliott's stinging words. She suddenly remembered Emma's admonishment from her first day at Johnny Dubs and her body deflated, asking, "She's gonna fire me, isn't she?"

"Nah, she *can't* do it now," Elliott scoffed. Considering his sister's stubbornness, however, he hedged his bet by adding, "But even if she did, I can get you another waitressing job."

"At *your* bar?" asked Nora. She partook of her coffee but watched Elliott disbelievingly.

"My buddy owns a bar-," Elliott began.

"I'm not working for Neil," insisted Nora good-naturedly. She handed Elliott her mug, which he accepted, and then dramatically stretched her body. Her sensual movements aroused him but, ignoring his leering, she took back her coffee and said, "Brandy's there, anyway."

"My *other* buddy owns a bar. Up in Dearborn Heights," Elliott expounded. Rebuffed by Nora, he retrieved his mug and drank from it before saying, "He owes me a big favor and he'd hire you in a second."

"A big favor?" asked Nora.

"I got him laid once in high school," Elliott replied with smirk.

"You think a guy you got laid, *in high school*, is gonna give me a job, *now*?" queried Nora. She tilted her head and rebuked him, "*Elliott.*"

"I didn't just get him laid, I got him laid by the hottest girl in school," Elliott explained with pride. The memories of high school flooded his mind as he explained, "Shirley Adams. She was a friend of Em's . . . of my sister . . . she helped a little, I admit it . . . but anyway, the two of 'em clicked. And that one-night stand turned into a seventeen-year marriage and three kids."

"You're crazy," said a grinning Nora despite slowly coming around to Elliott's plan.

"Seventeen years. Three kids," Elliott repeated. His countenance dimmed and he conceded, "The money won't be as good."

"I'm hardly making it as it is," said Nora as her shoulders slumped, the distress evident in her voice. She handed her coffee to Elliott again and stood up. Pacing and gesticulating, Nora continued, "I've gotta cut my schedule some at work 'cuz 'a my class load this semester, plus my rent's, like, going up *and-.*"

"Just move in here," Elliott suggested without hesitation.

"Oh, come on," Nora protested. Elliott placed her mug on the end table next to his own.

"I'm serious," Elliott asserted. He rose to his feet and inquired, "You got a religious objection to shackin' up outside 'a marriage?"

"What about Toni?" asked Nora bluntly, her demeanor darkening.

Elliott winced as if stuck with a needle. The mention of Toni stirred strong emotions within him but also brought a conversation he had with her into his mind. The words seemed to fit the circumstances so he walked to the window and repeated them to Nora.

"I think it's possible for you to have strong feelings for a few different people at the same time," Elliott said in strong, clear voice, "but the right moments for each person come and go, and the time frames overlap."

Elliott's heartfelt wisdom wafted over Nora. She felt oddly calmed, almost hypnotized, by his explanation and observed him with a blank expression.

"They're like strands blown in the wind, and they flutter all around you, all the possible endings," continued Elliott with his glazed eyes staring forward. He took a deep breath and continued, "Some people grab one and hold on for dear life, other people move from strand to strand. Some decide which strands to grab and others just flail around and grab whatever ones they can."

"So you couldn't grab Toni's strand so I'm next in line," replied Nora in a wounded tone. Elliott spun around and it startled her.

"Do you remember the first night we met in Em's office?" Elliott asked while gazing at her intensely. Nora bowed her head and nodded. Elliott stepped forward, took both of her hands in his own and declared, "I fell for you the second I saw you."

Nora's face flushed with embarrassment. She tried to extricate herself from Elliott's grasp but he maintained it.

"You can't tell me you didn't feel the same way that night," Elliott declared. He attempted to pull her closer but she resisted as he said, "And you wouldn't've come here, hell, you wouldn't still *be* here, if you didn't still feel it."

Nora hesitated. She then jumped into Elliott's arms and kissed him deeply.

"You'd better not tell me in six months you're still hung up on her," Nora challenged Elliott. She took his chin in her hand and squeezed it forcefully, saying, "I mean it, Elliott."

"So do I," Elliott answered though the words pained him. He hid his hurt and buried his feelings for Toni deep inside. His feelings for Nora flooded over them and rose to his emotional surface. She shook his chin.

"And listen. Emma's not just my boss, she's my friend," said Nora. Relinquishing her grasp, she declared, "So *I* decide what we tell her and when ... and I'm not ready to tell her *anything* yet."

"Whatever you say, kiddo," Elliott answered despite knowing Emma would interrogate them both in the coming hours.

"Don't call me that, *grandpa*," replied Nora. Elliott walked to the couch and gently tossed Nora on it. She squealed and the lovers, suddenly awash in mirth, playfully tussled with each other. The physical contact soon turned sexual and they spent the morning in each other's arms.

• • • •

NORA SLUMPED IN HER seat and stared out the car window while nervously stroking the long, loosely braided ponytail in which she tied her hair. She occasionally fiddled with the small, red bow affixed to its end. Elliott recognized her anxiousness, grabbed her thigh and shook it gently.

"Ya' okay, there?" he inquired.

"Uh-huh," mumbled Nora in unconvincing fashion. Elliott shifted his gaze between his girlfriend and the road and appreciated her youthful comeliness. She wore a red, oversized velour top with black trim underneath her jean jacket and black leggings. Red makeup adorned her lips and fingernails.

"You know, you don't have to dress up just to go to Em's," Elliott advised Nora as he surveyed her outfit. The comment distressed her.

"You don't like how I look?" Nora whined while sitting up straight.

"I *love* how *you* look," replied Elliott with a smirk. He waved a hand towards himself to note the battered pea coat, the old, collared shirt and the worn jeans and added, "It's how you make *me* look that's the problem."

Elliott laughed. Nora frowned. He shifted tack.

"This car turns eleven this year," Elliott said as he drove his red 1975 Ford LTD down Goddard Road. He patted the dashboard, entertained a few thoughts of the past and uttered, "Hard to believe. That time went fast."

"It used ta' be your Dad's, right?" asked Nora gingerly. The question momentarily discombobulated Elliott and he nearly missed the turn into Emma's neighborhood. Hitting the brakes, he turned sharply with squealing tires and his arm held up to protect Nora.

"Yeah, though not for very long," Elliott said after completing his turn. He withdrew his arm but not before Nora noticed the chivalry.

"Sorry," apologized Nora. She felt foolish.

"You're fine," Elliott said as he grasped her hand. Lifting and kissing the back of it, he smiled sadly and added, "We'll talk about John Warden someday. Just not today."

Nora grinned weakly and nodded in assent. She squeezed Elliott's hand.

"Yeah," agreed Nora. The pair gazed forward and remained mute as Elliott drove past Emma's house, turned around in her neighbor's driveway and parked on the street. Nora wrung her hands.

"I'm really nervous, Elliott," Nora confessed as she turned her head towards him. She squirmed in her seat and said, "I mean, what if Emma has, like, second thoughts?"

Elliott lunged into Nora and kissed her. The sudden affection rendered her lightheaded.

"And I thought *I* worried too much," said Elliott. He slid back across the front seat, opened the driver-side door and urged her, "C'mon."

Nora placed her hands in her lap and sighed. She watched Elliott exit the car, walk around its hood and open the passenger door. Nora looked to Elliott with the face of a child going to her first day of school. She unfastened her seatbelt.

"I only carry you into the house if you're under five-feet tall and asleep," advised Elliott with a smirk. He held out his hand. Nora giggled and pretended to fall asleep. Elliott chuckled in return and said, "Don't make me break out the tape measure."

Nora exhaled dramatically, steeled her will and debarked. Walking hand-in-hand with Elliott and buttressed by his presence, she allowed him to lead her towards the house. Nora stopped on the porch and turned to Elliott.

"Don't tell her anything you don't have to," Nora instructed Elliott. She disentangled herself from his grip and placed her hands in her jacket pockets, saying "Em knows I stayed with you last night but that's, like, *all* she knows."

"I'm sure she figured *that one* out," said Elliott. Acutely aware of Nora's anxiety, he threw a reassuring arm around her shoulders and said, "We just gotta get through the first hour or so, and then we're home free."

Elliott paused to consider his assertion. He shrugged.

"That's my theory anyway," Elliott said.

"*Elliott*," pouted Nora.

• • • •

EMMA ALWAYS SLEPT WELL into the afternoon on New Year's Day but insisted on a casual family dinner after she recovered from the last of the previous year's festivities at Johnny Dubs. Her first familial gathering of 1986, however, would be a small one as her in-laws spent the New Year's holiday in Chicago.

"Gonna miss your mom and dad this year," Emma said to David with a hint of disapproval in her voice. She wore a hooded Wayne State sweatshirt and grey leggings. Her husband, clad in his familiar baggy jeans and Tigers jersey, picked up a stack of plates on the counter.

"Hey, even they need a break from our craziness once in a while," David scolded her gently. Emma sighed away her displeasure.

"Yeah, I guess," replied Emma. She pulled out her hair tie, shook out her hair and then reaffixed it. David moved into the kitchen doorway and paused.

"Can we just eat wherever since Mom and Dad aren't here?" suggested David carefully. His thoughts rested on the broadcast of the Rose Bowl game.

"Absolutely not," Emma stated firmly. She began unbagging long loaves of bread and added, "This family eats *at the table, as a family.*"

Emma stopped. David's hopes rose.

"God, I sound like my mother," Emma said while drifting into memories of Lillian Warden. David waited for a dispensation to continue his duties but it did not arrive. Emma finally returned to the present and admonished him, "Doesn't change anything. But you can watch the game until the subs are ready."

David shook his head and departed into the dining room with the plates. Looking out the kitchen window, Emma saw Elliott's car pull up to the house.

"Well, here we go," Emma sighed. She took a deep breath to center herself, reached her hands towards the ceiling and performed an elaborate stretch. She avoided another glance out the window, walked into the foyer and opened the door. Elliott's appearance, though much improved from the day before, stunned her.

"Happy New Year, Sis," Elliott greeted her with a shit-eating grin. Disregarding the cold cement on her bare feet, Emma stepped onto the porch and closed the door. Nora took a diagonal step backward to partially shield herself behind Elliott.

"You look terrible," Emma declared. Elliott's skin remained pale and dark circles ringed his eyes. Emma appraised his form and asked, "Have you lost weight?"

"You shoulda' seen what I looked like yesterday," replied Elliott with a widening smirk. Emma reached out and rubbed the collar of his shirt between her thumb and forefinger.

"You are wearing a shirt with a collar, though," Emma added in an impressed tone. She switched to a displeasured one and said, "I bought it for you in 1980, but better *really damn late* than never."

Nora felt an unfamiliar twinge. It was a protective instinct, one that spurred her into action.

"Hi, Em," Nora interjected as she stepped fully into Emma's view. She moved to hug her boss, hesitated and then embraced her. Emma, to the surprise of both Nora and Elliott, returned it.

"You, on the other hand, look absolutely adorable," Emma commented bluntly. She pulled away from Nora but retained her grip on her elbows, the older woman appraising her with shining eyes and saying, "Like a model straight outta the JC Penney catalog."

"Aww. Thanks," an embarrassed Nora cooed. David opened the front door and lumbered up behind his wife.

"She's right, Nora, you look great," said David, his gaze conveying a message of approval to Elliott. He set a large, strong hand on Emma's shoulder and asked, "You guys comin' inside or what?"

"She's one of us now so she has to," Emma said with a firm tone and pointed expression. The light in her eyes told Elliott she was, at least initially, resigned to – perhaps even supportive of – his relationship with Nora. Beckoning them into the house with a wave, Emma urged, "C'mon inside. It's effin' cold out here."

• • • •

EMMA FREED DAVID ONCE the dining room table was set and he and Elliott settled into the living room with beers to watch the Rose Bowl. Nora, meanwhile, remained in the kitchen with Emma and assisted with the dinner preparations. Submarine sandwiches were to be the main course.

"Good thing you went over there," Emma said as she stood at the kitchen island and arranged layers of ham and turkey on the bottom half of the loaves. Nora sliced tomatoes at the counter.

"He hadn't showered in like a week," Nora said with a wrinkled nose. Emma grimaced at first but, as her mind processed Nora's words, she guilefully smiled. Finished with the lunch meat, she re-wrapped it, placed it in the refrigerator and retrieved a package of American cheese.

"He gave that up pretty quickly," Emma remarked while walking past Nora. She playfully allowed her shoulder to brush against the twentysomething who failed to acknowledge it and continued slicing tomatoes.

"Oh, well, yeah," Nora said sheepishly as she remembered her nude enticement of Elliott. Emma added the cheese to the sandwiches.

"Men are suckers for the . . . *attention* of younger women," Emma said. Nora turned to her, the knife still in her hand, and struggled to find an explanation. Emma held up her palm and assured her, "Don't worry, Nora, I *don't* wanna know."

"Are you mad?" asked Nora after rotating back to her original position. She set down the knife and picked up the cutting board.

"How can I be mad?" Emma replied. She tossed down the last slice of cheese and stated sardonically, "This is the first New Year's dinner he's shown up for showered, shaved and, most importantly, bimbo-less."

Nora grinned with a sibling's love and offered Emma the cutting board of tomato slices. Feeling uncomfortable with the emotion, she pointed towards the sink.

"Lettuce first," Emma instructed her. Her daughters bounded into the kitchen as Nora set the board on the counter and obtained the colander full of washed lettuce. Elliott appeared in the doorway, leaning against its frame and holding his beer.

"Is dinner ready yet, Mommy?" inquired Tessa. She and Lanie noticed Nora and eyed her suspiciously. The young woman pretended not to notice as she added lettuce to the sandwiches.

"Where's Toni?" asked Lanie bluntly. The adults in the room winced.

"Yeah, where's Toni?" queried Tessa.

"This is Nora," Elliott quickly answered. Motioning towards his new love interest, he said, "My girlfriend."

Elliott offered Nora a muted smile. She trembled with sudden elation.

"But I thought you and *Toni-*," began Lanie. Elliott threw optical daggers at her.

"Toni is just Uncle Elliott's friend, and she has a fiancée," Emma interrupted her daughter. Lanie inhaled to ask another question but her mother beat her to the punch, saying, "Which means the man she's going to marry. So, Toni and her fiancée, Bobby, are together today because it's a holiday."

Lanie snickered.

"He's the guy I kicked in the nuts at your party," Lanie declared proudly. Even Nora giggled.

"That's right," Emma said while displaying the same pride as her daughter. She exchanged the colander that Nora held for the board of tomato slices and politely nudged her towards the sandwiches, saying, "So Toni's with her family, and Uncle Elliott is here today with his family and . . . ."

Emma hesitated for a fraction of a second. Nora held her breath.

". . . that includes his new girlfriend, Nora," she said. Elliott smirked but Nora exhaled in relief as Emma reminded Lanie, "You met her at my party, too, remember? She works at my club."

"Oh, yeah," Lanie said. She and Tessa grew quiet and pondered the new information while the adults nervously waited for them to respond. Tessa stepped forward first.

"You're pretty. Not like Toni, but like Mommy," said Tessa. The adults' collective skin crawled and Nora turned white. Tessa, however, defused her loaded comment by asking, "Wanna play Nintendo with us?"

"Uh, okay," said Nora. She and Elliott exchanged glances as Tessa grabbed her hand. Lanie bolted down the hallway.

"Dibs on the good controller!" yelled the ten-year-old on her way to her room.

"I'll help with the subs," Elliott said as Tessa pulled Nora from the kitchen. He turned to Emma and waited. When she said nothing, he asked, "What, no shot about all the kids playing video games together?"

"Nope," Emma answered as she applied the final touches to the subs.

"Thanks, Sis," Elliott said.

"You've finally got what you wanted from the beginning," replied Emma. Remembering similar advice she gave him about Donna, she said, "So don't screw it up *this* time."

"Right," Elliott said. Emma let several seconds pass and he felt her emotional temperature sharply drop.

"That means 1986 is a whole new year," continued Emma gravely with scintillating eyes, "and you've got to forget about 1985."

Feeling the veiled reference to Toni like a knife in the kidney, Elliott lingered in a brief trance before he raised his eyes to his sister. Unable to speak, he simply nodded his head in agreement.

When You Close Your Eyes

T oni wallowed in a hot shower after an exhausting day of delayed flights and a harrying layover. It was late when she and Bobby finally arrived in Miami from Detroit and checked into their hotel. Running her hands through her short, brown hair, she let the water soak it and thought of Bobby.

"I still can't believe he agreed to separate beds," Toni said to herself. Bobby indulged her desire to shield her virginity until marriage, so much so that he reserved two single rooms on different floors of the hotel when no adjoining rooms were available. She distinctly remembered their conversation about it.

"Just get a rollaway and I'll sleep on it," Toni suggested when Bobby told her of the double booking of single rooms. She reasoned, "We're gonna be sleeping in the same cabin on the cruise anyway."

"I want to sleep on a real bed, not some crappy rollaway, and I don't want you sleeping on one, either," Bobby responded. He chortled and added, "Besides. It'll be good practice for the night before our wedding."

"Thank you," said Toni as she insinuated herself into his arms and grasped the back of his neck. She planted a grateful kiss on his lips and stated, "You don't know how much this means to me."

"Just make it worth my while on the wedding night," said Bobby. Toni laughed, gently pinched the skin of his cheek and shook it.

"Deal," Toni said suggestively before engaging Bobby in a longer, sultrier kiss.

Replaying the memory made her heart flutter and her libido engage. She doused her desire in cool water and said aloud, "Okay, time for bed, Toni Amanda."

Exiting the shower, Toni meticulously dried herself and then wrapped the plush, white hotel towel around her body. She moved to the vanity, squeezed toothpaste onto her toothbrush and looked to the foggy mirror. She wiped some of the condensation away with her hand and studied her face.

"January in Miami and my birthday on a cruise with the man I love . . . *my fiancée*," Toni stated thankfully. Grinning, she raised her toothbrush and asked herself, "What else could I possibly ask for?"

Toni commenced brushing her teeth but then abruptly froze. Her mind answered the question with an unpleasant image of Elliott's devastated countenance.

"*Please* let him be okay," Toni prayed. Her spirits fell and her heart ached as she brushed her teeth in deep contemplation, saying to herself, "With everything going on I forgot."

Thoughts of Elliott suffering back in Michigan plagued her as she completed her nightly routine, discarded the towel and slipped into her cream-colored nightgown. She exhaled and rubbed her eyes.

"Get some sleep," Toni instructed herself as she clicked off the bedside lamp. Pulling back the covers, she tucked herself into bed and let her heavy eyelids fall. She then danced in and out of an uneasy sleep and ran from Elliott in both her dreams and her waking moments. Irritated by her inability to escape him, she sat up, pulled her knees to her chest and hugged herself.

"Stop it," Toni scolded her mind as if it were a separate entity. When it refused to obey, she sighed and reasoned in a quiet voice, "He'll be okay. He's got Em and she'll find him someone."

The telephone's shrill ring startled Toni and derailed her consideration of Elliott. She turned on the light and answered the call.

"Hello?" Toni said with uncertainty.

"You get settled in?" inquired Bobby. His strong voice comforted her.

"Yeah, I did," Toni replied with a smile, "but I can't stay asleep for some reason."

"You'd sleep better in my arms," said Bobby. Admonishment, albeit gentle, arose on Toni's tongue. She squelched it, however, and instead decided to appreciate Bobby's desire for her.

"Soon," Toni said wistfully. She grew serious and gushed, "And then I'm never leaving them. I'll be completely yours, forever. You ready for that?"

"Yeah, I think so," said Bobby in an intentional understatement of his feelings.

"I love you," Toni said, the words seeming inadequate.

"See ya' in the morning, beautiful," replied Bobby.

"Good night," Toni said. She hung up the telephone, clicked off the lamp and settled into bed. Thinking of Elliott a final time, she said, "I have my own man to take care of. *Elliott'll be okay.*"

Toni closed her eyes. The hotel became silent.

"He'll be okay," she whispered as sleep finally overtook her. Her consideration of Elliott, like her consciousness, gradually slipped away into the night and she did not see him again in her dreams.

• • • •

"OH MY GOODNESS, *Bobby*," Toni gushed when she first saw the *Song of America*, the Royal Caribbean Cruise Lines ship that would whisk them from Miami to Nassau in the Bahamas. Its massiveness astonished her and she felt as if she lingered in a fairytale. Toni grasped Bobby's arm and whispered, "How much was this trip?"

Bobby engulfed Toni in his arms and kissed her. She melted into him.

"That's nothing you need to worry about," replied Bobby. He extricated himself from her embrace, took her hand and led her into the check-in area. White signs, each lettered with a range of the alphabet and supported on tall columns, guided cruisegoers to the appropriate desk. Inundated by swarms of buzzing passengers, the paramours completed the procedures necessary to board the ship.

"This is too much," Toni insisted as the couple walked hand-in-hand. Toni wore a white sundress decorated with flowers of green, yellow, blue and pink. Its wide hem brushed her knees and long spaghetti straps tied into large bows graced the smooth skin of her shoulders.

"You're worth it," Bobby said. He donned deck shoes, khaki shorts and a blue polo shirt. Fellow cruise-goers noticed the handsome couple and, with Toni's engagement ring gleaming in the light of the hot Florida sun, sensed the passion and love between them.

Their boarding experience and orientation to their home for the next seven days proved magical for Toni. She marveled at the massive common areas and the amenities the ship offered and repeatedly thanked Bobby with copious affection.

"Separate beds, just as you requested," Bobby announced when they arrived at their cabin. Noting the tinge of disappointment in his tone, Toni decided to set him on his heels.

"So I'm worth a cruise but not the wait?" asked Toni with a glance at Bobby as she sauntered past him and through the cabin's doorway.

"I got the separate beds, didn't I?" Bobby countered. He entered the room in her wake, closed the door and hugged her from behind.

"You did," responded Toni as she laid her head on his shoulder. She soon broke away from him and curiously examined every inch of the room. Bobby dropped himself onto one of the beds, placed his hands behind his head and watched Toni's meticulous inspection in amusement.

"Oh, wow, look at how small the bathroom is," Toni remarked. Her blue eyes sparkled and she beamed. Flushing the toilet, she jumped and squealed when it emitted a high-pressured whoosh. Laughing, she said excitedly, "Let's go up to the top deck. I wanna see the ocean, and feel the heat, and the breeze."

"And get a cocktail," added Bobby with a smirk.

"Oh, Bobby, this is gonna be the trip of a lifetime," Toni declared breathily. She felt lightheaded.

"No, it's not," disagreed Bobby with a feigned grim mien.

"Why's that?" pouted a surprised Toni.

"This is gonna be the status quo, sweetheart," asserted Bobby with serious eyes. Toni offered him an adoring expression.

"You're gonna spoil me," Toni playfully scolded Bobby. She walked to him and said, "But don't forget, I'm a simple girl, and I want to build a loving home, and fill it with kids."

"Fill it?" queried Bobby with a dubious expression. Toni reached out her hand, which he took, and pulled him onto his feet.

"Let's go," Toni urged him.

. . . .

DESPITE A WHIRLWIND first day on *Song of America*, and from the moment she closed her eyes, Toni spent another night running from Elliott in her dreams. She slept in spurts of varying lengths, sometimes forcing herself to wake up to escape his advances, other times starting out of a deep sleep to a surge of anxiety. Bobby slept soundly and gave no indication he noticed Toni's restlessness. She flipped a final time and faced him, her head lying on her pillow and her arm perched atop the curve of her hip.

"*Look at him.* Think about what he's done for you, what he's given up, how he's changed . . . all because *he loves you,*" Toni rebuked herself. Her persuasion successful and her angst evaporating, she settled into sleep. It did not last long, however, as Bobby slid into bed with Toni and spooned her. Waking out of a deep slumber, she felt his erection against her buttocks. Toni screamed and jumped.

"Bobby!" Toni protested.

"Hey, take it easy!" exclaimed Bobby. Toni rolled over the top of him and onto her feet. She scalded Bobby with a harsh look.

"We talked about this and *you promised,*" Toni admonished him. She suddenly realized the volume of her voice and, gesturing to her full-length nightgown, said quietly, "It's the whole reason I'm wearing *this.*"

"It's tough to be on a romantic cruise with my fiancée and not want, ya' know, *that,*" said Bobby with desperate eyes.

"Then we should have waited until our honeymoon for the cruise, too," an undaunted Toni replied. She exhaled dramatically and slumped her shoulders in exasperation. The simultaneous pursuit of two men – one in her dreams and one in reality – wore on her.

"Hey, c'mon," said Bobby as he rose from the bed. He attempted to hug her but she folded her arms and pulled away from him.

"I'm going for a walk," Toni announced. She circumvented the bed and moved to her open suitcase.

"Okay," said Bobby as she procured a pair of jean shorts.

"Alone, Bobby," Toni replied quickly with a glare. Bobby's old ways warred against his new policy of restraint. He wallowed in frustration for a few seconds before surrendering with a sigh.

"All right," relented Bobby. Remorse crept over his heart and he said, "Look, I know I screwed up. I'm sorry. You just, well, you know how guys get."

"Turn around," Toni said as she pulled on the shorts underneath her nightgown. Bobby hesitated but she insisted, "Turn around, Bobby."

Bobby turned his back to Toni. She slid off her nightgown over her head and revealed her long, slender back. Swiftly pulling a bra from her suitcase, she wrapped it around herself and fastened the hooks.

"I just need a little air and I'll be back," Toni informed Bobby. She grabbed a gray, long-sleeved Detroit Tigers t-shirt and pulled it over her head. Sliding her arms into the blue sleeves, she then pulled the shirt down and said, "Okay, you can look."

Bobby turned around. He chuckled while leering at her.

"You didn't get it right," said Bobby. Her prominent curves and girl-next-door appearance reignited his arousal.

"Didn't get what right?" Toni asked with a puzzled mien.

"You look even sexier now," answered Bobby. He started to walk around the bed but Toni froze him with a pointed finger.

"Get some sleep," Toni instructed him firmly. She gave him a loving, earnest glance, motioned towards his bed and assured him, "I won't be long."

Toni stepped into her sandals and exited the cabin. Sitting down on the bed, Bobby watched the door for several minutes after she departed. Suspicion gripped him.

"Something's not right," Bobby said aloud, "and I think I know what."

• • • •

TONI STEPPED QUIETLY on the varnished flooring of the vacant promenade deck while running her hand gently along its white railing. Choosing a spot with minimal lighting, she placed her elbows on the railing and clasped her hands together. Toni inhaled deeply and indulged in the pleasant sea breeze. The moonless sky formed a dark fabric dotted with thousands of twinkling stars.

"Maybe we should've gotten separate rooms," Toni posited as she pondered Bobby's licentiousness. She sympathized with his plight nonetheless and conceded, "I know this is tough on him. Saving oneself for marriage just isn't that big of a deal anymore."

Elliott was ever present in her mind, lingering in the shadows of her thoughts as if patiently waiting for the right moment to step forward. Toni's solitary presence in such a spiritual setting provided him the perfect opportunity: she, nestled in his car on a rainy fall night, laid her head on his lap and her heart bare.

"Why can't I stop thinking about him?" Toni whispered as one of the deck's lights glinted off her engagement ring. She suddenly realized she was crying.

"What the hell, Toni?" asked Bobby. He slowly approached her with his hands in the back pockets of his shorts.

"*Bobby*," gushed a surprised Toni as she angled her body away from him and hastily swiped at her tears. Bobby angrily folded his arms.

"It's Elliott, isn't it?" demanded Bobby. A tremor ran through Toni at the mention of the name. She panicked.

"Let's not do this," Toni begged, the soon-to-be twenty-eight-year-old refusing to face her fiancée. Her mind raced and her heart thumped as she pleaded, "*Please*. Not here, not now."

"Then when?" queried Bobby sharply. He hesitated before turning around with his hands on his hips. The lovers spent a tense thirty seconds with their backs to one another. Bobby abruptly groaned and began to depart.

"Bobby, wait," Toni implored him. He stopped and lifted his chin.

"What?" asked Bobby in frustration. Toni whirled around with one outstretched hand still draped on the railing.

"You've done so much, and changed so much, for me," Toni explained. Uneasy about the conversation to come, she sighed and then said, "I can do this for you."

Bobby languidly turned back towards Toni. She looked at him with love in her eyes and grinned weakly. When Bobby remained stationary, Toni proceeded to a blue-and-white deck lounger and sat down on it. She pulled an adjacent lounger closer to her and patted its seat.

"Come. Sit with me," Toni encouraged Bobby. Accepting the gesture, he slowly walked to the lounger opposite her, paused and then seated himself on it. Their gazes met and she stated, "Let's talk about Elliott."

Bobby became uncomfortable and averted his steely grey eyes. Toni bit her lip.

"I don't know where to start," grumbled Bobby. Toni set her hands on his knees in a gesture of support.

"I do," Toni said. She carefully constructed her question and then asked pensively, "Did I have feelings for Elliott?"

Bobby clenched his jaw. Toni shrugged.

"Yeah, I did," Toni admitted. Bobby seethed but said nothing. Toni squeezed his knees.

"But the only reason our friendship started to become, well, something else," Toni said as she released his knees and straightened her body, "was that *I thought we were over, Bobby*. When you punched him, and I saw the anger and hate in you, I doubted for the first time that you were the man for me. That day was horrible and sad and just . . . *jarring*."

Toni's emotional distress caused her face to contort but she held back her tears. Bobby squirmed in his own skin.

"But that's all behind us now," Toni assured Bobby. Her countenance gradually relaxed and she explained, "You've more than earned my forgiveness, and you never lost my love. You're a better man today, and I want to spend the rest of my life with you. And only you."

"Did you love him?" Bobby interjected bitterly. It was Toni's turn to squirm. She stood up and gazed out over the ocean. Bobby watched her closely.

"As a friend, yes, and I know that may be hard for you to accept, but my relationship with Elliott never matured beyond that point," Toni replied. Her anxiousness subsided and, while happily examining her ring, she continued, "But when you came back, with a proposal, and this beautiful ring, and made all those changes for me, well . . . ."

Toni sensed the small, secluded space in her heart that still clung to Elliott and refused to let him go. She decided to isolate it, and hide it, and hope it faded out of existence. Toni turned back to Bobby.

"Elliott became my past," Toni stated flatly.

"Aren't you still gonna be friends?" scoffed Bobby. His vitriol for Elliott was palpable.

"No," Toni answered sadly, "because he made the very wise decision that we couldn't be anything anymore."

"Yeah, right," said a skeptical Bobby. Toni paused to let a couple quietly meander past.

"He knew I couldn't be his girl and he couldn't be my friend," Toni stated bluntly. She planted herself next to Bobby, their bodies pressed together, and continued, "He even said he was meant to meet me so you'd get jealous and get your act together."

"Asshole," grumbled Bobby. Toni wriggled an arm in between Bobby's arm and his torso and clutched him tightly.

"It's hard to say he was wrong," Toni reasoned. Bobby contemplated her assertion and then he, too, relaxed.

"So why are you out here crying?" inquired Bobby astutely. Toni exhaled and trembled. She laid her head on his shoulder.

"I don't know," Toni answered. She pondered her emotions and then said feebly, "Maybe I just feel bad for him, ya' know, how hard he took it, and how there just doesn't seem to be anyone for him."

An awkward moment of silence arose between Toni and her betrothed. She lifted Bobby to his feet.

"No more tonight," Toni insisted with a quick shake of her head. She kissed Bobby on the cheek and led him, arm-in-arm, away from the loungers. A sleepy Bobby acquiesced to her wishes as she said, "We'll talk more but, tonight, we're getting some sleep and then, tomorrow, we're gonna have a fabulous day together."

Leaving her memories of Elliott behind her, Toni escorted Bobby to their cabin. The couple disappeared below deck and the soothing sounds of the ocean and the wind once again overtook the night.

• • • •

BOBBY'S EYES OPENED and he groggily acclimated himself to his surroundings. Toni laid next to him with her head on his shoulder. They both wore the clothes from their late-night stroll.

"Good morning, handsome," Toni greeted Bobby melodically. She tightened her grip on his body but then let it go and set her chin on his chest, cooing, "It's time to start our fabulous day."

"You're feeling better this morning," said Bobby. He caressed her cheek and asked, "How long've you been awake?"

"An hour or so," Toni answered happily. She said with adoration in her big eyes, "I've just been lying here, enjoying being alone with my guy. Listening to your heart, and your breathing."

"And in the same bed," said Bobby as he pulled her into a hug of his own.

"We fell asleep like this," Toni replied. Much to Bobby's surprise, she dismissed their sharing of his bed, saying, "But no harm done."

Toni extricated herself from Bobby's arms and left the bed. She bounced around the room and began preparing for the day ahead. Bobby let his eyelids fall.

"Time to wake up and get going," Toni sang as she grabbed his foot and playfully shook it. She finished making her bed and walked into the tiny bathroom.

"Wow, you're *really* feeling better," Bobby said. He sat up and massaged his eyes. Toni stepped back into the cabin.

"I figured it all out, Bobby," Toni gushed in relief. She plopped down on her bed and expounded spiritedly, "I was crying last night because I felt so guilty about Elliott. Because, even though I shouldn't've, I let him get too close. I was hurting over us and he was there for me. And I blurred the lines when it was convenient for me. At a time I felt terrible, he made me feel . . . ."

Toni stopped herself before she uttered the word "special".

". . . *better*," Toni said emphatically. She returned to her feet and began selecting her outfit for the day, adding, "I gave him hope and then crushed him."

"And you're happy about that?" asked Bobby with a puzzled expression.

"No, of course not," Toni objected. She tossed a light blue sundress on her bed and said, "Don't you see, though? I feel terrible about what I did to him, and this trip, and our engagement, well, it'll kill him when he finds out. Thinking about it made me realize that, and it all hit me at once."

"So you led him on," Bobby said bluntly. Toni winced at his phrasing.

"Yes, and it was wrong," Toni whimpered guiltily. Her demeanor dipped but swiftly rebounded as she explained, "But – and listen to this – I don't have any lingering romantic feelings for him. I was crying because of guilt, because I *do* care about him. But I don't love him, and I don't miss him, not in that way. And that should make you feel good, Bobby. *Really good.*"

"So whaddaya gonna do?" queried Bobby. The finer points of Toni's reasoning were lost on him but he made an effort to understand and accept her platonic feelings for Elliott.

"Go to Confession, and talk to my priest about the right way to handle it," Toni replied confidently, "and accept my penance."

"Is leading someone on even a sin?" asked Bobby doubtfully. A thought struck him and he asserted, "He'll make you see him again. He'll probably want you to apologize."

"I don't think so," Toni countered thoughtfully, "because seeing him again would just make things worse."

Bobby gave her a suspicious look. Toni decided Bobby had reached his limit.

"For him, not me," Toni said. She said firmly but good-naturedly, "But all that matters Bobby is I love you and I'm marrying you and there's no need to belabor the issue. Elliott Warden is just not my concern anymore."

"So what is it now?" asked Bobby.

"Breakfast," Toni said with a smirk and a pillow thrown at Bobby. She laughed and directed him eagerly, "So get dressed!"

E lliott smiled. He remembered the late spring and early summer of 1985, sitting on his reserved bar stool at Johnny Dubs and hawking Nora as she worked her shifts. This time, however, there were more mutual grins and playful banter whenever she passed him.

"What have I done?" Emma asked ponderously when she saw Nora affectionately peck Elliott on the cheek. She rued the day she sent the waitress to rescue him.

"They seem pretty happy, Em," remarked Sean, Emma's younger second-in-command, as the two women completed tasks at the far end of the bar. She was six-feet tall with her thin, blonde hair tied in its usual ponytail, a round face and a small, pointed nose. Sensing her employer's irritation, Sean quickly added, "And it's not like they just met."

Emma sifted Sean's comments and her countenance softened. She shrugged and, to Sean's surprise, accepted her logic.

"Yeah, I guess," Emma sighed. She swiftly fixed Elliott a Grumpy Old Man and walked to the other end of the bar. Sliding the drink in front of Elliott, she asked pejoratively, "You two're laying it on pretty thick, don't ya' think?"

Elliott glanced at Nora and smiled softly. Emma's negativity failed to dampen his spirits.

"Hey, I need to ask you something," said Elliott in a serious tone. It snared Emma's attention and she watched him with anxious anticipation.

"Don't you dare," Emma thought as the specter of a marriage proposal arose in her mind. Elliott leaned forward and stared directly at his sister. His gravity melted away and he offered her a shit-eating grin.

"Do I look happy to you?" queried Elliott in haughty earnest. Emma, relieved that his query did not include an engagement, ignored his smile and gazed on him intensely. He was glowing.

"You do," conceded Emma. She located Nora flitting amongst her customers and glowing in much the same manner as Elliott. He sampled his drink as Emma further confessed, "And she's been in fairy princess mode since New Year's. Floating around here, all bubbly and happy."

Emma wrinkled her nose. Elliott chuckled.

"But that's good, right?" inquired Elliott. He took a long drink from his cocktail as he awaited his sister's answer.

"Yes," Emma admitted begrudgingly. Unable to resist her brother's infectious positivity, she shook her head and beamed, saying, "*Really good.*"

"What are you guys up to?" asked Nora as she swept up to them. She shifted her tray to her left hand and rested her elbow on Elliott's shoulder. He wrapped an arm around her waist.

"Nora has something to ask you, too," Elliott announced. Nora's eyes grew wide and then she froze. Elliott goaded her, "Well, go on."

"What're you talking about?" replied Nora while feigning ignorance. She shifted from paralyzed to panicked, the twentysomething trembling and squirming under Elliott's grasp.

"Em, Nora's gonna need next weekend off," Elliott said. Despite her light resistance, he pulled Nora closer.

"No, Elliott, *don't*," whined Nora. She loathed the thought of a confrontation with Emma, especially one that occurred in public.

"What are *you* guys up to?" Emma asked, her interest piqued by Nora's desperate plea but her mood soured by the expected unpleasant news. She held words of chastisement on the tip of her tongue.

"We're moving her into my apartment," Elliott answered. Nora ceased her attempts to wriggle out of Elliott's grip, reversed course and clung to him.

"The hell you are," snapped Emma before she could stop herself. Nora wilted, broke Elliott's hold and tried to flee. Elliott hopped off his bar stool and caught her in an embrace. He hugged Nora tightly and then gently rotated her towards Emma. Standing behind her, he wrapped his arms around her stomach.

"You both need to calm down," Elliott encouraged them. The strength in his voice eased Nora's angst and she leaned into him as he continued, "I know this is a big step, for all of us, but everything's gonna be just fine."

Emma marveled at Elliott's composure and the way he lovingly buttressed Nora. She wondered if her negative reaction was truly intended for Nora or if it was mere habit when Elliott dated anyone not named Donna.

"The herd's thinning out in here," stated Elliott with a nod towards the seating areas, "so why don't we all go up to your office and talk about it."

Nora looked up to Elliott and then to Emma. The two women exchanged affirmative nods and then offered them to Elliott. He took Nora's tray from her, set it on the bar and took her hand. He then escorted her towards the stairwell leading to Emma's office while Emma shadowed them on the opposite side of the bar.

"Cover them for a bit, will ya', Sean?" asked Elliott as he passed her. She slung a tray of drinks onto her shoulder.

"You got it," Sean affirmed.

"Thanks," Elliott said with a wink. Sean remained rooted to the floor.

"That can't be good," said Luke the bartender when the trio disappeared into the stairwell and the door closed. He wiped down the bar with a white towel.

"I don't know, Luke," Sean replied while staring at the door. Her countenance became envious and, before whisking away the cocktail-laden tray, she said, "There's just something about those two."

• • • •

ELLIOTT BREEZED PAST his sister when she unlocked her office door and pushed it open. His nerves crackled with a tingling elation and he felt a supreme confidence. Taken aback by Elliott's uncharacteristic demeanor, Emma and Nora lingered around the doorway.

"Have a seat, ladies," Elliott said as he walked behind Emma's desk and claimed her high-backed chair. She and Nora shared a puzzled glance and then slowly entered the room. It was not lost on Emma that Elliott resembled John Warden and the resemblance stirred her emotions: she realized one of them was jealousy.

"Uh, that's *my* line," protested a perturbed Emma when she stopped in the middle of the room, "and *my* chair."

"You can sit on the other side today. Ya' know, just like in the old days," Elliott countered without hesitation. Emma narrowed her eyes and threw optical daggers at him. Undeterred by her ire, Elliott leaned back in her chair and warned with a smirk, "But keep your feet off the desk, Little Sis. I wouldn't want you leaving shoeprints all over it."

Emma defiantly folded her arms and shifted her weight to her left foot. Nora, meanwhile, took a seat to Elliott's right and waited expectantly for him to speak. She sheepishly glanced at Emma.

"Humor me, Em," Elliott urged his sister. She fumed for ten seconds before taking a seat next to Nora. Refusing to look at Elliott, she lowered her unfocused eyes as he said, "Now, look, Nora and I are together now and we all need to get on the same page about it."

Emma rolled her eyes and then aimed them at Elliott. They raged with blue-green fires and Nora subtly leaned away from her to avoid their heat.

"Even though this whole . . . ," began Emma as she searched for the right word, " . . . *thing* has been going on for months, you two've only been . . . *together* . . . for a few weeks, and you guys are movin' way too fast."

Emma cooled her frustration and looked upon Nora with a serious mien. Nora bit her lip and guiltily averted her gaze.

"Em, I'm gonna level with ya," an undaunted Elliott countered. Nora hung on his every word, desperate to be rescued from Emma's cold logic, as he declared, "This *thing*, well, it was love at first sight, at least for me."

Elliott's use of "love" shocked Nora and Emma alike. The younger woman gaped at him while Emma's eyes darted to her to gauge her response.

"And, yeah, we're movin' at light speed," Elliott continued. He smiled at Nora, saying, "but, when's she's with me, I feel nothin' but good. And I haven't felt that way in a long time, Em. *A long damn time.* And ya' know what? It's nice. And I wanna keep feeling it as much as I can, and as often as I can, for as long as I can."

Entranced by Elliott's heartfelt explanation, Nora melted into a puddle of adoration. She scooted to the edge of her chair.

"You love me?" squeaked Nora, her palpable excitement bubbling just below her emotional surface.

"That's right, princess," Elliott replied with a goofy expression and a few affirmative head nods, "I love ya."

Elliott's faith in their relationship emboldened her and, circumventing the desk, she plopped into his lap. The fledgling lovers kissed passionately and then indulged in an affectionate display of cuddling and nuzzling. A realization struck Emma like a hard slap to the face.

"Oh my god," thought Emma as she watched the paramours wallow in each other's arms, "she just single-handedly pulled him outta the dark shell."

The couple waited for Emma's response. She leaned back in her chair and threw one leg over the other.

"Got *that* one wrong," admitted Emma to herself.

"So whaddaya say?" Elliott asked. Emma decided on a final volley and her determined gaze fell on Nora.

"You didn't say you love him," observed Emma shrewdly.

"*Emma Renee*," Elliott rebuked her. While he stewed over his sister's stubbornness, Nora slid out of his lap and walked around the other side of the desk. She stopped in front of Emma, hopped onto it and grasped its edges with her hands.

"I do," asserted Nora. Emma squirmed under the younger woman's attention. Nora, meanwhile, laid her hands in her lap, swung her legs like a child and shrugged, saying, "I love your brother."

Elliott exhaled deeply as a future with Nora blossomed before him. Emma's resistance melted away and her face became neutral.

"And that makes me one of you now," added Nora stoically, "just like you said."

"I never shoulda' said that," griped Emma. She rubbed her face with both hands. Rising to her feet, she relented, "All right, you maniacs. You obviously make him happy, so I'm behind you. Both of you."

"So I can have next weekend off?" queried Nora cautiously.

"Dave and the girls can help," replied Emma without directly answering the question, "but *my* boss'll never give me an entire weekend off."

Emma offered her a muted smile, reached out and took Nora's hand. She squeezed it.

"Now, you, get back to work," said Emma and, peeking around Nora to view Elliott, continued, "and you get the hell outta my chair."

"Whatever you say," Elliott replied as he stood up. Emma offered him Nora's hand which he took. Graciously accepting the win, they exited the office.

"Oh, and Nora," beckoned Emma. She released Elliott's hand and stopped on the landing while Elliott continued his descent. Emma folded her arms again and expounded, "I usually shut the club down on the day after the Super Bowl, ya' know, give the crew a break. I also keep the girls outta school for a special shopping day with lunch and the whole thing."

Nora stifled a joyous smile. She eagerly awaited the invitation.

"So, if you can play hookie from college for a day," said Emma, "you should come with us."

"Yeah," said Nora with a bobbing head and a glowing countenance, "sure."

"Don't get ahead of yourselves," warned Emma gravely.

"We won't," Nora assured her, "I promise."

Nora waved at Emma and then hurried after Elliott. When Emma heard the door at the base of the steps close, she chortled.

"They'll be married by Christmas," Emma sighed with a shake of her head. She closed the door and locked it, returned to her desk and poured herself a shot of vodka. Lifting the glass, she said gratefully before downing the alcohol, "Here's to you, Nora. For turning his life around."

• • • •

"BYE, UNCLE ELLIOTT!" Tessa yelled as she gave him a passing pseudo-hug and bounded out the front door of his apartment. She made it to the entry of the hedge surrounding the patio and stopped. Whirling around, she charged back into the apartment to where her father, her uncle and Nora stood. Tessa hesitated, studied her briefly and then gave her a deliberate embrace, saying, "Bye, Aunt Nora."

Tessa's unexpected classification of Nora as family stunned the adults. Nora recovered first and hugged her would-be niece.

"Bye, sweetie," Nora said. Touched by Tessa's welcoming of her into the Hastings clan, she praised her effusively, "You were a *big* help today. Thank you *so* much."

"You're welcome," replied Tessa. She once again bolted from the open door of the apartment and yelled over her shoulder, "C'mon, Daddy!"

"Tess, hold up!" shouted David after his daughter. Elliott shook his head and Nora giggled.

"Have fun livin' in sin, man," said Lanie as she nonchalantly patted her uncle on the shoulder and followed her sister. Her precocious comment caused David to wince. Stopping on the porch, Lanie turned around and waved, adding, "Bye, Aunt Nora."

"Bye," replied Nora with a feeble grin and a weak wave.

"She didn't get that from me," insisted David as he held up both of his large hands.

"Eh, she's right. But sinnin's the fun part," Elliott replied with a smirk. He hugged his brother-in-law and said, "Thanks, man. You guys made this a helluva lot easier."

"Yeah, thank you, Dave," said Nora sweetly as she, too, embraced him.

"Anytime, you guys," said David. His truck horn honked three times.

"C'mon, Dad!" yelled Lanie.

"Emma Junior calls," Elliott said with a dubious smile.

"We bribed 'em with having friends over tonight," explained David as he exited the apartment. He waved on his way towards the hedge and said, "Catch you two later."

Elliott clicked the lock on the base of the storm door and it gradually closed out the cacophony of the Hastings family's departure. He lifted a cardboard box from the floor.

"You sure as hell picked the right weekend to move," Elliott said as he dropped the box in the small kitchen area. Two pizza boxes, paper plates, used napkins and cans of Coke littered the table, the Dominoes feast serving as the Hastings reward for a job well done. Wiping the sweat from his brow, Elliott said, "The temp's jumped like twenty-five degrees since Wednesday."

"We just got lucky," Nora said while sitting on the couch and considering the unseasonably warm temperature of nearly fifty degrees. Elliott dropped onto the cushion next to her and she rested her head against his shoulder, explaining, "The NFL conference championship games were last weekend and the Superbowl's next weekend. Johnny Dubs will be crazy busy so it *had* to be this weekend."

Elliott leaned back and closed his eyes. Nora sighed.

"So, you wanna start unpacking?" Elliott asked despite dreading the prospect. He opened his eyes and scanned the crowd of boxes on the living room floor.

"Nope," Nora answered. Elliott gave her a confused look but she expounded, "We can unpack tomorrow. I wanna go to the Senate for chili cheese fries and then come back here, take a shower and get in my PJs for popcorn and a movie."

"How specific," Elliott commented after a chuckle. Nora crawled into Elliott's lap and kissed him. He queried, "What movie are we watching?"

"Whatever," replied Nora with a shrug. Offering him the most precious face he had ever seen, she said, "I just wanna watch it with you."

"How did we not do this earlier?" Elliott asked. Nora offered him a guilty expression.

"Guess I was kinda wrong on that one," admitted Nora. Her distress burgeoned but Elliott swiftly comforted her.

"Why don't you just go ahead and shower and we'll get takeout?" Elliott suggested. Nora stood up as he added, "I'll go pick it up while you figure out what we're gonna watch."

"Really?" asked Nora. Elliott rose to his feet.

"Sure," Elliott said. He embraced Nora and, when he released her, she offered him a suggestive grin.

"It'll probably take 'em a while to get it ready on a Saturday night," hinted Nora. She placed her open palms on Elliott's chest and continued, "You could call it in and then, ya' know, like, we could . . . ."

Nora trailed off as she felt Elliott's arousal. Her face flushed.

"Be up there in ninety seconds," Elliott stated. The couple shared an affectionate smile before Nora broke away from him. Elliott gently smacked her butt as she ascended the stairs.

"Hey! Dirty old man!" objected Nora in jest. Her mien became serious and she requested, "Get me extra cheese? Please?"

"You got it," Elliott answered.

"Thank you!" said Nora over her shoulder and she bolted up the stairs like Lanie or Tessa. Elliott watched her disappear into his bedroom. He then made his way to the telephone hanging on the kitchen wall.

"My girl sure likes to do it in the shower," Elliott said. Chuckling softly, he picked up the phone and began dialing, saying, "*My girl.*"

• • • •

THE REPETITIVE THUDS of a heavy hand knocking on Elliott's front door jarred his consciousness as he slowly descended the stairs. He wore a white t-shirt and gray sweatpants and felt the chilliness of winter on his sockless feet. Arriving at the front door, Elliott shook his head to clear it and peered out the peep hole.

"This can't be good," Elliott said. He rapidly unlatched the deadbolt and unlocked the main door. Making an emphatic gesticulation, Elliott asked Emma through the glass storm door, "What the hell are you doing here?"

"I w-w-wanna see N-Nora," stuttered Emma while watching Elliott through heavy eyelids. He attempted to open the storm door but Emma's drunken lack of coordination prevented her from moving out of its path.

"Em, it's 3 o'clock in the morning," griped Elliott. Opening the storm door slightly, he managed to grab her by the arm and maneuver her around it. Twice she nearly stepped off the porch and toppled over, her poor balance causing Elliott to grumble, "Damn it, Em."

"Elliott?" called Nora from the middle of the stairs. Elliott managed to pull Emma inside the apartment and close the storm door. Nora, her arms folded as a ward against the cold air, risked two more steps and asked, "Who is it?"

"Nora?!" shouted Emma excitedly. Nora wore her usual nightshirt, this time a white one with blue sleeves and the words "Sack Time" printed above a picture of the cartoon cat Garfield in a brown sack. Emma struggled against Elliott's hold and insisted loudly, "I need to t-t-*talk* to Nora."

"Bring it down a notch," Elliott ordered in a quiet yet harsh tone. He released his sister's arm, closed the main door and locked it. Noticing her lack of coat, he inquired, "And where the hell is your coat?"

Emma held up her arms and examined herself. She wore only a long-sleeved Detroit Lions t-shirt and blue jeans. Looking around the room in a futile attempt to find her missing coat, Emma finally let her arms drop to her sides.

"I don't know," replied Emma with a sad shrug.

"Did you *drive* here?" Nora asked as she entered the living room.

"*Oh, Nora*," Emma whimpered while ignoring the question. She sobbed, recovered and then sobbed again. A forceful embrace followed.

"*Oh, boy* is more like it," Elliott grumbled.

"I'm *sooooo* sorry," gushed Emma as she cried on Nora's shoulder. The younger woman glanced at Elliott and saw the irritation on his face.

"Maybe you should go back to bed," Nora encouraged Elliott. She escorted Emma to the couch, sat her down and said with another glance, "I got this."

Elliott hesitated. Emma rarely engaged in risky or foolish behavior and her intoxication worried him.

"You go back to bed. I'll sober her up," replied an annoyed Elliott. Emma exploded from her stupor and jumped off the couch.

"*Noooo*, Elliott!" objected Emma. Her body swaying like a tree about to fall, she deliberately enunciated each word and demanded, "*I need to talk to Nora.*"

"Really, it's fine," Nora implored Elliott. She slowly guided an unsteady Emma back to the couch and advised, "Maybe you should call Dave, though, and let him know she's staying here tonight."

"*Noooo*," whined Emma, "I can't stay here."

"Good luck," relented Elliott with an exhale. He kissed Nora on the cheek, headed for the stairs and then stopped, saying edgily, "Good night, Sis."

"Goodbye, Elliott," said Emma with a wave as if Elliott embarked on a long journey. Shaking his head in disapprobation, he climbed the stairs and telephoned his brother-in-law.

"I'll get you some water," Nora said. Emma sat up and grabbed her arm.

"No, don't go!" begged Emma. Tugging on Nora's elbow, she insisted again, "I have to talk to you."

"Okay, I'll stay," Nora assured her concernedly, "and we can talk."

"I'm sorry, Nora, I'm so sorry," Emma apologized. She pulled her legs underneath her and leaned a shoulder into the back of the couch.

"For what?" a befuddled Nora asked.

"I tried to keep you and Elliott apart," whined Emma. Her tears fizzled as she commenced a sad, meandering and surprisingly clear monologue: "But I was *wrong*, Nora. *So wrong.* I thought Donna was better. He used to love her, I think, and she *really* loved him. She was his *widdle puppy dog.* But she wasn't better. *She changed.* It's so weird. And now she's with Ben and, without you, Elliott wouldn't have had anyone. And now that you two're shackin' up, it hit me. He loves you, and I almost messed that up, Nora. I almost messed it up."

The torrent of tears resumed. Nora took Emma's hands in her own and squeezed them supportively.

"There's no reason for you to feel bad at all," Nora reasoned. She beamed and shook Emma's hands, declaring happily, "It all worked out. Elliott and I are together now, and things are good. *Really good.*"

"Yeah, I guess," replied an unconvinced Emma while wiping away her tears with her sleeves. Demonstrating uncharacteristic confidence, Nora grabbed Emma's cheeks.

"I love your brother, too, Em. I swear it," Nora promised her. She released Emma's cheeks and let a hand caress the length of her arm, saying, "And remember, you're the one who sent me over here in the first place. So, in a way, you're the one who got us together."

An epiphany struck Emma. She perked up as she pondered Nora's assertion.

"Yeah, I guess I did," Emma said. It was her turn to touch Nora's cheek and she lauded her, "You're so sweet, and nice, and pretty . . . so pretty. You and Elliott are gonna make *beauuuuuutiful* babies."

"*Em,*" Nora scolded her with reddening cheeks. Emma stretched out on the couch with her legs across Nora's lap, adjusted a throw pillow and laid her head on it.

"You watch," said Emma with weak, sleepy eyes. She babbled on with steadily lowering volume, "He'll propose to you before Easter and you guys'll be married by Christmas. You guys should get married *on* Christmas. Or New Year's Eve, because *that's* when you got together."

Emma closed her eyes. She laughed.

"Baby number one in 1987," said Emma with a lazy smirk. Her eyelids lifted and she said determinedly, "But you have to name him John."

"Let me get you a better pillow," Nora replied. Emma's predictions elated her but also came with a healthy dose of anxiety.

"*No.* I'm just gonna rest here for a minute," announced Emma as her eyelids again fell. Nora gave her a look of pity but, by the end of the minute, she slumbered deeply. She carefully slid out from underneath Emma's legs, rose to her feet and then covered her with a blanket from the back of the couch. Nora's mind raced with thoughts of an impending proposal.

"She's just drunk," Nora said to herself. Trying to squelch the smile on her lips and the flutter in her heart, she argued, "He's not gonna propose. Not this year, anyway."

$$\cdot\ \cdot\ \cdot\ \cdot$$

"DAMN IT'S COLD OUT there," Elliott complained as he stepped into Johnny Dubs from the frigid January air. Conveniently finding himself near the club after his last morning appointment, he ducked inside to spend his lunch with Nora. Elliott hated wearing his McClean Hunter Cable garb at Johnny Dubs but his love for his girlfriend proved the stronger emotion.

"Hey, beautiful girl I don't deserve," Elliott said after his vision adjusted to the darkness and he acquired Nora's slender figure. Before he could process her distressed countenance and bleary eyes, she tossed her tray on the bar and crashed into him.

"Oh, my god, Elliott," whimpered Nora as she squeezed him for dear life and wept in his arms. So great was her regular patrons' love of their sweetheart, they made no jokes. Elliott noticed their unusually somber expressions before they returned their attention to the television suspended over a corner of the bar.

"What's wrong?" Elliott queried with a surge of anxiety.

"It blew up," mewled Nora. Elliott looked to the television. It showed a recording of the Challenger Space Shuttle breaking apart shortly after launch. Nora said hoarsely, "They're all dead."

"Oh, man," Elliott uttered. The dark, depressive cloud inundating Johnny Dubs settled over him. He watched the screen intently but was unable to speak as it displayed the tragic fireball that tore apart the shuttle. Elliott said with a contorted face, "That really sucks."

Another whimper from a crying Nora wrested Elliott from his stupor. Keeping his arms wrapped around her, he gently guided her to his barstool. She resisted his efforts to place her on it.

"*Noooo*," objected Nora pathetically as she maintained her tight grip on his body.

"C'mon, Nora, just sit down for sec," Elliott implored her. He glanced at the nameplate on the bar, which read "RESERVED ELLIOTT WARDEN", and assured her, "Everything's gonna be okay."

"How can you say that?" asked Nora. Elliott firmly yet carefully extricated himself from her grasp. She permitted him to manipulate her body and, after a brief, futile attempt to remain standing, to sit her on his barstool.

"Look, I know that was scary to see, and it's terrible those people died, and it's okay to be sad about it," Elliott said as he rested his hands on her shoulders and massaged them lovingly, "but you and I, and everyone we love, we're all good."

Nora's tears lessened. Elliott searched the vicinity and, locating a stack of napkins, quickly grabbed several of them.

"But *they're all dead*, Elliott," insisted Nora. She allowed him to dry her eyes and said, "Death is so scary."

"You're a twenty-three-year-old waitress who someday'll be a counselor or a shrink," Elliott with a dubious expression.

"So?" whimpered Nora.

"So," Elliott answered with a hint of incredulousness, "you're young, *and* healthy, *and* gonna work in a career field that doesn't require you to ride rockets into space. You'll be sittin' safe n' sound in an office somewhere."

Nora grew quiet and contemplated Elliott's reasoning. His face became taut and grim.

"I've been punched by death, Nora," Elliott stated. His countenance further hardened and he declared, "Right in the gut. Twice."

"Oh my god, Elliott, I'm sorry," blurted Nora when she realized her *faux pau*.

"Don't even worry about that," Elliott swiftly replied with a dismissive wave.

"I'm being so silly and stupid," whimpered Nora as her eyes watered. Elliott hugged her and then set her back on her feet.

"No, you're not," Elliott countered. He placed a curved index finger under her chin and continued, "You've just got a stupid big heart. But I think you can be tough, too. *You're gonna be fine.*"

"Yeah. Yeah, I will be," Nora agreed with burgeoning inner strength. Emma leaned against the doorway with her arms folded. She had watched her brother comfort Nora and his caring efforts made her smile.

"That's the Lillian in him," thought Emma in reference to their late mother. She remembered her mother fondly and felt a twinge of guilt. John Warden always loomed large in her heart and mind but she loved her mother just as much.

"Now, go get me a club sandwich," Elliott quipped as he turned Nora around and lightly spanked her. She spun around, kittenishly smacked his chest and then walked away backwards.

"Get it yourself," said Nora. The couple beamed at each other, the happiness emanating from them and brightening the bar. Emma could not stifle a laugh.

"And all that's just Elliott," she remarked.

"Oh, it's you," Toni's mother, Katherine, said disappointedly after opening her front door. Built on the same frame as her daughter, she closely resembled her though her hair was longer and graying and her visage was aged beyond her years. She wore light gray leggings with an oversized, matching sweater and held a bowl-shaped glass of white wine in her hand.

"Hello, Katherine," replied Bobby while putting on a respectful air. When Katherine failed to extend an invitation to enter, Bobby gestured towards the inside of the house and asked, "Can I come in?"

Katherine sipped her wine and methodically studied Bobby with skeptical eyes. She exhaled dramatically at the end of her examination.

"I suppose so," Katherine relented. Turning around and waving Bobby forward, she said, "You *are* going to be my son-in-law after all."

Katherine led Bobby into her kitchen and motioned towards the refrigerator. He followed her at a safe distance.

"I think Toni still has some beer in there," Katherine said. She then seated herself at the kitchen table. Uncorking the green bottle setting upon it, she poured herself more wine. An unfinished, handwritten letter and a pen sat in front of her.

"I'm fine, thanks," responded Bobby. He pulled out the chair opposite Katherine and lowered himself onto it.

"So, to what do I owe the pleasure of this unexpected visit?" Katherine inquired with heavy sarcasm. Bobby hesitated. Disinclined to assist him, she waited patiently and attended to her beverage.

"I want to talk to you about the wedding," offered Bobby cautiously after working up the nerve to speak.

"Why is that?" Katherine asked as she leaned back in her chair. She set her glass on the table and folded her arms, saying snidely, "You didn't talk to me about the proposal."

"Well, ya' see, I, uh, well," stammered Bobby.

"*But about the wedding,*" Katherine interjected as she whisked her glass off the table and rose to her feet. She walked to the kitchen counter, leaned her back against it and again folded her arms.

"I, uh, well, I, um, kinda already planned it," admitted Bobby nervously, his body tensing as if he expected a physical attack.

"Excuse me?" Katherine queried in surprise.

"I already planned the wedding," repeated Bobby with burgeoning courage. His body relaxed as he explained, "Everything's booked and the deposits are down."

"Really?" Katherine asked with a curious, muted grin. She indulged in a large gulp of wine but kept her eyes on Bobby. Resuming the amused smile, she urged him, "Do tell."

"Well, when I realized that Toni was the most important thing in my life, I knew I had to prove it to her," Bobby expounded, his love for Toni and newfound commitment to unselfishness on full display. He clasped his hands together on the table and continued, "And when it came to our marriage, that meant the Christmas Day proposal, the cruise to celebrate it . . . and a wedding in Hawaii."

Katherine's jaw dropped. She set her wine aside.

"An *April* wedding in Hawaii," added Bobby. Katherine returned to her seat at the table and leaned forward on folded arms.

"I'm impressed, Bobby," Katherine remarked though the words tasted bitter on her tongue. Suspicious of Bobby's motives, she asked, "But why the advanced notice for Mom?"

"I've let my close family know and they're all able to make it," answered Bobby. Discomfited by his physical proximity to Katherine, he adjusted his chair backward.

"And you need to make sure the Family Cullen can do the same," Katherine said with a knowing expression. She stood up and retrieved her wine glass from the kitchen counter, stating, "Well, there are only two of us, including the bride, so I think we can swing it."

Bobby smiled and nodded. She set her glass on the table and obtained a beer from the refrigerator.

"Although," Katherine said as she pulled a magnetic bottle opener from the refrigerator door, "I'm sure she has some friends she'd like to be there. I mean, you can probably do it without them, but it'll make it better for her if they can attend."

She set the bottle in front of Bobby but he did not touch it. The ghost of Elliott floated through the room and slithered around both their minds. Bobby felt his blood pressure tick upwards.

"But I can handle those invitations without revealing your secret," Katherine advised, her statement chasing Elliott's specter from the room. Her countenance became serious and she said, "She'll want a Catholic wedding, Bobby, and that's not a process you can squeeze into three months."

"Already got it handled," replied Bobby. He and Katherine settled into a rare comfortable conversation, mother and fiancée discussing details over the next hour and downing several cocktails each. When Katherine finally escorted Bobby to the front door, she found herself developing a fondness for him. She did not like the feeling.

"I've never liked you, Bobby," Katherine stated bluntly, "and I've certainly never thought you were the one for my Toni."

"I know," conceded Bobby. Katherine suddenly yet awkwardly hugged him. Unprepared for the sudden expression of affection, Bobby weakly returned her embrace.

"Your last three months have been stellar, though, young man," Katherine said as she released him, "so keep it going."

"I'm a changed man, Katherine," asserted Bobby with a hand held to his heart. The air momentarily chilled around them.

"I'm counting on it," Katherine warned while repeatedly poking Bobby in the chest. The pointed finger turned into a reassuring hand on his shoulder and she said, "Good night, Bobby."

"Good night, Katherine," replied Bobby. He donned his coat before descending onto the porch and then the front walk. Despite the January cold, Katherine kept the door open as he departed.

"Bobby," Katherine called to him. Bobby stopped halfway down the front walk and rotated towards her.

"Yeah?" asked Bobby.

"Keep in mind," Katherine answered with a wicked smile and a wink, "that it's a *helluva* lot easier to dispose of a body in the ocean."

. . . .

TONI SAVORED HER RED wine and adored Bobby with stars in her eyes. She wore a black dress overlaid with floral print while he donned a sport coat *sans* tie and sipped on a Gin Gimlet.

"This is perfect, Bobby," gushed a beaming Toni with her chin set in her hand. She soaked in the ambiance of Sibley Gardens, the dining room a soothing blend of predominantly brown earthtones, leather upholstery and dim, soft lighting. Amid the hum of nearby conversations and the occasional clinks of dinnerware, she stated, "I've been craving good Italian for weeks."

"Happy Valentines Day, sweetheart," Bobby said as he lifted his cocktail glass. Toni clinked her wine glass against it. Bobby grinned self-assuredly and declared, "I love you."

"I love you more," replied Toni earnestly. The lovers leaned across the table and shared a short yet ardent kiss before Toni expounded, "What you've accomplished for us, *and for yourself*, is nothing short of incredible. I'm so proud of you."

"Oh, I'm not done yet," Bobby said, his conceited streak flashing in the pan. He finished his drink and then informed Toni, "I have a surprise for you."

"Another one?" asked Toni as Bobby set his glass on the edge of the table. She smiled coyly and said, "Now you're just spoiling me."

"I booked our wedding," Bobby announced proudly, "*in Hawaii*."

A speechless Toni stared at Bobby and her grin disappeared. The waiter passed and plucked his glass from the table. The pause in the conversation did not help Toni process Bobby's words.

"What did you say?" asked Toni as she set her wine glass aside.

"I booked our wedding. In Hawaii," Bobby repeated with a smirk. He grabbed her hands and said, "In April. With a honeymoon afterward, of course."

Toni's head spun. Unable to muster a response, she wriggled her hands free and reacquired her wine glass. Lifting it to her lips, she took a long, slow drink.

"Something wrong?" Bobby inquired. Toni kept the glass in front of her mouth, seemingly paralyzed by the moment. She finally set down her glass demonstratively.

"Uh, well," replied Toni after fifteen-seconds of silence, "I don't know."

"You don't know?" Bobby queried incredulously.

"Bobby, it's a generous, and incredibly romantic, gesture," began Toni with growing distress, "but you know I want a *Catholic* wedding, and I'd really like to have it at St. Alfred."

"Yeah, and that's why I found a great little Catholic Church for it," an undaunted Bobby answered. He pulled a picture from his jacket pocket and handed it to Toni, stating, "St. Peter's by the Sea. It's right on the ocean. I mean, this is it, sweetheart. It's perfect."

Toni took the photograph from Bobby. The tiny, white-walled, blue-roofed church was nestled on the shoreline of the Pacific Ocean with palm trees towering over its cross-tipped steeple.

"It's beautiful," uttered Toni as she studied the picture of the quaint building. She imagined the ocean breeze and the crash of the waves on the rocky shore.

"And *Catholic*," Bobby added with a pointed finger. Toni set down the picture and raised her eyes to her fiancée. Bobby read the mild discomfort on her face.

"Bobby, there's more to a Catholic wedding than just the church," advised Toni gently. The waiter passed the table in the opposite direction and, without disturbing their conversation, set another Gin Gimlet where the empty glass once rested.

"Like what?" a puzzled Bobby asked.

"Like six months of marriage counseling with my priest," stated Toni. She stared at the table as the gears of her mind spun, saying, "And I think I have to get married in my own parish, so that means St. Alfred. I'm sure there's some other stuff, too."

"I didn't think you had to do all that because I'm not Catholic," Bobby countered. Toni looked to him and winced when he protested, "Hell, I'm not even Christian."

"You could be," offered Toni gingerly. She had hoped to introduce Bobby to the Catholic wedding process slowly and struggled to find the right approach on short notice.

"Hey, we've talked about all that," Bobby replied as the first traces of frustration appeared on his face and seeped into his words. He grabbed his second cocktail and said, "You know I'm not into the religious stuff. Not with the way my parents were about it. Ya' know, the parents who got married in the Catholic Church and still divorced?"

The couple once again fell into silence. Bobby downed half his drink.

"Look, let's not worry about it tonight," suggested Toni. She affectionately rubbed his leg with her shoeless foot and said, "Let's just enjoy our night and talk about it later. We'll figure it out."

A pensive Bobby set down his glass. Toni retrieved her wine and finished it.

"We'll schedule a meeting with my priest as soon as he can see us," said Toni confidently. She set down her glass and added, "He'll know what to do. *I promise.*"

"All right," Bobby relented. The couple shared a weak smile and drifted into small talk. The issue of their wedding, however, remained on their minds throughout the evening.

• • • •

EMMA IMPATIENTLY TAPPED her foot on the ground as she waited in a hard plastic chair at the Taylor Police Station. She was due to give a statement regarding a recent fight in Johnny Dubs' parking lot. Regretting her agreement to provide it, Emma exhaled in frustration and looked at the analog clock on the wall.

"Katherine Cullen," announced the fit yet aging desk sergeant wistfully. His use of the surname caught Emma's attention.

"Sergeant Reynolds," Katherine greeted him. Her appearance was noticeably enhanced with extra makeup and a tasteful yet alluring outfit. Sergeant Reynolds stood up and circumvented his desk.

"Oh my god," thought a curious Emma while studying Katherine and envisioning Toni, "that's gotta be her mom."

"So, why are you gracing me with your presence?" asked Sergeant Reynolds as he ogled Katherine. She sauntered up to him and, taking her extended hand chivalrously, he kissed it.

"Always the charmer," Katherine playfully scolded him. She retracted her hand and said bluntly, "I need a favor."

"And here I thought I might get another shot at ya," replied Sergeant Reynolds. He shook his head in defeat and chuckled while returning to his seat. Emma watched their interaction with rapt attention.

"If I ever open that door again, you'll be the first to know, Sergeant," Katherine said with a little seduction added for good measure. His ego boosted, Sergeant Reynolds melted and began effusively praising her. Emma tossed her purse onto an adjacent chair and stood up.

"Excuse me, Sarge," interrupted Emma upon arriving at the desk. She wagged a finger at Katherine and said with confidence, "You're Toni Cullen's mother, aren't you?"

Katherine squared her shoulders to Emma. She cursorily examined her before her attention fell upon the younger woman's brilliant eyes.

"That's me," Katherine answered with a quick tilt of her head. She grinned subtly and said with amusement, "And with those incredible eyes, you must be Elliott's bar-owning, ball-busting sister."

Emma threw Katherine an edgy smirk of mock offense. Sergeant Reynolds cringed.

"Ball-busting's my word, not Toni's," Katherine added. Emma nodded her head in agreement.

"Yeah, that girl blushes when *someone else* says it," replied Emma with a chortle. She lauded her brother's former flame, "She's really a great person, though. My girls *loved* her and they still mention her once in a while."

"Oh, she's talked about them, too. Especially that little firecracker, Lanie," Katherine said. She responded with a tinge of sadness in her voice, "She'll be a wonderful mother someday, despite having a poor role model in that department."

"Hey, now, that's not true at all," objected Sergeant Reynolds. Katherine waved him off and sealed the emotional breach by offering him an appreciative grin.

"Thank you, Sergeant, but it *is* true. Some of it anyway," Katherine said resignedly. She looked to Emma and stated, "Now Toni just has to find the right father."

"Yeah, she does," Emma agreed. Unable to withstand each other's gazes, the women looked away and suppressed the uncomfortable thought on both their minds. Emma recovered first and, motioning to Sergeant Reynolds, inquired, "So, what brings you to see Taylor's finest?"

"To find out who Bobby Aurello really is," Katherine answered bluntly. Emma's face lit up.

"Oh, you're a fellow schemer," said Emma with a gleam in her eye. She folded her arms and shifted her weight to her left foot, saying, "Ya' know, I might be able to help you with that."

"Oh, boy," muttered Sergeant Reynolds. The prospect of Emma Hastings and Katherine Cullen joining forces was truly frightening.

"Why?" Katherine queried with a small measure of suspicion.

"Elliott's no longer on the table, so don't worry about that angle," replied Emma though the words did not ring as true as she expected. Her face contorted with anger and she balled her fists, sneering, "And let's just say I owe that asshole Bobby a little payback."

"Ah, yes, a broken nose and a wounded ego," Katherine replied knowingly.

"Lanie avenged Uncle Elliott," said Emma proudly. She stuck her hands in the back pockets of her jeans and explained, "I owe him for ruining my birthday party. Then there's the fact that Toni deserves better than that jerk."

"That's why I thought Sergeant Reynolds here could assist me," Katherine advised. She was still uncertain of Emma's sincerity and thought the sergeant a safer option.

"Oh, definitely, Sarge could help," said Emma with several nods. Her tone and her countenance became devious and she stated with relish, "But I know someone who can dig a little deeper."

"Em, Em, Em," sighed Sergeant Reynolds while disapprovingly tapping his pen on the desk.

"Am I wrong?" queried Emma unapologetically. Sergeant Reynolds leaned back in his chair and grasped the ends of the armrests.

"No," conceded Sergeant Reynolds reluctantly.

"I like where this is going," Katherine said with a quick glance at Sergeant Reynolds.

"There is one condition, though," added Emma thoughtfully.

"Which is?" Katherine asked.

"If you break 'em up, you have to keep *your* daughter the hell away from *my* brother," stated Emma firmly.

"Oh, is your brother too good for my Toni," an offended Katherine replied.

"Nope," answered Emma. She stated without hesitation, "She's too good for him."

· · · ·

"ANOTHER FIVE MINUTES and I'd have been asleep, young lady," griped Katherine when she answered the front door in a baby blue bathrobe. Light streamed from the outdoor fixture onto the porch, the illumination touching on the gentle, intermittent snowflakes that drifted to the ground. Toni shivered in the cold but, with an open coat and without a hat or gloves, she did little to combat it.

"I'm sorry, Mom," bleated an apologetic Toni. The wind tussled her purple scrubs as she hung her head and whined, "I can talk to you tomorrow. Go back to bed."

"Don't be ridiculous," Katherine grumbled, her irritation merely an act. She reached towards Toni and waved her into the house, demanding, "Get in here. Where are your hat and gloves?"

"I forgot them at work," Toni answered as she crossed the threshold. She shook out of her coat and hung it on a hook while kicking off her shoes.

"You'd think a nurse would know better," scolded Katherine as she closed the door behind her daughter. Wrapping her arms around Toni, she rubbed her to warm her and asked, "Did you miss the day they covered hypothermia and frostbite?"

Katherine guided Toni into the kitchen as if she were a young girl. She then pulled a pair of glasses from the front pocket of her robe and looked at the clock on the wall.

"You're late for an after-work visit," commented Katherine quizzically. Leaving the glasses on her face, she moved past the kitchen table while pulling out a chair. Katherine arrived at the refrigerator, opened the door and produced a casserole dish.

"I covered for Joan for a couple hours, so . . . ," Toni explained. She slumped into the chair.

"I have leftover ham and mashed potatoes," Katherine informed her. She set the dish on the kitchen counter, procured a plate from a cupboard and said, "I cut up the ham and mixed it into the potatoes, though. I didn't expect a visit this weekend."

"You don't need to make anything for me, Mom," Toni replied without affect. Katherine opened a drawer and produced a large serving spoon.

"I'm only going to heat it up," countered Katherine.

"I just need to talk," Toni said. Katherine let the spoon fall to her side and shook her head.

"So, what did you manage to find wrong with a Hawaiian wedding?" asked Katherine with an irked look.

"You know?" a surprised Toni asked.

"He ran it by me before he told you," answered Katherine. She set down the spoon and approached the table, saying, "Wanted me to help with making family arrangements."

"That'll be easy with just the two of us," Toni said.

"Why do you think I said I'd help?" quipped Katherine as she sat down in the chair next to Toni.

"Hawaii's a, a . . . a *dream*, Mom. I mean, who wouldn't want to get married in Hawaii?" Toni said with burgeoning emotion. She began gesticulating demonstratively and reasoned, "The problem is he really wants to get married *in April* in Hawaii. He's made all the deposits and reservations. But that's just not enough time for the Catholic marriage preparation and I want to get married in the Church. I want us to fulfill the Sacrament, together, and be married in God's eyes, not the State of Hawaii's."

"Just do a civil wedding and then get it recognized by the Church," suggested Katherine with a shrug. She urged Toni, "Tell your priest Bobby pressured you into it. Bobby'll probably do it anyway, and that way it's not a lie."

"*Mom!*" Toni chastised her mother. She stood up and added, "It's still dishonest. It's still a sin."

"What can you expect from a lapsed Catholic?" Katherine asked dismissively.

"Which still makes you a Catholic," Toni rejoined. She walked over to the counter and pulled a metal spoon from a drawer.

"Toni, if you don't want to get married in April, then don't get married in April," argued her mother in frustration. She removed her glasses and set them on the table before continuing, "I don't see what the problem is. I'm sure Bobby can reschedule it."

Toni scrunched her face to ward off tears. She closed the drawer and lifted the lid off the dish.

"It's just . . . he's done *so* much for me in the last few months," Toni stated. Her stomach growling, she scooped up some potatoes and said, "I feel like lately he's been doing all the giving and I've been doing all the taking. I don't want it to be like that."

"Bobby took more than he gave for a long time, my dear," sneered Katherine. She stood up and walked to her daughter, insisting, "He has a lot of catching up to do."

"He was never *that* bad," Toni countered. Katherine took the spoon from her as she expounded, "Some men are just a little more selfish than others, and that includes my Bobby. But it's not like he's completely self-centered, not by a long shot. I mean, I feel safe with him. I know he'd risk his life to protect me. I know he loves me, and he's strong . . . ."

Toni smiled. The twinkles in her large eyes made Katherine nauseous.

" . . . and handsome," she said adoringly, "and he's a good provider, and he'll be a rock for our family."

Mother and daughter settled into silence, Toni feeling the effects of fourteen hours on her feet and Katherine contemplating her pact with Emma. The older woman decided to punt.

"Maybe you should talk to your priest," suggested Katherine while stifling a sour expression. She began scooping ham and potatoes onto the plate and said, "He *is* supposed to be your spiritual guide, especially when it comes to the Sacraments."

Toni exhaled dramatically and nodded her head. Katherine finished scooping and put the spoon back in the casserole dish.

"You're right," Toni said. She folded her arms and stated confidently, "Of course, you're right."

"Why don't you stay here tonight?" asked Katherine. She obtained some plastic wrap and covered Toni's plate, continuing, "I'll fix you dinner while you shower. Do you work tomorrow?"

"No," Toni said as part of a yawn.

"Good, then you can sleep in, and I'll fix you a big breakfast," said Katherine, "and we'll sit around and drink coffee all morning."

"Would you go to church with me?" Toni inquired gingerly. Katherine turned to her with the plate in her hand and a scowl on her face but, despite her mother's disapprobation, she offered, "Maybe we can talk to Father Bernard for a few minutes?"

"You're really pushing it, Toni Amanda," replied Katherine. She collapsed under the weight of her daughter's hopeful gaze and said, "Fine. But that means you make *me* a big breakfast tomorrow."

"Deal," Toni said with a bubbly smile. She hugged her mother with girlish affection and kissed her cheek before asking politely, "Can I use your bedroom phone? I wanna call Bobby and say goodnight."

Katherine opened the microwave door and popped the plate inside. Toni watched her expectantly.

"Go ahead," said Katherine. Toni departed with a spring in her step but Katherine threw an annoyed glance at the ceiling, closed the microwave door with a little extra force and stated, "Whatever I'm supposed to do, just let it come from that priest's mouth tomorrow."

. . . .

FATHER BERNARD, A GANGLING priest with the paunch of middle age, stood over six-feet tall but his long, violet vestments made him seem even taller. The balding cleric wore glasses on his kindly face which he occasionally adjusted as he conversed with parishioners.

"Well, I've had enough Catholic Calisthenics for this year," griped Katherine as she dramatically stretched her aching knees. She and Toni stood in the vestibule of St. Alfred Catholic Church after Sunday mass with congregants mulling around them.

"*Mother*," Toni scolded Katherine. Fidgeting as she waited for the priest, she said with uncertainty, "A lot of people want to talk to him today. Maybe I should schedule an appointment."

"Just give it a few minutes," advised Katherine as she read her daughter's distress. Toni trembled.

"I'm so nervous," Toni said with a jittery sigh.

"Toni, the world's a different place now," Katherine stated matter-of-factly, "and it changes more every day. Who knows? Maybe people won't even get married thirty years from now."

"I don't think 'the world does it that way' is a legitimate excuse," Toni argued in frustration. She folded her arms and pretended to read notices and flyers on a bulletin board, saying, "Besides, what about our family tradition? I know it doesn't mean much to you, but it meant a lot to Aunt Agnes."

"*The tradition*," scoffed Katherine. She explained with disdain, "Yes, the women in our family have been married in the Catholic Church for over two hundred years. But I haven't seen one picture where any of them looked truly happy. *The tradition*."

"That's not true," Toni interjected wistfully. She turned to her mother and continued, "Aunt Agnes seemed very happy, and always talked about how much she missed Great Uncle Lou after he died."

"*After* he died, which was *thirty* years before she did, and absence makes the heart grow fonder," retorted Katherine, the topic of discussion raising her level of irritation. Composing herself for her daughter, she said after the pause, "You don't have to shoulder that burden anyway. I broke the tradition by getting a divorce. First one ever."

"You didn't have a choice, Mom," Toni countered in defense of her mother.

"You're not those women and they're not you," declared Katherine steadfastly, the older woman unwilling to further discuss her past. The chill of the opening entry doors seeped into the church so she slid into her coat, saying, "I'm not saying you should abandon your faith, Toni, but you also don't have to abandon Bobby because of it."

Toni studied her mother closely. Katherine sensed her scrutiny and, when she turned her attention to her daughter, she offered her a wise, muted smile. Toni returned it; her mother's composure buttressed her and she felt at ease.

"See, here we go," said Katherine as she tugged Toni forward. Father Bernard, after ending a conversation, moved in their direction and Katherine maneuvered she and Toni into his path. She beamed and beckoned, "Father Bernard."

"Oh, Toni. I was hoping I'd run into you," Father Bernard greeted her. He examined Katherine and said, "And this *must* be your mother. The resemblance is remarkable."

"You're supposed to say that I must be her older sister," stated Katherine coquettishly as she introduced herself. Settling into her role, she offered her hand to the priest and said, "*Katherine.*"

"Hello, Katherine," Father Bernard replied, "pleased to meet you."

"Did you want to talk to me about something, Father?" Toni asked to derail what she considered inappropriate behavior by Katherine.

"Rumor has it that you have a country band," Father Bernard said as if Toni kept Morning Cloak a secret, "and that you're pretty good."

"We just enjoy performing," Toni answered humbly. Momentarily forgetting the weighty issue on her mind, she lamented, "But, actually, we haven't played in a few months."

"Ya' know, a little concert at the Fall Festival might be a big draw for the parish," Father Bernard suggested. Katherine intervened by wrapping her arm in the priest's arm.

"I'm sure it won't be a problem. Those boys are pretty easy-going," said Katherine. A stunned Toni stood mute. Her mother's physicality with her priest embarrassed her but not as much as Katherine's blunt statement: "But we have a little marriage question for you."

"I see," said Father Bernard with piqued interest.

"Well, go ahead, dear," prompted Katherine impatiently. Toni guiltily lowered her eyes and clasped her hands behind her back.

"My fiancée, Bobby, well, he's not Catholic," Toni admitted uneasily.

"He's really not anything," added Katherine with veiled dislike for Bobby.

"He was raised Christian," countered Toni with a critical glance at her mother, "he just doesn't practice anymore."

"That's not a problem at all, Toni," Father Bernard assured her. He gestured as he explained, "It's called 'disparity of cult' in Catholic law. It just takes a little more preparation and effort but, if both parties truly love each other, and you maintain your faith in God, the Church will accept your marriage."

"He's reluctant about getting married in the Church, Father," Toni admitted. Recognizing the angst on her face, Father Bernard laid a comforting hand on her shoulder. Katherine hid her skepticism and remained measured.

"Call the rectory, schedule an appointment and the three of us can discuss it," Father Bernard advised, the confidence of her spiritual guide settling Toni's emotions. He added with a squeeze of her shoulder, "And most importantly, ask for guidance. *Pray.*"

"I will, Father," Toni replied obediently. She felt relieved.

"I look forward to meeting Bobby," Father Bernard said with a smile. He nodded to Katherine and said, "And I hope to see more of you, too, Katherine."

"That depends on how good the coffee and donuts are," quipped Katherine. Toni winced but Father Bernard laughed.

"Have a blessed afternoon, ladies," he said before walking away. Toni watched him depart while Katherine watched her.

"Am I gonna be able to get Bobby into a meeting with Father?" Toni asked with a dubious mien.

"Depends on how good the coffee and donuts are," repeated Katherine. Toni shot her a playfully annoyed look.

"Let's go, funny lady," Toni replied.

Nora gracefully glided towards the lane, proceeded through all the motions Bart taught her and then released the bowling ball. It rolled down the alley and caused eight pins to fall. Nora abruptly spun around after the clatter.

"Yay!" cheered Nora while jumping up and down and clapping. Elliott laughed at her childish reaction though no one else noticed; attendance at the bowling alley, as expected early on a weekday, was sparse.

"Usually *that* kinda celebration is reserved for a strike, or at least a spare," Elliott said with a smirk. While he wore his usual dark t-shirt and blue jeans, Nora shined in high-waisted, acid-washed jeans and a tiny pink top. A long barrette held back her golden hair; its lengths were curled and bouncy.

"*Hey*," objected Nora. She proudly addressed Elliott, "I've been practicing for months and I'm actually getting better."

"I'll forgive ya' this time," Elliott said with a chuckle. The return spit out Nora's ball and she swiftly retrieved it. Taking a long drink of his beer, Elliott watched her carefully align herself for her next throw. She threw the ball with too much English and it swirled into the gutter just before reaching the two remaining pins.

"Nooooo!" pouted Nora with a stamp of her foot. Her shoulders fell and she dejectedly returned to the seating area.

"Eight outta ten's a passing grade," Elliott reasoned sympathetically. He managed another sip of his beer before Nora dropped into his lap and wrapped her arms around his shoulders. Her mood improved.

"I'm *soooo* glad you took today off," gushed Nora. She purloined his beer and drank from it before saying, "I thought we'd see each other a lot more once I moved in but *that* hasn't happened."

"Yeah, our schedules don't exactly mesh well, do they?" sighed Elliott as he accepted the bottle back from Nora and set it on a nearby table.

"You're okay with it though, right?" asked Nora. Her bowling ball emerged from the return and whirled onto the rack. She energetically hopped up and said, "Your turn."

"I can take days off like this all the time," Elliott said as Nora reached out with both hands. He took them and she pulled him to his feet. Feigning the groan of an elderly man, Elliott added, "Hell, I'll take tomorrow off, too, if ya' want."

"I wish," pouted Nora as Elliott made his way to the ball return. She rested a knee on the scorer's table chair and said, "I got a Sociology test tomorrow."

"Eh, you'd probably just make me bowl again, anyway," Elliott quipped. He picked up his bowling ball and turned back to Nora.

"Come on, you know you're having fun," said Nora with a tilt of her head.

"Yeah, but not as much as you," Elliott said with a nod. Nora's addiction to her former boyfriend's favorite sport tweaked his ego.

"I don't know what it is," Nora said with a certain glow, "I just really like to bowl."

"Because of Bart, right?" Elliott asked. He slowly lowered his bowling ball and held it one-handed at his side.

"Stop it," scolded a miffed Nora. She sat in the chair and remarked, "Geez, guys get jealous so easy."

"He was the one who introduced you to bowling. Am I wrong?" asked Elliott, the question sounding more like an accusation.

"Yeah, he got me started, and showed me how," expounded Nora with a pointed finger, "but I'm here playing it with *you*. So stop being jealous and bowl."

Rotating back towards the lane, Elliott moved into position and paused. He then stepped forward and hurled the ball which, with the extra momentum provided by his envious angst, struck the pins. They all scattered and fell in a cacophonous display. Elliott turned to Nora and shrugged.

"Do I jump up and down now?" Elliott deadpanned.

"*Show off*," said Nora with a dubious mien. She shifted gears as Elliott returned to the scorer's table and explained, "I didn't break up with Bart because he was a bad person or wasn't fun to be with. Seriously, Elliott, he's a really great guy."

"Em said it was because he was getting too serious too fast," Elliott replied. He leaned against the table, intensely gazed at Nora and said, "Which is exactly what I'm doing."

"I broke up with Bart because I couldn't stop thinking about *you*," confessed Nora. She reached out and touched Elliott's arm, continuing, "He may be a great guy but he's just not *my* great guy."

"Then who is?" Elliott asked. Nora withdrew her hand and rolled her eyes.

"You're hilarious," said Nora.

"You're incredible," Elliott countered. Studying every inch of the young beauty that was now his, he shook his head and inquired dramatically, "How in the hell is Elliott Warden gonna hold on to you?"

"He doesn't have to, because I'm holding onto him," asserted Nora with confidence, with tenderness and with love. She stood up and moved to hug Elliott. He prepared for an embrace but, instead, Nora spun him around and pushed him towards the lane. Playfully patting him on the butt, Nora said with a grin, "You're up, *Elliott Warden*."

· · · ·

"OKAY, OPEN YOUR EYES," Nora said with a desperate sigh. The twentysomething wore a brown bomber jacket, a grey, hoodless sweatshirt and blue jeans. She also donned pink knitted gloves and a scarf to ward off the chill in the air.

"That's the surprise?" asked Elliott when he gazed up at the sign on North End Bar, its black lettering hard to discern against its blue background. Traffic on Ecorse Road motored past in both directions so he raised his voice and said, "Neil's shitty bar?"

"I never said it was a surprise," Nora reminded him. The anxiety she masked during the car ride began oozing from her.

"So then what're we doing here?" inquired Elliott as he thrust his hands into the pockets of his peacoat. Elliott's and Nora's cheeks and the tips of their noses reddened in the February cold.

"There's something I need ta' do," Nora answered sheepishly. She waited patiently for Elliott to connect the dots. He exhaled and let his chin fall to his chest.

"Oh, no," objected Elliott. He turned to Nora, raised his chin and, considering the possibility that both Brandy and Macayla were inside, stated firmly, "*Bad idea.*"

"I need to make peace with her, Elliott," Nora insisted ardently, "and maybe I can smooth things out between her and Em."

"*Really* bad idea," said Elliott with a discouraging mien.

"But I feel really guilty about, like, messing up their friendship," mewled Nora. The temperature-induced wateriness in her eyes worsened.

"Friendship's a strong word," argued Elliott with doubt in his tone. He added with growing frustration, "And I think you're forgetting she hit you."

"Yeah, but I could've handled the whole thing differently and then that wouldn't've happened," Nora countered. Elliott hesitated and squirmed under the prospect of Brandy's wrath.

"Look, Nora. You, as usual, are a sweetheart for thinkin' it," Elliott said while staring at the sign. He turned to Nora and explained, "But Brandy and Em'll never bury the hatchet. Trust me. That party's over."

"*Please*," Nora begged. She took his hands in her own and, tugging them gently, urged Elliott, "I really think I can fix it. And she won't even, like, let me start talking if you're not there."

"You just want me to keep her from slappin' you again," Elliott replied with a smirk and a shake of his head. Nora emphatically yanked on his hands and gazed at him with puppy-dog eyes. Elliott, his resistance melted by her naïve adorableness, relented, "All right. Let's get this disaster over with."

The couple moved to the metal entry door and, after a pregnant pause, Elliott opened it and held it for Nora. Hot, stale air tinged with a smoky-scent and the sounds of seventies rock rushed over them both.

"Yuck," Nora muttered with a wrinkled nose.

"Just like his apartment," Elliott commented blithely before adding, "before the whole 'marriage-and-kid' thing, anyway."

Elliott ushered a nervous Nora inside the bar and let the door creak closed behind them. It took several seconds for their eyes to adjust to the darkness which exceeded that of Johnny Dubs.

"You got real balls, comin' in here, honey," said Brandy loudly when she noticed Nora. The petite, raven-haired forty-one-year-old was attractive but aged beyond her years. Her big, hazel eyes lit up when she gazed on

Elliott and, with a hand on her hip and a tray in the other, she uttered in astonishment, "*No effin' way.*"

A bespectacled man in his late thirties and wearing a flannel shirt stood behind the bar. Shaggy-haired and even shaggier- bearded, the tall brunette tossed a white bar towel over his shoulder.

"Slummin' it today, huh, Elliott?" the man queried. He grinned mischievously and ogled Nora before realizing her identity. The man threw up his arms, the sudden motion causing the towel to drop to the floor, and asked, "Really, man? You're gonna start a chick fight in my bar?"

"Hello, Neil," responded Elliott.

"Chick fights're okay with us," announced a grizzled regular sitting at the other end of the bar. Laughter ensued from the other two barflies perched on their stools and the motley trio watched the unfolding interactions with great interest.

"I'm taking my break now," advised Brandy as she untied her pocketed apron and tossed it onto the bar.

"Ya' just took one," Neil protested. He swooped down and picked up the bar towel.

"So I'm taking another one," snapped an incredulous Brandy. She shook her head and chastised him, "Damn, Neil, don't be such an asshole."

"Yeah, Neil," said the grizzled regular. Nora stood still and gawked at the scene, the cutting back-and-forth rendering her speechless.

"Have a seat, kids," said Brandy as she motioned to a nearby table. Sitting down in one of the four chairs, she pulled a pack of cigarettes from one front jeans pocket and a lighter from the other. She procured a cigarette and then tossed the half-empty pack onto the table, asking smugly, "So, you two here to announce a weddin' or somethin'?"

"Not exactly," Elliott answered. He moved to the table and pulled out a chair for Nora. Meanwhile, Brandy lit her cigarette and took a long, slow drag on it. She stretched out her short legs and set her feet on the chair next to her.

"Well, come on, princess," Brandy taunted Nora while laying her lighter next to the cigarette pack. The younger woman hesitated. Elliott gestured towards the chair.

"This is what you wanted, *princess*," Elliott said dubiously.

. . . .

"SO WHAT'S THIS ALL about?" inquired Brandy in a plume of smoke directed at Nora. She rested her elbow on the arm of the chair and held her cigarette aloft. Scrunching her face in disgust, Nora coughed and waved the smoke away.

"C'mon, Brandy," Elliott rebuked her. He and Nora sat opposite Brandy with two beers in front of them.

"Sorry," said Brandy unconvincingly as she made a lackadaisical effort to fan the smoke away from Nora.

"It's okay," Nora said while laying a hand on Elliott's arm. Her countenance contrite, she stated, "I know you're mad at me."

"And you thought comin' to see me at work would help?" inquired Brandy with a healthy dose of skepticism. She snickered and added, "At least ya' had the good sense to bring this handsome bastard with ya' so I wouldn't smack ya' again."

"Damn it, Brandy, will ya' just listen," Elliott snapped. Brandy laughed loudly, her outburst momentarily drawing the attention of the bar patrons.

"Well look who else is feelin' ballsy today," announced Brandy after another hit of her cigarette. Elliott scowled and moved to retaliate but Nora again placed her hand on his arm.

"*It's okay*, Elliott," Nora repeated. Sensing Elliott's angst and Brandy's annoyance, she blurted sincerely, "Brandy, I'm really, really sorry I got you fired."

Elliott's gaze darted from Brandy to Nora and back again. Brandy's irritation melted away.

"Sickeningly adorable 'til the end," replied Brandy with a chuckle and a shake of her head. She rested her head on her fist and indulged in her cigarette.

"What?" Nora queried with a puzzled mien.

"Damn it, you're so cute and innocent I can't be pissed at you," confessed Brandy begrudgingly with a burgeoning smile. Nora's cheeks warmed with embarrassment but Brandy continued, "Nora, you were stupid for not snaggin' Elliott earlier and you deserved all the shit I gave you. Except the smack. I'm sorry about that, I guess. But, in the end, *I* got me fired, not you."

"Do you mean that?" Nora queried. She was taken aback by Brandy's admission.

"Well, the booze helped, too," replied Brandy before blowing smoke towards the ceiling. A dubious look from Elliott, who was well aware of the older woman's alcohol tolerance, caused her to admit, "But it was mostly me."

Elliott watched his girlfriend in wonder. Defusing the bomb that was Brandy was an impressive feat for one so young.

"She's just . . . *somethin' else*," Elliott thought, the phrase seeming an inadequate characterization of his girlfriend.

"So what about Emma?" Nora queried as she pressed her advantage. Elliott winced.

"Don't push it, kid," warned Brandy. Much to Elliott's surprise, the threesome left the topic of Emma and settled into a cordial if not pleasant conversation. He and Nora finished their beers and, when the conversation ended, Brandy hugged them both.

"Hey, kid," beckoned Brandy as Elliott and Nora departed. They stopped and Nora took a step towards the older woman.

"It's *Nora*," Nora replied. Brandy rolled her eyes but played along.

"Hey, *Nora*. Remember: keep his balls empty and his belly full," advised Brandy. Several laughs echoed throughout the bar and Nora's cheeks again turned red. Seriousness hardened Brandy's face and she added, "But don't let that fool wait too long to seal the deal, either."

Brandy snapped her fingers before Elliott could react. The eerie click tore through the room and paralyzed everyone who heard it.

"Things can change just like that," Brandy stated. Nora nodded her head in the affirmative and, after a brief pause, she turned on a dime and hurried from the bar.

"See ya', Neil," Elliott yelled, the call garnering a wave from Neil as he talked on the telephone. He and Brandy shared a dubious smirk before he disappeared through the door. She chortled.

"Now I just gotta find me a stud in his twenties," remarked Brandy to no one in particular. Her eyes lingered on the door for a few seconds but, feeling buoyant, she returned to her duties and her customers, muttering, "Eh, the old man'd never have it."

. . . .

THE EXISTENCE OF ELLIOTT'S recent girlfriend and former high school sweetheart, Donna, slipped Nora's mind after the whirlwind beginning of their new relationship. When she stepped into Johnny Dubs on an ordinary February day, however, it was like a car crashing into Nora's heart.

"She *is* Em's best friend," Nora thought when she wondered at Donna's unexpected arrival. Before she had any opportunity to be jealous of her, and despite the opinions of others, she decided Donna was not attractive. Her eyebrows seemed too prominent, her jaw too angular, her eyelashes too dark and the highlights in her curly brown hair too "young". Feeling remorse over her negative appraisal of Donna, she forced out the compliment, "She does have pretty hazel eyes. Not gorgeous like Emma's. But still pretty."

Nora purposefully avoided Donna and retreated into the far corner of the bar to clean a table she had already cleared. Her efforts were aided by Emma who emerged from the stairwell leading to her office. She greeted her best friend and quickly ushered her up the stairs.

"That was close," Nora said quietly. Discombobulated by Donna's impromptu appearance, she meandered around the dining areas and pretended to tidy tables while falling prey to her suspicions. She stopped at a table she had yet to clear and thought worriedly, "I wonder if Emma changed her mind about me and Elliott."

Nora jumped and squeaked when two arms wrapped themselves around her stomach from behind. Several barflies buzzed with laughter.

"Relax," Elliott said as he set his chin on her shoulder, "it's just me."

Nora inhaled Elliott's manly scent and indulged in the sensation of his arms holding her tightly. She tilted her head sideways and affectionately rested it against his temple. Elliott beamed.

"Aren't you supposed to be at work?" asked Nora as she rotated to face Elliott. He pulled her into a passionate kiss and she went weak in the knees.

"I was drivin' by and just wanted to see you," advised Elliott while holding Nora upright.

"*Elliott*," Nora cooed, the romantic gesture touching her very spirit. She set her arms on his shoulders and asked, "Can you stay for lunch?"

"Nah, I gotta get to my next appointment, like, *now*," Elliott advised disappointedly. He hugged Nora and pecked her on the forehead before saying, "Love ya'. See ya' at home."

Nora's heart sank when she noticed Donna lurking behind the partially closed stairwell door and watching her embrace Elliott. He, however, did not see her.

"Love you, too," Nora said as she reluctantly released Elliott but kept her attention on Donna. She failed to see him hustle towards the front doors and disappear into the light of day, saying to herself, "I don't think she liked *that*."

Donna made no effort to hide her jealousy and purposely approached Nora. The young waitress feigned ignorance of Donna's presence while wiping a table.

"So you and Elliott, huh?" asked Donna. A chilliness arose between the two women.

"Yeah," Nora replied sheepishly. She queried in a jittery voice, "Didn't Em, like, tell you?"

"No, she, like, didn't," replied Donna as she appraised Nora.

"I'm sorry," Nora apologized. Looking for avenues to flee the conversation, she said, "I didn't know he was stopping by."

Donna's mood became fey. Nora took a step backward and left the rag on the table.

"I wonder what you have that I don't," pondered Donna aloud. She said pejoratively, "Other than being a lot younger, of course."

A speechless Nora became visibly anxious as she felt Donna's displeasure ooze over her. Donna, meanwhile, considered whether to plant the seeds of doubt in Nora's mind.

"I mean, I used ta' have what you did," said Donna with a yearning for the past. Loathe to surrender Elliott, especially to a younger woman, she made her decision and asserted, "*I was you*. Young, and sweet, and deferential."

"Deferential?" Nora queried. The "young and sweet" label had been affixed to her so often as to be meaningless in her mind; *deferential*, however, was new.

"You just puppy-dog after him," expounded Donna as she walked through old memories, "following him everywhere. Doing what he wants to do. Liking the things he likes. Always worried that someone else'll catch his eye."

Donna smiled a half-smile but it was not a happy one. Nora's expression soured.

"Hell, always *terrified* someone will," continued Donna. She returned to the present and her envious eyes flashed to Nora.

"It's not like that," Nora objected with a discomfited expression. Emma emerged from the stairwell door with her coat and purse.

"What's going on here?" Emma inquired as if catching Lanie taking advantage of her little sister.

"Just sharing some notes on Elliott," confessed Donna. The admission surprised Nora.

"Really," Emma said suspiciously. She and Donna exchanged bizarre, almost hostile, expressions. Nora, her tolerance at an end, finally found her out: one of the regulars held up his glass and rattled the ice cubs inside.

"Nooooorrrra," he beckoned.

"I'd better go check on the guys' drinks," Nora quickly interjected. She grabbed the rag with which she wiped tables and swiftly fled the tense situation.

"Yeah, you do that," Emma droned while studying her best friend. Donna lost their optical battle and quickly looked away. Stepping closer to her, Emma asked, "Do you really think it's a good idea for you two to talk Elliott 101?"

Donna returned her gaze to her friend. The intensity of Emma's eyes and the edge in her tone betrayed her displeasure.

"C'mon, Em, it was just girl talk," deflected Donna though with a guilty mien. She squirmed under Emma's disapproval and explained, "I figured a little advice on Elliott couldn't hurt. Just helpin' her out, ya' know?"

"Anything that keeps that sweetheart in his life makes him happy," Emma stated. She leaned toward Donna in an ominous manner and asked, "And that's what we all want, *right?*"

"Of course," replied Donna nervously though her response seemed forced to Emma. She made a mental note of her best friend's bizarre behavior.

"Well, I'm ready," Emma said with a softening demeanor and raised arms, "so let's go."

"Let's go," repeated Donna as she watched Nora in her peripheral vision.

· · · ·

TAKING UP HIS USUAL position on a Saturday when Nora was working, Elliott dozed in his recliner with both living room lamps blazing and the television tuned to NBC. An eleven o'clock news preview for the local affiliate, WDIV, transitioned the commercial segment into the television show *Remington Steele*.

"Such bullshit," Elliott complained as he drifted out of sleep. His favorite show, *Hunter*, was on a temporary hiatus and it irked him. Elliott closed his eyes and his head slumped to the side. Fighting off sleep, he raised his eyelids and acquired a gray ring box in his vision. Elliott studied it and said, "I shouldn't leave you out. She gets off early one night and I'm busted."

Elliott languidly sat up, retrieved the ring box from the end table and popped it open. The engagement ring once meant for Donna was tucked safely inside and sparkled in the light of the lamps. He examined it meticulously, noting each and every facet and sparkle, and thought of Nora.

"This is really it," Elliott said as the warmth of his love washed over him. He grinned weakly and stated, "She's really the one."

A knock at the door startled Elliott. The instinct to hide the ring flared within him and he swiftly closed the box with a soft thud.

"Who the hell is it at this hour?" Elliott asked aloud. He began to rise but froze when he remembered Toni's August 1985 visit. A chill rippled down Elliott's spine and he uttered, "*No way.*"

Elliott stood up and quickly stashed the ring box in the end table's small drawer. Hesitantly proceeding to the front door, he moved his head towards the peephole. He paused halfway, exhaled and then traveled the rest of the distance.

"You gotta be kidding me," Elliott said when he gazed through the peephole and identified his unexpected guest. His anxiety morphed into mild irritation and he opened the main door, muttering, "My god, it's like it called to her or somethin'."

"Hi, Elliott," said Donna with a warm, eager smile and a raised hand of greeting. She wore a stylish maroon coat with a white, winter pattern across the chest and a matching ivy hat and gloves. Elliott, in contrast, wore a white t-shirt and gray sweatpants.

"You come from a fashion show or somethin'?" Elliott asked through the glass storm door. It began to fog as the heat from his apartment warmed the cold glass.

"Just out and about. Thought I'd stop by," answered Donna with feigned innocence. When Elliott did not respond, his hand still on the handle of the front door, she asked, "Can I come in?"

"Where's Ben?" Elliott inquired suspiciously. His first inclination was to admit Donna into his apartment but better judgement and love for Nora squelched it.

"In Florida," Donna answered as she stuck her hands in her coat pockets, "at a conference."

"And you passed up the chance to escape Michigan in February?" Elliott asked. He subtly began closing the door and added, "Ya' know, get the hell away from this cold."

"I'd like to get away from the cold right now," replied Donna coyly as she exhaled a steamy breath and shivered.

"I'm not really up for a visit," Elliott advised her. Quickly devising a cover story, he added, "Long week at work, think I'm fightin' a cold, I'm tired. You know how it goes."

"Liar," said Donna with distaste. Elliott immediately suspected she knew of his relationship with Nora. Pressing her advantage, she opened the fogged storm door and stepped inside.

"Seriously, Donna, I'm not up for company right now," Elliott replied while retreating a step. Donna swept the room with her gaze and noted the signs of his cohabitation with Nora: a jacket hanging on a kitchen chair, a pair of shoes tossed heedlessly aside and new knickknacks throughout the apartment.

"She's living with you?" inquired Donna accusatorily. She began to move further into the apartment but Elliott reclaimed lost ground and blocked her advance.

"It's none of your business," Elliott began firmly, "but, yeah, she's living here. And that's why you can't stay."

Donna's angry eyes flashed to Elliott. He gave her a quizzical look.

"What're you doing here, Donna?" Elliott asked.

"Correcting mistakes," stated Donna as she placed her open hands on his chest. He grabbed them and, despite her struggling, removed them from his body. Donna whimpered, "*I miss you, Elliott.*"

"I don't need this right now," Elliott said tersely. Shocked by the rejection, Donna went on the offensive.

"You're just chasing the old me," argued Donna while pulling off her cap. She attempted to remove her gloves but Elliott prevented it.

"Time to go, Donna," Elliott insisted. He used his entire body to usher her towards the door. Donna resisted.

"She's just like I was," Donna asserted as she set her feet and refused to depart. She shoved Elliott, the sudden contact catching him by surprise, and darted underneath his left arm. Planting herself on the couch, she reasoned, "And just like me, she'll grow up Elliott, and then you'll be right where you are now with me. She won't be all sweet and naïve forever."

"C'mon, Donna, let's not do this," Elliott begged as he took pity on her. Donna's desperation tugged at his heart.

"Be an adult," pleaded Donna. Elliott grew angry as she implored him, "Have an adult relationship, *with me.* You and Nora won't work. And I'm not waiting for you forever. But there's no need to wait. We can always try therapy to smooth out the rough edges. The immaturity."

"Oh, sure, and Ben can be our therapist," Elliott scoffed. He abruptly lunged at Donna, grabbed her by her arms and yanked her to her feet. The move stunned her and, with a strong grip, Elliott pulled their faces together. Misreading the situation, Donna expected a kiss and closed her eyes. Elliott instead growled, "Get this straight, Donna."

Donna's eyelids flickered and opened when she felt the heat of his acrimony and the sting of his words. He riveted his gaze to her countenance.

"I loved you once, but it was a long time ago, and I don't now," Elliott explained. Donna dropped her hat and squirmed uncomfortably in his grasp but made no effort to escape. She kept her eyes on his face but turned her cheek away from him.

"*You do,*" whimpered Donna.

"No, I don't," Elliott stated brusquely. Donna began crying as he escorted her to the door. He scooped up her hat on the way and continued, "But

I do love Nora, and I'm not giving her up for anything. So you're leaving, right now, and going home, and calling Ben, and telling him you love him or whatever you two say to each other. And you're not coming back here. *Got it?*"

Intermittent tears lazily rolled down Donna's face, her shock temporarily dulling her emotional pain. Elliott held her arm with one hand, opened the storm door with the other and deposited her onto his porch. Donna attempted to turn towards Elliott but he kept her facing the front walk.

"Now *I'm* going back to my chair to sleep until my girl gets home," Elliott said. Setting Donna's hat on her head, he added, "And *you're* going home. Good night."

Elliott closed the door and noisily locked it. The cold made Donna shiver but the shivers soon morphed into rage-induced trembles and she shed angry tears.

"You'll love me again," vowed Donna eerily, "*you will.*"

"Toni!" yelled a wide-eyed Tessa when she saw Toni sitting at a small table in the Heritage Hospital cafeteria. Darting through a maze of tables and chairs and dodging several surprised cafeteria customers, she bounded towards the nurse.

"Oh, damn it, not today," Emma lamented with slumping shoulders. Lanie's broken elbow and visit to the Emergency Room had, after seven straight long days at Johnny Dubs, drained the last of her energy reserves. Emma called out weakly, "Tessa, get back here!"

"Mommy, look, it's Toni!" exclaimed Tessa in the middle of her circuitous route, the nine-year-old emphatically pointing at Toni's table. Emma's mien and mood soured when she saw her companion.

"And Bobby's with her," Emma sneered quietly. She watched Toni, who wore her usual, long-sleeved scrubs, rise to her feet and open her arms. Bobby, meanwhile, pretended not to see Emma, who clenched her teeth and muttered, "*Great.*"

"Hi, Toni!" gushed Tessa as she crashed into Toni with an emphatic embrace.

"Hey, Tess'!" Toni replied while lovingly returning the child's hug. The pair ended their embrace and she asked, "What're you doing here?"

"Lanie broke her elbow ice skating this morning," Emma advised upon arriving at the table. Tessa pointed to her own elbow to demonstrate the injury.

"Oh, no," Toni replied, "that's terrible!"

"She cried a lot," offered Tessa. She attached herself to Toni's side and grasped her hand.

"Lanie's gonna be fine," Emma sighed with tired eyes. She folded her arms and, glancing at Bobby, added, "Thankfully, the bone's still in place so no surgery."

"Oh, thank you, God," Toni prayed aloud. Her spirits dipped when she realized Emma and Bobby were in dangerous proximity to one another. The prospect of a confrontation cast a sudden pall over the table.

"Do you wanna see her?" asked Tessa eagerly, the child blissfully unaware of the tension among the adults. Toni's eyes flashed to Bobby and her heart sank. She held her breath in anticipation of his response.

"Sure, go ahead," answered Bobby earnestly and without the veiled aggravation Toni expected. He shrugged and reasoned, "The kid'd probably love to see you, and we were about done with lunch anyway."

"Thank you," said Toni in adoring surprise, her love for Bobby overflowing. She maneuvered around the table, kissed her fiancée on the lips and said, "See ya' tonight?"

"You bet, sweetheart," Bobby replied. He caressed Toni's cheek and she beamed. The moment struck Emma: Toni seemed truly happy.

"Let's go!" insisted Tessa as she tugged Toni's arm. She relented and allowed the chattering child to drag her towards the cafeteria exit.

"Slow down, maniac. I don't need another broken arm," Emma shouted after her. Turning to Bobby, she felt her skin crawl but said, "Thanks for being cool about it. It'll mean a lot to Lanie."

"I just don't want her to kick me in the nuts again," joked Bobby with smirk. The levity caught Emma off-guard.

"Right," Emma said with an uneasy half-grin. Feeling uncomfortable, she stated, "Well, I'd better catch up with them."

"Yeah," said Bobby as the tension between them thickened. Emma turned to leave but he beckoned, "Hey, Emma."

"Yeah?" Emma replied as she rotated to face Bobby. He hesitated as if debating his next move but, after several seconds, stood up. Emma took a reflexive step backward.

"I'm sorry . . . about your birthday party," apologized Bobby clumsily. The tension between them vanished. Bobby looked to the floor, thrust his hands in his pockets and said, "I was a jerk, *a huge jerk*, and I never should've hit your brother, and . . . I'm just sorry."

"Uh, okay, thanks," Emma responded with several nods. She struggled in the moment, her anger over Bobby's assault on Elliott warring with her gratitude for his gesture towards her daughters and his contriteness. Emma forced herself to say, "Congrats on the engagement."

"Thanks. I'm a lucky guy," said Bobby, his apparent transformation stunning Emma. The two adults lingered in a discomfiting limbo for ten seconds.

"Well, I gotta go," Emma interjected into the stalemate. Discombobulated by the odd and unexpected encounter with Bobby, she waved awkwardly.

"Hope Lanie has a speedy recovery," said Bobby. He and Emma exchanged muted grins before she hurried after Tessa and Toni. Bobby watched her depart and, once she disappeared, fell into his chair and drifted into thoughts of Toni.

• • • •

"TONI!" LANIE SHOUTED when she saw Toni enter her small emergency department room. The movement of her excited response tweaked her casted forearm. She grimaced and griped, "Ow."

"See, Toni, I told you she broke her arm," said Tessa as if Toni doubted her truthfulness. The nurse walked to Lanie's bedside, grasping the railing with one hand and caressing the child's head with the other.

"Oh, Lanie," Toni said. Lanie allowed the first caress but dodged the second.

"I didn't break my arm. It's a greenstick fracture of my ulna," Lanie corrected her sister in irritation. She gingerly lifted her blue-green cast which ran from just below her fingers on her right hand to just below her elbow.

"*Ouch*," Toni said with a pained, sympathetic expression. She gripped the railing with both hands and commented with an uncertain grin, "Your cast is a really pretty color, though."

"Just like Mom's eyes," stated Lanie matter-of-factly. Toni's attention turned to Dave who sat in a chair in the corner of the room and shook his head at Lanie's precociousness.

"Hi, Dave, good to see you," Toni greeted him affably. She offered him a dubious expression and trailed off, "Could be under better circumstances, I guess . . . ."

"Yeah," acknowledged a tired David with a sigh, "but good to see you, too."

"This cast sucks, Toni," complained Lanie while again holding it aloft. Tessa insinuated herself under Toni's left arm. David noticed and chuckled.

"I know, I broke – fractured my ulna *and* radius – when I was little. Twice, so *two* casts," Toni said as her sympathy morphed into empathy. She toyed with Tessa's long, brown hair and reasoned hopefully, "At least it's winter so it'll be off in plenty of time for swimming this summer."

"I wanna go swimming now!" shouted Lanie impetuously.

"Yeah, me, too!" yelled Tessa.

"Gotta keep it down, girls," Lanie's ER doctor scolded them before David could calm his daughters. When the doctor noticed his colleague, he smirked and jabbed her, "And you should know better, Ms. Cullen."

"Sorry, Doctor," Toni replied. The doctor turned heel and walked away just as Emma approached the room. She halted in the doorway. Watching Toni interact with her girls stirred something within her.

"She's ready to be a mamma," said Emma to herself. A depressive thought arose in her mind and she continued, "Too bad it can't be with Elliott, 'cuz I don't think Nora's there yet. Probably won't be for a while, either."

Emma's mind went quiet. She then shrugged and entered the room.

"She'll get there," Emma assured herself. Lanie keyed on her mother the second she appeared.

"I wanna go home, Mom," pouted Lanie. Emma sensed her family's fraying patience.

"Any luck on those discharge papers?" Emma asked David. She walked to him and wrapped an arm around his broad shoulders.

"Nothin' yet," answered David weakly. Toni scanned the room, her eyes moving from tired face to tired face, and felt the Hastings's exhaustion.

"I'll pull some strings," Toni stated firmly. She gave Tessa a mini-hug and promised, "We're gonna get you guys outta here."

"You don't have to do that," Emma replied though the assertion was merely a pleasantry. The prospect of Toni's assistance enheartened her.

"Hey, anything for my favorite family," Toni insisted with an engaging smile. The statement tweaked Emma's heart: she saw a pregnant Toni in her mind and loathed the prospect of it not being Elliott's child. The nurse gently hugged Lanie's head and kissed the top of it, saying, "Get better, monster."

Toni's use of the word "monster" struck her; it was the same term of endearment Elliott used for his nieces. She hid her emotion and quickly embraced Tessa while reaching out and grasping David's hand.

"Thanks so much, Toni," David exhaled, "we're all *burnt*."

"Any time," Toni replied. She released Tessa and, in a surprise for both women, hugged Emma.

"I wish I could say it," Emma said when the women separated but held onto each other's forearms.

"I know," Toni said with barely perceptible squeezes. She relinquished her grip and stated, "I'll get those discharge papers rolling *pronto*."

The women said no more but shared a knowing grin. Toni disappeared into the hallway.

"Say what?" asked David with a furrowed brow.

"Don't worry about it," Emma answered dismissively. She shook her head and lied, "Not important."

The impromptu intervention by Toni moved the Hastings to the front of the discharge line. Already late returning from lunch, she then hurried past Lanie's room. A laugh from the ten-year-old stopped her in her tracks.

Looking into the room, Toni observed the loving family that was the Hastings. Tessa jumped into David's arms, the six-foot-four dad easily holding her aloft, and Emma slipped into the hospital bed with Lanie who laid her head on her mother's shoulder. The foursome discussed what special treat the girls would receive after their taxing hospital visit.

"It's so *wonderful* what they have," Toni thought enviously. She folded her arms and continued to watch the Hastings while ignoring the hospital traffic flowing past her. Several minutes elapsed before Tessa noticed Toni in the hallway and waved at her. She returned the wave and, with her arms still folded, slowly walked away in deep contemplation.

· · · ·

"OH, SHIT," EMMA HISSED when she saw Katherine glide into Johnny Dubs. The older woman, who wore a long, charcoal winter coat with knit white gloves and a scarf, looked very much out-of-place as she scanned the club. Hurrying up to Katherine, a ponytailed Emma asked in irritation, "What're you doing here? There's *always* a chance Elliott could pop up."

"That'd be a nice surprise," replied Katherine licentiously. She reminisced about earlier encounters with Elliott, saw his handsome face in her mind and said, "I've liked your brother since the day I met him. If I were just a decade younger-."

"You'd still be too old for his tastes," Emma rudely interrupted Katherine.

"My goodness it's hot in here," replied Katherine while ignoring the slight. She shed her gloves and scarf.

"Cigarette-smoking drunks give off a lotta heat," Emma said brusquely. Katherine removed her coat, set it on a barstool and carefully sat on the one next to it. Emma took Katherine by the arm and guided her to her feet, griping, "Uh, we're *not* talking out here."

"Then lead on," said Katherine in irritation as Emma's pushiness tweaked her ego. She whisked her coat off the stool.

"No, wait," Emma said while holding up a palm. She took Katherine's coat from her and set it on a different stool, gesticulating and explaining, "It'll look suspicious if we go up to my office. We'll talk out here. It's gotta look casual, like it's a coincidence or something."

Katherine exhaled to center herself and chuckled. She gestured to a barstool and then occupied the one next to it.

"I'll take whatever red wine you can have here the quickest," advised Katherine while tapping the bar. Emma resisted the suggestion, folded her arms and stomped her foot.

"Aren't you worried about getting caught?" Emma demanded. Katherine titled her head and gave her a dubious look. Keeping her sparkling eyes on her guest, Emma called out, "Luke, two bourbons on the rocks, please."

"Oh, that's better," said Katherine with a smirk and no effort to correct the order. She again gestured to the open bar stool and stated, "Now, to answer your question."

"That'd be nice," Emma grumbled. Acceding to Katherine's request, she dramatically slumped onto the bar stool.

"No, I'm not worried about getting caught," replied Katherine. Luke approached, slid two full cocktail glasses towards the conspirators and melted into the background.

"And you're not worried about it *why*?" Emma asked incredulously. Katherine, in an uncharacteristic moment of doubt, delayed her answer by partaking of the bourbon.

"Because I can't do it," Katherine answered remorsefully.

"Can't do what?" Emma queried.

"I can't dig up dirt on Bobby. I can't interfere," answered Katherine staunchly. She took another drink of bourbon, a drink in which Emma joined her, and then stated bluntly, "*She loves him, Emma.* And it's her caring, and compassion, and love, that will make that marriage work. It isn't about him. I mean, look at what she's accomplished with him already. I just can't do it."

Emma's eyes glazed and she contemplated her recent encounter with Bobby and Toni. Katherine allowed the pause and waited silently. Emma drained her glass and returned it to the bar with a thud and the clinking of ice cubes.

"You're right," Emma agreed begrudgingly, her face contorting in response to the liquor's strength.

"I am?" asked a puzzled Katherine.

"That daughter of yours is a natural matriarch, kinda like my mom was, and she'll create a *wonderful* family," Emma declared ardently. Her confidence waned and she said in a meandering explanation, "And then there's, well . . . it's entirely possible – and I hate to say this – but, I think . . . it just might be that, well . . . Bobby may actually be an okay guy."

"Are you serious?" inquired Katherine. The dissent she expected from Emma did not materialize.

"Lanie broke her arm the other day and Tessa and I ran into Toni and Bobby having lunch in Heritage's cafeteria," Emma expounded. She turned her barstool so that she faced the bar and, while staring into her empty glass, continued, "Well, you know how much my girls love Toni, so, of course, my little princess just charges right up to her."

The beginning of the story brightened Katherine's face. Emma rested her folded arms on the bar and her feet on the bars of the stool.

"So, we intruded on Bobby's time with Toni," Emma said, "and Tessa asks if Toni wants to go see Lanie, and then Toni asks Bobby if she can go see her and then . . . and then he said 'sure' and was totally cool about it."

"Unbelievable," said Katherine, the words the only response she could muster.

"And that's not all," Emma said. She stuck her finger in her cocktail glass and lazily stirred the ice cubes, saying, "He apologized for ruining my birthday party, and hitting Elliott, and even made a joke about Lanie bustin' his balls."

Katherine laughed heartily. Emma smirked.

"I love that story," Katherine said. Emma joined her in a laugh and then became serious again."

"The point is he acted like a good guy," Emma stated in disbelief, "so . . . maybe he is one."

"This is a sight I never thought I'd see," Toni said when she appeared behind her mother.

"Oh, hey, Toni," offered a suddenly flustered Emma. She pulled her finger from the glass and rotated her stool towards Toni.

"Hello, dear," Katherine said while flawlessly feigning composure.

"What're you doing here, Mom?" Toni inquired with a healthy dose of suspicion.

"Seeing if this club was available for a little party to celebrate your wedding. You know, so some of your friends can be a part of the festivities," explained Katherine in believable fashion. Buttressed by the older woman's performance, Emma centered herself as Katherine added, "I know how much you love playing here, and I thought you'd like to put on a little show."

"I *was* gonna ask if we could start playing again soon," began Toni as the joy of her upcoming marriage flooded her heart, "but, now that I think about it . . . ."

Toni trailed off and looked at her mother. Emma waited with bated breath for her to continue.

". . . I'm getting married in April," Toni declared proudly. Her statement mystified her mother who inhaled sharply. Smiling widely with glistening eyes, Toni said, "So, though I hate to be away from the mic for so long, we should probably wait until May. Maybe we could do the party then?"

"Uh, yeah, sure," answered Emma, "that'd be great."

"Hey, how's Elliott by the way?" Toni asked. She, like her mother, managed a convincing performance, one in which she showed only friendly interest in Elliott. Katherine saw through it but said nothing.

"He's good. Really good, actually," said Emma while intentionally omitting Elliott's relationship with Nora. She said no more and, sensing the presence of another woman in his life, Toni did not question her further.

"That's great," Toni said, "*really great.*"

. . . .

TONI SWEPT INTO CARL'S Chop House in Detroit and desperately scanned the crowd for her beloved fiancée. She felt underdressed in a colorful, geometric sweater and jeans but her desire to speak to Bobby overruled her fashion sense.

"He said they were meeting at six-thirty, so they should be almost done by now," Toni thought as she glanced at a clock on the wall. Several minutes later she located Bobby in a sea of tables sitting with a white-haired man. Both men wore shirts and loosened ties with their suit jackets hung on their chairs and their sleeves rolled up. The pair sipped after-dinner cocktails and seemed to be engaged in small talk. Toni's heart fluttered as she watched Bobby and she said quietly, "He's so handsome."

Taking a seat at the bar, Toni waited eagerly for Bobby to finish his dinner meeting. She began to feel self-conscious due to her casual dress so she ordered a glass of red wine instead of a beer. The restaurant was similar to Sibley Gardens though without the Italian feel; its tablecloths appeared like white flowers in the copiousness of earthy tones and soft, warm lighting.

"Just be patient," Toni admonished herself. She held the neglected wine glass in her hand and anxiously tapped her foot. Several well-dressed, interested men passed her but, failing to establish eye contact with the preoccupied nurse, each one continued on his way. She assured herself, "He'll be done soon."

Twenty minutes later, Bobby and the older gentleman rose to their feet, donned their suit jackets and shook hands. Toni absentmindedly set her wine glass on the edge of the bar and it nearly toppled over. She failed to notice, however, as she rushed after Bobby.

"Bobby!" Toni beckoned, the volume of her voice barely carrying over the multitude of conversations. Hearing his name, Bobby stopped and turned around. His business associate noticed Toni and lingered by the table.

"Toni?" said a surprised Bobby. He gestured with upturned palms and queried, "What're you doing here? Weren't you supposed to work tonight?"

"I called off," Toni said as she hurried to Bobby. Embracing him as if her life depended on it, she then enraptured him with a powerful, loving kiss. Remaining in his arms, she insisted, "I had to talk to you."

"What's wrong?" demanded Bobby after recovering from Toni's ardent affection. His dinner companion smirked.

"Looks like everything's just fine to me," said the older man in a deep yet polished voice. Toni's eyes grew wide when she noticed he remained at the table.

"Oh, no. Did I interrupt?" asked a mortified Toni. She extricated herself from Bobby's arms and said, "I am *so* sorry! When you both stood up I assumed you were done with your meeting."

"Of course not, young lady," objected the older man. Greatly intrigued by the situation, he expounded, "When a man gets a greeting like that, there must be good news to tell. I wouldn't dare deprive Bobby of that. The name's Roger Morton, by the way. And you *must* be Toni."

Toni maneuvered around the table and took Roger's extended hand. His handshake was unexpectedly vise-like and she winced.

"Yeah," Toni replied sheepishly, "that's me."

"You're every bit as beautiful as Bobby described, if not more," stated Roger while appraising Toni's figure. He pulled out his chair for her and motioned to it, saying, "Please, have a seat. I'll let you two talk."

"Thanks, Roger," replied Bobby. Though irked by Toni's intrusion into a business meeting, he remained levelheaded.

"Actually, I'd like to say this in front of someone, if you'd like to join us," Toni suggested. Her offer befuddled Bobby.

"I'd love to," replied Roger. Toni returned to Bobby and, before he could stop her, she made the announcement.

"I want to get married in April, Bobby, in Hawaii, just like you planned," Toni cooed with excitement bubbling below her emotional surface. An astonished Bobby simply gaped at her. Toni grabbed his hands, trembled and pleaded, "I want to be your wife, as soon as I can."

"Well, now, this calls for a toast," said an entertained Roger. He halted a passing waiter and stated as if in a movie, "Waiter, a bottle of your finest champagne. And another chair, please."

The betrothed shared another kiss before the waiter promptly returned with a third chair. Bobby chivalrously escorted Toni into her chair and pushed it into the table.

"Bobby tells me you're a singer, and a damn good one at that," said Roger after the threesome settled into their seats.

"It's just a little country band," Toni replied as her cheeks flushed with embarrassment. Downplaying her own talents, she lauded her bandmates, "The guys are awesome musicians, though."

"But it's Toni's voice and energy that make the difference," interjected Bobby proudly, "and she's one helluva guitar player, too."

"I just really love to perform," Toni said while glowing.

"Interestingly enough, I do have an acquaintance in the music industry, though, admittedly, he doesn't handle any country music acts," advised Roger. Toni looked to Bobby who raised his eyebrows as the sixty-something added, "At least not yet."

"I'm not sure I'm cut out for that," Toni replied humbly.

"I beg to differ, my dear," Roger countered before regaling them with a winding story about the music industry. Bobby remained attentive but Toni's focus soon waned. She watched Bobby and Roger in their suits, drinking champagne in an upscale restaurant, and suddenly felt isolated in her casual outfit.

"I'm gonna have to get used to that world," Toni said to herself. She sipped her champagne, squelched the urge to grimace and rejoined the conversation.

• • • •

TONI AND BOBBY WALKED hand-in-hand to her car with the ubiquitous sounds of the city cutting through the cold evening air. The lights of Detroit sparkled around them.

"Roger's definitely a talker," Toni commented with a pleasant smile. She was perfectly contented to be with Bobby and feel the strong, warm grip of his hand. He, conversely, seemed pensive.

"Yeah, I thought we might close the place down," agreed Bobby. He stopped, released Toni's hand and turned to her, inquiring in a serious tone, "Why the change of heart?"

"I knew you were gonna ask that," Toni said as her grin evaporated. Projecting a confidence that Bobby acutely felt, she gazed on him with her big, energetic eyes and answered, "Bobby, I love you, *so much*, without any doubt, and I know you love me, especially because you've made so many positive changes in your life *for me*. Big changes."

The cold nipped at Toni's ears and nose. She took Bobby's hand again and they continued into the parking lot.

"So let me ask you this: do you trust me?" Toni asked. They walked past a line of cars and she added, "Deep down, really trust me?"

"Yeah, of course I do," answered Bobby emphatically.

"I feel the exact same way about you," Toni asserted. The couple arrived at her car and, standing in front of it, clasped hands as she continued, "The love and trust are there, Bobby, and we're gonna build a strong, loving family on that foundation."

Toni pulled Bobby forward and they embraced. She placed her lips near his ear.

"I think God'll forgive us a few formalities if we get the big stuff right," Toni reasoned convincingly, "so let's get married."

The lovers said no more and, stepping out of place and time, remained intertwined in each other's arms. Neither felt any doubt about anything; their die was cast.

Glittering Prize

Emma, with the assistance of Nora, put the finishing touches on Easter dinner. The two women buzzed around the Hastings' dining room table, Emma prattling about minor irritations inherent in the operation of Johnny Dubs while Nora completed her duties in a trancelike state.

"Thanks for helping with dinner," said Emma when she noticed Nora's mental distance. Nora did not respond and continued absentmindedly placing silverware on the table. Emma set down the last cloth napkin and beckoned, "*Nooorrraaa.*"

"What?" a spacey Nora replied as she returned to the present. She subtly shook her head to clear it.

"What's up with you today?" asked Emma with a hand on her hip. Nora, eager to avoid discussion of her thoughts, continued placing silverware. Emma stated suspiciously, "You've been in la-la land since you got here."

"Sorry, I, like, didn't sleep well after work," said Nora with a shrug and without further elaboration. The silverware distributed, Nora quickly fled to the kitchen. Emma sighed in frustration and followed on her heels. She carried a metal serving spoon in her hand.

"Seriously, what's going on with you?" asked Emma firmly as the pair entered the kitchen. Nora stopped with her back to her and trembled, the response prompting Emma to demand, "Nora, tell me what's wrong. Did Elliott do something stupid?"

"*Noooo!*" Nora exclaimed as she spun around to face Emma. Emma's head jerked up and she scanned the backyard patio. Elliott, David and David's parents conversed at the patio table while Lanie and Tessa noisily played in the yard. Satisfied that no one heard Nora, Emma stepped out of the view of those outside. Nora hugged herself and insisted, "He didn't do anything. Not yet anyway."

"What's going on?" inquired Emma sharply as she gripped Nora's arm. Nora lowered her gaze, hesitated, and then raised it to Emma's comely countenance.

"I think Elliott might propose at dinner," Nora said carefully. Emma gasped, released her arm and dropped the metal serving spoon. It hit the kitchen floor with a clatter.

"Say that again," said Emma calmly though her hands shook and her eyes scintillated like blue-green embers. Nora, stunned by her reaction, found it difficult to speak but the older woman waited patiently for her response.

"I, I think that . . . ," Nora began slowly and uncertainly, "that Elliott might, like . . . propose . . . at dinner."

"Why do you think that?" Emma inquired as she grabbed Nora's upper arms and shook them. Her intensity cowed Nora and she trembled.

"*Em*," whimpered Nora. Cognizant that she intimidated her employee, Emma again released her. She exhaled dramatically to center herself, guided Nora into a chair at the kitchen table and then sat down in the one next to it.

"I'm sorry," Emma said contritely, "but you know you gotta tell me everything."

"Yeah, I know," answered Nora as she smiled for the first time during the conversation. An elation burgeoning within her, she stated, "He's been acting kinda, like, weird, lately and-."

"Elliott always acts weird," interrupted Emma, her impatience flaring. Dissatisfied with the scant evidence of an impending proposal, she demanded, "What else?"

"*Em*," Nora whined, "you're getting crazy."

"*I'm sorry*," apologized Emma dismissively. She forced herself to query in a neutral tone, "What else?"

Nora squirmed under her scrutiny while Emma bit her lip to keep herself from speaking. The younger woman sighed and rested her arms on the table.

"I saw the ring box," Nora answered with a sudden rush of joy. Emma emitted a truncated squeal and then slapped her hand to her mouth.

"You okay in there, hon?" shouted David from the patio.

"Yeah," Emma replied swiftly. She leaned back in her chair and yelled, "Dinner in fifteen, family!"

Emma absorbed the cacophony of responses and then returned her attention to Nora. Her heart suddenly dropped.

"You're gonna say yes, right?" asked Emma anxiously. Nora looked at her indignantly.

"Yeah, I'm gonna say yes!" Nora replied as if Emma should have known the answer. Emma sighed in relief and Nora expounded with a growing grin, "It's just so weird to think about *marriage*, and it's a such a big step. But, yeah, I wanna marry Elliott. And I didn't know what you'd think about it."

"I'm . . . *so* happy for you guys," gushed Emma while pulling Nora into an emphatic embrace.

"You don't think it's too soon?" queried Nora cautiously. Emma ended their hug but kept her hands on Nora's shoulders.

"You two've been doin' this dance for almost a year now," Emma answered supportively, "and it's not like you're getting *married* today."

"What're you girls up to?" asked a playfully suspicious David as he entered the kitchen. Nora grew embarrassed and remained silent but Emma stood up and left one hand on her shoulder. David opened the refrigerator.

"What're *you* up to?" countered an undaunted Emma. David held up two bottles of beer and closed the refrigerator with his foot.

"Just beer," said David as he read Emma's mood. Departing the kitchen, he said over his shoulder, "And never mind. I don't wanna know what you're up to."

· · · ·

NORA FIDDLED WITH HER fingers in her lap, relentlessly bounced her leg and stared into the table. She watched Elliott in her peripheral vision for any sign of a ring box or a descent to one knee. He, as usual, sat at the end of the table farthest from the kitchen but made no moves.

"You alright?" Elliott asked his girlfriend with a comforting hand on her thigh. She flashed him an anxious smile.

"Just a little jittery," answered Nora as she grasped Elliott's hand. Squeezing and then releasing it, she explained rapidly, "I didn't sleep well, and I should've eaten more than half a bagel for breakfast, so I think I'm just tired and hungry. I'll feel better after dinner."

"All right, then," Elliott replied. Nora tensed when he studied her; it was as if he suspected she concealed the true source of her concern. Tom, David's father, came to her rescue.

"So, Elliott, you ready for opening day next week?" asked Tom before Elliott could interrogate Nora further. The fifty-something man resembled an aging version of his son and dressed in a shirt and tie. His question gave Elliott a sense of déjà vu as he remembered the previous Easter. Macayla nudged her way into his mind but he pushed her out of it.

"Oh, we're going, too!" blurted Nora as she eagerly accepted the distraction.

"You didn't tell me that," Tom replied in mild offense. He pointed to the kitchen and asked, "Does Davie know?"

"I just got the tickets the other day and, honestly, it slipped my mind," Elliott answered. He lost track of Nora's worry and fully engaged with Tom, stating, "Hopefully this weather'll hold and we won't freeze our balls off like you guys did last year."

"Davie and I haven't missed one in over thirty years," Tom informed Nora proudly after taking a long pull from his bottle of beer. Elliott remembered Tom speaking the exact sentence the previous Easter.

"Okay, that's just weird," thought Elliott with a furrowed brow.

"You and Dave look so much alike," commented Nora, her remark sending a chill down Elliott's spine. The conversation tracked the one of a year ago and it unnerved him.

"You should see pictures of Tom in his thirties," responded David's mother, Rose. Attractive, tall and long-faced with lengthy blonde hair, she studied Nora approvingly. Despite the age difference, she found Nora a breath of fresh air after Elliott's past dalliances. She added, "They look like the same person."

Stunned, Elliott grabbed his beer and downed it. The rapid movement caused some of it to dribble down his chin and drip into his lap.

"Damn it!" an irritated Elliott whispered. Lanie jumped into the room from the hallway.

"Swear jar!" Lanie shouted. Elliott froze, her accusation sounding identical to the one she made one year earlier. He pondered the moment and, in response to her upturned palm, pulled a dime from his pocket and set it demonstratively on her hand.

"There ya' go, profanity Nazi," Elliott grumbled. Lanie looked at the dime and then offered Elliott a dissatisfied expression.

"*Elliott*," Nora rebuked him lightheartedly.

"You usually pay a dollar so you can swear more," stated a puzzled Lanie.

"Not today, kid," Elliott replied. Lanie shrugged.

"Whatever," said Lanie. She closed her fist around the coin and walked out of the room.

"Get your sister, Lanie. It's time to eat," said Emma as she set a large dish of steaming scalloped potatoes on the table. David entered the dining room behind her with a huge platter of sliced ham. A chorus of delighted compliments followed.

"This all looks and smells so awesome," said Nora while offering Emma a grateful smile. The words, spoken identically by Macayla on Easter 1985, slapped Elliott in the face.

"I'm in the god damn twilight zone," thought Elliott. Lanie and Tessa entered the room and took their seats. Abruptly rising to his feet, Elliott said, "Got any whiskey, Em?"

"Yeah, did you want me to make you a Grumpy Old Man?" Emma replied as she seated herself next to David. Her husband took his spot at the head of the table.

"No, I'll get it," said Elliott said. He left the room and, despite his efforts to hide it, did so with a deliberate pace, thinking, "What *the hell* is going on?"

Emma and Nora exchanged glances and barely contained their excitement. Nora attempted to serve herself some cooked carrots but her hands shook. David noticed the furtive glances between his wife and Nora and he, too, suspected an engagement ring was imminent.

"Almost forgot," announced Elliott when he suddenly returned to the dining room. All heads save Nora's turned to him; her eyes remained on her plate. Emma tensed as she visualized the engagement ring in her mind.

"Incoming, monsters," Elliott said to the confused expressions of Emma and Nora. He tossed a plastic egg to each of his nieces. Rose winced.

"Must we do this every year, Uncle Elliott?" Rose scolded Elliott for again breaking the rule against throwing objects at the dinner table. The girls eagerly snagged the eggs from the air and popped them open.

"Happy Easter, munchkins," Elliott said despite the phrase's contribution to his sense of déjà vu.

"Wow, *fifteen* bucks!" blurted Lanie. She held up one ten-dollar and one five-dollar bill, one in each hand, and waved them like flags.

"No way!" yelled Tessa while examining the bills closely.

"Aunt Nora decided you two needed an Easter raise," advised Elliott. Both girls jumped up as Elliott added blithely, "Cost of living, I guess."

"Thank you, Aunt Nora!" said Tessa while harrying Nora with a hug. The familial affection overwhelmed Nora and she temporarily forgot about the absent proposal.

"Awww, you're welcome," gushed Nora as she embraced Emma's daughters. Their responses made Elliott smile and engendered a deep feeling of love for her.

"You're awesome," said Lanie bluntly while placing a hand on Nora's shoulder.

"Hey, are you forgetting who threw the eggs at you?" asked Elliott with mock incredulity and outstretched arms.

"Thank you!" chirped Tessa while bounding up to Elliott and crashing into him with an embrace.

"You're welcome," replied Elliott. He returned the hug and waited for Lanie to approach.

"Thanks, man," Lanie said with a nod. She patted Nora on the head and advised Elliott, "Keep this one."

"What're you, thirty?" queried Elliott as he playfully disentangled himself from Tessa's embrace and pushed her away with his foot.

"I'm gonna put mine in my room, okay, Mommy?" requested Tessa as she inched towards the hallway.

"Sure, sweetie," Emma replied. Lanie, however, waved her money at David.

"*I'm* gonna hire somebody to open the pool," Lanie said snottily.

"I'm not opening the pool in March," replied David. He motioned to the dining room's bay window and declared, "It'll probably be snowing tomorrow."

"*Awww, Dad-dy*," mewled Tessa. The dining room settled into eating, small talk and the antics of Lanie and Tessa. Emma and Nora, their expectations of a ring dashed, shared only fleeting glances throughout the rest of the meal.

"I'll be damned. They thought he was gonna propose," said David to himself. He shoveled some ham into his mouth, turned his attention to his brother-in-law and thought, "Em'll be on your ass until you do it, now. *Poor bastard*."

· · · ·

"THIS WEATHER IS SO awesome, Elliott," gushed Nora as she soaked up the rays of the setting sun. They shone through her golden curls and illuminated them in an angelic radiance. The temperature settled into the middle seventies and a cool, declining wind cleared the clouds from the sky.

"Nothing like warm days in March," Elliott replied. He and Nora laid on the hood and windshield of his LTD, the couple parked in the farmer's field near Detroit Metropolitan Airport. Elliott pulled Nora closer and added, "And nothing like being here . . . *with you*."

Elliott winced, the words sounding foolish as he spoke them. Nora, whose head lay on his shoulder, looked up to him.

"Did you ever bring Donna or Toni here?" inquired Nora. Elliott's hesitation and his guilty expression provided her with the answer.

"Well, uh, I, um . . . ," Elliott stammered.

"Which one?" asked Nora, her voice tinged with jealousy. Elliott exhaled but, before he could respond, Nora sat up and whined, "Really? *Both* of them."

Elliott found no words but managed to nod his head in the affirmative. Nora, who suffered from a similar inability to speak, tucked her legs underneath her and folded her hands in her lap. Unable to look at one another, they remained silent as an airplane roared nearby. Elliott sat up.

"Believe it or not, you were here first," Elliott said when the airplane landed and the noise of its engines faded into the distance.

"No, I wasn't," countered Nora with a frown.

"Yeah," Elliott insisted as he touched her knee, "*you were*."

Elliott's staunch declaration caused Nora to doubt herself. She attempted to recall a visit to the field. Elliott chuckled.

"Remember that night we fought at Mexican Gardens?" Elliott asked. Nora lifted her gaze to his face.

"I don't want to," pouted Nora. Elliott maintained eye contact with her until she relented, "Yeah, I guess."

"I came here after all that," Elliott declared. His skin crawled as the jealousy and emotional hurt of that fateful evening reignited. He remembered Toto's "I Won't Hold You Back" playing on his car radio, its application to Nora and its manipulation of his mood, saying, "I lied to myself, and said I'd give you up. But I never did. *And you were with me.*"

Elliott, once again feeling foolish, twice thumped a fist into his chest. His words captivated Nora.

"In here," Elliott said hoarsely, "you were with me in here."

"Oh my god, Elliott," Nora replied. Feeling as if Elliott sought to distract her from the other women of his 1985, she scoffed, "That's cheesy. Even for me."

"Hey, I'm baring my soul here," Elliott complained in partial jest. Nora decided to test him.

"Donna says I'm just like she was when you guys dated in high school," advised Nora with a rare, penetrating gaze.

"She said that? When?" Elliott pressed Nora.

"Actually, she said *she* was *me*," said Nora, the ugliness of the experience tormenting her.

"She was wrong," Elliott stated confidently.

"No, she wasn't," rejoined Nora. She yearned to believe him but the specter of Donna, and her long romantic history with Elliott, haunted her.

"Nora," Elliott said as he scooted closer to her. Grasping her wrists and squeezing them gently, he queried, "Remember when you told me you wanted to date me *and* Bart?"

"Let's not go there," begged Nora. She tried to extricate her wrists from Elliott's grasp but he firmly yet carefully held her fast.

"Just stay with me on this," Elliott urged her. They stared at each other, neither one wanting to surrender.

"*Okay*," relented Nora reluctantly. Elliott waited for her to answer until she said, "Yeah, I remember it."

"Donna never would've stood up to me like that," Elliott argued ardently, "let alone actually *considered* someone else. If I said jump, she wouldn't just ask 'how high', she'd jump twice to make sure she did it right and then obsess about it regardless of whether she did or not. I'm not sure she really loved me. It was more like . . . desperation."

Nora appraised Elliott's countenance and judged him to be sincere. She slid into his arms and hugged him tightly.

"I don't want to talk about this anymore," said Nora. Elliott kissed her on top of her head.

"Good," Elliott said. He stated, "Because we have something else to talk about it."

Chills rippled down Nora's spine as the prospect of a marriage proposal reentered her mind. Elliott used his left arm to reach behind himself.

"It's not the way most guys would do it, or the way most girls would want it, but this has been a special place for me since high school," Elliott explained in a serious tone, "and it's the only place that still means something to me – well, the only one not stuffed full of emotional baggage – and it's where I'm asking you. I just can't think of any other place I'd rather be, or any place I'd rather ask you to marry me."

Elliott revealed the ring box. Nora caught her breath.

"Will you marry me, Nora?" Elliott asked with a surge of emotion that overwhelmed her. Nora began crying and her first attempt to answer failed.

"Yes!" exclaimed Nora on her second attempt. The couple kissed as Nora's tears of joy-soaked Elliott's shirt.

"Em's gonna be *so* mad you didn't do it at dinner," said Nora though she cared little for Emma's wishes. She cleared her eyes.

"You didn't think I was gonna ask you during the Hastings Show, did ya'?" Elliott asked with a smirk. He removed the ring from the box and ceremoniously placed it on Nora's finger.

Ensconced in Elliott's arms, Nora clung to him, rested her head on his chest and massaged her engagement ring with her thumb. The betrothed said no more, focused exclusively on one another and, bathed in the comforting rays of the setting sun, forgot about the rest of the world.

• • • •

ELLIOTT OPENED THE front doors to Johnny Dubs, paused and then stepped inside. He let the doors slowly close behind him but the click sent a chill down his spine.

"Uh-oh," muttered Elliott with a shiver. Emma waited in front of his barstool as if she expected his appearance at that very moment. A freshly prepared Grumpy Old Man accompanied her.

"You suck," Emma greeted Elliott when he slid onto his barstool and hung his head. She set the cocktail on the bar with a *thunk*.

"That I do," agreed Elliott facetiously with a nod of resignation. He removed his coat and laid it on the corner of the bar as the adjacent barstool was occupied. Its occupant paid the siblings no mind and chattered about drunken nonsense to her male companion.

"You couldn't have proposed at Easter dinner?" Emma inquired sharply with an imposing lean towards Elliott.

"Not happy about it, dear sister?" replied Elliott. He wrapped both hands around his drink but did not partake of it.

"Eh, it's fine," Emma confessed as her frustration fizzled. Resting her elbows on the bar and clasping her hands, she reasoned, "Would it've been nice to celebrate my big brother's engagement with the entire family? Yes. But you settling down with the princess? I don't care if you asked her on the moon."

"Speaking of my beautiful princess, where is she?" queried Elliott as he attended to his drink.

"Errands," answered Emma. She stood up straight and added, "But she'll be back soon. So whaddaya want for dinner?"

"This," Elliott replied. He grasped his glass by its bottom and presented it to Emma.

"Wrong answer," stated Emma bluntly. She gently pushed the glass back towards Elliott.

"And what's the right answer?" said an annoyed Elliott.

"If you're drinkin', you're eatin'," Emma advised. She added with satisfied smirk, "Princess's orders."

"It's not like we're married already," Elliott complained. Emma switched a customer's empty beer bottle for a full one.

94

"It's about time is what it is," Emma declared in a snarky tone. She made her way to the kitchen and shouted over her shoulder, "I'll go put your order in."

"And that concludes today's episode of 'Whipped Before the Wedding,'" said Elliott in the voice of a television announcer. The patron next to him prattled endlessly, her relentless flow of words irking him. He glanced at her, took another drink and muttered, "*Shut up.*"

A sudden affectionate hand on Elliott's shoulder improved his mood and he set down his glass. The press of lips on his cheek stoked his libido but the familiar scent that tickled his nostrils instantly dashed it.

"Damn it, Donna," Elliott barked as he spun towards her and, rising to his feet, shoved her away from him. Donna stumbled backwards a few steps but seemed unaffected by the rejection. Elliott sneered, "What're you stalking me now?"

"Who's getting married?" asked Donna with a disturbing grin. The altercation drew the attention of the surrounding patrons but her blunted response caused them to quickly lose interest. Exhaling his frustration, Elliott pulled Donna closer to him and sat down.

"Seriously, Donna, why are you here?" Elliott questioned her while maintaining his grip on her arm.

"I'm not here for you, Elliott," lied Donna. She pulled free of his grasp and declared haughtily, "I'm just grabbing a quick bite with Em."

Donna languidly reached out and caressed Elliott's cheek. He recoiled from her touch.

"But I could be," added Donna seductively. She attempted to move into Elliott's body but he blocked her advanced with a stiff arm.

"Whatever's going on with you," Elliott said as he held her at bay, "needs to stop. I'm with Nora now, and that's all there is to it."

Donna fumed at the mention of his relationship with Nora but maintained her composure. Angered by her uncharacteristically aggressive behavior, Elliott decided to deliver the killing blow.

"And to answer your question," Elliott continued while moving Donna backward, "*I'm* getting married. To Nora."

Donna threw off Elliott's arm, the wild expression of an injured animal on her face. Nora, unnoticed by the former lovers, appeared next to Elliott. The look on Donna's face told her all she needed to know.

"Donna, I know you're hurt," reasoned Nora with pity, "but not here. Why don't I go get Em for you?"

"Go to hell, little girl," snapped Donna. Elliott stood up and Nora saw his hand twitch. Reading his intention, and then seeing the desire on Donna's face, she acted reflexively. Her open hand flashed outward and struck Donna's cheek, the smack drawing the startled looks of the crowd.

"Oh, shit," Elliott uttered as he grabbed Nora, wrapped her arms and torso in his own and pulled her into his body.

"Let go of me!" demanded Nora while struggling against Elliott's grasp. Donna raised her hand to strike back.

"Donna!" Emma barked. She marched down the length of the bar and ordered with a nod towards the stairwell, "*Get upstairs.*"

Nora squirmed out of Elliott's arms. She and Donna went nose-to-nose and glared at one another while a stunned Elliott awaited the impending clash between his past and his future.

"I said get upstairs, Donna," reiterated Emma. Donna relaxed her body and walked away.

"You two aren't gonna make it," jabbed Donna as she passed Elliott and Nora.

"Upstairs!" Emma barked with a pointed finger. Donna marched to the door like a pouting child while Emma walked parallel to her down the bar.

"What the hell's her problem?" griped Nora as remorse for her impetuousness washed over her. Elliott raised his palms in a calming gesture.

"Just relax," Elliott advised her with a sigh, "Emma'll handle it."

• • • •

"I MISS THE DAYS WHEN my waitresses only slapped horny drunks," Emma lamented. She took a seat in her chair, kicked her legs up on her desk and let her hands hang over the edge of its armrests. Donna folded her arms defiantly and remained standing so Emma instructed her, "Have a seat."

"You should've let me hit her back," grumbled Donna. Emma gazed at her in disbelief.

"What's wrong with you?" Emma queried in exasperation. Removing her feet from the desk, she leaned forward on her elbows and said, "You've never acted like this before, Donna."

"You're supposed to be on my side," pleaded Donna as she dropped into one of the guest chairs.

"I was until you decided you didn't want him anymore," Emma countered. Pointing a finger at Donna, she said, "I even tried to give you a golden opportunity but you refused it, because of Ben. Ya' know, *your boyfriend*."

"I made a mistake, Em," whined Donna, "a big mistake."

"No, you didn't," Emma insisted. She leaned back in her chair and said, "You're in a relationship. A good, healthy relationship."

"Not anymore," replied Donna. Her lips quivered as she held back tears and said, "I ended it."

"You've lost your mind, girlfriend," Emma admonished her.

"I want Elliott back," declared Donna in despair.

"Why? Because some pretty, young girl caught his eye?" Emma asked bitingly. She again let her hands hang off the ends of the armrests and inquired, "What about all your maturity bullshit?"

"I should've gone to his apartment on New Year's Eve, not her," mewled Donna.

"But you didn't," Emma snapped. Gesticulating as she spoke, she ranted, "You two're done, Donna. He doesn't love you anymore, and I don't think you love him. You're just panicking, that's all. He was always your safety valve, but all of a sudden, he's not. And it scares the hell outta you and it's making you crazy. *Really damn crazy*."

Donna's eyes fell to the floor and she pondered Emma's argument. Emma waited patiently for her to reach the same conclusion.

"Maybe you're right," admitted Donna. She slowly lifted her gaze to Emma.

"I am," Emma stated confidently, "and you're gonna be just fine, and I'll always be here for you."

"I should go apologize," said Donna. Emma doubted her contrition.

"No," Emma corrected her. She stood up and motioned to the door, saying, "I'm going to walk you to your car and then you're going to Ben's house and you're gonna fix it."

"No, I'm not," countered Donna. She leaned forward with her elbows on Emma's desk, let her forehead touch its surface and whimpered, "Not tonight. I just can't."

"Well, you'd better do it soon," Emma warned her while placing a reassuring hand on her best friend's back, "or you're gonna lose him."

Donna buried her face in her arms to hide it from Emma. She descended into jealous thoughts, thoughts which she concealed from her best friend, and wondered how to get Elliott back.

If You Were Here Tonight

S t. Peter by the Sea, a small Catholic church built in the 1880s, was nestled on the shoreline north of Keauhou, Hawaii. A blue roof covered the twelve-pew building with a separate section for the later additions of a belfry and a porch. Its white siding contrasted starkly with the green lawn and dark volcanic rocks that comprised its grounds. Palm trees towered above the church and swayed in the warm ocean breeze as traffic whizzed past on Alii Drive.

"Oh, Bobby!" Toni exclaimed as she wrapped him in her arms and kissed him several times. Wearing a blue sundress with a long skirt that fluttered in the wind, she scurried towards the Church and shouted, "This is *perfect*!"

"She's right," said Bobby as he watched Toni explore the grounds. Clad in a Hawaiian shirt, a tan belt and board shorts, he wrapped his arm around Katherine's shoulders and declared, "This is gonna be *perfect*."

"Her dress even matches the Church," Katherine added with a slow shake of her head. Bobby's affection irked her but she endured it for Toni's sake and altered her tack, asking, "How much is it to rent this place for a wedding?"

"That's the good part," Bobby replied. He gestured towards the church and explained, "Our wedding party's so small we're just gonna stop by, get married on the porch and then it's straight to the reception, which is also on the ocean."

"*That's* the good part?" Katherine inquired. Cognizant of the skepticism in her tone, she sweetened it and queried, "What if there's another *scheduled* wedding here tomorrow?"

"There's not," stated Bobby confidently. He squeezed Katherine's shoulder and then released her, saying, "I called and checked. Plus, you know my brother. He's good at running off unexpected guests."

"Guess you've got it all handled," Katherine said, the admission akin to eating glass. A persistent splinter of doubt needled her but she thought, "You're holding his past against him. He's a changed man, and he's shown it time and time again. *Let it go.*"

"Isn't it adorable, Mom?" Toni called from the Church's covered porch, her voice contending with the sound of the surf. She wrapped an arm around one of the blue porch posts, waved to Bobby with the other and beckoned, "C'mon, Bobby! Come see this!"

Toni seated herself on one of the two benches flanking the front door, both of which were built into the porch. Bobby took a few steps towards St. Peter and turned to Katherine with a determined glance.

"Nothing's gonna stop me from marrying your daughter tomorrow, Katherine," vowed Bobby with serious eyes. The long, loose shirt Katherine wore blew in the same, stiff wind that tossed her hair as she pondered the man before her. Several seconds later, she relented, relaxed her body and smiled.

"Well, don't keep her waiting," Katherine playfully admonished him. Bobby grinned in response, turned and walked to the porch. He took a seat next to Toni and threw an arm around her as she cuddled into his body. Watching the couple's tender interactions, Katherine engaged in a long, slow exhale and stated aloud as if to tempt fate, "This marriage, the one I never thought I'd see, is actually gonna happen."

Katherine closed her eyes and indulged in the heat of the early afternoon and the massage of the salty air. Reopening them, she left her doubt in the narrow roadside parking lot and walked towards the church.

· · · ·

"WHY CAN'T I SLEEP?" Toni thought as her eyelids opened for the hundredth time. Bobby slept next to her and held her closely. Toni allowed him to sleep in the king bed with her on the condition he refrain from sexual advances; to her mild surprise, he refrained from even mentioning sex. She said to herself, "I guess it's like Mom said. I'm just nervous about tomorrow."

Bobby stirred and tightened his grip on her to the point of his hold being uncomfortable. She squirmed and he unconsciously loosened his grasp.

"Maybe it's sleeping with someone else," Toni thought with a sigh. She cautiously maneuvered out of his arms in fits and starts, thinking, "That'll be a big adjustment."

Toni, confident that Bobby slumbered deeply, finally escaped him. She carefully slid off the bed and crept across the bedroom until she reached a chair. Retrieving a pair of white shorts from it, she squiggled into them before removing her full-length nightshirt and donning a blue-and-white striped, long-sleeved top. Bobby suddenly and dramatically flipped over in the bed.

"Shoot," Toni whispered as she froze. Bobby did not move again, however, and she sighed, "That was close."

Pausing each time Bobby stirred and then slipping further away when he settled down, Toni eventually opened the screen door. She stepped onto the lanai, gently closed the door behind her and then exhaled in relief. Toni looked back at Bobby.

"Be back soon, love," Toni said softly. She kissed two fingers and used them to touch the screen, adding, "Sleep well."

The temperature settled into the mid-seventies but the breeze steadily blew. Toni listened carefully for sounds in the night but heard only the waves crashing on the shore. She stepped lightly in bare feet through the sand and, upon nearing the waterline, sat down on the beach. Safely hidden by the shadows falling upon the sand, she let her mind wander.

"No, no, not now," Toni lamented as Elliott meandered through her thoughts. She felt a surge of guilt and her tears fell unabated. Toni looked to the sky: the moon was absent but the stars blazed by the thousands. She opened her heart to God and asked, "Why am I doing this again? Here I am, in a tropical paradise with a man who loves me, and's changed so much for me, *because I asked him to*, but instead of clinging to him, I'm out in the night, under the stars, thinking about Elliott."

Toni cried for several minutes before inhaling sharply and inadvertently gazing at her engagement ring. Her tears made her vision fuzzy but it slowly came into focus.

"Get yourself together," Toni rebuked herself. She wiped her watery eyes, returned them to the heavens and said, "Elliott knew. *He knew, didn't he?* You put him in my life so Bobby'd get his act together, and be more mature, and become the man I was meant to marry."

Toni hugged her knees to her chest and reminisced about Elliott's brief foray into her life. She smiled.

"He's a special guy," Toni said aloud with a fluttering heart. She heard Emma's words in her head.

"*He's good. Really good, actually*," said Emma of her brother.

"She meant it, too," Toni said quietly. She stood up, brushed the sand from her shorts and continued, "He's got somebody. I've got somebody. It's all the way it's supposed to be."

Her confidence swelling, Toni stood up and walked purposefully back to her room. Moving as noiselessly as possible, she changed into her night shirt, slipped into bed with Bobby and entwined herself in his arms. His strong grasp made her feel loved and protected.

"The way it's supposed to be," repeated Toni. Minutes later, she drifted to sleep and did not wake again during the night.

· · · ·

ELLIOTT AWOKE BEFORE his alarm, his eyelids opening and closing several times before he emerged fully from his slumber. Nora uncharacteristically slept on her side of the bed instead of clinging to Elliott in some manner, a behavior to which he had yet to acclimate. He glanced at the alarm clock.

"You don't hafta get up yet, idiot," he scolded himself. He closed his eyes and, to his great shock, Toni waited for him there. Elliott immediately opened them to quash her image. Carefully rolling out of bed, he thought, "You don't need *that* right now."

Fearing Toni's return, Elliott walked like a zombie to the stairs and then, with slowly improving balance, descended them. By the time his bare feet hit the living room carpet, he craved coffee. Elliott walked to the kitchen, turned on the coffee maker with a click and leaned against the counter to await its caffeinated nectar.

"It's entirely possible she's married by now," Elliott mused carelessly. The prospect froze his heart. Ten seconds later, the appearance of Nora at the base of the steps thawed it.

"You okay?" asked Nora, her voice angelic in the silence of the morning. Elliott's sleepy-eyed princess was adorable with her disheveled curls, a girlish nightshirt and white bobby socks.

"Yeah," Elliott replied with a weak grin. Nora shuffled to him and leaned her body against him, laying her head on his shoulder and yawning. Elliott wallowed in her affection and said earnestly, "Better than okay."

"I'll have coffee with you," advised Nora despite maintaining her grasp on her fiancée. Elliott engulfed her in his arms as the coffee maker percolated loudly behind him.

"*So* much better than okay," Elliott thought.

. . . .

KATHERINE KNOCKED ON Toni's hotel room door. Toni opened it and, upon seeing her mother, gave her a welcoming hug.

"Good morning," Toni greeted Katherine.

"Hello, my dear," replied Katherine. She examined Toni with a gaze of discernment.

"Who is it?" asked Bobby from the bed. Katherine raised her eyebrows. Toni winced.

"Just my mom," Toni replied while refusing to look at her mother.

"Well, now," said a surprised Katherine. She offered her daughter a mock scandalous expression.

"We slept together in the literal sense of the word only, Mother," Toni insisted strenuously.

"So much for not seeing each other before the wedding," said Katherine.

"That's just a silly superstition," Toni scoffed. Katherine continued to study her daughter's countenance.

"Have you been crying?" Katherine inquired. Toni's eyes widened and she swiftly stepped into the hallway.

"Of course not," Toni stated as she eased the door closed.

"You've been crying," asserted Katherine.

"No, I haven't," Toni replied with a look of confusion.

"Don't lie to your mother," warned Katherine. Toni's façade cracked ever so slightly but it was enough for her mother to read. She waited for several hotel guests to traverse the hallway before speaking.

"I'm not lying," Toni insisted as she turned away from Katherine and reached for the door handle.

"Look at me," said Katherine as she stopped her daughter in the middle of her turn and rotated her back to her original position. Toni offered only light resistance.

"Please, just let it go," Toni begged, her voice cracking as she spoke.

"You're lucky that fiancée of yours is a sound sleeper," said Katherine ominously. Toni straightened her body as her mother expounded, "Not many men would want to find their new wife crying on the beach the night before their wedding. Makes them think about being left at the altar."

Toni froze. She did not know if she should reveal her secret to Katherine or, if she did, whether she could maintain her composure.

"I, on the other hand, am not a sound sleeper. Never have been," said Katherine. Toni's clenched her jaw and her eyes watered. Supportively grasping her daughter's arm, Katherine explained, "So, I get up, and I sit, and I watch. You'd be surprised what you see at night, when everyone else – or almost everyone else – is asleep."

Toni's heart began beating rapidly and her palms felt sweaty. Bobby suddenly opened the door.

"Everything okay out here, ladies?" inquired Bobby with a smirk. It melted when he saw Toni's misty eyes.

"Everything's fine. Just a little emotional mother-daughter moment," declared Katherine. Tugging Toni's arm, she moved her away from Bobby and said, "I need a little wardrobe advice, dear. You won't mind if I borrow your bride for a while, will you?"

"Not at all," replied Bobby with an unconcerned shrug. He stepped forward, kissed Toni's cheek and asked, "Breakfast in about thirty?"

"Sure," Toni managed to respond while Katherine nodded in the affirmative. Bobby, none the wiser, disappeared into their room. Katherine pulled Toni down the hallway.

"Keep it together until we get to my room," said Katherine. The pair moved quickly past three rooms containing Bobby's family before arriving at her door and slipping inside. Toni seated herself on the queen bed and the waterworks resumed.

"So *my* guess is that a certain cable installer we both know and love is hanging onto your heart tighter than you thought," Katherine stated bluntly while she watched her daughter weeping. Her tone became more flippant and she added, "Running around and planting little seeds of doubt here and there in your head."

"How did you know that?" an astonished Toni queried. Her tears lessened. Katherine seated herself next to her daughter.

"Bobby's been a model fiancée," explained Katherine, "so it couldn't be him. And *I know* you love him, so it's not really you, either."

Toni lowered her gaze and contemplated her mother's words. Katherine permitted her a few moments to think.

"So that said, it must be someone else," continued Katherine pointedly, "and there's only one other man you've felt so strongly about."

"*Oh, Mom*," Toni mewled as she hid her face in her hands. She said in a muffled voice, "Most women don't find *one* man they want to marry."

Katherine exhaled in mild frustration. Though Toni did not know it, her heart bled for her offspring but she decided on a tougher course.

"Do you want to get married today or not? Because only one of those men is on this island," demanded Katherine impatiently. Toni pondered the question for over a minute.

"Yeah, I do," Toni stated firmly as she returned her attention to Katherine. Her mother patted her on the thigh and stood up.

"Then let's get you fed, and dressed, and dolled up – *forget all about Mr. Warden* –," instructed Katherine gravely as she took Toni's chin in her hand, "and, unless there's a bolt from on high, get you married."

. . . .

"WHERE *is* that girl?" griped Katherine as she saw Bobby's parents arrive in a rental car at the main doors of the hotel. She paced the tropical-themed lobby and waited impatiently for Toni. Her daughter soon appeared, an enchanting vision in a silky, spaghetti-strapped wedding dress and elegant white sandals. Her annoyance evaporating, Katherine appraised Toni adoringly and said, "Aren't you a tall drink of water?"

"*Enough*," an embarrassed Toni replied. Katherine nodded to the front doors.

"The Aurellos are waiting for you," advised Katherine. She did not see the approaching hotel employee and nearly careened into him as she ushered Toni towards the car. She stopped, gave the employee a frustrated look and asked, "May we help you?"

"Ms. Cullen, there's a call for you," said the employee dutifully. The young, attractive Native Hawaiian, who wore the expected Hawaiian shirt and colorful lei, seemed undaunted by Katherine's angst.

"A call for me?" asked Toni with a shiver and a vivid image of Elliott in her mind.

"It's for Katherine Cullen," replied the attendant with a trickle of doubt in his tone.

"I'm Katherine Cullen," Katherine said as she pointed Toni in the direction of the doors. She gave her a nudge and added, "This is *Toni* Cullen, soon to be Aurello, and she was just leaving."

"Who'd be calling you here?" Toni inquired. She struggled against Katherine who, suspecting Elliott crept into Toni's mind, immediately intervened.

"No one you'd need to worry about, now *go*," answered Katherine while pushing Toni forward. She made it to the doors and abruptly spun around.

"What about the flower for my hair?!" Toni exclaimed in a panic. She started to retrace her steps.

"I'll bring it," insisted Katherine while glaring at Toni and holding up a palm that stopped her in her tracks. She slowly lowered it and demanded, "*Now go.*"

Toni hesitated. Her mother's countenance softened while the hotel employee patiently waited for their spat to resolve.

"Everything you need is in your bag in our rental car," advised Katherine calmly, "and I know that because *I* packed it and *I* put it in there and *I* will bring it."

"Alright," Toni uttered with a nod in assent. Katherine extended a hand to Toni which she took. After an assuring squeeze, she released her grip and her daughter obediently passed through the doors and into the sultry Hawaiian air.

"Sorry about that," Katherine apologized. Ogling the attractive young man, she said, "You're quite the patient man, and very handsome."

"This way, Ma'am," said the man while gesturing towards the front desk and ignoring the compliment. Katherine allowed him to lead her to the telephone which sat on the desk's high counter.

"Katherine Cullen, wedding planner extraordinaire," Katherine announced after lifting the receiver to her ear. She kittenishly waved her fingers at the departing attendant.

"You're a talented woman," replied Sergeant Reynolds.

"Sergeant Reynolds?" Katherine said, the voice on the line astonishing her. She leaned against the front desk and asked, "How in the world did you find me here?"

"Well, I knew you were in Hawaii, and you said you'd be on the big island, and told me about St. Peter by the Sea," Sergeant Reynolds answered. He reclined in his desk chair and added, "Luckily, I only had to call a few resorts."

"You should've been a detective," Katherine responded cheekily.

"Now you sound like my ex-wife," countered Sergeant Reynolds before shifting the telephone to his other ear.

"So what was so important that you tracked me down thousands of miles away on my daughter's wedding day?" Katherine inquired edgily.

"Well, ya' know how you and Emma Hastings were gonna do a little checking into your daughter's fiancée?" queried Sergeant Reynolds.

"Yes," Katherine answered, the slow unraveling of the Sergeant's story irking her. She tucked one arm into her body, set her opposite elbow on top of it and stated, "We decided against it."

"Oh, I didn't know that," said Sergeant Reynolds, the revelation giving him pause. He sat up, rested his elbows on his desk and continued, "Well, since I've got you on the phone anyway . . . I took the liberty of running a background check on him, and it came back, but my daughter had her baby that same week, and it kinda got buried on my desk for a while. I was doing a little desk cleaning today and I came across it and-."

"Oh my god, did you find something?" Katherine interrupted him. The volume of her voice garnered glances from several lobby patrons.

"No, no, nothing like that," stated Sergeant Reynolds. He opened the file sitting on his desk and perused it, saying, "He's clean as a whistle."

"Thanks to Elliott not pressing charges," Katherine muttered. Satisfied with the information provided by the sergeant, she impatiently tapped her fingers on the desk.

"What's that now?" asked Sergeant Reynolds. Leaving the file folder open, he again leaned back in his chair.

"Nothing. Never mind," Katherine deflected. Her disinterest in the conversation burgeoning, she inquired, "So you called to tell me you found *nothing*?"

"I thought it might put your mind at ease, and your daughter's, too," explained Sergeant Reynolds in a wounded tone.

"I suppose it does," Katherine sighed. She turned towards the desk in the belief that the call was about to end, saying, "Thank you, Sergeant. I appreciate the effort."

"Anything for you," replied Sergeant Reynolds. A corporal approached to speak with him but, holding up a finger, he opined, "I'm sure those two'll be very happy together. Sometimes young men need to get that first one outta the way and it matures 'em a bit."

"Yes, very happy," Katherine repeated. The import of Sergeant Reynolds's words suddenly hit her and her heart dropped like stone. She walked away from the desk and stretched the telephone cord, saying, "Wait, first one?"

"Bobby's first marriage . . . which, don't worry, ended in divorce," answered Sergeant Reynolds. Katherine looked upward.

"Kinda short notice, don't ya' think?" Katherine lamented to the ceiling.

"Excuse me?" queried Sergeant Reynolds with a puzzled mien.

"I wish you would've told me this yesterday," Katherine said with a shake of her head and a smile of resignation.

"Why's that?" asked a confused Sergeant Reynolds. Katherine's eyes glazed.

"I just spent twenty-four hours thinking I was wrong," Katherine mused, "when I could've spent them knowing I was right."

• • • •

KATHERINE'S ABRUPT opening of the rental car door surprised Bobby and he jumped. She dramatically dropped herself into the passenger seat and slammed the door shut. Bobby jumped again.

"Damn, Katherine, you scared the hell outta me," complained Bobby. He felt a coldness greater than the air conditioning and shivered despite the hot air that briefly gushed into the car. Supposing Katherine was upset about his tardiness, he mustered an apologetic tone and said, "Don't worry. We'll get there in time, or maybe just a few minutes late. No big deal."

"No big deal," Katherine said with a chuckle. Bobby became stone-faced and pale when she added, "Like your first marriage is no big deal?"

"What're you talking about?" queried Bobby as he turned to Katherine. Her countenance hardened and she stared through the windshield with narrowed eyes. A long, deep exhale followed.

"You know, your first marriage, the one you've been keeping from Toni," Katherine said in a clear, deliberate voice. Bobby recovered from his initial shock and feigned befuddlement.

"I don't know what you're talking about," replied Bobby with a gesture of his hand. He shifted the car into "Reverse", dutifully checked his mirrors and backed out of the parking space.

"Oh, yes, you do," Katherine objected while continuing to stare forward. Her tone elevated beyond her familiar sarcasm and became acerbic as she snarled, "So spare me the bullshit."

Bobby held Katherine in his gaze for several seconds but she refused to look at him. His expression soured as he turned his attention to the parking lot, shifted the car into "Drive" and let it trundle along the pavement.

"What, you run a background check on me?" asked Bobby acrimoniously. He braked at the entry to the main road and surveyed both directions of traffic.

"More or less," Katherine remarked guiltily. Bobby waited for the traffic to clear, turned right and accelerated away from the hotel.

"You just couldn't leave it alone," grumbled Bobby while shaking his head. He fumed for a moment before punching the steering wheel and barking, "Damn it!"

"What are you, a child?" Katherine inquired cuttingly with a glare. She pointed a finger at Bobby and demanded, "Get a hold of yourself."

"I'm not telling her," declared Bobby with a defiant shrug.

"Oh, yes, you are," Katherine insisted as she threatened him with the pointed finger.

"Or what? You'll tell her?" sneered Bobby. Sensing an advantage, he smirked and parried, "You really ready to do that, Katherine?"

Katherine mulled Bobby's response for several seconds. Thinking he won the round, he haughtily glanced at her and then back at the road.

"I am," Katherine announced. Bobby's blood ran cold and he glanced at her again. Katherine throttled him with grim yet courageous eyes.

"I thought you were supposed to wait for the 'forever hold your peace' part," said Bobby, his own eyes waving the white flag.

"This isn't a movie of the week, Bobby," Katherine snapped. Bobby parked the car at St. Peter's roadside lot and they surveyed the small crowd of his family. Her heart hemorrhaging for Toni, she explained gravely, "You're not going to embarrass my daughter during her wedding, in front of her future in-laws. *At* the wedding is bad enough."

"How do we do it?" asked Bobby, a cauldron of anxiety boiling beneath his calm veneer. Katherine pondered her next move as Toni noticed her and waved excitedly. The twenty-eight-year-old floated on a cloud and beamed from ear to ear.

"I'll send her back to the car," Katherine began. The gears of her mind turned and then she explained slowly, "You two can take a drive while I keep your family occupied. I'll tell them it's a little family tradition. Yes, that should do it."

"We don't have to do this, Katherine," pleaded Bobby. He kept himself from looking at Toni. She waved repeatedly to attract his attention.

"You're right, Bobby, we don't," countered Katherine. A perplexed Bobby looked to her as she added, "*You* do."

· · · ·

TONI REACHED FOR THE door handle, hesitated and then pulled her hand back. Her entire body trembled; her mother's odd demeanor tripped her inner alarms and she did not like it. Summoning all her courage, Toni grabbed the handle firmly and cast open the door. Her burst of confidence evaporated, however, and she could only bring herself to lean her head into the vehicle.

"What did she do?" Toni asked with an apologetic expression and slumping shoulders. Unable to muster a response, Bobby sat mute with his gaze forward. Toni furrowed her brow and urged him, "Bobby?"

When Bobby again failed to respond, Toni sat in the front seat and closed the door. She grabbed Bobby's right hand and squeezed it supportively.

"Tell me what's wrong," Toni implored her fiancée. Bobby struggled with his emotions and, sensing his inner turmoil, she suggested, "Let's drive."

Neither Toni nor Bobby looked at the crowd of his relatives watching the car expectantly as Katherine attempted to herd them towards the church. He turned the vehicle south onto Alii Drive.

"Okay, we're away from all that now," Toni said with a parting wave to the Church. She shifted in her seat to face him and placed her hand on the back of his neck, saying, "So tell me, *please*, what's going on."

Bobby said nothing. He flipped on his turn signal, entered the parking lot of Kahalu'u Beach Park and rolled into an empty spot. He permitted himself an extended exhale and rubbed the radix of his nose.

"I didn't wanna tell you this, not yet, but Katherine's kinda forced my hand," said Bobby bitterly. He looked to Toni and confessed with a heavy heart, "I was married before, Toni. The divorce was finalized about a year before I met you."

Toni's face went deathly white and she deflated. She withdrew her bare feet onto the seat, supported her back against the door and let her arms hang limp. Gazing on Bobby like a child who just learned the truth about Santa Claus, Toni made several failed attempts to speak. A thought struck her and she tensed.

"Do you have kids?" Toni queried apprehensively.

"God, no," protested Bobby as he fidgeted. He touched her left foot and she reflexively pulled it away. Bobby grimaced and began, "Look, it was your mother's-."

"Don't do that," Toni interrupted Bobby. She hugged her legs into her chest and asserted, "This is between us, and no one else."

"I was gonna tell you. I *wanted* to tell you," asserted Bobby though without much confidence in the truth of his statement. He shifted the car into "Park" and turned towards Toni, continuing, "But it's always tough in the beginning, and then the more I learned about the whole Catholic thing, and how much you're into that stuff, I, well . . . I just didn't wanna screw things up."

Beachgoers mulled around the vehicle. Their presence discomfited Toni.

"Let's drive again," Toni whimpered. She set her feet on the floor and sunk into her seat while her eyes became hazy. Bobby complied and, within seconds, the couple traveled north towards St. Peter. He swallowed hard.

"Do I stop?" asked Bobby as they neared the church. Toni shook her head with short, quick motions.

"No," Toni answered. She watched the road ahead and said pensively, "This is my fault. I disobeyed God and the Church."

"C'mon, Toni," objected Bobby. He gestured with his forearm resting on the steering wheel and asked, "How could it be your fault?"

"I knew better," Toni stated. She bit her lip and then released it, expounding, "Had we done this the right way, through the Church, and with marriage counseling, this would've come to light and we would've had time to deal with it."

Toni lowered her chin in shame. Her remorsefulness sent a chill down Bobby's spine.

"But I rushed into things, and instead I'm finding out about it on our wedding day," Toni continued sadly.

"I haven't seen her in a couple years," insisted Bobby, "I swear it."

"I know, sweetheart," Toni replied with a resigned expression. She pointed at a road-side park on the coast and directed Bobby, "Let's stop here."

"Here? Why?" asked Bobby. He read the sign identifying the small beach as "La-Aloa Bay Beach Park".

"Bobby, please," Toni insisted. Bobby obeyed, slowing the car and deftly hanging a U-turn into a parallel parking spot.

"I suppose there's a lotta talking to do," said Bobby blithely while again shifting the car into "Park". He affectionately grasped Toni's thigh.

"There is," Toni agreed. She removed his hand from her leg, gripped it and returned it to him, saying, "Pick me up here in two hours."

"You want me to just leave you here? At the beach? By yourself?" inquired an incredulous Bobby. Leaning into him, Toni kissed him and then playfully tapped his nose.

"Yeah," Toni replied with compassionate composure. She retreated into her seat.

"Alright," relented Bobby with an exasperated exhale. He confirmed, "Two hours."

Leaving her sandals and purse behind, Toni disembarked from the vehicle, scurried across the hot pavement and then meandered through the warm sand. She rotated around, looked to Bobby and held up two fingers in a "V". He nodded when she brought them together and then separated them again.

"Hang in there, Bobby," Toni said as she watched her fiancée depart. She meandered south down the beach, letting the waves tickle her feet. Arriving at Haukalua Heiau, the remains of a small, ancient Hawaiian temple constructed of volcanic rocks, she felt the spiritual nature of the site wafting around her like the humid air. She prayed, "So what do I do now?"

Careful not to disturb the holy site, she seated herself on a large rock on the shore. Toni tucked her legs into her chest, hugged them to her body, rested her chin on her knees and thoughtfully gazed at the ocean. She let the gentle touch of the breeze soothe her emotions, and the crashing of the waves ease her mind, and the sacred setting center her spirit.

"The next two hours are yours," Toni said to God, "and I'm listening."

That Was Yesterday

The third of May dawned cold yet fair. The temperature climbed from the twenties into the fifties by the afternoon but the air retained an elusive chilliness. Elliott shivered and squirmed in his jacket.

"I can't believe we're at the Zoo," Elliott said as he walked hand-in-hand with Nora down one of the Detroit Zoo's broad, black-topped lanes.

"I love the Zoo!" protested Nora with a trace of offense in her tone.

"Which is why I'm here, darlin'," Elliott replied as he playfully pushed Nora away from him. She stumbled and nearly fell but he swooped to her side and steadied her. Elliott teased Nora, "Sorry, I forgot how clumsy you are."

"Meanie," whined Nora with a mock pout. She squiggled out of his arms, returned the gentle shove and ran away from Elliott. Watching her scurry onto the massive patio that surrounded the Rackham Fountain, he smiled warmly.

"Still so much like a kid," Elliott said to himself. He pursued Nora and quickly closed on her, wrapping his arms around her stomach and scooping her into the air. She squealed.

"Let go!" yelled a laughing Nora. Elliott set her on her feet and embraced her from behind. Relaxing into his arms, she studied the Fountain with wonderous eyes and gushed, "The fountain's so pretty."

Constructed in 1939, the Horace H. Rackham Memorial Fountain was in the center of the Zoo. It resembled a bulky, elaborate streetlight with a huge, shallow bowl positioned three-quarters of the way up its column. Water exploded from its small, domed apex and then cascaded into the bowl, over the two ten-foot bronze bears that held the column and into a 75,000-gallon pool. Life-sized turtles guarded the Fountain's circular, multi-level base, the reptiles looking outward at the immense, rectangular pool and the semi-circular extensions on each of its short sides. A life-sized sea lion, spewing water with its head held high, guarded each extension.

"I wanna sit," declared Nora as she walked to the Fountain's stone wall, the barrier comprised of creamy-hued columns and equidistant square supports. She plopped onto the ground and said, "Right here."

Despite loathing the touch of the cold, hard concrete, Elliott acquiesced to her wishes and seated himself next to her. Nora leaned into his body and laid her head on his shoulder.

"How cozy," Elliott remarked while futilely seeking a more comfortable position.

"When're we getting married, Elliott?" queried a suddenly serious Nora. Elliott stopped moving.

"Uh, I don't know," Elliott answered. He subtly shrugged to avoid displacing her and added, "I guess I figured you'd tell me."

Elliott and Nora grew silent and the couple pondered the issue. He stirred first.

"When do you wanna get married?" Elliott asked bluntly.

"Soon," answered Nora.

"I guess it depends on how big you wanna go," Elliott said with money on his mind. Nora surprisingly took his meaning.

"I don't have the best relationship with my parents," explained Nora sheepishly, "and my dad wouldn't be able to help much anyway."

"We'll figure it out," Elliott said without a trace of doubt. Nora failed to perceive his confidence and cuddled into him.

"I don't need a big, expensive wedding," stated Nora matter-of-factly. She tightened her grip on Elliott and thought out loud, "I don't want one. But I want it to be different. *Unique.* Yeah, unique. "Ya' know, *special.*"

Elliott marveled at Nora's heart and pecked her on the top of the head. She hopped into his lap.

"But I *do* want to be married by Christmas," continued Nora as her countenance brightened, "so we can spend it with Emma, and Dave, and the girls, and be a big, happy family."

"Em'll give us Johnny Dubs for the reception," Elliott stated. Offering Nora a dubious grin, he added, "In fact, she'll probably insist on it."

"How about in the fall?" inquired Nora. She saw an outdoor wedding in her mind, with brilliant flashes of red, yellow and orange, and said, "When it's cool, and the leaves are changing. But not too close to Halloween."

"What, no Halloween wedding?" Elliott asked. Receiving a disapproving look from his fiancée, he swiftly added, "An early October wedding sounds great."

"You're such a guy," said Nora. She agilely jumped to her feet while holding Elliott's hand and said, "C'mon, old man, let's go."

Feigning a grunt and difficulty rising, he let Nora pull him up. She looked to the fountain and did a double take.

"Let's do it here!" exclaimed Nora.

"Sure, but we'll probably get arrested," Elliott deadpanned. Several nearby zoo patrons laughed at his jest.

"*Elliott*," scolded an embarrassed Nora. Lowering her voice and waiting until the patrons departed, she said, "I mean it. Right here at the fountain."

"That's unique, I guess," Elliott replied as he surveyed the vicinity of the Fountain. Nodding his head with approval, he said, "Sure. Let's get married at the Zoo."

"Yay!" shouted Nora as she jumped into Elliott's arms and kissed his cheek. Glowing with love, she cooed, "I can't wait to be Mrs. Elliott Warden."

Elliott shook his head at Nora's youthful enthusiasm. His face became neutral, however, and Nora heard the mechanics of his mind.

"What?" Nora pressed him. Elliott set her on the ground.

"Don't quote me on this," Elliott began as he continued to ponder, "but I think, on his day, a year ago . . . ."

"Yeah?" said Nora eagerly.

"I think we kissed for the first time," Elliott said with a burgeoning smile.

"That night in the parking lot," said Nora as the light bulb in her mind illuminated. She waved forcefully and griped, "That stupid cat jumped outta the dumpster at me."

"You'd a' thought it was a bear," Elliott said with a nod over his shoulder at the bronze fountain guardians. Nora offered him a pouty expression but it soon melted into a grin.

"We *have* to get married here," declared Nora.

"Guess we do," Elliott said before the couple celebrated the anniversary of their first kiss.

• • • •

TONI KNEELED IN A PEW at St. Alfred Catholic Church and prayed. Outwardly, her face was weak and careworn and no makeup could completely conceal it. Turbulence wracked her inner world; the prospect of confessing her disobedience to Father Bernard was a daunting one. She exhaled and trembled when it was her turn in the confessional.

"In the name of the Father, and of the Son, and of the Holy Spirit, Amen," began Toni as she performed the Sign of the Cross. Moving two fingers as she spoke, she first touched her forehead, then the middle of her chest and left shoulder, and finished with her right shoulder.

"Why, hello there," an unfamiliar voice greeted her. Toni recognized the Detroit accent of an elderly black man.

"Oh," said Toni, the presence of someone other than Father Bernard or his subordinate priests surprising her.

"Expectin' somebody else?" the priest asked, the amusement evident in his voice. A fear of appearing racist caused Toni to panic.

"No, not at all!" pleaded a mortified Toni. She moved closer to the screen between them and added desperately, "I'm so sorry, Father, I just, I just . . . ."

"You just came to the right place," the priest stated to astutely calm Toni. His tactic worked and, as she relaxed and settled into the confessional chair, he asked, "Now, what can I do for you today?"

Toni paused, the priest's casual approach to confession discombobulating her. He patiently waited for her to speak and, when she regained her composure, the proper words came to her remembrance.

"Bless me, Father, for I have sinned," said Toni, the reason for her visit coming into focus and the sentence chilling her soul. She took a deep breath, the inhale choppy as her body shook, and continued, "My last confession was six months ago."

Toni tensed as if physically struck. She usually attended Confession every month and her neglect of her faith saddened and shamed her.

"And it's been way too long, Father," said Toni with tears arising in her eyes. One fell as she whimpered, "I'm so ashamed of myself."

"You're here now," the undaunted priest reasoned, "and so'm I, and so's God. Easy fix."

The veteran priest's positive, accepting attitude set Toni at ease. A long, slow breath of air expelled the last of her trepidation.

"Father Bernard – you know Father Bernard, I'm sure," began Toni, her words flowing faster like a torrent of water bursting through a crumbling damn, "well, my fiancée, who's not Catholic, or really even Christian, proposed on Thanksgiving, and Father Bernard told me to schedule an appointment to meet Bobby – that's my fiancée, Bobby – and schedule marriage counseling before our wedding, and-."

"Let me guess," the priest interjected shrewdly, "Mr. Bobby didn't wanna wait."

"No, he didn't, and he had already booked a wedding in Hawaii," conceded Toni. She felt a pain in the pit of her stomach as she said, "And the trip was, well, pretty expensive."

"Oh, boy," the priest remarked.

"Yeah, so, even though I knew it was wrong, I went along with it," said Toni. Feeling a surge of guilt, she explained, "Don't get me wrong. I'm not blaming Bobby. It was on me to obey God and do things the right way. I guess I got caught up in my emotions, and how perfect and romantic a Hawaiian wedding would be."

Toni remembered the beauty of Hilo and smiled. The priest said nothing.

"He was so sweet, though, and he made so many changes in his life for me. I felt like I'd be punishing him if I made him wait," said Toni as she sat up. She folded her hands in her lap and continued, "He planned the whole thing as a surprise. Can you believe it? A manly guy like Bobby planned a surprise, Hawaiian wedding on his own. He even found a cute little Catholic church on the ocean for it. I still can't believe he *did* that. My Bobby did that."

"You know what I'm gonna have ya' do, right?" queried the priest rhetorically. Though behind the screen, Toni heard him sit up in his chair and advise, "We need to get that wedding recognized by God, and the Church, and maybe even get that husband of yours into the club."

Toni laughed but she did not know why. It was the priest's turn to be puzzled.

"I miss somethin'?" the priest asked.

"Sorry, Father, I don't know why I laughed," replied Toni. The laughter felt good, though, and she wiped away her tears, expounding, "The wedding didn't happen. It almost did. But it didn't."

"So your sin's not as big as ya' think," the priest stated. He leaned towards the screen and queried in a low voice, "Any premarital sex?"

The question embarrassed Toni and her face reddened. Fidgeting in her chair, she forced herself to answer.

"Thankfully, that's a sin I didn't commit," stated Toni with a measure of pride.

"Ya' narrowly avoided disaster, girl, but narrowly still counts," the priest mused.

"I'm so sorry Father for what I've done," Toni said earnestly.

"Then I absolve you of your sins," the priest stated in a more official manner, "and your penance is simple. *Not easy*, but simple. From now on, before you make any decisions in your love life, you talk to God about it first, and listen to his guidance with an open, obedient heart."

"That's sounds wonderful, and I absolutely will, Father," Toni gushed. She felt her connection to God strengthen and basked in his love.

"You know what comes next," the priest said.

"*O my God, I am heartily sorry for having offended Thee . . .* ," said Toni as she began the Act of Contrition prayer. When she finished, the priest's stomach suddenly growled and broke the silence.

"Sorry 'bout that. I ain't eaten yet today and I'm starvin'," the priest declared unceremoniously. Toni giggled. She found the priest's down-to-earth yet wise manner endearing.

"If this isn't appropriate, Father, just let me know," began Toni gingerly, "but, I kinda feel like God answered my prayers by bringing me here today, and, well, that maybe you're the one to help me. How about a late lunch, my treat."

"The bishop'd have my ass for lettin' penitents buy me lunch right after confession," the priest replied in a comical tone, "but I'm hungry and poor ole' black priests need ta' eat, too."

"I know the perfect place," said Toni with a reminiscent grin.

• • • •

ELLIOTT AND NORA ENTERED Johnny Dubs to the approving looks and glances of the regular patrons. The upcoming nuptials of its owner's brother and its beloved sweetheart were common knowledge and only those harboring a secret crush on Nora disapproved. The rest of the crowd was sparse as the Saturday lunch rush ended and the Tigers' first pitch was scheduled for 7:35 pm.

"How come we never sit at a table?" asked Nora as Elliott slid onto his reserved bar stool. He cringed inwardly; her tone was like the one Donna used when trying to reform him during their brief reunion.

"Why would we do that?" Elliott replied with mock befuddlement. He threw a quick finger at the next barstool and said, "Besides, I was gonna get Em to slap a 'RESERVED' nameplate on that one, too."

"Really?" asked Nora, her face illuminating with a glow of appreciation. The light alleviated Elliott's fear of another betterment campaign.

"Really," Elliott confirmed. Nora proudly hopped on the bar stool, the young woman oblivious to the approach of her employer.

"Here with twenty-seven minutes to spare," Emma said as she arrived in front of the couple. Wiping down the bar with a ubiquitous white towel, she sniped, "That's not like you two."

"Sorry again about last week," apologized Nora with a wrinkled nose. Emma's gaze fell on Elliott.

"Just don't take advantage of our relationship," Emma warned.

"I'd never do that!" objected Nora in an injured tone.

"Relax, Nor," Elliott interjected with a dubious expression for his sister, "she was talkin' to me."

"You're so smart, Big Bro," Emma said as she tweaked his nose. Elliott's attempt to dodge was late.

"Damn it, Em," Elliott griped as he slapped the air in front of his face.

"The girls started doing that to me and Dave lately, and I guess it's kinda caught on," Emma explained without remorse. She exhaled as she tossed the towel aside and asked, "So, I guess you guys wanna eat, huh?"

"Em's famous tacos?" suggested Nora impishly.

"I thought I said don't take advantage," Emma complained with an unforgiving stare despite fully intending to grant the request. Elliott swooped to Nora's rescue.

"You're not exactly swamped right now," Elliott said with a nod towards the dining areas.

"Fine," Emma replied with an eye roll.

"Yay!" exclaimed Nora. Emma grabbed the towel and swiped it at Elliott but, cognizant of her irritation, he avoided it.

"I'd curb your enthusiasm," Elliott advised as Emma journeyed to the kitchen. He expounded with a histrionic stretch of his arms and upper body, "She'll probably bring 'em out two minutes before your shift."

"I'm *hungry*," countered Nora with two hands on her stomach, "so they won't last that long."

"I gotta hit the john," Elliott stated as he rose to his feet.

"Maybe you should get up on stage and announce it," jabbed Nora with a smirk. Grabbing her head, Elliott kissed her on top of it.

"You're so damn cute," Elliott said, "*mouthy*, but cute."

"I'll go check on our tacos," stated Nora as she stood up though Elliott knew she wanted to reveal their marriage news to Emma. The couple walked the length of the bar, turned right into the back hallway and then diverged: Elliott veered left into the men's room while Nora continued forward before turning right into the kitchen.

"Grab me some shells, will ya," Emma requested while browning ground beef in a pan. The women were alone; the day cook indulged in a cigarette break in the parking lot.

"We're getting married in October," announced a bubbly Nora as she entered the large pantry, "at the Rackham Fountain at the Detroit Zoo."

Emma scrunched her face to stifle a smile. Nora, approaching her with a package of taco shells, noticed and offered one of her own.

"We're having the reception here," Emma stated as if the matter were settled.

"I know," replied Nora. She stole a leaf of lettuce and bit into it. Watching her future sister-in-law preparing the ingredients, Nora queried, "Do you think Donna's gonna be a problem?"

"No," Emma answered brusquely, "even if I have to lock her in my trunk and drive her back to Arizona myself."

"Good," said Nora, Emma's determined response soothing her worries. She moved towards the kitchen door and stated, "I'll go fix Elliott a drink."

"You do that," Emma said, "because it's *your* job now."

Nora exited the kitchen as Emma continued fixing the couple's tacos. A thought crept into her head, a thought she tried to push out, but it stubbornly clung to her brain. She addressed it directly.

"*That* problem ended on a beach in Hawaii," Emma whispered to herself, "so *that* is *that*."

• • • •

"SO HOW LONG'VE YOU been retired?" asked Toni as she and her new friend, Father Maurice Jenkins, sat down at the last available table. The Senate Coney Island teemed with patrons amid the sights, smells and sounds of conversations, cooking food and clinking tableware.

"Too long," Father Maurice answered unabashedly. He allowed the waitress to fill his mug with coffee and said, "Diocese still has me pinch hit, though."

"I'm glad they did today," replied Toni with a bright countenance. The waitress moved to her coffee cup and she asked, "Where was your parish?"

"East side," Father Maurice answered. His mood dimmed and he added bitterly, "St. Margaret Mary. Closed in 1982. So I retired."

"Be back in a few, kids," said the waitress before departing. Father Maurice shook his head at her.

"Shit, *kids*," Father Maurice muttered. He lifted the mug to his mouth and quipped, "*You?* Yeah. *Me?* Moses and I went to seminary together."

Toni laughed. Father Maurice drank.

"Well, we've got coffee, so let's hear it," Father Maurice urged Toni. Her demeanor darkened and she drank her coffee to delay telling her story.

"It actually starts a long time ago, at least a long time for me," Toni began sadly. She recounted the Montana years – the neglect and emotional abuse at the hands of her father, his physical abuse of Katherine and her brave struggles to raise her child, and the intervention of her Great Aunt Agnes – and continued into their new start in Michigan. The waitress occasionally interrupted her account by refilling mugs, taking their orders and delivering their food.

"I gotta meet this mamma of yours," Father Maurice interjected mischievously while chewing the last bite of cheeseburger.

"You will," replied Toni with a grin and a warm sensation in her heart, "I promise."

"But I digressed you," the old priest said while holding up several French fries.

"I think it was a good time to do that," said Toni with a glance at her uneaten Chef Salad. She took her first bite of it.

"So what gift'd God give you outta all that?" Father Maurice queried. He took a sip of coffee and added, "Other than Mamma Cullen."

Toni gazed at him in wonder until a weak smile emerged on her face and slowly spread like the rising sun emerging from the dark clouds of a morning storm. A yearning, suppressed until the moment, suddenly welled within her soul.

"*My music*," gushed Toni. Father Maurice watched her intently, the twenty-eight-year-old bubbling with appreciation and saying, "Dad had this old, beat-up guitar, and he gave it to me for my eighth birthday . . . two weeks late, but he still gave it to me. So I just started singing and playing – terribly at first, just ask my Mom – but I learned pretty quickly. By the time I was nine, it was as easy as breathing, playing all those old country songs Dad listened to. Once in a while, he'd even ask me to play something for him. Usually Hank Williams, Jr. or Waylon Jennings or . . . ."

Toni stifled a sob and tears formed in her eyes. Her thoughts moved from the past to the present and she recovered.

"Ya' know, I haven't played since Bobby proposed," said a deflated Toni. She pondered that fact while indulging in a few more bites of salad and then continued, "I've messed around a few times on my guitar, sang a little to myself, but not really played. We certainly haven't played any shows."

"Who's we?" Father Maurice asked.

"I was, *I am*, in a band. At least I think I still am, if the guys haven't given up on me," expounded Toni guiltily. Feeling as if she wanted to perform right then and there, she said with pride, "Morning Cloak."

"And what's that mean, Morning Cloak?" Father Maurice queried.

"Well, a *Mourning* Cloak is a big, pretty butterfly with brown wings," answered Toni.

"Brown butterflies're pretty?" Father Maurice said with a dubious expression.

"Yeah! They're beautiful!" insisted Toni. She imagined Mourning Cloaks fluttering during a hot Montana summer in her mind and described, "The edges of their wings have a line of black with blue splotches and then another line at the ends with this creamy yellow color. I saw them all the time when I was little. Most kids would chase them, but I'd just sit there and watch them. I loved the blue dots. That was my favorite part."

"So which morning we talkin' about?" the priest asked. Toni offered him a knowing look.

"Nobody usually catches that. Mourning as in grieving," said Toni. She became sheepish and explained, "But I don't like that word, so I convinced my boys to change the name to Morning Cloak, as in the am. Guess it reminded me when I was a girl, and used to wake up before dawn, and I'd hear the birds chirping but the dark, though kinda fadin' away, was still covering up the morning. Like a cloak. I know, it's dumb."

"Ain't nothin' dumb about you, young lady," Father Maurice corrected Toni. He drained his coffee mug, aimed his deep brown eyes at her and stated, "Looks like we found the first thing ya' gotta fix."

Toni straightened her body and gazed on the priest quizzically. His stare did not waver.

"Why not start with somethin' small? Get a little momentum under your belt," Father Maurice suggested, "and a little joy in that big heart a' yours."

"Only if you come see me play," Toni said buoyantly.

"You play that country stuff, don't ya?" queried Father Maurice with distaste. Toni laughed yet again, the old cleric a delightful May surprise after a brutal April. Her levity was contagious and garnered multiple grins from surrounding patrons. Father Maurice relented with a dismissive wave, "Oh, all right."

· · · ·

EMMA CONVERSED WITH a customer at the north end of the bar when she heard Toni's voice call her name. It briefly stunned her; thinking the sound was an auditory illusion in the background noise of the club, she nonetheless hesitated before turning towards it.

"Didn't expect to see you 'round here again," Emma said when she confirmed Toni's presence. Both women were visibly uncomfortable.

"I know," advised Toni while averting her gaze. Her rough countenance made her more closely resemble Katherine and it unnerved Emma. She scanned Johnny Dubs to ensure her brother was gone and, cognizant of her concern, Toni said, "I waited until he left."

"That red boat a' his is kinda hard to miss, isn't it?" Emma asked with a smirk and a fond memory of her father. She settled into the conversation and asked, "So . . . what's up, stranger?"

"I know we've been – *I've been* – pretty scarce lately, but I'd like to get Morning Cloak back on the stage again," explained an anxious, apologetic Toni. She looked to the stage longingly.

"Oh, trust me, I want that, too," Emma quickly replied. She eased onto a vacant barstool with her hands folded at her knees and expounded, "You guys are the best rainmakers I've ever had in here. But I think you'd agree we've got a few sticky issues to work out first. Like I can't have that hotheaded husband of yours punching out my brother 'cuz he didn't like the way he looked at you."

Toni bowed her head, embarrassed by Bobby's assault on Elliott and ashamed of her ruined wedding. The moment struck her: if Elliott was unattached, the path to his heart was unobstructed.

"How is he?" asked Toni sheepishly despite knowing she treaded on dangerous ground. She saw Father Maurice's disapproving expression in her mind.

"Believe it or not, my big brother is engaged," Emma said with a sigh. Toni's spirit plummeted and her eyes watered.

"Already?" asked Toni with a squeak in her voice. Regret soaked her to the bone and she uttered woundedly, "Wow."

"That's right," Emma said. Toni's reaction both puzzled and intrigued her.

"So he made the changes Donna wanted?" asked Toni as she processed Elliott's betrothal.

"Not a one," Emma stated bluntly.

"Boy, she really loves him," commented Toni with a frown. She folded her arms and shifted her weight to her right foot.

"Yeah, she does," Emma replied. Sliding off the stool, she said to Toni's great shock, "But I wasn't talkin' about her. My thirty-eight-year-old brother is engaged to my twenty-three-year-old waitress. A girl who was born when he was a sophomore in high school."

"Not thrilled about it, huh?" inquired Toni cautiously. She felt a welling of emotion in her chest but, uncertain of what emotion it was, she struggled to suppress it.

"Actually, I'm good with it," Emma confessed. She pulled Toni out of the aisleway to allow several patrons to pass and elucidated, "She might be young, and a little naïve, but she's good for him. Someway, somehow, she's good for him."

Every word Emma spoke was a dagger in Toni's heart. Her approval of Elliott's union with Nora proved too much for Toni to bear and she panicked.

"Excuse me," blurted Toni as she burst into tears and attempted to flee towards the women's restroom. Emma, however, grabbed her arm and directed her into the stairwell leading to her office.

"Use the *upstairs* bathroom," Emma instructed Toni. The younger woman swiftly ascended the steps and, reaching the top, turned a sharp right into Emma's office. The bar manager, Sean, approached her boss who lamented, "Why am I always cleaning up his messes? *Idiot.*"

"You're probably not gonna like that, either," added Sean while hooking a thumb at the entrance. Following it to the doors, Emma saw Toni's bandmates walk into the bar: the lanky, shaggy-haired Eddie; his portly, bristly-mustached brother, Oscar; and the tall, dark and brooding Ryan.

"Beer 'em up on the house and tell 'em I'll be down in a few minutes," Emma sighed as she lifted a finger in the air and whirled it in a circle. She then pointed the finger at Sean and added, "And don't let Eddie talk you into a second freebie."

"You got it, Em," replied a dutiful Sean as she moved to the beer cooler.

"I always got it," Emma muttered with a shake of her head.

• • • •

EMMA CAUTIOUSLY ENTERED her office. She heard sobs and sniffles coming from the bathroom at its far side. Stopping just outside the door, she watched Toni desperately wiping her eyes.

"Damn it, Elliott," Emma quietly griped to herself. Draining the irritation from her voice, she called, "The band's here, Toni."

"Thanks, Em," replied Toni after a pause. Managing to stanch her tears she made a final dab of her left eye and tossed the tissue in the garbage can. She rotated around to face Emma.

"Wait a minute. Why are you crying?" Emma inquired suspiciously. Toni clenched her jaw and squinted her eyes to stave off further tears as Emma queried, "Aren't you married to Bobby?"

"*No*," whimpered Toni. She spun around, grasped the sink with her hands and resumed weeping.

"No?" a disbelieving Emma said. She stuck her hands into the back pockets of her jeans, lingered outside the bathroom and asked, "Are you bullshitting me?"

Toni bowed her head and an unusual hardness crept over her heart. Her knuckles became white as she squeezed the porcelain.

"I'm not," declared Toni in a strong tone. She wiped her eyes free of her sorrow, attended to her makeup and ran a hand through her short hair. Turning around, Toni gazed directly at Emma and advised, "I called it off at the last minute. Long story."

Emma gaped at Toni for thirty seconds, her mind unable to comprehend the news. When she recovered from her stupor, she slowly walked to the office door and closed it. Emma dropped herself onto the worn leather couch.

"Wanna drink?" Emma offered.

"No, I'm good," replied Toni. She, too, made her way to the couch and plopped onto it. The two women, sitting on opposite ends, stared forward and sat silently for over a minute.

"What happened?" Emma inquired.

"I'm stupid," answered Toni acerbically.

"And you're stupid because . . . ," Emma said.

"Oh, a lotta reasons . . . ," responded Toni, ". . . because I didn't see what was right in front of me. Because I ignored my faith and God and didn't do the right thing."

Toni exhaled. Emma remained mute.

"Because I fell in love with your brother," replied Toni with a haunting smile, "but I blew my chance with him, and now it's too late."

"Oh, shit," Emma thought. She threw optical daggers to heaven and silently chastised her higher power, "You gotta be kidding me with this right now."

"Feels good to say it," said Toni with a widening grin, "*I love your brother.*"

"You don't love him," Emma insisted despite knowing her statement to be false. She threw an arm over the back of the couch, crossed her legs and turned her body towards Toni, saying, "He came on really strong when you and Bobby were on the rocks and it made you feel good. But it was just a honeymoon period and-."

"A what?" interrupted Toni in puzzlement. She slipped off her shoes, pulled her long legs onto the couch and hugged them to her chest while facing Emma.

"You know. A honeymoon period," Emma continued. Toni's blank stare prompted Emma to continue, "That first six months or so where everything's wonderful with the physical electricity every time you see him . . . the fun dates, the long phone calls . . . and the great, romantic sex."

"Em!" objected Toni as her cheeks flushed and her eyes widened.

"I know he's my brother and all but, like, c'mon," Emma said. She hoisted her legs onto the couch and mimicked Toni, stating, "And I *know* my brother. You two had to've done it at least once."

"We didn't," protested Toni. She slowly shook her head in the negative and added, "And neither did me and Bobby."

"Okay, now you *are* bullshitting me," Emma scoffed.

"I'm dead serious, Em," declared Toni. Her seriousness became pride as she said declared steadfastly, "I'm a good Catholic girl and I've saved myself for marriage."

"Oh my god, you *are* serious," Emma said. Taken aback by Toni's chastity, she lowered her voice and asked, "You're, like, a virgin? At twenty-eight?"

It was Emma's turn to display hazy eyes as she pondered the new information. The club's speakers roared to life and spurred her onward.

"But didn't you guys go on a cruise together?" Emma queried.

"We did," Toni answered, "but we got a cabin with two beds."

"Wow," Emma said, "that's hardcore."

"I actually spent the night at Elliott's place once," confessed Toni, her smile returning as she remembered the care Elliott rendered on a hot August evening.

"And got out with your virginity intact," said Emma sardonically.

"He was the quintessential perfect gentlemen when I was the quintessential vulnerable lady," reminisced Toni. Emma opened her mouth to comment on Elliott's feelings for Toni but a knock on the office door interrupted her.

"Come in," Emma said after receiving a nod of approval from Toni. Nora opened the office door and stepped inside. Toni stifled a gasp.

"Em, Laurel's gonna be late," stated Nora. She continued speaking until she noticed Toni: "She got caught by the train and-."

"*Perfect*," Emma complained to herself. The sight of Toni petrified Nora while Toni looked at Nora sadly; Emma felt as if she sat in the eye of an emotional tornado. Toni recovered first and forced a pleasant grin.

"Congratulations on the engagement, Nora," said Toni sincerely. She stood up, walked to Nora and extended her hand, saying, "You got yourself a great guy, and you two're gonna be so great together."

"Thanks," replied Nora uneasily as she weakly shook Toni's hand.

"The band's here, Em, so I'll see ya' downstairs," said Toni as she flawlessly performed the role of a woman disinterested in Elliott Warden.

"Should I be worried?" asked Nora when Toni disappeared down the steps.

"No," Emma answered, "Toni's a totally different bird than Donna."

. . . .

THE REMAINDER OF NORA'S shift was an eternity to her, the time crawling forward and the clock seemingly unwilling to move. The ride home proved unbearable and Nora found herself speeding more than once. When she finally arrived, she threw open the storm door and fumbled with her keys as she tried to unlock the main door.

"Damn it," Nora snapped when her keys hit the porch. After she retrieved them and turned the lock, she burst into the apartment while still wearing her shoes and jacket. Nora jumped into Elliott's lap and embraced him fervently despite the fact he dozed in his recliner.

"What the hell, Nora?" Elliott griped as she jolted him from sleep. Nora grasped his cheeks and engaged him in a long, passionate kiss. Maintaining her grip on his face, she pulled away from Elliott and gazed deeply into his eyes.

"I wanna get married soon," said Nora. She kissed him again and then insisted, "I don't wanna wait."

"Okay," Elliott replied. He moved her hands away from his face but kept his grip on them, inquiring, "Like how soon?"

"As soon as we can," said Nora emphatically.

"I thought you wanted a fall wedding," Elliott said. The mental fog slowly lifted from his mind and he stammered, "Ya' know . . . with the, the, uh, like leaves changing colors and, like, all that."

"I changed my mind," said Nora as she held onto Elliott for dear life. His exhaustion and the late hour prevented him from further questions.

"All right, but we're not having a kid this year," Elliott quipped. Nora laid her head on his chest and focused on his heartbeat.

"Deal," Nora said happily.

What Is Love

The scene was a familiar one for Uncle Elliott. He sat at the patio table, underneath its large umbrella, with his long legs stretched out before him and crossed at the ankles while he watched his nieces splash and play in Emma's inground pool. The Grumpy Old Man she set on the table next to him was the cherry on top.

"Okay, we're packed and ready to go," advised Emma as she dropped herself into the chair opposite Elliott and added, "and Dave's ordering the pizza now."

"So, whaddaya gotta tell me?" an amused, suspicious Elliott inquired.

"How'd you know?" asked Emma blithely.

"Mom, watch!" Lanie shouted. She charged towards the pool and flipped into water.

"Don't do that again," warned Emma with stern glance when Lanie surfaced. She swam to the shallow end and rolled her eyes at her mother who said, "You'll crack your head open on the edge of the pool."

Elliott's eyes remained on his sister despite the interruption. She felt his stare but did not acknowledge it.

"Look, you got me over here to watch the girls on a night Nora's working *so she won't hear it*, you and the old man are headed outta town *so you won't have to deal with it*, and you brought me a drink *so I can handle it*," Elliott said with a goofy grin. He held up his drink in a mock toast and added, "Something's up, Sis."

Emma flashed him a snarky expression. An undaunted Elliott partook of his cocktail but kept his gaze on his sibling.

"Fine," grumbled Emma with a labored exhale. She stretched out her long legs before her, crossed them at the ankles just like her brother, and stated, "Morning Cloak's gonna start playing the club again."

"I knew that'd happen eventually," a surprisingly even-keeled Elliott replied. He took another sip and added, "I'm just surprised Bobby's letting her near Johnny Dubs after all our history. But the stage is where she belongs. Maybe he realizes that."

A shriek from Tessa as she leapt into the pool broke the flow of the siblings' conversation. The momentary reprieve gave Emma no pleasure; it would be short-lived and she wished to spit out the words on her tongue. They felt like glass shards crammed in her mouth.

"Good work conning Dave into opening the pool early," Elliott said while watching Lanie follow her sister and cause a spray of water. The farthest-reaching drops hit him but Emma withdrew her legs to avoid them. She made a sour face as he continued, "It makes babysitting really damn easy."

"Elliott, they're not together anymore," Emma blurted. She tensed her entire body in anticipation of her brother's response.

"Who's not together?" asked Elliott. Failing to take Emma's meaning, he sat up with drink in hand and a furrowed brow.

"Toni and Bobby, idiot. They didn't get married in Hawaii," snapped Emma. She added in a slow, grim voice, "*And they're not together anymore.*"

"So *that's* why Nora hit the accelerator on the wedding," said Elliott. He drained his glass and added in annoyance, "Little shit didn't say a word."

"She doesn't know. I least I don't think she does," Emma replied. She settled into her chair and relaxed her muscles, saying, "But she walked into a conversation Toni and I were having about it."

Emma's tone made Elliott's spine tingle. He set his elbows on the table with both hands wrapped around his glass.

"Toni was upset so she had to know something was up," said Emma with a glance at Elliott. He stared at the ice cubs in his glass as she speculated, "I think that's what may have spooked our little princess."

Emma turned to face Elliott and encompassed his hands in her own. He tightened his grip on the cold, condensation-glazed glass.

"What're you gonna do, Elliott?" asked an uncharacteristically anxious Emma. Elliott let several seconds pass.

"Not a damn thing," Elliott answered stoically. He returned his attention to his sister's comely face.

"Really?" queried a skeptical Emma.

"Em, they both had a choice between me and someone else," Elliott reasoned. His face hardened and his gaze intensified as he explained succinctly, "As great as Toni is, she chose the other guy and Nora chose me. That's really all there is to it."

Emma shook her head in silent acceptance of Elliott's declaration. She squeezed his hands and then released them. Turning their attention to the frolicking children, they spoke no more of Toni Cullen that day.

• • • •

TONI ARRIVED IN BISHOP Park in Wyandotte on a warm Saturday. She carried a brown sack with grease stains and a carboard tray with two lidded Styrofoam cups. Scanning the riverside benches for Father Maurice, she soon located him and hurried towards the elderly priest.

"Well, if it isn't Miss Cullen," Father Maurice greeted Toni as she strode to the bench. He was dressed in his usual cleric's clothing while Toni wore a loose-fitting, blue jumpsuit with a white blouse underneath. Giving her a once-over, he remarked, "Looking as good as ever."

"You realize we were at a Coney Island last time," said Toni playfully while ignoring the compliment, "and you could've had coney dogs then, right?"

"If I wanted someone tellin' me what to eat, *I* would've gotten married," Father Maurice replied.

"I never told Bobby what to eat," Toni countered with a smirk. She sat down and set the tray and bag between them. Toni then handed the priest his drink and a straw before opening the bag and reaching inside.

"Let me guess," Father Maurice said, "the skinny white girl got a salad?"

Toni laughed. She produced a chili-smothered coney dog wrapped in white paper and displayed it.

"No, she actually ordered a coney dog, too," replied Toni, "*and* got extra onions, so watch out."

"Uh-oh," Father Maurice said with a raspy chuckle. Toni, like an attentive mother, distributed the food and napkins and the priest noted her maternal instinct. Carefully unwrapping a messy chili dog and lifting it to his mouth, he paused and asked, "So what's the 4-1-1 on Mr. Bobby?"

Father Maurice consumed a large bite of his lunch and watched Toni while he voraciously chewed it. She sipped her Diet Coke through a straw and pondered the question.

"We never really did talk about the present, did we?" said Toni, her mood disappearing behind a cloud just as the sun did the same. She set down her coney dog on the flattened paper bag and expounded, "We talked in Hawaii and it didn't go well. He just didn't seem to understand why hiding a previous marriage was a big deal."

"Oh, it is," Father Maurice stated in between bites of his coney dog and swipes at his mouth with a napkin.

"That's what I told Bobby," said Toni in a distressed tone. She retrieved her coney dog and continued, "I explained how I was already turning my back on God and the Church by not following the rules, and that our marriage wouldn't ever be valid in the Church because his marriage hadn't been annulled."

"And what'd he say ta' that?" asked the priest as Toni indulged in a bite.

"Nothing," answered Toni with a hand held to her mouth. When she finished chewing, she swallowed and said, "We've hardly spoken since that day. It's just tough. I feel he's been dishonest and it worries me how casually he dismisses it. He feels he's made so many sacrifices for me that I should just be grateful and let it go."

"If you ask me, you ain't too broken up over the dude," said Father Maurice pointedly. He crumpled the white wrapper into a ball and threw it into a nearby garbage can. Father Maurice queried with his usual shrewdness, "So who's the other guy?"

"It's like you're in my head," said Toni, the priest's perceptiveness unnerving her. Father Maurice did not relent, however, and his intense gaze prompted her to answer, "That would be one Elliott Warden."

Toni's heart fluttered and she felt tingly. Father Maurice recognized the look and, sensing the avalanche of words on Toni's tongue, he picked up his second coney dog.

"He was a really good friend, my best friend, even more than Bobby," began Toni wistfully. Speaking over the noise of the priest unwrapping the next course of his meal, she said, "He fell head over heels for me, and I, well, I guess I let him get too close. It just wasn't fair, on my part I mean. Bobby and I went through a rough patch, and I pulled Elliott over the line a few times – the *emotional* line – and then begged him to go back across it when it suited me. Bobby ended up punching Elliott in the face and broke his nose. In two places."

"Hot-headed honky," Father Maurice commented through his food. The little man finished his second coney dog and washed it down with his Coke.

"That's when I took a break from Bobby. Elliott and I got even closer, but we agreed that we'd give it some time and then talk about us," continued Toni. She grabbed her soft drink, wet her whistle and then said, "*Until 1986.* But Bobby had a complete change of heart, got his act together and proposed, Elliott gracefully bowed out, and when 1986 came, I was engaged to Bobby."

"Young people, always in a hurry," Father Maurice scoffed. He lowered his chin, cocked an eye at Toni and added, "That's why we do the counseling."

"I know," sighed Toni with remorse. She set down her drink and stated emphatically, "That's why I wanna do it the *right* way this time, whoever my guy turns out to be. And why I need your help."

"If you can't fix your relationship with your man – and you think this Elliott's the one – you're gonna hafta take it slow this time," Father Maurice advised, "follow God's plan and God's clock."

"Elliott's engaged now, Father," advised Toni with watery eyes. Father Maurice gave her a hard look.

"Doesn't change the analysis," Father Maurice stated firmly, "so work on your relationship with God. Just don't bitch about what ya' don't got but be thankful for what ya' do. Everything else will fall into place after that."

The unlikely pair sat quietly as Toni contemplated the priest's advice. They watched the passing Detroit River, and the seagulls, and listened to the sounds of children playing in the park. Upon finishing her lunch, Toni bagged their garbage and set it aside.

"You're right, as always," announced Toni. She embraced him and said, "Thank you, Father."

"You definitely got extra onions," Father Maurice joked as he returned the hug.

"*Fa-ther,*" objected Toni. Her embarrassment lessened when she saw the grin on his face. She returned the smile and said, "I'd say you're terrible but it wouldn't be true."

"St. Patrick Church's just down Superior," Father Maurice informed Toni with a point of his skinny arm to the west. He suggested politely, "Why don't we pay the Boss a visit?"

"Let's," replied Toni as she stood and offered a hand to Father Maurice. Pulling him to his feet, she took his arm and they strolled through the late spring day.

• • • •

THE JUNE THURSDAY BROUGHT wind and rain with temperatures easing into the seventies but Elliott, *sans* jacket, ignored the precipitation and casually walked towards North End Bar. After striding through the front door, he let his eyes adjust to the darkness and his nose to the strong smell of cigarettes. The bar was moderately busy for a weekday but only Brandy served customers. She noticed Elliott while delivering four beer bottles to a rowdy table and set her hand on her hip.

"Warden, whadda *you* want?" Brandy chastised him in her usual surly manner.

"To ruin your break," answered Elliott as he seated himself in a lonely corner. Brandy returned to the bar area.

"Damn it," Brandy complained. She dramatically slapped the white towel hanging from her shoulder onto the bar and yelled, "All right, losers. Last call before my break."

Elliott chortled and shook his head. The bar patrons, unoffended by Brandy's slight, placed their orders and she deftly filled them before making a Grumpy Old Man for Elliott. She dropped it in front of him and some of it sloshed onto the table.

"So, where's the princess?" Brandy asked as she slid into one chair and kicked up her left foot on another. She quickly produced a cigarette and a lighter. Elliott sipped his cocktail.

"Drove her parents to Ohio to see relatives," answered Elliott. He pulled some napkins from the dented metal dispenser, tossed them onto the table to soak up the spilled drink and then set his glass on top of them. Brandy lit her cigarette and indulged in it as Elliott added, "She wasn't happy about it but her heart's pure gold."

"And I'm supposed to care why?" a vexed Brandy inquired. A plume of white smoke followed.

"You asked," countered Elliott pointedly.

"Alright, spit it out, Warden," Brandy demanded. She threw her off arm over the back of the chair and added, "I ain't got all day."

"Toni's back," said Elliott with his eyes trained on Brandy.

"So what?" Brandy snapped with a shrug. She secretly worried about the development but deflected, "She's married, you're engaged. Doesn't mean a damn thing."

"She didn't go through with it," advised Elliott. He took a drink before expounding, "She's not with Bobby *and* she's gonna start playin' at Johnny Dubs again."

"Again, so what?" Brandy asked as she set her cigarette in the crook of the ashtray. She tilted her head back and urged Elliott, "You got a good thing goin' with Nora. Don't screw it up."

"It's not like that," said Elliott while leaning forward. He let his chin hover above the table and explained, "I'm not giving her up for *anything*. But, I don't know, I just needed to tell someone that . . . ."

Elliott tapped his chest. His heightened emotion prickled Brandy.

". . . . there's still a little something in here for Toni," confessed Elliott.

"And I drew the short straw?" Brandy grumbled.

"You're the only person I trust enough to tell who isn't emotionally invested in Nora," stated Elliott bluntly. He leaned back in his chair, set his arms on the armrests and said, "Emma finally thinks she's got me married off. She'd murder me."

"I'm close," Brandy replied as she leaned forward and gazed directly into Elliott's eyes. Her countenance softened and she implored him, "Look, I get it. I know you two got close when princess was playin' around with the boy toy and Bobby was, well, bein' Bobby."

Brandy leaned back while retrieving her cigarette. She smoked it in dramatic fashion, expelled the smoke through her nostrils and ran her tongue over her bottom lip.

"But she was outta your league then, and she still is now," Brandy opined, "so it's time to let that one go."

Elliott nodded his head in agreement and took a large gulp of his cocktail. Brandy smoked and watched the gears of his mind spin.

"Seen Macayla lately?" asked Elliott as he returned his attention to Brandy. She threw optical daggers at him but he caught them and hurled them back, saying, "C'mon, Brandy. Even I'm not that stupid."

"Sometimes I wonder," Brandy replied. She sighed and revealed, "No, I ain't seen her in months. She's probably high as a kite and shackin' up with some blue-collar sugar daddy."

Elliott finished his drink and stood up. Brandy remained seated.

"Why don't ya' hang out here for a while?" Brandy suggested. She nodded over her shoulder and said, "I need someone to abuse for a while and none of these assholes fight back anymore."

"Thanks," replied Elliott with an appreciative grin.

· · · ·

EMMA ENTERED JOHNNY Dubs after an extended break in the middle of the day to visit her daughters. She stopped at the hostess stand and surveyed her club: the years of blood, sweat and tears had paid great dividends and her pride burgeoned. Her eyes fell on the picture of John Warden behind the bar.

"I hope you're proud of me, Daddy," thought Emma with a tingle in her spine. The sight of a drunken Elliott interrupted her reverie; she marched to him and inquired sharply, "What the hell are you doing here?"

"Tryin' to get a drink," Elliott replied loudly with an angry look at Luke. The bartender flipped him the bird. His clumsy mannerisms betraying his intoxication, he held up his glass and yelled, "Empty!"

"Keep it down!" ordered Emma. She asked Luke accusatorily, "How many'd you serve him?

"Just one," replied an annoyed Luke. He turned to the cash register and opened it, saying, "He was already drinking it when I realized he came in here lit."

"I was convincing," said Elliott with a goofy grin. Emma slapped him on the back of the head, the hit prompting him to object, "Hey!"

"If you drove here drunk I'll-," began Emma. Elliott quickly raised his palms and made a shoving motion towards her without contact.

"*I didn't,*" Elliott interrupted her acerbically. Emma's intense glower tempered his anger so he lowered his hands and his voice, repeating, "I didn't."

"Then how'd you get here?" demanded a skeptical Emma. She displayed a swift smile as a group of patrons entered the bar and greeted them with the usual pleasantries. Her welcoming demeanor quickly vanished.

"I may've paid Brandy a lil' visit at North End," Elliott admitted with the slightest slurring of his words. He braced for the expected chastisement of his sister and added, "And she may've given me a, me a lift, after her shift. Hey, that rhymed."

Emma moved into Elliott's personal space. He did not retreat.

"And you were drinking with Brandy why?" queried Emma brusquely. She smelled the liquor on his breath.

"Technically, she wasn't drinking," Elliott answered matter-of-factly. He raised a finger and continued, "She was smoking like a damn chimney, though."

"*Elliott,*" griped Emma.

"Look, I'll just leave," Elliott conceded as he attempted to rise. Emma placed her hand on his shoulder and pushed him back onto the barstool.

"You can't leave now, idiot," scolded Emma, "you're drunk and ya' don't have a car."

"Eh, I'll figure it out," Elliott said. Emma's ire melted away.

"Please just go up to my office and sleep it off," begged Emma, her patience waning. Elliott weighed his options and his attention drifted to a banner hanging on the wall. Breaking Emma's resistance, he stood up.

"I'm leaving," Elliott said firmly. Emma glanced at the banner promoting Morning Cloak's schedule.

"They don't go on until nine," said Emma. She assured Elliott, "Go catch some Zs and I'll get you outta here before sound check."

"You'd better," Elliott warned Emma with a pointed finger.

"Yeah, yeah, just you sober up," grumbled Emma as she nudged Elliott onward.

"I mean it, Em," Elliott growled. She shook her head.

"Alright, alright," relented Emma in irritation. With a push towards the stairwell, she urged him, "Just *go*."

. . . .

MORNING CLOAK'S SOUND check woke Elliott from his slumber. He lay on his back on the leather couch in Emma's dark office with his feet propped on its arm. The first traces of a headache arose in his skull, his body felt hot and his mouth was uncomfortably dry.

"Damn it, Em," a groggy Elliott muttered as he set his feet on the floor with a thud. Though it hurt to concentrate, he managed to devise a plan and muttered, "She'll be up on the stage. I can probably sneak out the back doors."

After a stop at the bathroom, Elliott languidly descended the steps. He cracked the door open and peeked into the club. Eddie, Oscar and Ryan were on the stage but there was no sign of Toni.

"She must not be here yet," Elliott whispered. Deciding the noise and commotion in the club would mask his flight, he steeled his will for a dash to the doors and said, "Time to go."

Elliott slunk from the stairwell door and carefully closed it behind him. He squared his shoulders to the exit and took a single step forward.

"Hi, Elliott," said Toni. She sat on a stool at the end of the bar and watched Elliott with a disapproving smirk. He watched her in his peripheral vision and heard her ask, "Hiding from me?"

"Damn it, Em," Elliott muttered again. He slowly rolled his eyes to her and said, "Hey, Toni."

Luke poured coffee into a mug and slid it to Toni. She sensed the angst underneath Elliott's forced smile.

"Em said we should get this over with," said Toni who slid the coffee towards Elliott. She motioned to the empty barstool next to her and reasoned, "Ya' know, two friends can say hello and talk a little, *in public*, and not worry about anything else. There don't have to be any consequences, and no one has to get hurt."

"Yeah, I guess," a discomfited Elliott said. Unable to resist her charm, he took the seat next to her. Nodding towards the band, Elliott remarked, "Glad to see you'll be back on stage again."

"Elliott, it's gonna be so awesome," replied Toni with a brilliant smile. She gripped his arm and gushed, "Singing and playing, and performing. It feeds my soul. I need it like I need air."

Elliott pretended not to notice the incredible sensation of Toni's touch. Realizing the awkwardness it caused, Toni released her grasp on him. Elliott lifted the coffee mug to his lips.

"You haven't played anywhere else or like, on your own?" Elliott inquired. He sipped the coffee before taking several gulps and enjoying its strength; however, it was the adrenaline pumping through his veins that heightened his senses.

"No, been a little busy," answered Toni sadly. Uncertainty plagued her but she forged ahead, saying, "I'm sure Emma told you what happened."

"Yeah, the basics," Elliott replied as he turned his stool towards the bar and grasped his cup with both hands. Intentionally avoiding any direct mention of Toni's failed nuptials, he asked, "Whaddaya gonna do now?"

"Work on me and be grateful to God for all I have," answered Toni in a confident, positive tone. She mimicked Elliott, though her hands grasped a Diet Coke, and declared, "My life is good. Right here, right now."

"How's Katherine?" Elliott asked quickly to change the subject.

"Cantankerous as ever," said Toni, "and still my rock."

"She's one helluva lady," Elliott remarked with a chuckle.

"That she is," Toni said. The band began coordinated warm-ups on stage. Reluctant to leave Elliott but unsure of what else to say, she advised, "Well, that's my cue. Gotta go."

"Break a leg," Elliott replied as he gave her a once-over. Toni hesitated, let her grin grow and then spun her stool towards the stage. She stopped in the middle of her rotation to glance at Elliott. The two words she wished to speak stuck in her throat.

"Congratulations, Elliott," said Toni as she forced them out. Regaining her composure, she stated sincerely, "You two're gonna be so happy together."

Elliott said nothing but simply nodded his head. Toni hopped off the barstool and scuttled away through a sea of tables and chairs.

"If only you'd said no to him," Elliott thought as he watched Toni wade through the crowd and ascend onto the stage. He conjured an image of Nora in his mind and said to himself, "But that's just not the future anymore."

. . . .

THOUGH SHE DID NOT notice it, Eddie hawked the brief reunion of Toni and Elliott closely and his gaze followed her to the stage. She slung her guitar over her shoulder and strummed a few chords. Cheers rippled through the crowd.

"So how'd that go?" asked Eddie with great interest. Toni blushed and he added, "You two good?"

Toni gazed on each of her bandmate's faces and acutely felt their anticipation of her answer. She lowered her eyes and took a moment to center herself. Her confidence rapidly grew.

"We're good, and we always will be," Toni declared. She smiled her trademark, captivating smile and said with gusto, "Now let's blow the roof off this place."

N ora rapidly descended the apartment stairs but stopped on the lower landing. She wore overall denim shorts with a white t-shirt beneath them and her curls held back by a sparkly, red-white-and-blue headband. Elliott examined her outfit and chortled until he saw the tears streaming down Nora's face.

"What's wrong?" Elliott inquired as he leapt off the couch and hurried to Nora. She jumped into his arms from the landing and nearly knocked him to the ground. Nora sobbed.

"Everything's ruined!" bleated Nora. She buried her head in Elliott's chest and held him tightly.

"Ruined?" Elliott asked as he adjusted his grip on Nora. He returned to the couch and sat down with her on his lap.

"It's g-g-gonna be in the nineties with th-thunderstorms on Saturday," mewled Nora. She continued weeping and muttered forlornly, "The w-wedding'll be a d-d-disaster."

"Take it easy, Nor," Elliott urged Nora while brushing away her tears. He caressed her hair and reasoned, "We're getting married in the morning. It won't be ninety then and those summer thunderstorms never hit 'til the afternoon. By the time it rains, we'll be married and drunk off our asses at Johnny Dubs."

Elliott's smirk broke Nora's melancholy. Though a tear or two still fell, she giggled. The laughter was short-lived.

"There's something else," whined Nora sheepishly.

"Oh, shit, what now?" Elliott thought. He feigned composure but waited on pins and needles for Nora to speak.

"I think I might be . . . ," began Nora. Elliott's blood ran cold. Nora finished the sentence by saying hoarsely, "Be . . . *pregnant*."

The news numbed Elliott's body. He had never been so close to the possibility of a child.

"You might be *what* now?" Elliott asked to stall for time. Nora grabbed his cheeks, shook them and went nose-to-nose with him.

"Pregnant, Elliott, pregnant!" replied Nora hysterically. She squeezed his face and said, "I'm late."

"How late?" Elliott asked as he grasped Nora's hands and pulled them from his cheeks. He tried to shift her out of his lap but she fought the attempt.

"Three days," said a disquieted Nora. Though three days did not strike Elliott as a long time, he, in truth, had no idea how long was too long. He decided to avoid the technicalities.

"You're just stressed out because of the wedding," Elliott assured her, "and that's got your body all outta whack."

"You think so?" asked Nora.

"Yeah, I do. We've been careful," Elliott answered with as much confidence as he could muster. Moving Nora onto the adjacent couch cushion, he explained, "But, to be safe, just pick up one of those pregnancy tests on the way to work and you can take it tomorrow. I think they're supposed to be pretty accurate now. It'll be negative and then you'll feel better."

Nora became calm but snuggled into Elliott and laid her head on his shoulder. He wrapped his arm around her.

"I'm not ready for a baby," said Nora with a sigh. Her body trembled before relaxing.

"Me either," Elliott replied as he, too, relaxed. He leaned back and said, "We've got the rest of our lives for that."

• • • •

"I'M NOT EVEN TAKING a shower tonight," Nora sighed as she drove through the green light at Goddard and Allen Roads. Despite being exhausted from a hectic night at Johnny Dubs, she offered a ride to the new waitress. Nora remembered her first few weeks on the job and empathized with her coworker. She blinked her eyes repeatedly and added, "And I'm sleeping all day tomorrow."

Nora now made the westward journey out of Allen Park and back home, the worn-out waitress simply wishing to crawl into bed with Elliott and fall into a deep sleep. Flashing red lights in the distance caught her eye.

"*Noooo*," Nora moaned, "not tonight."

The lowering gates and alternating lights of the railroad crossing tweaked Nora's fraying emotions. Rolling slowly up to the tracks, she stopped her car.

"I'm never gonna make it home," Nora whined while feeling like she might cry. She considered shifting the car into "Park" but instead readjusted her foot to get a firmer command of the brake pedal. Her mouth felt dry so she grabbed her purse from the passenger seat and rummaged through it, asking, "Where's that gum?"

The train blared its horn to announce its approach. Nora continued to search her purse, occasionally removing an item and placing it in the cupholder between the seats.

"Yeah, yeah, I hear ya," Nora grumbled. She mishandled a tube of lipstick and it fell to the floor. Nora's attempt to whisk it off the mat caused her to miss the fast-approaching headlights behind her vehicle. Unable to reach the lipstick, Nora sat up and tossed her purse into the passenger seat, griping, "Screw it."

Nora screamed upon seeing another car in her rearview mirror and, realizing the excessive speed at which it travelled, braced for the impact. It careened into her bumper with bone-shattering force and violently threw her forward as the train again sounded its horn. Its lights illuminated the crossing.

"Brake," thought Nora; it was the only word she could form in her mind. Despite her nose being broken and bloodied by the steering wheel, Nora managed to depress the pedal. Her car, however, lurched forward as the other car continued to accelerate and push it into the path of the train. The gate snapped and her vehicle skidded onto the tracks as she screamed, "Noooo!"

The train blared its horn in warning but it was too late. The locomotive slammed into Nora's vehicle and hurled it down the tracks. It rolled repeatedly, was struck a second time by the train and spun into the underbrush to the west of the tracks.

The second car, meanwhile, hit the train and its hood was pulled underneath it. The crumpled vehicle was dragged along with the train until it engaged its brakes and gradually screeched to a halt. When it finally stopped, all that could be heard was the blaring of a car horn. Its eerie announcement of the devastation caused by the crash echoed into the night.

. . . .

THE SOUND OF THE DOORBELL followed by forceful knocking jarred Emma from sleep. She had only recently descended into deep slumber and it took her several seconds to fully awaken. Opening her eyes, she rolled over and shook David.

"Dave, someone's at the door," Emma said with continued shakes. He responded with a truncated snore as a second round of knocking ensued. Emma tugged on his ear and whined in a raised yet exhausted voice, "Dave, get up."

"I'm up, I'm up," groaned David. He reflexively sat up on the edge of the bed, paused and swayed, and then rose to his feet.

"Make them go away," Emma moaned. Clad in a white t-shirt and boxer shorts, David meandered like a zombie out of the bedroom and shuffled heavily down the hallway. Emma quickly lost consciousness in his absence.

"Em, ya' gotta get up," David said when he returned a few minutes later. He was fully awake and spoke with an urgency that quickly roused his wife from sleep. She rolled out of bed and turned on the bedside lamp.

"What is it?" Emma demanded. She wore a dark blue, jersey-like nightshirt with two white stripes on each of its sleeves. Moving past David, she pulled her bathrobe off the hook on the bedroom door.

"Clay's here," advised David. Emma threw open the door and marched down the hallway while donning her robe. When she arrived in the foyer, Sergeant Clay Clifford stood there. The massive, middle-aged man was taller and larger than David and seemed to block the illumination from the overhead light.

"Oh, my god, Clay," Emma blurted with wide, scintillating eyes, "what is it?"

"I got some really bad news, Em," said Clay with a somber expression. Emma grabbed his uniform.

"Elliott?" Emma replied in a sudden panic. David appeared from the hallway.

"No, not Elliott," replied Clay. Gently removing her hands from his shirt, he set his own huge, meaty hands on her shoulders and said, "You know that young blonde waitress ya' had workin' for ya'? Nora I think her name was."

"Yeah, Nora Billingsley," Emma said in puzzlement. She wrested herself from his grasp and demanded, "Clay, what happened?"

"I'm really sorry, Em," began Clay. David tried to hug Emma but she histrionically dodged the attempt. Clay paused to collect his words and then advised, "She was killed in a train accident tonight. At the Goddard tracks."

"*No*," Emma hissed; it was the only word she could muster. She wobbled and nearly fell but David's strong arms caught her and held her upright. Allowing her husband to engulf her, she wept quietly to avoid waking her daughters. Clay bowed his head and waited patiently.

"They're still investigating, but it looks like a drunk rear-ended her and pushed her onto the tracks," Clay expounded when Emma's crying lessened. Her vulnerability proved to be short-lived. Clay added, "She managed to survive the accident but died at the hospital."

"Thanks, Clay, for letting me know," Emma said as she extricated herself from her husband's affection. Straightening her body, she cleared away her tears and asked stoically, "Have you told her parents?"

"Lieutenant's at their house now," said Clay. He rested his hands on his gun belt and queried, "She wasn't married, right? No kids?"

Emma's eyelids fell and she shook her head. She saw her brother's future crumbling.

"Only engaged," Emma answered as she opened her eyes, "to Elliott."

"Oh, man, Em," said Clay with a wince, "I'm so sorry."

"You want some coffee or something?" Emma offered as if Clay's arrival was merely a friendly visit. David leaned against the wall and marveled at his wife's inner strength.

"Nah, I'd better get back to the scene," responded Clay, "see if the guys need any help."

Emma hugged him, stood on her tiptoes to kiss his cheek and then retreated to David. He wrapped an arm around her waist.

"Thanks, man," said David. He moved Emma to one side and shook Clay's hand.

"You got it," Clay said. He waved to them, lumbered to the door and let himself out. Emma sighed deeply.

"What can I do, babe?" asked David though he was uncertain what assistance he could provide. She rested her forehead on his chest with her arms hanging at her sides. Pondering the next twenty-four hours, she remained in the position for over a minute.

"Get the girls through today without them finding out," Emma said when she lifted her head from David's chest. Beginning to nod as she formulated her plan, she stated, "We'll tell them this afternoon."

"You sure you wanna wait that long?" inquired David.

"I'm sure," Emma answered with absolute certainty. Her countenance hardened and she said grimly, "I'll need time to recover from what I'm about to do."

· · · ·

SURGING ADRENALINE kept Emma's exhaustion at bay as she drove to Elliott's apartment. The sun rose, the breeze blew and the birds sang, the dawn oblivious to the tragedy. Emma's journey from the car to his porch was one of the longest of her life and she stood upon the stoop for several minutes before ringing his doorbell. The living room lamp shed light behind the blinds and Emma figured her brother dozed in his recliner.

"I don't know if he'll recover from this," Emma said to herself with a brief dip in her confidence. Ringing the bell again seemed to rouse Elliott, his movement betrayed by the passing of faint shadows on the closed blinds. Stoking her inner fire and ferocity in defense of her family, Emma said aloud, "*He will*, and I'll be there every step of the way."

Emma opened the storm door just as Elliott opened the main door. Her disheveled brother wore only red athletic shorts.

"Em?" said Elliott, his eyes barely open and his hair mussed. He shook his head to clear it and asked, "What the hell are you doing here?"

Emma stepped inside the apartment, her advance causing Elliott's retreat. She allowed the storm door to close behind her, paused, and then closed the main door. Noticing the light of morning, and Nora's absence, Elliott tilted his head and furrowed his brow.

"What time is it?" queried a tired, befuddled Elliott. He whisked a white t-shirt off the back of the recliner and clumsily donned it, asking, "Is Nora with you?"

"I don't know how to say this, Elliott, or if there even *is* a right way, so I'm just gonna say it," Emma said dourly. She ran her tongue along the bottom of her teeth and then bluntly stated, "Nora was killed in a train accident early this morning."

Elliott failed to process Emma's words. He craned his neck towards her and folded his arms.

"What're you talking about?" replied Elliott with a shrug and a shake of his head.

"Her car was hit by a train at the Goddard tracks a few hours ago," Emma answered in a slow, clear voice, "and she died at the hospital."

Elliott felt the room begin to spin and his body swayed. Emma rushed to him and, with his legs giving way, guided him to the floor. He pushed the base of his palm into his forehead.

"What was she doing at the tracks, and why the hell was she *on* 'em?" inquired Elliott as if he could reason Nora back to life. His body went limp.

"She took that new waitress home – she lives in Allen Park – and was probably on her way back here," Emma said while wrapping her arms around Elliott. A tear escaped her eye, languidly rolled down to her chin and hung from it. Brushing it on her shoulder, Emma continued, "Taylor PD thinks she was hit by a drunk driver, and he pushed her in front of the train."

All emotion bled from Elliott, the news of Nora's demise rendering him hopelessly numb. The siblings sat together on the floor and Emma remembered a similar scene after the death of their mother.

"Except it was Dave holding me," Emma said as she recalled the emotional roller coaster that was nineteen seventy-five. Lamenting Elliott's sporadic emotional support during that time, she asked herself, "Who was holding Elliott?"

"Why, Em?" asked Elliott, his question interrupting Emma's thoughts. He struggled to speak above a whisper, continuing, "Why now? Two days before. *Two days.*"

"I don't know," Emma replied with a dramatic exhale, "I just don't know."

• • • •

EMMA WATCHED ELLIOTT speaking with Nora's mother from a distance with her arms folded and her shoulder leaning against the hallway wall. She bristled at the treatment her brother received at the hands of his once-future mother-in-law, the middle-aged Mrs. Billingsley acting as if Elliott's presence was an intrusion. Only Elliott's plea for her to "stay out of it" held Emma's wrath at bay.

"Boy, she and I woulda' tangled," muttered Emma, her ire warding off her sadness over the loss of her friend. Elliott finished his conversation with Nora's mother and pointed to a bank of chairs near where Emma stood. Mrs. Billingsley nodded and disappeared into a room while he returned to his sister.

"She gave the doctor the okay to talk to me," advised Elliott, the relief evident on his haggard face. He fell into a chair and deflated.

"How nice of her," remarked Emma facetiously, "letting the doctor talk to Nora's *fiancée*. It's not like you guys were living together or anything. *Bitch*."

"I don't have a leg to stand on unless she says so, not without a wedding ring," Elliott said. He interlocked his fingers in his lap and stared at the floor, muttering in resignation, "Let's just take what we can get."

"Fine," Emma conceded though she knew something was on Elliott's mind. She dropped into the chair next to him and, upon seeing a doctor approach, thought, "All right, Elliott, let's hear it."

"Are you Mr. Warden?" asked the Pakistani doctor in perfect English. The tall, handsome man wore light-blue scrubs and the expected stethoscope around his neck.

"Yeah, Doc, that's me," confirmed Elliott while rising to his feet. The men shook hands and he added, "Elliott."

"Dr. Pakatul. My condolences on your fiancée," began Dr. Pakatul earnestly. A wave of emotional pain washed over Elliott. Cognizant of it, Emma grabbed her brother's hand and squeezed it to stem the tide.

"Thanks," muttered Elliott feebly.

"As I'm sure Mrs. Billingsley told you, Nora was brought here after her accident," said Dr. Pakatul, the physician leaving no time for an awkward moment, "but, unfortunately, she passed away shortly after her arrival due to internal bleeding."

Elliott lowered his eyes to the floor and did not immediately respond. His silence puzzled both Emma and the doctor. Elliott stirred and then returned his attention to Dr. Pakatul.

"Was she conscious?" inquired Elliott thickly.

"No," answered Dr. Pakatul with a grave mien. Elliott made several attempts to speak but no words came from his mouth. While Dr. Pakatul waited patiently, Emma felt like every molecule in her body might explode in anticipation.

"She thought – she wasn't sure – but, she thought she might be . . . be," Elliott began slowly. The doctor narrowed his eyes and read Elliott's face. Emma inhaled sharply and felt nauseous before Elliott uttered, ". . . *pregnant.*"

A grim-faced Dr. Pakatul shook his head in the negative. Emma exhaled and grabbed her forehead.

"She wasn't," replied the doctor.

"That's all I needed to know," Elliott replied. He again fell into the chair and said, "Thanks, Doc."

"Of course," said Dr. Pakatul. He again avoided an awkward moment by simply walking away.

"Doctor," beckoned Elliott. Dr Pakatul stopped and turned around.

"Yes?" replied Dr. Pakatul.

"Her mother doesn't know," Elliott stated. The doctor acknowledged that fact with several nods and then departed.

"Why didn't you say anything?" Emma asked when the siblings were alone again.

"I kinda wished she was until now," Elliott said while ignoring his sister's question. Allowing himself to think of Nora, he pictured her holding an adorable, towheaded child and continued, "And that'll be my last memory of her. Seeing our kid in her eyes when she told me."

Elliott warded off tears though a few breached his eyes. He angrily wiped them away. Emma barely held back her own waterworks.

"I'm sorry, Sis," Elliott said with a scowl.

"What in the *entire world* could you be sorry about?" asked Emma as she grasped his arm with both hands.

"I'm always the black cloud, always the screwup, always bringing this shit down on your family," Elliott replied, his nieces first experience with the death of a loved one plaguing his conscience. Emma grabbed his cheeks with one hand.

"First of all, it's *our* family," asserted Emma with blue-green fire in her eyes. Her fingers pressed into Elliott's flesh as she lectured him, "And second of all, we're survivors, Elliott, all of us. We made it through Daddy and Mom's deaths and will make it through Nora's. Together. As a family. Like we always do. *Like we always will.*"

"*You're* a survivor," Elliott countered with plummeting confidence. He pulled his face from her grasp and uttered, "I'm just lucky you've got the strength to drag me through with ya.'"

Emma leapt up while pulling Elliott with her and then slapped him. The smack echoed in the hospital hallway and drew the attention of several staff members. They uneasily watched the siblings' tense interaction.

"Remember that," insisted Emma forcefully, "'cuz I won't do it again for a while."

"Gee, thanks," Elliott said with a healthy dose of sarcasm. Emma became fey and eyed him closely.

"You can mourn her all you want," said Emma unrelentingly, "but *don't* start feeling sorry for yourself."

Elliott removed Emma's hands from his shirt, affectionately squeezed them and then let them go. He lightly touched his hand to Emma's cheek in a feigned smack.

"Yeah, I guess you're right," agreed Elliott, his sudden recovery surprising Emma. Her lack of sleep hung heavily on her countenance so he said, "Why don't you go home and get some sleep? You gotta be exhausted."

"What're you gonna do?" asked Emma.

"Stick around here for a bit, see if they need anything," Elliott advised with a nod towards the room where Nora's parents were. He pondered his options and added, "I can catch a ride home. Hell, maybe I'll walk."

"Okay," consented Emma reluctantly. The siblings embraced and she added, "But you'd better call me later. We're just gonna be home today, so if you need anything . . . ."

"I will," Elliott responded. Buttressed by Emma's strength, he composed himself and said, "Love ya', Sis."

"You'd better," Emma replied with a slight smirk that Elliott returned. She watched him walk down the hall before glancing upward.

"You can't keep hitting him like this, knocking him down all the time," pleaded Emma, "'cuz one a' these days, he won't get back up."

• • • •

ELLIOTT FLOATED AIMLESSLY throughout the hospital like a ghost as the morning languidly progressed. His head ached from caffeine withdrawal but nausea killed his desire for coffee; his appetite was nonexistent and all he consumed was a small cup of water to cure his dry mouth.

Torpified by the loss of Nora, Elliott's desire to be conscious vanished. He slumped into a chair haphazardly placed by itself against a vacant nurses' station. Elliott leaned the back of his head against the station, closed his eyes and settled into a hazy, surreal mental state. A radio sitting on the station's counter spewed inane commercials but Elliott only heard them as a distant droning.

The noise soon transitioned into a song and its words became clear; as they drifted into Elliott's ears, he recognized Christopher's Cross's ballad "Think of Laura". Its lament for a young woman taken far too young paralyzed him and, in place of 'Laura', his mind changed the name to 'Nora'. The haunting words ushered him into sleep and then deserted him, leaving Elliott to wander aimlessly in troubled dreams.

• • • •

TONI MADE A NOTATION on the sleeping patient's chart and then hung it on the end of her bed. Carefully rolling the tray table away from the elderly woman, she glanced at the partially eaten breakfast upon it.

"At least she ate something today," Toni whispered as she made gentle adjustments to the covers. She stood back, appraised her improving ward and smiled at her before departing the room. Stopping in the hallway, she absorbed the quietness of the hospital and said, "July 4th. Should be a quiet shift."

Toni giggled. Firework-related injuries were an Independence Day tradition at Heritage Hospital.

"As long as I stay outta the ER," Toni quipped. She immediately felt guilty and scolded herself, "That's not funny."

Snippets of a song playing on the radio distracted her and she looked towards their source. Her gaze drifted to the nurses' station where a person sleeping in a chair piqued her interest.

"Elliott?" Toni asked quizzically when she recognized her friend. She approached him with quickening steps and nearly ran into a doctor walking in the opposite direction. After apologizing to the doctor, Toni beckoned softly, "Elliott."

Toni's mellifluous voice lured Elliott out of his dreams. He gradually awakened, stirred and stretched.

"I thought you promised not to show up here unannounced," Toni playfully chastised Elliott, a warm rush of elation flooding her body and a brilliant smile coming to her lips. Shaking off the cobwebs of sleep, Elliott became cognizant of Toni's presence. Her joy vanished when he recoiled as if he planned to crawl backwards onto the nurses' station. A shocked Toni assured him, "Hey, it's okay. It's just me."

Toni processed his pale skin, the dark stubble on his face, his bleary eyes and the sunken, gray circles beneath them. His pathetic appearance throttled her and she took a backwards step.

"What's wrong?" Toni asked anxiously.

Groggy and numb, Elliott did not immediately answer. Remembrance scuttled over him like a thousand prickly spiders and, suddenly weak, he collapsed into the chair. A fraught Toni fought the compulsion to comfort him.

"Nora was in a car accident this morning," replied Elliott hoarsely. He pushed his tongue into his cheek to ward off a sob, bit it and then uttered, "She's gone."

"*Oh, no*," Toni mewled. She instinctively rushed to Elliott, kneeled in front of him and embraced him. Overcome by sorrow, Elliott made no response to her affection as she whimpered, "That's terrible, Elliott. I'm so sorry."

"Some drunk asshole hit her from behind and pushed her onto the Goddard tracks," explained Elliott, Toni's mere presence extracting the words on his tongue. The strength of her caring and compassion washed away his numbness and he continued in a stronger tone, "Somehow the kid made it here alive . . . but she didn't last long."

A hybrid emotion of bitter anger and utter sadness arose in Elliott. His face hardened and a few tears fell.

"Didn't even get to say goodbye," said Elliott, the sudden surge of emotion-fueled energy bleeding from his body. Toni touched his face.

"Let me see if I can get someone to cover for me and I'll take you home," Toni suggested. Her caress rekindled old feelings but they engendered guilt that rankled Elliott. He immediately stood and freed himself from her arms.

"During your shift? On the Fourth of July? I appreciate it but I can't put you in that spot," replied a skeptical Elliott. He felt drawn to Toni but also panicky and uncertain. Wishing to flee the hospital, he said quickly, "Actually, I think I'm just gonna walk."

"At least let me call Em," Toni suggested. She, too, felt the awkwardness between them and the pull of competing emotions.

"She's the one who brought me here," responded Elliott as he turned away from Toni. Sticking his hands in the back pockets of his jeans, he expounded, "But she was runnin' on fumes so I kicked her loose."

Elliott turned back to Toni and grinned weakly. She watched him on tenterhooks.

"My little sis' is the toughest person I know," mused Elliott. His mood darkened and he added, "But even she needs a break once in a while. Hell, she's still gotta tell the girls their new aunt is dead."

The word "dead" caused Elliott to shiver. Toni, meanwhile, felt every ounce of Elliott's pain.

"You shouldn't be alone right now," Toni pleaded. She searched her mind for a solution, settled upon one and suggested hopefully, "Hey, how about you stay here? It'll be slow, and I'll probably be bored anyway. I'll find you a quiet place to sleep for a while, maybe we can get ya' somethin' to eat. And I'll be here if you need me . . . I mean, need someone."

"Always the angel," Elliott stated with adoration. The reference to the afterlife brought thoughts of Nora crashing back into Elliott's head. He stifled a grimace and muttered, "Had one a' those until this morning."

"Stay, just for a little while," Toni implored Elliott, the nurse wishing to soothe his hurts. Her offer tempted him but, in his final analysis, to accept it would dishonor Nora's memory.

"Maybe some other time," Elliott replied in a solemn voice. Seemingly reading his mind, Toni nodded and had pity on the wounded and withered being before her. Unable to endure her beneficence any longer, Elliott simply turned and walked away as her watery eyes hawked his departure.

• • • •

ELLIOTT EMERGED FROM the hospital and was greeted by a stiff southwest wind. It partnered with the July sun to rapidly warm the morning as it trundled towards midday; in his state, its rays felt almost painful on his skin. Elliott's stomach gurgled and groaned as a reminder that he skipped breakfast.

"Nothin's gonna be open today," Elliott griped; even the simple prospect of preparing a meal seemed daunting. He continued to the curb while entertaining Toni's offer and said, "Eatin' here might be my best bet."

A white, convertible Ford Mustang GT rolled up to Elliott and blocked his path. Its top was retracted.

"Need a ride, handsome?" Donna inquired cheekily. Clad in a top resembling lapis lazuli and white, high-waisted shorts, she also sported sunglasses and a devil-may-care attitude. She wore her hair pinned up with numerous windswept strands messily hanging from her head.

"What're you doin' here, Donna?" asked Elliott, his tone thick with acrimony. She removed her sunglasses and gave him a pointed look.

"Taking you home," answered Donna as if the matter were resolved. His pathetic appearance tweaked her heart.

"I can walk," Elliott grumbled. He turned on a dime and walked along the edge of the sidewalk. Donna lifted her foot from the brake pedal and rolled along with Elliott.

"Just get in, Elliott," pleaded Donna. Elliott's exhaustion caused him to stumble but he managed to steady himself. Donna shifted the car into "Park", threw open the driver-side door and rushed to his side. Wrapping an arm around his waist, she urged, "C'mon, let's get you home."

Donna guided him to the car, opened the passenger door and tucked him inside. Returning to her seat, she slid on her sunglasses, shifted the car into "Drive" and sped through the parking lot. Elliott closed his eyes.

"God, he looks terrible," Donna thought with constant, worried glances at Elliott. The pair said nothing during their brief trip down Telegraph Road. When they reached Goddard Road, Donna flipped on her turn signal and braked behind a line of cars in the right lane. Elliott's eyelids slowly rose.

"When'd you get this?" inquired Elliott as the wind noise died. He ran his fingertips along the front facing of the dashboard.

"Last month," Donna answered proudly. Encouraged by his focus on the Mustang, she asked, "Like it?"

"Yeah, I guess," replied Elliott. He closed his eyes again, pressed the back of his skull against the headrest and asked, "How's Em?"

"Burnt," said Donna, her expression one of concern. The light changed and she followed several vehicles onto Goddard Road, saying, "I could hear it in her voice. But, as always, she was worried about you. So I volunteered to come to your rescue."

"I coulda' walked," Elliott insisted. Donna scolded him with a glance.

"Look, Em's still gotta tell the girls, and that's gonna be rough, and Dave's trying to prop *her* up," Donna explained as she steadily increased the volume of her voice to compete with the road noise. Shifting her left hand to the steering wheel and taking Elliott's hand with the other, she continued, "*I* can be there for you today and take some of the load off her."

"Little early to pick over the corpse, don't ya' think?" asked Elliott bitterly. The accusation offended Donna and her countenance contorted.

"That's just mean, and not true," Donna objected. She resisted Elliott's attempt to extricate his hand, stating firmly, "And it's not like that."

Donna and Elliott fell into an uncomfortable silence but she refused to release his hand. She turned her Mustang onto Beech Daly Road and headed north towards Continental Apartments. Elliott stared at the passing ground as the car entered his apartment complex. Less than a minute later, Donna pulled into a parking space next to Elliott's red Ford LTD. She killed the engine and turned towards Elliott.

"Look, I know I came on too strong before, and I'm sorry," Donna admitted as Elliott stared forward. She squeezed his hand repeatedly as she continued, "But you need someone right now, someone who can focus on just you, and not get pulled in a hundred different directions. *Let me get you through this.* For Em's sake if nothing else."

Elliott pondered the offer and then shifted his gaze to Donna. Though the arguments were more articulate, the look on her face – the insatiable desire to please – resembled the girl Elliott once dated. Its return gave him pause.

"It's one less thing on her plate," Donna reasoned. She implored Elliott while shaking his hand, "Let me be there for you, like I should've been before."

Elliott assumed Donna referred to the death of his parents. She, however, thought of the more recent past.

"All right," Elliott conceded with a dramatic exhale. His surrender exhilarated Donna but she managed to contain any outward expression of it.

"There we go," said Donna with a widening smile. Elliott's stomach growled a long, horrid growl. Donna chortled.

"Hey, I'm starvin'," Elliott complained, his immediate physical needs and the distraction of Donna climbing over his sorrow.

"I can fix that," replied Donna.

Morning Cloak began Mel McDaniel's "Baby's Got Her Blue Jeans On" to raucous applause. Toni switched the gender roles in the song and became its fictitious ogler, her eyebrow raises, sexy glances and provocative sways driving the male-dominated crowd wild. The lyrical alteration, however, also conjured vivid images in her mind of a jean-clad Elliott. Thoughts of him fueled her performance to new heights and hurled the crowd into a tizzy.

"That was pretty hot for a good Catholic girl," Eddie ribbed Toni when she walked to her stool, whisked up the glass on it and took a swig of water. He raised an eyebrow and asked, "Who were you singin' about?"

Toni offered Eddie a guilty smirk but said nothing. She set down the glass, spun back towards the crowd and lifted the microphone to her lips.

"Okay, so we've got a new one for ya', though it might be a little poppy for a country crowd," Toni said. Her fans, thinking she could do no wrong, roared their approval. She added, "It was popular a few years ago but . . . *you tell us*."

Morning Cloak launched into Sylvia's "Nobody", a song about a woman fighting for her man against a clever usurper. She performed the role with her usual flair but, as the words left her lips, she wondered where she would stand in such a love triangle with Elliott. When the song concluded, the audience cheered its approval.

"Thanks, guys. Thank you," a beaming Toni said as her bandmates took their bows. She returned her microphone to its stand and advised with a wave, "We're gonna take a quick break and then we'll be back."

Applause followed but soon died as the room broke out into numerous conversations. While her bandmates eagerly accepted cold beers from a waitress, Toni hopped off the stage and onto the dance floor. Dodging tables and chairs and politely but hurriedly accepting adulations from her fans, she made her way to the bar.

"Sean!" Toni yelled with a wave to Emma's second-in-command.

"What's up?!" shouted Sean as she finished filling a line of shot glasses with whiskey. The group of rowdy men at the bar downed their shots and yelled excitedly for more.

"Can I use the phone?!" replied Toni. She mimicked a telephone with her hand.

"Yeah, no problem!" said Sean as she whisked the telephone from underneath the bar, hustled to Toni and set it in front of her. A retreating Sean shouted, "Good luck hearin' anything though!"

"Thanks!" yelled Toni though Sean never heard the word. Training her gaze on the telephone, Toni hesitated and stared nervously at it. She reached for it, pulled back her hand and then grabbed it. Toni quickly dialed Elliott's number while pressing the receiver into one ear. It rang three times.

"Hello?" Donna answered. Barely able to discern the greeting, Toni covered her other ear with her hand to muffle the noise of Johnny Dubs. Jarred by the cacophony blasting from the receiver, Donna repeated in a louder voice, "Hello?"

Recognizing to whom she spoke, Toni froze and said nothing. The commotion around her faded from her consciousness.

"Who is this?" demanded Donna. Her territoriality rattled Toni.

"Um, hi," Toni said uneasily. Forcing herself to continue, she queried, "Is Elliott there?"

"May I tell him who's calling?" asked Donna snidely.

"Uh, well, it's, uh, uh . . . never mind," Toni answered before abruptly hanging up the telephone. She cringed and grimaced. Feeling morally slimy, her face soured and she called to Sean, "All set, Sean, thanks!"

Sean glanced at her and nodded before delivering the three large beer glasses she precariously held in two hands. Toni slunk away from the bar and pondered Donna's presence in Elliott's apartment.

"Why the long face, boss?" asked Oscar when Toni returned to the stage. She looked at him disappointedly.

"I think *I'm* nobody," Toni replied.

· · · ·

THE RINGING OF A DISTANT telephone found Elliott in a dream but he recalled nothing of it when he awoke. The day of Nora's death was a day of numbness but the day after was a day of intensifying pain and slowly passing time. When Elliott finally fell asleep his slumber was fitful and pockmarked with many unremarkable and elusive dreams.

"I just don't get it, kid. *Why?*" Elliott whispered hoarsely as he ran his hand over her side of the bed. Donna's voice suddenly emanated from the first floor of his apartment and momentarily distracted him from his emotional ache. He wondered aloud, "Why is she still here?"

A groggy Elliott heaved himself out of bed after several attempts, stumbled out of his bedroom and unsteadily descended the stairs. When he hit the landing, he saw Donna nestled on the couch watching television.

"I thought you were going home," Elliott said. Donna's presence annoyed him; he considered her care a pretense for weaseling her way into his life.

"I didn't feel right leaving you alone," replied Donna while hugging a throw pillow.

"Did you just get the phone?" Elliott queried as he rubbed his face and shuffled to the kitchen.

"Yeah, wrong number," Donna answered quickly. Elliott procured a glass and filled it from the faucet. Slipping off the couch and leaving the pillow behind, Donna joined him in the kitchen and watched him drain it. Elliott set the glass on the counter with a "thunk" and opened the refrigerator door, his action prompting Donna to say, "I can make you something."

Elliott closed the refrigerator door and turned to Donna. She expectantly watched him and oozed an absolute desperation to please him, a desperation he had not seen in many years.

"Look, I appreciate the concern," Elliott said while feeling sorry for Donna. The emotion evaporated, however, as he considered the affront to Nora she represented. Elliott shivered as reality soaked him like rain and continued, "But I only went along with you bein' here today for Em's sake."

"Lanie and Tess' took Nor- . . . took *it* pretty hard, harder than Em expected," advised Donna sadly. Nausea washed over Elliott but, recognizing his angst, she wrapped her arms around him. His tears fell as Donna argued, "Let me get you through this so she can get them through it."

"It wasn't right for you to be here when she was alive," Elliott countered despite desiring Donna's support. He swiped at his tears and said, "And it's still not right for you to be here when she's dead."

"I'm here as a friend and that's it," insisted Donna with feigned offense. Her own irritation burgeoned and she inquired, "Why can't you just accept that?"

"Don't lie," Elliott snapped. Donna kept one arm wrapped around the small of his back and repeatedly poked him in the chest.

"Admit it," insisted Donna steadfastly, "you felt better when I showed up. You felt better not being alone."

Elliott contemplated Donna's argument. Her presence, while irksome on his emotional surface, was comforting on a deeper level. His will to resist faded.

"You know you don't want me to leave," added Donna in a more consolatory tone.

"What, are you gonna sleep in your clothes?" Elliott countered feebly.

"I got an overnight bag in the car," said Donna. When Elliott offered her a dubious look, she raised both palms and said with a smirk, "It was Em's idea. I swear it."

Elliott's exhaustion bested him and he swayed but Donna reestablished her grip on him and held him upright. Allowing the moment to linger, the couple eased into an embrace. Donna wallowed in it until Elliott squirmed.

"You stink," Donna commented with a wrinkled nose and a giggle. She reluctantly detached herself from Elliott and said, "Go take a shower. I'm gonna go get my stuff and then I'll make you something to eat."

The mention of a shower brought Nora's New Year's Eve rescue to Elliott's mind and his remorse welled. The conflict tore at the very fibers of his spirit.

"I'm not hungry," an agitated Elliott said.

"You will be," declared Donna.

"We can't make a habit of this," Elliott warned.

"We won't," replied Donna, the barely perceptible waver in her voice stoking Elliott's inner turmoil. Desperate to flee the moment and hide her guilty countenance, Donna whirled around and headed to the door. Elliott watched her quickly slip on her shoes and scurry outside.

"Don't lie," Elliott repeated softly.

• • • •

THE JULY MORNING DAWNED warm and cloudy, the sun fighting a losing battle against the clouds. Wearing his usual sleeping getup of shorts and a t-shirt, Elliott trudged onto the porch with his radio and a cup of coffee. The light stung his eyes and his head throbbed with every step.

"Hope that Tylenol kicks in soon," Elliott groaned as he set his radio on the patio table. Days of Donna's constant, intrusive coddling distracted him from Nora's impending funeral; however, the previous night his numbness became pain again and he drank it into submission. The resultant hangover was a steep but necessary price to pay and Elliott uttered as he sat in a patio chair, "At least I slept."

Elliott spent several minutes sipping coffee with his eyes closed. The haunting piano opening of "I Won't Hold You Back" by Toto emanated from the radio and struck him like a cold wind. Elliott shivered.

"Well, that's a kick in the balls," muttered Elliot in grim resignation. The ballad took him back to the beginnings of his relationship with Nora: the cool night, the farmer's field, the solitude, Nora's first date with Bart. Elliott set his foot on a chair and said, "And her first fight with me."

That night in 1985, the song for longtime lovers ending their relationship highlighted the sorrowful solitude Elliott felt with Nora in Bart's arms. Now, in 1986, it underscored the finality of their relationship's tragic end.

"Damn it," griped Mrs. Franklin, Elliott's elderly, chain-smoking neighbor as she emerged from her apartment. The usual coughs and grumbles carried over the low hedge and bounced the lit cigarette hanging from her weathered lips. The music on the radio soon reached Mrs. Franklin's ears.

"Them sad songs ain't doin' ya' no good, young man," the old woman admonished him. Forsaking her usual curlers and housecoat, she wore a floral print dress and a blonde wig. Mrs. Franklin attempted to speak again but the remainder of her advice was cut short by a coughing fit.

"Mornin', Ms. Franklin," uttered Elliott. Mrs. Franklin moved to the hedge and threw a disapproving glance at a car arriving in the parking lot.

"Neither is that Donna hangin' 'round," Mrs. Franklin rumbled in her raspy yet strong voice. Elliott turned off the radio as she added, "Your little cutie ain't even in the ground yet."

Elliott cringed at Mrs. Franklin's crude phrasing. He heard Donna's car door close.

"Thanks for the reminder," Elliott answered bitterly. The accusation threw fuel on the fire of his guilt.

"Hi, Mrs. Franklin," said Donna with a wave as she stepped onto the walkway leading to Elliott's patio. She held a McDonald's bag and a tray with two large coffees in the other hand. Mrs. Franklin retreated from the hedge and ignored Donna.

"She doesn't like you hanging around here," Elliott advised Donna when Mrs. Franklin disappeared into her apartment without returning the greeting.

"It's none of her damn business," declared Donna indignantly. Glowering at Elliott in his hungover state, she scolded him, "I leave you alone for one night. How much did you drink?"

"I think it's safe to say too much," Elliott answered with a grimace. He stretched and added, "Ya' know, it's the first time since, since . . . ."

Stating Nora's name was impossible and even its formation in his mind made Elliott feel ill. He set down his mug, the scent of the coffee suddenly nauseating.

"I got breakfast," announced Donna cheerfully as she held up the bag and the tray. Seeking to lift Elliott's spirits, she said, "That should help."

"You know this doesn't look good," Elliott rebuked Donna, "you comin' over here so much so soon."

"There is *nothing* wrong with a friend caring for a friend," declared Donna with another sneer directed at Mrs. Franklin's apartment. Immediately improving her demeanor for Elliott, she set the bag and the tray on the table and began arranging Elliott's breakfast in front of him, saying, "That's what friends do."

Elliott watched Donna finish setting out their meal. She dropped a stack of brown napkins in the center of the table, took a seat and smiled at him.

Appreciative of her kindness regardless of her motives, he sighed and offered her a weak grin in return.

"You've been great this last week," Elliott began, "but I'm not sure when I'll ever be ready for anything. With anybody."

Elliott picked up one of the large cups and sent some caffeine into his veins. Donna fidgeted and waited eagerly for him to continue.

"Hell, I may never be ready," Elliott muttered.

"You don't need to worry about me, Elliott," replied Donna compassionately. She leaned forward, unwrapped a breakfast sandwich for Elliott and handed it to him, saying, "Just know, from now on, I'll always be here. No matter what. No conditions, no ultimatums . . . no expectations."

Having someone's unwavering, undivided support eased Elliott's cares but he did not believe her claim of "no expectations". His headache faded and his appetite returned, its reemergence chasing away his concerns for the time being.

"Now eat," ordered Donna playfully.

· · · ·

A CONFLICTED TONI TURNED left from Beech Daly Road onto Continental Circle. She wished to comfort Elliott in his time of need but also harbored a selfish desire to be close to him. A McDonald's bag sat on the passenger seat and two large coffees were in her cupholders.

"I should've talked to Father Maurice about this," Toni said as her vehicle rounded the large northern curve of Continental Circle. She glanced at the impromptu breakfast and reasoned, "He's probably at work anyway."

Toni braked as she reached Elliott's parking lot. She hesitated and a chill rippled down her spine.

"Well, let's answer that question," Toni said. She held her breath and entered the parking lot. Feeling a rush of emotion when she saw his car, she uttered nervously, "He's here."

Her heart dropped when she noticed Donna's Mustang next to Elliott's LTD. She rolled into a parking space shielded from his patio by the hedge and the north wall of his apartment. Tuning the key, Toni let the engine go dormant and lowered the passenger side window.

"I knew you needed to eat," declared Donna happily, her joyous voice carrying into Toni's ears. She laughed and added, "And there's nothing like McDonald's breakfast for a hangover."

Donna's voice sent another chill rippling down Toni's spine. Unable to endure Donna's gibbering over Elliott, she raised the passenger window.

"Guess that's my sign, huh?" Toni asked God with a frown. She restarted her car and swiftly fled the parking lot without looking towards Elliott's patio, saying, "Guess I took all this to the wrong person."

• • • •

ST. FRANCIS XAVIER Catholic Church in Ecorse reminded Toni of an old mission with its bell gable and red-bricked façade wall. The wall recessed twice as one moved from the main entrance's elaborate archway to the either end of the building, the arch constructed of the same cream-colored stone as the mitre-shaped window frames. The stained-glass windows were honeycombed with solder of the same hue.

"Wow, this place is kinda neat," commented Toni as she studied the building. The entrance archway housed two red doors, above which "ST. FRANCIS XAVIER" was engraved in the stone. Atop the stone were three windows with a statue of the saint standing on a two-layered, cylindrical dais in front of the middle window. Remembering the purpose of her visit, she felt uneasy and said, "Better go find Father Maurice."

The doors opened and, as if summoned by his name, Father Maurice emerged and strolled down the church's main thoroughfare. The broad walkway, more akin to a two-lane road, delivered him to Jefferson Avenue and Toni's parallel-parked car.

"Good morning, young lady," Father Maurice greeted Toni upon his arrival. Before she could respond, he opened the car door. Toni quickly scooped up the McDonald's bag and set it on the dashboard as he sat down and said, "I figured we'd go for a drive."

"Okay, sure," answered a discombobulated Toni. She pointed to the bag, and with a befuddled expression and a shrug, said, "I brought hour-old McDonald's and lukewarm coffee."

"Good enough for this ole' man," Father Maurice said as he grabbed the bag and rummaged through it.

"Take whatever you want," urged Toni. She pulled her car onto Jefferson Avenue, hung a U-turn and headed south, adding, "I kinda lost my appetite."

"This wasn't for me, was it?" replied the priest as he shamelessly procured a breakfast sandwich and unwrapped it. He set the bag on the floor between his feet, bit into the sandwich and said through his food, "You got lucky I was covering the early mass down here and they didn't send me to Southfield or Troy or somethin'."

"Sorry," apologized Toni, "I panicked."

"Bring me food and we're straight," Father Maurice explained. He again lifted the sandwich to his mouth, eyed Toni and asked, "Now, what's the story?"

"Something terrible happened," said Toni as her voice cracked. The priest continued eating and watching her intently. She paused and then spoke, expounding, "Elliott's fiancée, Nora, was killed in a car accident last week."

"No shit," Father Maurice said in surprise. He made the Sign of the Cross and then shook his head.

"It's so horrible. A drunk driver hit her car and pushed it in front of a train," Toni said while trembling. The impulse to drive to Elliott warred against her better judgement; she wanted nothing more than to soothe his hurts.

"So Mister Warden's on the market again," Father Maurice remarked, his tone one of warning. Finishing the sandwich, he crumpled the wrapper, dropped it into the bag and made another foray for his next course.

"Yeah," responded Toni with a healthy dose of uncertainty. Uncomfortable with the subject, she changed it and queried, "How do you stay so thin eating like you do?"

"You ain't gettin' off the hook that easy," Father Maurice said. He explained as if reading Toni's mind, "Now, my guess is you wanna help him out, so you offered, he declined . . . and then he kinda pushed ya' away."

"Yeah," squeaked a distressed Toni. She felt like crying.

"He needs space," Father Maurice stated. Knowing there was more to Toni's story, he advised matter-of-factly, "Let him have it."

Toni bit her lip and struggled with what to say next. She replayed her brief telephone conversation with Donna in her mind.

"I don't think he needs space," suggested Toni, visions of Elliott and Donna plaguing her thoughts.

"Why's that?" Father Maurice asked.

"Because," began Toni, "because he's letting his high school sweetheart back in the picture and she *really* wants him. Like marry him tomorrow wants him."

Father Maurice shook his head in disapprobation. His demeanor tweaked Toni's ego.

"What?" demanded Toni shrilly.

"You youngins', always so damn impatient," Father Maurice complained. He rested his arm on the window frame and admonished Toni, "First of all, Missy, it ain't the time for relationship buildin' when his girl just died. Second, you have no idea what this – what's her name?"

"Donna," answered Toni, the name tasting bitter on her tongue.

"What this Donna was doin' there, or what's goin' on," the priest said. Toni bobbed her head from side-to-side and her angst ebbed as Father Maurice added, "Maybe she's just bein' a good friend, just like you wanna be."

"You're right," conceded Toni while bowing her head in shame. She glanced at Father Maurice and asked sheepishly, "I overreacted, didn't I?"

"Yep," Father Maurice said before polishing off the second sandwich and licking his fingers.

"I just wanna be there for Elliott," said Toni. She recalled his appearance in the hospital and added, "He looked so pathetic, so devastated that day. I can't imagine what he's goin' through right now."

"Do you wanna be there *for him*?" Father Maurice inquired pointedly. Toni's shoulders fell and she grimaced as he continued, "Or *for you*?"

"Sometimes you're too wise," griped Toni. She answered with the countenance of a scolded puppy, "Both."

"Let me ask you another question," Father Maurice said. A pregnant pause followed as he gazed out the window and watched the world roll past. He finally inquired, "What's the hardest thing for people ta' do in times like these?"

"I don't know," answered Toni with a shrug.

"Nothin,'" Father Maurice stated bluntly. He tossed a finger at the roof of the car and said, "Trust the Big Man and let Him figure it out."

"So I'm nobody doing nothin,'" sighed Toni. She chuckled fatalistically and uttered, "*Great*."

· · · ·

EMMA AND DONNA EMERGED from the crowd surrounding the small Dairy Queen building with their treasures: a Peanut Buster Parfait and a Snickers Blizzard, respectively. It was a pleasant evening of fair, sunny conditions and comfortable humidity. The vicinity buzzed with the activity of pedestrians mulling about the sidewalks and traffic whizzing past on Ecorse Road.

"These new Blizzards are awesome," gushed Donna before consuming a spoonful of the ice cream treat. She and Emma crossed Cortland Avenue and waited for the light to change. Donna affectionately nudged Emma with her shoulder and added, "You shoulda' got one."

"I always get what Daddy always got," Emma stated before sampling her Parfait. The traumatic events of the past week drained the liveliness from her normally effulgent eyes yet, despite the emotional strain and her lack of makeup, her beauty remained intact. The light changed to green and permitted the Cortland Avenue traffic to cross Ecorse Road.

"I was surprised when you said you wanted to come out," commented Donna as the pair traversed the crosswalk.

"Dave ordered me outta the house," Emma replied with a sigh. Donna chortled at the prospect of David ordering his wife to do anything. Emma shrugged and said, "So here I am."

"How're the girls doing?" asked Donna with a fading grin. She and Emma left the roadway and continued south towards her house.

"Wishbone Chicken," Emma moaned as the wonderful scent of the restaurant inundated her. She wistfully watched patrons exiting the building with their meals and stated, "Pool party. Soon. You'll bring chicken."

"Sure," responded Donna with a weak smile, "but the girls?"

"The weekend was rough but they're back to their normal maniac selves . . . for the most part," Emma expounded. She took a bite of her Parfait, savored it and then continued with a dramatic flair, "Yesterday, Lanie – *Lanie* mind you – started *crying* about 'Aunt Nora' which got Tess' cryin' about her which got me cryin' about her. We were a mess, sittin' on the couch hugging and blubberin' about Aunt Nora. *Poor Dave.* He's been a trooper."

"You hit the lottery with that man," said Donna jealously though her envy related more to 'Aunt Nora' replacing 'Aunt Donna'. She asked about Nora's funeral, "Howdaya' think they'll do tomorrow?"

"I have no idea," Emma replied with a slow shake of her head. The women continued their walk to Donna's house in silence. When they arrived, Emma stopped on the sidewalk and studied Donna's small yet quaint home.

"You're gonna need a bigger house," Emma said thoughtfully. Her remark confused Donna who followed her friend along the walk. Emma plopped onto the stoop and Donna sat down next to her.

"What about Elliott?" asked Donna carefully while watching Emma in her peripheral vision. Emma set aside her Parfait and folded her arms on her knees.

"For him, it's not about tomorrow," Emma said cryptically, "but the day after, and the day after that, and the day after that."

"What does *that* mean?" asked a puzzled Donna.

"That's up to you," Emma answered. Donna gazed on her friend for several seconds before understanding the import of her response.

"Oh, so now that the fairy princess is gone, I get him," said Donna bitterly. She, too, set aside her Blizzard and muttered, "Gee, thanks."

"As much as I wanna say it's not like that," Emma said, "it *is* like that."

Emma's blunt assessment briefly stunned Donna. Her best friend's change of heart irked her, however, and she soon rose to her feet and faced her.

"'*You two're done, Donna. He doesn't love you anymore, and I don't think you love him,*'" quoted Donna with emphatic gesticulations. She pointed at Emma and sneered, "You said that, Em. *You.*"

"Things are different now, Dee, *way* different," Emma countered with uncharacteristic levelheadedness. She patted the spot on the porch vacated by Donna and said, "He'll carry this with him for the rest of his life, and you're the only girl who knew him, *who loved him*, before it all happened."

Emma let her words hang in the air. Donna's ire cooled and she returned to her seat.

"He'll start relying on you, and you two'll get closer, and it'll happen," Emma reasoned calmly. She wrapped an arm around Donna's shoulder and explained with waning hope, "Just like Dave and I, it'll happen. Things'll turn around and you two'll make it. *You've got to*, or my big bro's gonna turn into an old, bitter, lonely man."

Though Emma's eyes watered, their brilliance returned. Donna laid her head on her shoulder.

"We need to get you two married and you knocked up, ASAP," Emma said. Donna jerked up her head and her jaw dropped.

"Emma Renee!" objected Donna in the same manner as Lillian Warden.

"Face it, Donna," Emma said with a small crack in her melancholy. The faintest traces of a grin came to her lips and she argued, "It's what you want, and what he needs. And who else knows him like you do?"

Another period of silence followed as both women retrieved and finished their desserts. Donna set down her empty container and turned to Emma.

"There's still Toni," warned Donna gravely.

"That's not gonna happen," Emma countered sternly, "because she's *way* too far over his head."

"So he needs to slum it with me?" inquired an offended Donna. She playfully shoved Emma and said, "Way to make me the *third* choice."

"Oh, knock it off," Emma admonished Donna. Becoming encouraged as she spoke, she gently gripped Donna's arm, shook it and said, "You know him, you know his shortcomings, and you love him anyway. She doesn't, and she's just another heartache waiting to happen. They wouldn't make it. But you and Elliott . . . *you will*."

"Do you really mean that," asked Donna shrewdly, "or are you just desperate?"

"If you want him back, I'm behind you. One hundred percent and for good this time," Emma declared. She made an unpleasant face and added with distaste, "Even if I have to bump Morning Cloak to a different club."

"It feels like we're tricking him into it again," said Donna warily. She wanted to believe Emma but the specter of Toni haunted her.

"Do you want him," Emma asked in a slow, blunt voice, "or not?"

Despite her heart screaming an affirmative answer, Donna hesitated and feigned stoicism. The fire in Emma's eyes returned and melted Donna's brave façade. She exhaled and slumped her shoulders.

"*I do*," mewled Donna.

"What a great day for a funeral," Elliott quipped as he disembarked from Donna's Mustang and assessed the gray, dreary day. The temperature hovered in the high sixties – unusually cool for the middle of July in Michigan - and light, intermittent rain showers often struck without warning.

"Don't say that," scolded Donna as she emerged from the car and opened a tan-and-black umbrella. When Elliott made no effort to avoid the rain, she hurried to him and urged, "Here, take this."

Elliott insisted that he drive alone and Emma insisted that he not; the compromise was that Donna would ferry him to the church. They all agreed, however, that her attendance would be in poor taste and that she would remain in the car.

"Elliott, c'mon, take it," pleaded Donna while pushing the umbrella handle against Elliott's chest. His odd, irritated mood worried her. Donna shielded them both with the umbrella and sighed, "You're gonna have to go in there."

"I don't want to," Elliott muttered as he simply stared across the parking lot of Community United Methodist Church and at the black-clad mourners passing underneath its covered front walk. Bricks of varying shades of light brown and tan composed the church's outer walls while its roof and trim were white; a large, white triangular structure topped with a tall cross hovered above the south wing of the building. Elliott squirmed uncomfortably in his suit and insisted, "I'm pullin' an Irish exit as soon as the service is over."

"No, you're not," replied Donna. Elliott slammed the passenger door closed, the jarring noise causing her to jump.

"Just come in with me," Elliott pled firmly before Donna could rebuke him. He turned to her with fires in his eyes and, waving dismissively, snapped, "To hell with what everyone thinks."

Elliott's impromptu request surprised Donna. She entertained it for but a second before her better judgment prevailed.

"If you need me, I'll be right out here waiting for you," replied Donna. She assured him with an adoring grin, "I'm not goin' anywhere."

Catching herself, Donna curbed her enthusiasm and straightened Elliott's tie. Their eyes met and, to avoid kissing him, she quickly averted her gaze.

"And you won't need me, anyway, because the entire Hastings clan will be right there with you," explained Donna while smoothing Elliott's lapels. The grace with which she handled the situation touched him and his annoyance fizzled.

"You know," Elliott began uncertainly, "I've never actually said the words 'thank you' and-."

"You don't have to," Donna interrupted him. She patted his chest and added, "You'd better get in there."

"Yeah, I guess so," Elliott said with a nod. Sullen and pale, Elliott walked away from Donna without the umbrella. The light rain became a steady misting but she endured it to watch Elliott's journey to the church. Donna exhaled in exasperation when Elliott ducked into a smaller door instead of the main entrance. Suddenly feeling someone's gaze upon her, she looked to her right.

A tall, lanky figure, clad in a suit and wearing sunglasses despite the rainy weather, watched her with a scowl. He shook his head and walked purposefully towards the door which Elliott entered.

"Oh, no," said Donna when she recognized Bart. He opened the door and disappeared inside. She took a step to intercede, hesitated and then jogged towards the Church.

· · · ·

ELLIOTT LINGERED IN a narrow back hallway of the church building, its cinder block half-and-half walls painted yellow from the floor and white from the ceiling. He leaned against one of the walls with his hands in his pockets, his right foot pressed against the blocks and his head bowed.

"Already had another one in your back pocket, huh, Elliott?" asked Bart sharply. Elliott closed his eyes and sighed deeply.

"It's not like that, kid," Elliott grumbled.

"I'm not a kid," snarled Bart as he approached Elliott. He threw a threatening finger in the direction of the parking lot and said, "And she shouldn't be here."

"Not now, man," Elliott replied, his ire bubbling up to his emotional surface. He clenched his teeth and balled his fists in his pockets, advising, "Some other time. We can fight it out if that's what you want. But not now."

"Go to hell," sneered Bart. The young man's blood boiled as he excoriated Elliott, "You're a selfish son-of-a-bitch. You kept her away from me, wasted all that time I coulda' had with her, and now . . . she's gone."

Elliott's anger dimmed. He felt the same loss as Bart and begrudgingly pitied him. Turning his back to the younger man, Elliott began to depart.

"You shoulda' been drivin' her home that night," said Bart with an itching for a fight. His words kindled Elliott's rage as he intended and he added, "She'd still be alive if you had."

"Little shit," Elliott growled as he whirled around. Bart charged him and shoved him to the floor.

"Elliott, stop!" Emma barked as she appeared in the hallway. Ignoring her command, Elliott regained his focus, rose up and shoved Bart. The aggressor stumbled backward into a doorway and tottered on his feet.

"David," Emma said in an elevated tone as he turned the corner into the hall. His name alone conveyed Emma's command and he waded into the fray. Elliott and Bart reengaged and Bart took a swing that Elliott dodged.

"That's it, guys," David ordered sternly as his huge hands grabbed their collars. His great strength held them apart despite their struggling. Emma pounced.

"Knock it off, both of you," she snarled. Elliott deferred to his sister long enough for Donna to grab him in a half-hug and pull him away from Bart.

"Butt out, Emma," snapped Bart. She slapped his face and it echoed in the hallway. Donna winced but continued to hold Elliott at bay.

"I said knock it off," Emma demanded with her brilliant eyes scintillating like blue-green coals. The sting on his cheek and the heat of Emma's enragement cowed Bart as she backed him into the doorway, stating, "This isn't about you."

Emma looked to Elliott. He bowed his head in shame but kept his gaze on his sister.

"Or you," Emma continued. Alternating her attention between Nora's former suitors, she said gravely, "There's a mother in there grieving because her little girl is dead. *Dead.* Do you think Nora would want you idiots brawling at her funeral like drunks at the club?"

Emma's demeanor cooled. She held each man in her penetrating gaze for several seconds.

"If you both loved her *so much*," Emma said, "then act like it. Get in there, be adults and be there for her family like she would want you to. Otherwise, *get out.*"

David remained between Elliott and Bart but relaxed his body. Elliott straightened his collar, glared at his adversary and allowed Donna to lead him away. Bart hesitated and fumed.

"The service doesn't start for ten minutes, man," David suggested. He gestured towards the front entrance and said, "Why don't you step outside and cool down?"

Bart nodded in agreement. He moved towards Emma.

"Sorry 'bout that," Bart said with his eyes on the floor. He staved off tears, turned on a dime and hurried out of the church.

"That was close," commented David blithely. Emma wrapped her arms around his torso and laid her head on his chest. Her eyes watered.

"I don't tell you this enough," Emma began before sighing, "but you're wonderful."

David engulfed Emma in a bear hug and kissed the top of her head. The realization that she had lost not just a cherished employee but a good and trusted friend wafted over her. Surrendering her composure, she cried in her beloved husband's arms.

"What's a' matter, Mommy?" asked a concerned Tessa as she arrived in the hallway. Emma quickly composed herself and wiped away her tears.

"Mommy's just sad about Nora, sweetie," Emma replied. She knelt and opened her arms for a hug.

"It's okay, Mommy," said Tessa. She scurried to her mother and embraced her. Her heart touched, Emma stifled a sob and wallowed in her daughter's embrace.

"I can't imagine what that poor woman is going through right now," Emma thought. Never one to be religious, she nonetheless prayed, "Please be with her today, God, and please watch over my babies."

. . . .

DONNA DEPOSITED ELLIOTT at the entranceway to the church proper, lingered for a moment and then departed before anyone noticed her. He remained motionless, a dark, brooding figure standing at the threshold but unwilling to cross it and finalize Nora's death. The numbing melody of stock funeral music flowed past him.

"Keep walking," Elliott thought when he noticed Bart in his peripheral vision. The young man made no effort to engage him and swiftly passed from sight. Refocusing on the task at hand, Elliott swallowed and said to himself, "Guess I gotta."

When Elliott gazed into the chamber, he was taken aback by its ethereal appearance. To the far end of the church, the track lighting and oak wood that comprised the sanctuary furniture and adornments created a honeyed glow. To the near end, the black clothing worn by the seated mourners created an amorphous darkness that suppressed it.

"Like looking to the other side," Elliott muttered with a grimace. Houses of worship made him uncomfortable since childhood and his skin crawled as he thought, "I hate churches."

The church's broad main aisle led to the dais that housed the sanctuary, its altar containing a freestanding cross and an open bible bookended by candles. The sanctuary centered on a corner of the building with three sizeable, overlapping panels of oak hung on the wall behind the altar. Affixed to the foremost panel was a large cross and a smaller one; above it, the middle panel was unadorned and, below it, the hindmost one supported a second, smaller cross. Delaying the inevitable, Elliott shifted his vision from the pulpit and portrait of Jesus on the left side of the dais to the piano and choir chairs on its right.

"Do it," Elliott said before forcing himself to look at Nora's coffin, its silvery hue in stark contrast to the rest of the church. It was positioned in front of the two steps leading onto the dais and flanked by two oak handrails. Elliott panicked and, with a quick shake of his head, stated, "Nope."

Elliott turned to flee but Emma, with David and Tessa standing hand-in-hand behind her, blocked his advance with an open palm. His face contorted as he battled his sorrow.

"Can't, Em. Just can't," Elliott insisted.

"You have to," urged a sympathetic Emma. Tessa relinquished her grip on David, walked to her uncle and took his hand.

"I'll go with you, Uncle Elliott," said Tessa. Emma grasped her mouth to squelch a cry and even David became teary-eyed.

"Okay, monster," Elliott said with a short-lived smirk. Buttressed by his niece, he proceeded with her down the center aisle and locked his gaze on the coffin. The chamber went silent when he reached the center of the walkway and he felt the pressure of every eye upon him; only Tessa's presence gave him the strength to continue forward. Emma and David followed them at distance and quietly took their seats in the front row.

"How come the coffin's closed, Uncle Elliott?" asked Tessa innocently. The extent of Nora's facial injuries required a closed coffin so her high school graduation portrait was positioned on a table to its right, the photograph conveying her beauty and the exuberance of her youth. The image of his beloved's face rendered Elliott unable to speak.

Unwilling to be upstaged by her little sister, Lanie walked to her uncle's side and wrapped an arm around his waist. Elliott looked down to her, laid his arm on her shoulders and then returned his gaze to the coffin. Emma buried her face into David's chest and wept. She was not alone: the sight of Nora's fiancée standing before her coffin with his nieces comforting him overwhelmed many of the mourners. Her mother cried uncontrollably.

"Well, what now?" Elliott asked in his head. Tears blurred his vision as he repeated, "*What now?*"

• • • •

TONI DROVE SLOWLY DOWN Olive Street and warily viewed Community United Methodist Church. Braking at the four-way stop where it met Bibbins Street, she shivered and exhaled.

"Do it," Toni encouraged herself. She had already passed the church once, failed to convince herself to turn into its driveway and then circled the block. Turning right onto Bibbins Street again and rolling her vehicle past the church, she searched the parking lot for Elliott's car. She did not see it and drove another loop around the neighborhood. Upon reaching the driveway a third time, she said more forcefully, "*Come on, Toni, just do it.*"

Toni turned her car onto the lane and it trundled towards the parking lot. Donna, at the same time, pushed her way through the church's main doors and traversed the walkway. The women simultaneously arrived at its end. Toni braked.

"Wow, she's relentless," Toni remarked with a trace of bitterness in her tone. Donna responded with a veiled glower as Toni lowered her passenger side window. The sound and scent of the falling rain poured into the car.

"Well, if it isn't the singer?" said Donna with the slightest hint of contempt. She crouched so that she was eye level with Toni and queried, "What're you doing here?"

"Hi, Donna," Toni greeted her. Despite the older woman's clear disdain for her, she maintained a positive attitude and answered, "Just came to pay my respects . . . and let Elliott know I'm here for him if he needs me."

Toni's declaration of support for Elliott heartened her but tweaked Donna's ego. Donna attempted to lock her countenance in a neutral expression but failed.

"Look, I know you guys kinda had like a little *secret thing* goin' on last year," began Donna accusatorily.

"It wasn't like that," Toni objected, the implication that she was unfaithful to Bobby causing her considerable guilt.

"Oh, come on," said Donna as she folded her arms on the windowsill of the car. Ignoring the water that soaked her sleeves, she continued, "He wanted you, you wanted him. And I know you care about him."

"*That* is true," Toni said earnestly. Donna's snideness prickled her.

"And I totally get that," said Donna condescendingly, "but you don't have to worry about him. Will it be rough for a while? Yeah. I'm gonna be there for him, though, and things'll get better. *Much better.*"

"So I guess Em's back on board with you two," Toni parried in a surge of possessiveness over Elliott. Donna's eyes widened and her face tightened.

"You catch on fast," declared Donna tersely. Her tacit admission wounded Toni but she refused to give Donna the satisfaction of knowing it.

"Good," Toni said while nodding, "that's good. He deserves to be happy."

"Ya' know, the funeral's starting already, so it's probably not a good idea to go in now," advised Donna. She stated, "I'll let Elliott know you stopped by."

A retort formed on Toni's tongue but she suppressed it. Instead, she heard Father Maurice's words in her head.

"Trust the Big Man and let Him figure it out."

A peacefulness settled on Toni. She grinned subtly at Donna.

"That'd be great. Tell him if he needs anything, I'm here," Toni said. She added pleasantly, "Thanks, Donna."

A stunned Donna gaped at Toni for a few seconds and then stood up. Toni raised her window as she pulled away, circled the parking lot and drove past Donna with a wave. Donna shifted her scowl into a fake grin and waved in return.

"Bitch," muttered Donna. Toni read her lips in the rearview mirror and saw her face shift back into a scowl.

"That jealousy is gonna eat her alive," Toni remarked as she turned onto Bibbins Street and accelerated eastward. An uneasiness arose in Toni's spirit as she traveled further from Elliott and, needing more than Father Maurice's advice, she said aloud, "I need my mom."

· · · ·

HOLDING A GLASS OF red wine, Katherine opened the door on the rainy afternoon and found her daughter looking gloomier than the weather. A pall hung over Toni from her black funeral dress to her sullen, wan face.

"I need my mom," Toni whimpered like a child. She forcefully embraced Katherine who held the glass away from her body to avoid spilling it. She wrapped an arm around Toni's shoulders.

"Well, that's convenient," replied Katherine with a reassuring squeeze of her daughter, "because that's who I am."

The quip garnered a grin from Toni. She tightened her grip on her mother.

"I love you," Toni gushed.

"Come inside and we'll figure it out," said Katherine while ushering her daughter into the house. She maneuvered Toni to the kitchen table, deposited her into a chair and pulled one out for herself. Katherine paused.

"Hungry?" asked Katherine.

"Not really," Toni answered with a head shake and a frown. Katherine sat down and set her glass next to a corked wine bottle, an open crossword puzzle book and a purple pen.

"So, let me guess," began Katherine, "Donna was at the funeral as Elliott's shoulder to cry on . . . just waiting to strike."

Toni stifled her tears and made a mean face to ward against their return. Katherine waited patiently for her to speak.

"Father Maurice thinks I shouldn't do anything," Toni said, her dissatisfaction with his advice clear.

"*Father Maurice*," scoffed Katherine with a hint of envy. She reacquired her wine, sipped it and pondered the situation while Toni stared into the table. They remained quiet for over a minute before Katherine exhaled and continued, "I hate to admit it but he's probably right. Elliott just lost the woman he expected to spend the rest of his life with, Toni. His head's gonna be a mess for the foreseeable future. If anything, he'll rebound with Donna, it'll fall apart and he'll be available again when he's in a better mental state. You may not want to hear it, but waiting makes sense."

"Another loss is not what he needs," Toni countered, "and no matter how I feel about him, I don't want that for Elliott. I'd rather lose him to Donna than him take another hit like that."

"You do realize he may not need either of you, right?" offered Katherine, her words cutting Toni to the bone.

"Geez, thanks," Toni replied.

"I said need, not want," countered Katherine. Mother and daughter drifted into another contemplative silence. Toni pulled her feet up on the chair and hugged her knees to her chest. Katherine finished her wine.

"Joan wants me to go on a date with this guy she knows," Toni said.

"Is he handsome?" asked Katherine with renewed interest.

"Mother, please," Toni admonished Katherine.

"You're a beautiful young woman and you should be with a man who's your physical equal," insisted Katherine. She uncorked the wine bottle, refilled her glass and commented, "Bobby may have been an asshole but you two made a great looking couple."

"Do you really need another glass?" Toni rebuked her mother.

"Yes," asserted Katherine matter-of-factly. She held the glass to her mouth and, before drinking, added, "You and Elliott, well, clean him up and they could put you two on top of a wedding cake."

"You're supposed to be helping," Toni complained. She rested her chin in between her knees.

"*Go on the date*," urged Katherine.

"I don't know, Mom," Toni said. Becoming fidgety, she stood up and walked to the kitchen window, saying, "It doesn't feel right."

"Honey, it's a date," reasoned Katherine. Paying close attention to her wine, she said, "Go meet the guy, let him spring for dinner – get something expensive – and see how it goes. If you don't like him, don't see him again and, if you do, go on a second date."

"But I love Elliott," blurted Toni. She grasped the edge of the counter with both hands and stared through the window. Her vision blurred.

"Life is not a romantic comedy, Toni," said Katherine gravely, her inner angst over her own past surfacing. Hearing her mother's change of tone, Toni faced her as she continued, "Every second isn't magical, there's a lotta pain, bad mistakes, wasted time."

Katherine recalled Martin Cullen and scowled. Toni shivered.

"Poor decisions," added Katherine pointedly.

"Poor decisions," Toni repeated. She hopped onto the counter and stated, "I made mine when I chose Bobby over Elliott last year."

"That may've been your only window," replied Katherine, "and if it's closed, you're gonna have to move on."

"What about you, Mom?" Toni asked with a tilt of her head. She studied Katherine's aging yet comely countenance and said, "You haven't dated in a long time."

"That window *is* closed," answered Katherine darkly. She refused to let it linger and said, "Now I'm waiting on grandchildren and until then . . . ."

Katherine lifted her glass and indulged in Toni's disapproving expression. A sudden idea caused her to lower it.

"What if there was a way for you to do nothing but still do something?" inquired Katherine slowly and slyly. Her interest piqued, Toni leaned forward.

"I'm listening," Toni said. Her hands trembled with anticipation so she clasped them together.

"Something that lets him know how you feel but in a very public way that doesn't put any pressure on him, or intrude on Nora's memory," suggested Katherine, the older woman taking pride in the innovative solution. An almost smug satisfaction spread across her face and she said, "Write a song for him, and sing it when he's at the club."

"I'm no songwriter," Toni responded despite loving the idea.

"Then steal a song and sing it to him," countered Katherine in irritation.

Toni opened her mouth to dissent but froze; as her mind devised a plan, the glow on her face burgeoned. She leapt off the counter.

"*Poor decisions*," Toni said. She rushed her mother and exclaimed, "You're a genius, Mom!"

Katherine again held her wine away from her body but the expected embrace did not materialize. Toni pecked her on the top of the head and then headed for the door.

"Where're you going?" asked a perplexed Katherine.

"To steal a song!" Toni exclaimed as she ran out the front door. She inadvertently slammed it.

"Of course," said Katherine. Sitting alone at the kitchen table, she sipped her wine and marveled at Toni's zest for performing. Katherine laughed and muttered, "That man doesn't stand a chance."

• • • •

"THE IN-LAWS HAVE THE girls for the weekend, Dave's playin' poker until god knows when, Elliott's tucked into his apartment for the evening and Sean's runnin' Johnny Dubs," Emma announced as she reclined in her hot tub and stretched out her long legs before her. Tapping the blue-and-white cooler behind her with the tip of her beer bottle, she told

Donna, "You and I got the place to ourselves, the hot tub if the rain holds off and a cooler full of beer."

Emma wrinkled her nose.

"And a bottle of wine," Emma added with a dubious glance at Donna. She lifted her beer bottle as Donna lifted her wine glass and the friends clinked their drinks together. With the steady breeze tossing her dirty-blonde hair, Emma exhaled, "To the end of a rough week."

"Amen, sister," Donna said as she offered her best friend a warm smile. It faded when she noticed the wear and tear on Emma's countenance and she asked, "How're *you* doing?"

Donna, too, leaned back and stretched her body. She sipped her wine with a thoughtful expression.

"I mean, the focus's been on Elliott since it happened," stated Donna, "and Lanie and Tessa some, too, I guess, but she was going to be your sister-in-law, and you two worked together *a lot*."

Emma rested the back of her skull on the concrete and pondered the question while Donna watched her concernedly. Thirty seconds later, she lifted it and took a drink of her beer.

"Honestly, Donna, I'm okay," Emma answered. She shook her head slowly and explained, "I mean, don't get me wrong. I'm sad, and I'll miss her. But I only knew her for a little over a year and our relationship was really just gettin' started."

"Are you sure?" inquired Donna. She stretched out her arms on the edge of the hot tub, set her wine glass on the cement and turned it by its stem. Returning her gaze to Emma, she said bluntly, "You look totally fried."

"I'm sure I do," Emma replied with affirmative nods. She used the bottle to point to her face and said, "Most of this is helping other people through it: Elliott, the girls, my Johnny Dubs crew. She touched a lotta lives there, and everybody loved the princess. But starting tomorrow, I'm shifting *everyone* back into normal gear. I think that's best for all of 'em, and that includes you and Elliott."

"Nora was buried yesterday, Em," replied a skeptical Donna. She tilted her head and pressed her friend, "You don't think it's a little early for that?"

"*I don't*," Emma stated. The pair enjoyed a pleasant, impromptu break in the conversation as they indulged in the massaging effects of the hot tub jets and their beverages. The wind delivered the sounds of Friday evening's neighborhood bustle for several minutes before Donna stirred.

"Toni showed up yesterday," said Donna. She sipped her wine.

"She did? At the funeral?" Emma queried sharply. She sat up and demanded, "Why didn't you tell me?"

"There was too much goin' on yesterday," answered Donna. Surrendering to her guilt over her behavior, she confessed, "I wasn't very nice to her."

"Do what ya' gotta do to fend her off," Emma stated flatly as she moved her head from side-to-side to crack her neck. Her coldness ebbed, however, and she added in a kinder tone, "Just don't get carried away. Toni *is* good people."

"She's playin' nice now, Em, but she's still got the inside track on Elliott and that scares me," lamented Donna. She abruptly drained her glass and handed it to Emma who, during another break in the conversation, retrieved the wine bottle from the cooler and refilled it.

"Remember when you used to sing in high school and college?" Emma asked while wedging the bottle back into the ice. She closed the cooler.

"With Rick Newton's crappy band?" asked Donna in amusement. She accepted her beverage from Emma and said, "I wouldn't call that singing."

"I would," Emma encouraged Donna as she slid back into the bubbling, steaming water and drifted into machinations. Donna recognized the look.

"What're you up to?" asked Donna suspiciously.

"Nothing yet," Emma said.

"Uh-oh," replied Donna.

"How would you like to beat Toni at her own game?" Emma asked thoughtfully.

"Tell me what you're thinking before I answer that," answered Donna.

"It won't be easy," Emma said, "but if it goes the way I think it will . . . ."

Donna saw the wicked delight on Emma's face and, buttressed by her devious energy, settled into the hot tub and sipped her wine. Holding her glass away from her, she grinned with narrowed eyes.

"I'm in," declared Donna resolutely.

S erendipity favored Elliott and he arrived at Johnny Dubs just as a lone parking spot became available. He pulled into the space, killed the engine and exhaled in dread. An electricity, intense even for a Friday night, crackled through the vicinity of the club.

"This is not a good idea," Elliott stated aloud. Nearly a month had passed since Nora's death and, as July became August, the desire to return to Johnny Dubs burgeoned. Succumbing to Emma's relentless urgings, he swallowed his pain and made his emotional return to the scene of their first meeting. A wave of nausea hit Elliott when he disembarked and, thrusting the door closed, he uttered, "Just get it over with."

Elliott arrived at the front doors and stopped in his tracks. Raising his eyes above the front entrance, he read the "Country Night" banner and identified its headliner: Morning Cloak. The sound of the band beginning Eddie Rabbit's "Drivin' My Life Away" emanated from the club.

"Damn it, Em!" Elliott shouted without regard for who heard him. He made several retreats, each time stopping himself and comically regaining the lost ground to the upbeat tune. Unable to surrender his original plan, he gestured angrily and griped, "Why the hell would she pick tonight?!"

Elliott finally drove himself forward by sheer force of will. His reluctant entrance went largely unnoticed as the club roiled with activity and the packed dance floor teemed with patrons. There was only one seat available in the house: Elliott's reserved barstool.

"Sight for sore eyes," Elliott uttered as he gazed on his neglected sanctuary. He caught his breath, however, when he saw the young, blonde woman sitting on the next barstool. Her resemblance to Nora was fleeting but close enough to reopen the wound of Nora's death. Seeing the picture of John Warden, he thought, "Little help, Dad."

Morning Cloak's song ended. Elliott shivered as a chill ran through his body.

"How we doin' so far, Johnny Dubs?" asked a bubbly Toni, her voice carrying throughout the club via its sound system. The crowd cheered in response. Elliott shook his head.

"Geez, Dad, blunt as ever," Elliott thought with a smirk. He turned towards the stage. Though characteristically radiant, Toni exhibited an unusual flare as she spoke to the audience. She wore a flowing, white blouse adorned with long tassels hanging from the neckline, dark blue jeans, a black belt with a sparkly, gold belt buckle and cowboy boots. Elliott backpedaled and plopped onto his barstool, muttering, "Why does she hafta' look so damn good?"

Toni noticed Elliott and her brilliant smile exploded across the room. She waved excitedly at Elliott and, enraptured by her, he offered her a muted grin and uneasily waved back. He felt as if Nora grasped at him from the grave and pulled him into the past, his deceased fiancée struggling against Toni's attempts to yank him into the future.

"So we got a new one for you guys," said Toni to a raucous response. She signaled to her bandmates and then added coyly, "A little song by a man named Mr. George Strait."

The crowd roared its approval. Morning Cloak began "You Look So Good In Love" with Toni singing the lyrics from the prospective of a woman. Her voice cast a spell on Elliott and, when she declared she still wanted him via the song, he nearly toppled from his barstool.

"It's really good to see you sitting there again," said Emma as she appeared next to her brother with a loving glow on her face.

"Hey, Em," Elliott uttered. He kept his attention riveted to Toni.

"Am I bothering you?" asked Emma in annoyance. Her brother's focus on Toni irked her greatly as did his failure to immediately respond to her question.

"No," Elliott said as he clumsily patted Emma's shoulder. She, too, turned her attention to Toni and processed the song lyrics.

"It's like she knew," Emma thought as she studied Elliott's gawking countenance. She turned on a dime and hurried off into the crowd.

"Don't look at him," Toni urged herself as she finished the second chorus. She soon reached the spoken verse of the song and every word she said reverberated through Elliott's heart.

"This one's for me," Elliott said to himself as Toni launched into the ending choruses. His mind moved past his role in Toni's song and, with a puzzled expression, he thought, "But who's the other *her*?"

• • • •

MORNING CLOAK FINISHED "You Look So Good in Love" to the applause of Johnny Dubs. Toni's bandmates took bows but she surrendered to her desire for Elliott as she returned the microphone to its stand. Their eyes pierced the haze of cigarette smoke in the club and they exchanged longing gazes. A sudden commotion drew their attention: Emma leapt onto the stage and grabbed the microphone.

"Love that Morning Cloak!" Emma bellowed while stepping in front of Toni and blocking her view of Elliott. She alternated her gaze between the crowd and the band, explaining, "We're gonna give 'em a well-earned break – with a round on the house, of course – and bring out a little surprise for you guys."

The audience cheered again. A puzzled Morning Cloak slowly set aside their instruments as another band took the stage and began setting up.

"Watcha' doin', Em?" inquired Eddie as he passed her. Emma clicked off the microphone.

"Humor me," Emma replied with raised eyebrows. Eddie shrugged off her bizarre interruption, vacated the stage and headed for his free beer. Remaining rooted to where she stood with her guitar still slung on her shoulder, Toni watched Emma who turned to her and said, "Pop a squat. It's just for one song."

Toni hesitated. She and Emma watched each other warily, each woman uncertain of the other's intentions. Toni relented first and unslung her guitar.

"Sure, okay," said Toni before setting her guitar on its stand. The men of Morning Cloak seated themselves at a table to the right of the stage that Emma reserved for them. Intrigued by the proffered surprise, Toni retreated to the table but remained standing.

Elliott, meanwhile, received a Grumpy Old Man and stewed over his sister's interruption of Morning Cloak. He believed the action to be a punitive overreaction.

"I'm gonna give her hell for this bullshit," thought an unforgiving Elliott with a sneer. Emma clicked on the microphone.

"Our next performer is a Taylor girl who's been gone for a long time," began Emma as if a *Solid Gold* host introducing a resurgent act. All went eerily quiet as she swept the crowd with her stunning visage and continued, "But when she left, she left something behind: *her heart*. But now she's finally come home, and tonight, she's here to get it back . . . ."

Emma's theater drew the crowd to the edge of its seats. Elliott's ire melted into skepticism.

"She didn't," Elliott assured himself. A slack-jawed Toni gaped at Emma.

" . . . so, in her first public appearance in a *long* time, please welcome my best friend, Donna Kirkenshaw, with the help of One Shot Rifle!" Emma announced. She returned the microphone to its stand and departed the stage.

"Tell me she didn't," Elliott said with fading certainty. A prepositioned spotlight shined on the stairwell door leading to Emma's office. Donna, clad in a tasseled, green mini-dress and cowboy boots, emerged from it and strode towards the stage. The audience's vigorous adulations, which including whistles and catcalls, escorted her the entire way.

"*She did*," Elliott said. He glanced at Toni, who was already watching his reaction, but she averted her eyes.

One Shot Rifle commenced Deborah Allen's "Baby I Lied" as Donna ascended to the stage and stepped in front of the microphone's stand. She dislodged it from its clasp, kept her head down and waited for her cue. When it arrived, Donna lifted the microphone to her lips and began singing the opening verse. She then looked directly at Elliott and hit the song's first chorus.

"Geez, Dee, I totally forgot *you* could sing," Elliott thought with vague remembrances of her vocal dabbling in high school. Toni stifled a grimace as she, too, was wowed by Donna's performance. Ryan rose to his feet while keeping his attention on Donna and leaned into Toni.

"You know she had a voice?" asked Ryan. Unable to form words or even look at him, Toni merely shook her head in the negative. Ryan quickly added, "She's no you, but still, I mean, she ain't bad."

Though the beguiled crowd focused on Donna, she focused solely on Elliott and poured her desire for him into every word. Her emotional plea paralyzed him as she flawlessly performed the bridge and entered the third chorus. Donna's voice control stunned Toni.

"Take it home, Dee," an ecstatic Emma said from her vantage point off stage. Donna repeated the song's title several times as it wound towards its end. The crowd erupted in applause.

"Thank you," a blushing Donna said with a wave, "thanks."

"I picked the wrong song," thought Toni while refusing to look at Elliott. Clenching her jaw to ward off tears, she thought of "You Look So Good In Love" and its theme of lost love. She said to herself, "Or maybe I didn't."

• • • •

ELLIOTT FELT AS IF he were mired in the middle of a locust swarm and being physically ripped apart. Throttled by a panic attack, he abandoned his bar stool and his cocktail and darted towards the front exit.

"Elliott!" Toni shouted as he vanished through the doors. Emma also noticed his flight.

"Donna and One-Shot Rifle!" said Emma quickly into the microphone. She pulled Donna aside as the band took its bows and, holding her hand over the microphone to muffle it, leaned into her best friend and urged, "Go get him."

Donna hesitated. Chasing after Elliott meant surrendering to old instincts and setting aside her new feminist paradigm.

"*Go*," Emma ordered her. Resuming her performance, she announced to the patrons, "And now we have *another* surprise for you."

Donna leapt off the stage and joined Toni's race to Elliott. They struggled through the teeming, boisterous patrons while measuring each other's progress, Toni with a head start but Donna with a shorter distance to travel to the doors. Toni stopped in her tracks when a man suddenly blocked her advance.

"Bobby?!" Toni exclaimed.

"Hey, sweetheart," replied Bobby adoringly, Toni's ex-fiancée raising his voice to be heard above the uproar.

"All right, Morning Cloak, come on back!" Emma urged Toni's bandmates with a beckoning wave. Eddie, Oscar and Ryan reluctantly stood up and looked to their lead singer for guidance.

"What're you doing here?" Toni asked Bobby in astonishment. She searched the vicinity of the front doors just in time to receive a stinging look from Donna. Attempting to push Bobby aside, she saw her slip outside and insisted, "Never mind, I gotta go."

"Wait, Toni," pleaded Bobby as he engulfed her in his arms, "hang on."

"Let me go!" Toni demanded as she fought out of his grasp.

"I think Toni and the boys need a little encouragement!" Emma said to the audience. The club exploded in raucous applause and cheers directed at Morning Cloak.

Once free of Bobby's arms, Toni scanned the sea of patrons that blocked her path to either exit and clamored for Morning Cloak's return to the stage. She accepted the defeat as Bobby expectantly watched her and, waving the white flag by motioning towards the stage, directed her bandmates to return there.

"There we go!" bellowed Emma. The audience's approval was deafening.

"You're pretty cutthroat, Mrs. Hastings," said Eddie as he walked closely behind Emma.

Emma ignored Eddie and instead beamed at Toni while Toni forced a smile over her anger. She yanked the microphone from Emma's grasp and hawked her with narrowed eyes. Emma whirled back towards the crowd.

"So, for surprise number two," Emma began as Toni seethed, "we invited an old friend of Toni's to sing one of her very favorite songs with her."

"She's absolutely diabolical," thought Toni. She heard Father Maurice's sage words in her head: *Trust the Big Man and let Him figure it out.*

The crowd went wild yet again as Bobby ascended to the stage and hugged Toni. She permitted it briefly before ending the embrace and, preventing Emma from departing, Toni wrapped her arms around her and pulled her close.

"When you finally feel bad about it, remember I said this: I forgive you," Toni said in Emma's ear.

"Gee, thanks," Emma replied haughtily as Toni relinquished her hold. Bobby, meanwhile, moved two stools to the front of the stage. Emma descended to the dance floor while he and Toni took their seats. An idea formed in Toni's mind and she lifted the microphone to her lips with a grin.

"This song's dedicated to my best friend, Elliott Warden," Toni stated with love in her tone. Emma spun around and glared at her to no effect. Toni motioned for Morning Cloak to commence "Meet Me in Montana" and the start of the song cemented Bobby in place despite his obvious displeasure. Goaded forward by the crowd, Bobby sang the first verse as Toni's eyes glazed and remained that way during the first chorus.

"Hope she sings her part," Bobby thought when Toni failed to join it.

When Toni launched into the second verse, her emotion overwhelmed her and she began to cry. Her tears had no effect on her performance, however, and, as the second chorus arrived, she stood up and poured everything she had into the song. Emma cringed. Bobby struggled to match her energy and volume.

"Toni strikes back," Emma said aloud from her vantage point at the bar. Every face in the bar focused on Toni as she belted out the bridge and sang Bobby's line. Bobby lowered his microphone into his lap and gazed upon his former fiancée in wonder. Emma glanced at Elliott's empty barstool and muttered, "Good thing he's not here to see this."

Toni's performance became heart-wrenching as she finished the song on her own. When it ended, the weeping twenty-eight-year-old jumped from the stage and, deftly slithering through the crowd, headed for the front doors. Stunned by her flight, Bobby stood up, dropped his microphone in the process and helplessly watched her departure. Eddie stepped towards his bandmates.

"Looks like it's gonna be a short set tonight," quipped Eddie.

• • • •

"AREN'T YOU SUPPOSED to be with Elliott?" inquired Emma sharply after Donna burst through the doors of Johnny Dubs and marched up to her.

"I can't *find* Elliott," a panicky Donna replied.

"Whaddaya mean ya' can't find him?" Emma asked indignantly. She and Donna blocked the aisleway along the bar but, unwilling to step aside, they forced the flow of club traffic into the dining area.

"He's not at his apartment, or your place," Donna answered. Speaking in a breathy, jittery voice, she continued, "I checked North End, and he wasn't there, either, and he's not at the field."

"He still goes to that place?" asked Emma in mild surprise. She had no idea that Elliott still sought solace in his high school hiding spot.

"Em!" Donna protested anxiously. The telephone behind the bar rang, its shrillness arising over the cacophony of the club. Sean answered it.

"Okay, okay, relax," Emma said as she lowered her gaze and pondered Elliott's whereabouts. Her sibling intuition told her that her brother was safe and, looking to Donna, she said "I'm sure he's fine. We just gotta think. Where else would he go?"

"Em, Romulus PD's on the phone for you," shouted Sean while holding up the telephone receiver.

"Oh, god, Em!" exclaimed Donna as she broke down. Emma grabbed her and shook her.

"Get it together, Dee! I know where he is!" barked Emma. She stopped manhandling her friend but maintained her grip on her and added, "And, just like I told you, he's fine. Physically, anyway."

"Where is he?!" Donna mewled.

"Tell 'em on my way, Sean," yelled Emma. Sean responded with a thumbs-up.

"Emma, where is he?!" Donna demanded angrily.

"*Relax*," urged Emma. She released her friend, turned around and headed to her office, saying over her shoulder, "I'm gonna go get him, and you're gonna go home."

"Absolutely not," objected Donna. She followed on Emma's heels and insisted, "I'm going with you."

Emma abruptly stopped and whirled around. Donna nearly careened into her.

"We won tonight, Dee," Emma said firmly, "but you get up in his business right now and you'll screw it up."

Emma's commanding aura calmed Donna and her anger bled away. Emma patted her cheek.

"Now, I told you I'm with you, no matter what," Emma continued, "but I know him better than anyone, so trust me on this. You're gonna need to give him a couple days to sort some things out. *Be patient.*"

"Alright, Em," Donna replied with several affirmative shakes of her head. She offered Emma an odd grin, one which made her furrow her brow, and said, "But your days of telling me what to do about my man are coming to an end. *Soon.*"

"That's the plan," Emma replied in frustration.

· · · ·

EMMA TURNED LEFT INTO the southern drive of Romulus Memorial Cemetery and hung another left onto an access road which ran southwest. She parked behind a Romulus Police Department cruiser with its lights flashing; just beyond it sat Elliott's LTD. The red-and-blue illumination rolling over the grave markers and through the cemetery's trees created a nightmarish scene while the bright-white headlight beams punched a huge hole in the darkness ahead.

"*Idiot,*" an exasperated Emma grumbled. Disembarking from her vehicle, Emma slammed her door and walked up to the awaiting police officer. The mustached man leaned against his cruiser with his muscled arms folded and watched her approach. He grinned.

"You married?" asked the officer unabashedly.

"Happily," Emma answered. Moving quickly to the issue at hand, she inquired, "How much trouble's he in?"

"Not too much," replied the officer, Emma's rebuff having no effect on his ego. Elliott sat on the hood of his car with his head bowed and his legs hanging over the driver's side wheel well. Turning his body towards his detainee, the officer placed a hand on the top of his car and explained, "Other than the public intoxication and the trespassing, he's behaved himself. I'd a' just run him off if he wasn't too blitzed to drive."

The officer handed Emma an empty bottle of cheap rum. She tossed it into a nearby garbage can with a bang that echoed in the night.

"His drinking's getting outta control," Emma griped to herself. She placed her hands in her sweatshirt pockets and looked at the officer, saying,

"Thanks for being cool about it. Johnny Dubs, Goddard and Mortenview. You stop in whenever you want and we'll take care of ya."

"Sounds good to me, pretty lady," said the officer with a smirk.

"That was goddamn masterful, you devious little bitch," uttered Elliott in a loud, amused voice.

"Watch that language now," ordered the officer gruffly. He glanced at Emma and queried, "You gonna be okay with him?"

"Oh, yeah. I've been dealing with his bullshit for as long as I can remember," Emma answered. She moved past the officer with a thankful touch of his arm and said, "I'll get him outta here. And tell Curtis thanks for calling me."

"Oh, yeah," said the officer, "he told me to tell you he owed you one, anyway."

"Right," Emma said with a glint of remembrance.

"Night, Ma'am," the officer said with a tip of his hat. Emma winced at his use of "ma'am". Climbing into his cruiser, he switched off the spinning lights and slowly departed. Emma waited for the police car to disappear from view before approaching her brother.

"Little bitch? Seriously?" Emma chastised Elliott. The impulse to slap him arose in her but, when his face morphed into a pained look and sudden, angry tears fell, it faltered.

"I haven't been able to go to her grave yet," confessed Elliott with unexpected clarity. He dispensed with his tears by rubbing his hand from his forehead to his chin and expounded, "Not on the day of her funeral, not since and not now. Oh, I've parked right here, and stared at it, but I haven't been closer than that. I just can't do it. I can't go over there."

"*Elliott*," Emma whimpered. She moved to him and wrapped him in loving arms.

"Sorry 'bout calling you a bitch," apologized Elliott. The alcohol's effect waned and he simply felt exhausted.

"But not devious, right?" replied Emma. The siblings shared grins as she hopped onto the hood beside him and pleaded, "Stay at our house this weekend. You really need to be with family right now. Sean can run the club for the weekend. We'll all hang out by the pool, drink and-."

Emma stopped speaking. She could smell the scent of alcohol oozing from Elliott.

"We'll feed you at least," Emma added with a nudge.

"Thanks, Em, but I just wanna go home," replied a sobering Elliott. Gazing at the grave, he said forlornly, "I know what you did tonight, and I know why, but I'm just not ready for that. Donna's been great but, please, *call her off*."

Brother and sister sat quietly and listened to the nighttime insects sing their tunes. Unwilling to tear down her webs, Emma instead shifted tack.

"Look, I gotta feelin' tomorrow's gonna be rough for you, in more ways than one," Emma said as she appraised Elliott's rough condition, "but how about Sunday I bring you back here . . . and you can really say goodbye."

Elliott broke down, clung to his sibling and wept in her arms. Emma placed a hand on top of his head.

"You're just gonna keep losing unless you let me fix things," Emma said, "*for good*."

"You're half right," uttered Elliott in defeat.

· · · ·

TONI LET THE SHOWER head spray hot water directly into her face and brushed it over her head to soak her hair. She always felt like she left Johnny Dubs with a thin layer of grime on her body and cigarette odor clinging to her skin. Toni inhaled deeply as the steam thickened.

"If they outlawed cigarettes in bars," Toni said aloud as she rinsed her body, "I'd be one happy lady."

Languidly washing her legs, Toni drifted into contemplation of the evening's disheartening events. Elliott's anxious flight saddened her and Donna's unexpected foray into performing demoralized her.

"Donna's hat's in the ring now, and she's got Em in her corner, too," Toni thought. Cognizant that Donna sought to beat her at her own game, she continued, "That performance wasn't just for Elliott. She was firing a warning shot at me."

Toni shampooed her hair and weighed the pros and cons of a war with Donna and Emma. She took the opportunity to massage the tension from the top of her head and her temples.

"That's a lot of nastiness to bring down on Elliott," Toni thought as she considered the effects of an all-out conflict. Rinsing away the shampoo, she lamented, "He's been through so much already and Em gets so crazy about it."

Daunted by the prospect, Toni turned to lesser concerns. She unscrewed the lid of the conditioner bottle, squirted some onto her left hand, reaffixed the lid and set the bottle aside.

"She'll boot Morning Cloak from the club," Toni thought while applying the conditioner, "and I can't do that to the guys. They've put up with *a lot* of my guy problems this year."

Toni bit her lip and leaned against the blue-tiled shower wall while letting the conditioner set in her hair. The moist heat of the shower wrapped around her like a plush blanket and she wallowed in it.

"There's one really big pro, though," Toni said with an amorous grin. Conjuring an image of Elliott in her mind, she permitted herself the indiscretion of a shower fantasy and stated, *"Elliott Warden."*

Toni returned to reality, moved under the shower head and scrubbed the conditioner from her hair. She rinsed her entire body a final time, turned off the shower and procured a sea blue towel that matched the bathroom's color scheme. After studying it for a moment, Toni frowned and glanced upward.

"It's a bad joke, right, like I should just throw it in," Toni said forlornly as she dried off and then wrapped the towel around herself. Leaving the bathroom, she plopped onto her bed with a bounce and folded her arms. Toni said aloud, "But I don't want to."

Father Maurice's advice percolated into Toni's consciousness. She clasped her hands in her lap.

"I didn't listen again," Toni confessed to God. Shamefully shaking her head, she added, "I didn't let You handle it."

Toni's attention fell to the telephone on her nightstand. She stared at it as if she expected it to ring.

"She wouldn't be up this late," Toni attempted to convince herself. She hesitated but, pouncing on the telephone, she whisked up the receiver and quickly dialed Joan's number. The telephone rang several times.

"Hel-lo," answered Joan.

"I didn't wake you up, did I?" Toni inquired gingerly.

"Does it sound like you woke me up?" asked Joan with her usual energy.

"I guess not," Toni conceded. She laid down on the bed and twirled the telephone cord around her left index finger.

"Shouldn't you be playing right now?" queried a puzzled Joan.

"We ended early. Long story," Toni replied. She fidgeted nervously and inquired, "Ya' know that guy you wanted to fix me up with?"

Joan squealed happily. Toni started.

"You're gonna go out with him, aren't you?!" asked an excited Joan. Toni hesitated, thought of Elliott and then shoved the image from her mind.

"Yeah," Toni answered sheepishly, "I think I am."

"He's a *great* guy," chattered Joan, "and really cute. He's been divorced for like, a few years now, and does have two kids, but he does the every other weekend thing with their mom, so it's not like you'd be raising two kids. I think they're eleven and nine."

Toni wrinkled her nose as she was not ready to be a mother. She shivered when she considered the children were the same age as Lanie and Tessa.

"You're really gonna like him," insisted Joan happily. Toni sat up on the bed as her friend declared, "I promise you that."

"I really hope so," Toni said.

King of Pain

Defying the relentless, early August rain, Elliott trudged towards Nora's gravesite. The verdant green of summer persisted but the grayness of the clouds above and the mists below nibbled on its edges. Traffic passed heedlessly on Shook Road, each car emitting a swishing noise as it sliced through the water pooling on the roadway. Elliott's red LTD starkly contrasted with the dreariness of the cemetery.

"Elliott, wait!" insisted Emma as she exited the car and struggled to open her umbrella. Shifting her gaze between Elliott and the uncooperative umbrella, she called, "*Elliott!*"

Elliott ignored her and marched forward, every step he took squishing into the lawn as he passed grave markers. Many of them were timeworn and some even crumbled under the stresses of weather and time.

"From one extreme to the other," complained Emma. She succeeded at opening the umbrella and, shielding herself from the rain, pursued her brother. She inadvertently stepped in a deep puddle and snapped, "Damn it!"

Elliott arrived at the southeast corner of the cemetery, its border marked with chain link fence. There, beneath a rectangular patch of mud strewn with small, intermittent blades of grass, lay Nora. Sinking to his knees, Elliott let the wetness of the ground soak his jeans.

"Elliott, what're you doing?!" Emma scolded him. She rushed to her brother and held the umbrella over him while trying to pull him to his feet, demanding, "Your jeans are soaked. *Get up.*"

Elliott said nothing and remained rooted to the ground. Emma finally ceded to his stubbornness and left him on his knees. She quietly read Nora's heart-shaped, gray headstone: *'In God's Care, NORA JILLIAN BILLINGSLEY, September 30, 1963 ♥ July 4, 1986, Beloved Daughter, Granddaughter and Niece'.*

"They wouldn't add fiancée," Elliott droned. Nora's family decorated the grave with fresh, vibrantly colored flowers on a weekly basis but even they drooped under the pelting precipitation.

"I know," replied Emma sympathetically despite agreeing with Nora's family. The siblings remained quiet for five minutes as Elliott simply stared at the grave. Emma's attention drifted and she sighed.

"I just don't get it, Em," Elliott suddenly said. Emma's focus returned and she watched him closely as he expounded, "God brought Toni into my life, got her to the brink of a relationship with me – something I suffered for, emotionally and physically, and then just . . . ripped her away."

Elliott paused and Emma squirmed uncomfortably. She had no answers for her brother - no way to soothe his hurts, no balm for his wounds - and she struggled for words. None were forthcoming but Elliott came to her rescue.

"And then Nora, who I should've been with from the start, shows up on my doorstep and rescues me from all the Toni bullshit, and I get a second chance," Elliott continued. He straightened his body and his spirits seemed to rise. Elliott stated confidently, "And I can account for all a' that."

"You can?" asked a surprised Emma.

"Toni hurt. Hurt a lot," Elliott said as he pondered his recent relationships. Emma made a sour face as he asserted, "But me showing up made Bobby pull his shit together, and she was happy, and Nora pulled my ass outta that fire. And that girl was the princess of all princesses, the sweetheart of all sweethearts."

Elliott, the legs of his jeans sopping wet, stood up. He gesticulated wildly as he spoke and Emma could not keep him under the umbrella.

"And things are great . . . no, they're perfect," Elliott said emphatically.

"*Hey, take it easy*," Emma protested before again giving up her efforts. He ignored his sister's rebuke.

"But, right after we decide to take the plunge – hell, when we thought we might have a kid on the way," Elliott stated as the volume of his voice rose, "He doesn't just rip her away, *He kills her*. And then she's just gone and I can't do a damn thing about it."

Elliott's energy faded and his hands fell to his sides. Emma let the rain soak him as she tried to muster her strength for her brother.

"She's just gone," Elliott repeated forlornly.

The siblings said no more and, despite standing apart, wept together. Emma moved to again shield Elliott with the umbrella and placed a hand on his shoulder which he grasped desperately. Emma closed her eyes and addressed God.

"If it's not Nora," Emma silently prayed, "and it's not Donna – and we both know it's not Toni – then you've gotta give him *someone* to get him through."

Regaining her composure, Emma wrapped an arm around Elliott's shoulders. She escorted him to the car.

"*Someone*," she begged.

· · · ·

"MOM!" SHOUTED LANIE happily as David walked into the foyer holding her upside down. Emma grinned weakly with dim, exhausted eyes.

"What're you doin' home?" asked David. He immediately noticed his wife's drawn countenance and queried, "What's wrong?"

"Everything's fine," Emma assured him with an exhale. She tossed her keys onto the table near the door and they landed with a clatter. She walked further into the house and explained, "Sean's got Johnny Dubs today and I just wanna be home right now."

"Wow, okay," replied a surprised David while setting Lanie on her feet. She ran up to her mother and, after Emma crouched to her level, hugged her.

"Where's Tess'?" Emma inquired.

"She's at Brittany's house," answered Lanie. The mention of Brittany instantly brought the pairing of her mother and Elliott to Emma's mind.

"Give it a rest for the afternoon," Emma admonished herself. She stood up with Lanie attached to her side.

"Will you watch a movie with me?" asked Lanie as she eyed her mother expectantly.

"We've watched two movies already," David interjected with a pointed look, "so why don't ya' give Mom a break?"

"I wanna watch another one," insisted Lanie. She detached from Emma and threw a playful yet solid punch into her father's stomach. Though he easily withstood it, he grimaced and groaned in feigned distress.

"We can watch a hundred movies if you want. Just let Mom get some comfy clothes on," Emma informed her daughter in a tone betraying her fatigue. She walked past Lanie, tussled her hair and then caressed David's face, saying, "And stop punching your father."

"Whaddaya want for lunch?" asked David as Lanie scurried into the living room and jumped onto the couch.

"Pizza!" bellowed Lanie.

"Pizza it is," Emma droned as she shuffled wearily down the hall towards their bedroom.

"I was asking your mom," said David as he followed a pace behind Emma. Mesmerized by the television, Lanie did not process his words.

"Pizza's fine," Emma advised David. His wife's lack of feistiness and slumped shoulders concerned him.

"Does this have to do with Elliott?" inquired David gingerly.

"Yep," Emma said bluntly. She stopped at the bedroom door, turned to him and, before disappearing through it, added, "And I *don't* wanna talk about it."

· · · ·

SITTING AT A SIMPLE square table of dark wood, Toni sipped her bottle of Bud Light and small talked with Joan's friend, Howard. Their first date unfolded at Miller's Bar in Dearborn, an establishment famous for its mouthwatering hamburgers.

"I can't believe you've never been here before," said Howard as he leaned back in his chair. The attractive, brown-haired thirtysomething insisted on being called "Howie" and proved as affable as Joan promised. His blue eyes sparkled with adoration.

"Yeah, I know," Toni responded as she scanned the main dining room. It was narrowly rectangular in shape with a long bar running down the west wall. Miller's was more brightly lit than Johnny Dubs and possessed the wooden adornments, earthy tones and a white-tiled ceiling typical of a decades-old bar. Returning her attention to Howard, she stated, "Everyone I've talked to who's been to this place loves it."

"Well, here's to your first visit," said Howard as he offered his beer bottle for a toast. Toni lifted her beer and the pair ceremoniously clinked their bottles together. Howard added with a smirk, "And to me finally getting a date with Joan's *knockout* friend."

"Oh, geez," Toni protested good-naturedly. Her face flushed with embarrassment.

"Her word, not mine," replied Howard in amusement. He appraised the beauty sitting before him and gushed, "Though she wasn't lying."

"Joanie is something else," Toni said while shaking her head. Seeking to change the subject, she quickly inquired, "So why Howie and not Howard?"

"'Cuz Howard's an old man's name and *my* old man's name," answered Howard with a chuckle. Toni realized that he wore a perpetual grin on his face and found his positive demeanor endearing. Pausing for a drink of his beer, Howard then asked, "Is Toni short for anything?"

"No, it's just Toni," Toni replied.

"I find it hard to believe it's ever just Toni," said Howard. Setting his elbows on the table and clasping his hands, he continued, "So you know I'm divorced, and have two kids, but Joan was kinda tight-lipped on your story. Been married before?"

Toni's face went white. She set down her beer before her, grasped it with both hands and stared at the bottle. Words were not forthcoming.

"I just made a huge first date blunder, didn't I?" queried Howard as he sat up. Toni offered him a pathetic, hybrid expression of sadness, of embarrassment and of discomfort.

"No, you just have the misfortune of a first date with me and my messy love life," Toni replied. Feeling unconfident and anxious, she squirmed and unloaded her feelings, saying, "I'm sorry. I wasn't sure I was ready for this, but Joan begged me to go out with you, and I-."

"Yikes, guilted into seeing me, huh?" interrupted Howard. Toni realized the import of her explanation and cringed.

"It's not like that at all. I promise," Toni said. Shifting to effusive praise to soothe Howard, she expounded, "Joan said you're a great, good-lookin' guy and she wasn't lying about that, either. Plus, I'm having a good time."

"But?" inquired Howard, the compliments insufficient to assuage his ego. Toni scrunched her face.

"The truth?" Toni queried as if the prospect of telling it pained her.

"Please," said Howard. He grasped his drink and leaned forward with interest but his smile dimmed.

"Okay then," Toni said. She sipped her beer and used the brief pause to collect her thoughts. Committing to honesty, Toni threw caution to the wind and said, "Oh, what the heck? The short answer: I left a guy at the altar in April."

"So let me guess," interjected Howard. He held up his bottle with his index finger pointing at Toni and said, "*You're* still hooked on the guy."

"You're half-right," Toni acknowledged coyly. Her response puzzled Howard and he lowered his finger and his drink.

"Meaning?" asked Howard.

"I'm still hooked on *a* guy," Toni answered. Feeling relieved to speak the truth, she said, "And, trust me, you wouldn't believe that situation."

"Quite the soap opera life ya' got there, just Toni," remarked Howard as his interest steadily grew.

"You have no idea, and the last year's been . . . *insane*," Toni said. She paused to allow the waitress to deliver their burgers and fries and viewed them with wide eyes and a suddenly growling stomach.

"These look and smell amazing," a briefly distracted Toni announced. The scent of her meal enticingly tickled her nostrils.

"Guess you probably wanna get 'em ta' go, huh?" asked Howie. His tone, however, indicated he wished to extend their date.

"Not unless you do," Toni countered. She popped a fry into her mouth.

"I think I'd like to hear about this insane life of yours," said Howard. He took his burger in two hands, lifted it to his mouth and added, "If you're okay with telling it."

"You're kidding, right?" Toni queried uncertainly. She mimicked his movements and, with them both holding up a burger, said, "I mean, that's like breaking *a lot* of first date rules."

"What the heck?" replied Howard. The couple laughed and, as they enjoyed their food and another round of beers, Toni recounted her love life beginning with Bobby and ending with her vocal battle with Donna. When she finished her account and they both pushed aside their baskets, Howard became serious and inquired pensively, "Can I ask you one last question?"

"I can't imagine what I left out," an amused Toni said, "but, sure, go ahead."

"How do you know I'm not a better guy than Elliott?" inquired Howard pointedly. Toni's eyes glazed and she set her chin in her palm.

"You very well could be, Howie," Toni conceded as she compared the buoyant Howard with the brooding Elliott. Her answered befuddled Howard until she looked to him with a determined mien and stated, "But somehow, someway, I know he's the better guy *for me*."

"I never had a chance, did I?" asked Howard as his smile disappeared for the first time that evening.

"Well, if Queen Emma gets her way . . . ," Toni began but then trailed off. Deciding her love life had been adequately dissected, she said, "Ya' know, I've talked about myself way too much tonight."

"Not at all," countered Howard with the smallest traces of a returning smile. Uncertain on which topic to settle, Toni hesitated. The thought of seriously dating a man with children made her nervous so she decided to further investigate.

"How 'bout we order coffee and you tell me about your kids?" Toni suggested.

"I'd like that," replied Howie as his grin returned in earnest.

• • • •

"JOANIE'S GONNA KILL me," Toni said aloud as she made the right turn onto her street. Rod Stewart's "Love Touch" played on the radio and added fuel to the fire of her longing for Elliott. She yawned and added, "Spillin' the beans about him on our first date like that."

Toni realized she forgot to turn on her porch light. She lightly slapped the steering wheel.

"I hafta stop doin' that," Toni scolded herself. She heard Katherine's chastisement in her head and whispered along with it, "You're just inviting someone to kidnap you, dear."

Toni's headlights washed over her front porch as she slowly pulled into her driveway. She started and slammed on the brakes when she noticed someone sitting on the stoop. Lurching forward but then collecting herself,

Toni gazed on her unexpected visitor. A man sat with his arms folded on his knees and his head buried in them.

"Oh my gosh, Elliott," Toni gasped. Coming to her senses, she straightened the car in the driveway and, shifting it into "Park" but leaving it running, threw open the door and dashed to him. Elliott slept so she shook him, begging, "Elliott, wake up. *Wake up.*"

Elliott stirred and lazily lifted his head to gaze at Toni. Appalled by his bleak, grief-weathered face, especially as viewed in the shadows cast by the streetlights, she felt her heart break for him yet again. The car's radio played in the distance.

"I don't wanna be alone tonight," begged Elliott weakly. Crouching down, Toni wrapped him in her arms.

"You're not gonna be," Toni assured him. She held Elliott for thirty seconds before the upbeat, out-of-place song playing on the car radio reminded her of the running engine. Kissing him on the top of the head, she said, "Be right back."

Scurrying to the car, Toni quickly turned it off and closed the door. She heard Katherine's voice in her head, stopped and returned to the vehicle.

"Okay, Mom," Toni said in mild annoyance as she locked the door. Hurrying back to Elliott, she assisted him to his feet. His legs nearly buckled and he wobbled but Toni held him upright with a strength she did not know she possessed. She turned Elliott towards the house and, while supporting him with one arm, opened her storm door and used her keys to unlock the main one. Toni pushed the door open and coaxed him, "C'mon, careful. I got ya.'"

Once across the threshold, Toni pocketed her keys and reached behind her to pull the main door closed and throw the deadbolt. She then escorted Elliott to her living room couch and, sliding around him, sat down and guided his head into her lap. He cried uncontrollably, the grief of Nora's loss finally overwhelming him.

"S-s-sorry," muttered Elliott pathetically amid his tears. Toni caressed his head with her left hand and hugged him with her right arm as he explained in a strengthening voice, "It hurts, Toni, it hurts so damn much. And then I go numb, and feel nothing, and then it hurts again. It's driving me crazy and I can't make it stop."

"Don't be sorry. You're *exactly* where you need to be," Toni encouraged Elliott. Choosing her words carefully and infusing them with love, she expounded, "But you can't make it stop, Elliott, and there's no way around it. You've gotta feel your way through it and that'll take time."

Elliott shuddered and his full weight fell into Toni. His weeping resumed.

"But you're not gonna do it alone," Toni steadfastly declared. She held him tightly and promised, "We'll get you to the other side. *Together*."

· · · ·

TONI TOOK A SIP OF water from the half-full glass she obtained for Elliott and then settled comfortably onto the couch. Elliott laid his head on a throw pillow on her lap and she tucked him underneath a special afghan knitted by her Great Aunt Agnes.

"If you're tired, the guest room is ready to go," Toni suggested despite not wanting to part from Elliott. The desire to simply take him to her own bed warred against her desire to avoid any sexual situations in Elliott's vulnerable state.

"I just wanna be with you," replied Elliott, "and I know being in a bed together, well, *causes problems* for you. But if *you're* tired-."

"Couch's fine," Toni interrupted Elliott good-naturedly. The pair spoke no more, cuddled into one another and let the stereo fill the room with the soft, romantic music of WNIC's Pillow Talk. Toni soon heard Elliott's breathing become deeper as he drifted into slumber and she smiled, whispering, "There ya' go."

Toni contemplated Elliott's loss, one that to her was unfathomable, and walked into the past. It was not lost on her that, mere months before, she cried in her living room with Elliott comforting her.

"I thought I lost him that night," Toni said to herself. A realization struck her and she added, "But now he's back, right here, right where we left off."

Alan Almond's famous baritone voice garnered Toni's attention as Pillow Talk exited a commercial break. She listened to his poetic words on love and desire until the legendary host introduced "Hold Me" by Whitney Houston and Teddy Pendergrass. Its tender, gentle opening massaged Toni's heart and, when the first chorus spoke of not squandering precious time, she caught her breath.

"Is this it?" Toni thought as her spine tingled and only the stereo and Elliott's breathing could be heard. A long slow exhale followed and she asked herself, "Is this where it finally happens?"

Toni's questions remained unanswered as her consciousness faded and her heavy eyelids flickered for over a minute before falling for good. Escorted into sleep by the melody of "Hold Me", she soon joined Elliott in the world of dreams.

• • • •

AN UNEXPECTED NOISE rattled Toni from her slumber and she twitched. She heard a commotion in the kitchen.

"Coffee maker," Toni sighed when she heard it sputtering to complete its cycle. Beyond her white, translucent curtains, daylight burgeoned and the birds commenced their chattering. Toni tilted her head from side-to-side to stretch her neck and said quietly, "I must've set it yesterday."

The memory of a dream vanished from Toni's mind but she remembered the previous night's events. Elliott slept soundly on her lap with the throw pillow still tucked under his head and the dampness from his tears lingering on her jeans. Lovingly running her hand over Elliott's arm, Toni studied his worn yet peaceful face and kissed his cheek.

"Probably shouldn't have done that," Toni thought. She watched Elliott and contemplated his appearance for the next thirty minutes, her desire to let him sleep outweighing her craving for coffee and need to use the bathroom. Elliott finally stirred and opened his eyes. Blinking his way out of sleep, he exhaled.

"I am so sorry," apologized Elliott, his guilt rising with his consciousness. He rolled onto his back and was greeted with Toni's glowing countenance.

"I'm not," Toni replied, her two-word response penetrating the depths of Elliott's heart. She caressed his cheek with the backs of her fingers and said, "We got you through the night, didn't we?"

"*You* got me through," Elliott lauded Toni as he sat up. His closeness to her prickled him, the proximity feeling like disloyalty to Nora, and he added ashamedly, "All I did was blubber on your lap like some dumb high school kid about the other girl. That had to've really sucked."

Sensing Elliott's discomfort, Toni scooted to the other end of the couch and placed her back against its arm. Unwilling to completely surrender him, however, she let her feet touch his leg.

"I'm just here for you, Elliott," Toni declared. Pressing her sock feet into the denim of his jeans, she implored him, "We don't have to define anything, say what we are, be anything. I'm here, whenever you need me, for as long as you need me, for whatever you need me for. Tell me whatever you want to tell me, whatever you need to tell me. Anything. *I'm just here for you.*"

"That's a lotta anythings and whatevers," quipped Elliott. Toni's mere presence improved his mood and the color gradually returned to his face.

"There's my funny guy," Toni replied. Seconds later, she regretted her choice of words and her mirth faded.

"You serve coffee in this joint?" asked Elliott to wriggle free of the moment. Toni appreciated the diversion and rose to her feet.

"After a stop at the little girls' room," Toni said with a goofy grin, "yes."

· · · ·

COMFORTABLE AND YET uncomfortable, Elliott and Toni sat on opposite ends of the couch and drank coffee. They faced one another with their legs dangerously close to touching.

"I'm glad you called off today," Toni said after a sip of coffee. Elliott did likewise as she added, "Especially because I'm off today, too."

"Eh, my boss ain't a bad guy," replied Elliott. He yawned before explaining, "He told me if I needed a day here and there, ya' know, because of Nora, it was cool."

The mention of Nora silenced them both and they sat quietly for over a minute while imbibing their morning beverages. Toni began to speak, stopped herself briefly and then proceeded.

"So, what's next, Elliott?" Toni queried with a serious mien. She swiftly added, "I don't mean romantically."

"I know," said Elliott to preempt Toni's guilt. Her presence, as always, loosened his tongue and he explained, "And, to answer your question, I have no idea. We were just focused on the wedding and-."

Elliott stopped abruptly and distracted himself with caffeine. Toni, though his words pained her, coaxed him with an honest, encouraging expression.

"Elliott, it's okay, you can tell me," Toni assured him. His expression soured.

"Well, anyway, we were just focused on the wedding, and she had just moved in after New Year's, so we didn't talk much about the future," continued Elliott. He confessed with a heavy heart, "Except we thought she might be pregnant."

Toni tensed as her heart and jaw dropped like stones. Elliott waved off her shock.

"She wasn't," stated Elliott in relief.

"Oh, thank God," Toni gushed as her tension escaped like air from a balloon. She pulled her legs closer and grasped her mug in both hands.

"I don't know if you'd call that a silver lining, but, well, ya' know," said a nauseated Elliott. He set his coffee on the end table. Before Toni could comfort him, a knock at the door interrupted their conversation. She looked at it in puzzlement.

"Who could that be?" Toni asked aloud. Elliott shrugged.

"Katherine, maybe?" posited Elliott.

"Maybe," replied Toni. She placed her coffee on the end table, stood up and walked past Elliott. Looking through the peephole, Toni identified her unexpected visitor, spun around and pressed her back against the door. She scrunched her face and whimpered, "Oh, boy."

"Who is it?" inquired Elliott.

"Uuhhhhh, well," Toni said. There was a second round of knocking and a man's voice called her name. Elliott immediately knew it was not Bobby.

"*Oh*," said Elliott as realization smacked him in the face. He rotated into a sitting position, placed his feet on the carpet and picked up his coffee with one hand, urging, "You should probably answer the door."

Toni hesitated and gave Elliott an apologetic look. She slowly turned around and opened the door. Standing in between it and the open storm door was a suit-clad Howard; he held a bouquet of vibrantly colored gladiolus flowers of pink, red, purple and yellow.

"Good morning, just Toni," said an effervescent Howard as he presented his gift to Toni. He examined the flowers and rearranged them, explicating, "I didn't know what your favorite flower was, so I just kinda guessed, but I thought these were pretty enough for a pretty lady like you."

Caught between Elliott and Howard, Toni froze. Elliott, meanwhile, drifted into a mood of amused defeat. He chortled.

"Ya' gotta be kiddin' me," thought Elliott. Howard peeked into the house and noticed Elliott. His smile dimmed but did not disappear.

"Ahhh, you must be Elliott," said Howard knowingly. Elliott offered him a nod and a wave. Shoving his off hand into his pants pocket, Howard raised his eyebrows and said, "Guess I shoulda' called first."

An awkward moment followed. Determined to break the stalemate, Toni took a step back.

"Look, guys, none of this is what it looks like," Toni pleaded as her gaze swiveled between them. She shrugged and gestured, asking, "Can you both just believe that, for me?"

Howard and Elliott looked to one another, each man appraising the competition. They, as if by silent agreement, returned their attentions to Toni and nodded in assent.

"Here, these are for you," said Howard as he moved the flowers closer to Toni. She graciously accepted them.

"They're really beautiful. Thank you *so much*, Howie," Toni gushed.

"Howie?" mouthed Elliott dubiously. He took a drink of his coffee.

"I'll catch ya' later," said Howard. Much to Elliott's chagrin, Toni approached Howard, held the flowers aside and gave him a quick half-hug.

"Bye," said Toni feebly. She closed the door but could not bring herself to turn towards Elliott.

"You don't owe me anything, Toni," Elliott advised. She rotated to face him as he added, "I don't have any claim on you."

"We only went on one date, because Joanie begged me to," Toni insisted emphatically, "and I actually told him you're the man for me. *Whoops*."

The unintentional admission astonished Toni and she grabbed the lower half of her face. Elliott looked at her blankly and then guffawed.

"This is too much," said a weary Elliott. His laughter faded away.

"*You're* too much," Toni replied with a smirk. She took several steps toward him, folded her arms and inquired in exasperation, "Whadda we do now, Elliott?"

"That's easy. *I'm* gonna drink more coffee and *you're* gonna make us breakfast," answered Elliott matter-of-factly. His sudden shift to an innocuous topic released the pressure they both felt.

"Good answer," Toni said with a laugh.

Coming Around Again

The sound of the doorbell wrested Elliott from sleep. He sat up in bed like a vampire rising from its coffin with his eyes closed and his head heavy. The doorbell rang again.

"What the hell?" asked Elliott aloud. Woozy and discombobulated, he opened his eyes and threw his feet onto the floor. The doorbell rang a third time and he yelled, "Hold on!"

Rising from his bed but still tangled in the sheet, Elliott nearly toppled to the floor. He gradually regained his wits and his balance as he zombie-walked to the stairwell, wobbled down the steps and approached the front door. Elliott peered through the peephole and saw two police officers standing on his porch. He recoiled before recognition seeped into his brain.

"Wait, that's Em's friend. Uh, what's his name?" muttered Elliott. He sorted through related words and rambled, "Uh, soil, mud, dirt, clay...*Clay*."

Elliott's adrenaline surged when Officer Clay Clifford said his name in a deep, rumbling voice. He opened the door and admitted a rush of muggy air into his apartment, the humidity contrasting starkly with the air-conditioned chilliness at his back. Elliott suddenly panicked.

"Oh, shit. What now?" said Elliott with a flashback to Emma's visit on the morning of Nora's death. He desperately asked, "Emma? The girls? Dave?"

"No, no. As far as I know, they're all fine," Clay assured him with a raised palm. Elliott exhaled in relief and ran his hand through his messy hair.

"You're a friend of Em and Dave's, though, right?" inquired Elliott. Clay gripped his gun belt with both of his massive hands.

"Yeah, that's right," Clay answered. A commotion arose in the next parking lot and, losing interest in the visit, his young partner moved to the hedge as Clay said, "We've met a few times. Saw ya' get decked at Em's surprise birthday party last year."

"Oh, yeah. Good times," quipped Elliott with a quirky grin. He briefly and reflexively squeezed his nose before motioning to the kitchen and asking, "You guys want some coffee or somethin'?"

"Nah, thanks," Clay replied while his partner closely watched the nighttime revelers. Shifting his weight to the opposite foot, Clay said ominously, "I do have some bad news, though."

Elliott's thoughts instantly jumped to Toni. His fear proved unfounded.

"Macayla Barnes died tonight," Clay advised. The news took a few seconds to sink into Elliott's mind.

"Wow, that sucks," said Elliott with a sad expression. Feeling no real sense of loss, he continued, "But why're tellin' me? I mean, it's terrible and all, but she and I haven't been together for a while now."

"You were at least once," said the other officer in a raised voice. Clay shot him an annoyed look.

"What?" asked Elliott. The young officer's blithe attitude irked him.

"So you really didn't know," Clay said in mild surprise.

"Know *what*, Clay?" demanded Elliott. His weariness feeding his irritation, he gestured with an open hand and queried sharply, "What the hell are you talking about?"

"I don't know how else to say this, so I'll just give it to you straight," Clay said. He paused, collected his thoughts and explained grimly, "Macayla was pregnant, Elliott. She had the baby two weeks ago, but the birth was rough on her and, well, she didn't make it. Thankfully, the baby's alive and, before Macayla passed . . . she identified you as the father."

Elliott stepped onto the porch but stumbled in the attempt. Clay caught him and held him upright until he reestablished his footing. Elliott's reaction caused the young officer to reengage with the conversation.

"They were at Children's in Detroit," the young officer said.

"Ya' know, because the baby was premature and all," Clay expounded. He pointed to the northeast and said, "A friend of mine on Detroit PD called me and asked if I'd let ya' know."

Elliott drifted into a dream-like trance. Clay gave him a minute to process the information, much to the chagrin of his impatient partner, and then grasped Elliott's arm.

"The hospital wants you to come down there, tonight," said Clay while shaking Elliott back into the moment.

"Yeah, that's probably a good idea," Elliott said as he patted Clay's hand. He then removed it from his arm.

"Think you should call Em," suggested Clay while appraising Elliott's mental state, "maybe have her drive you down there?"

Feeling centered in a way he never had before, Elliott shook his head in the negative. The officers sensed the change.

"Nope," Elliott said matter-of-factly, "this one's mine."

• • • •

ELLIOTT BECAME A NEW man the second he saw his child. The sight of his tiny daughter rendered him inert; the sight of her in an incubator tore his heart. Wires were attached to her skin with clear tape, a small diaper seemed vastly oversized on her minute body and the stub of a black, shriveled umbilical cord stubbornly clung to her navel. Her starkest feature, however, was the nose that belonged to her mother.

"Oh, man," Elliott groaned. After the initial shock, however, he moved closer to the incubator and read his child's nametag, "Lillian Warden." He chuckled and said, "She remembered."

Elliott's quiet chortle abruptly became a joyous laugh. Elliott's mirth caused Dr. Zhou, an attractive Asian woman in her fifties, to start while baby Lilian squirmed in response.

"Take it easy there, little one," Elliott said. Seemingly obeying her father, she yawned and then settled back into sleep. Elliott turned to the doctor and inquired with a hidden anxiousness, "What kinda odds we lookin' at, Doc?"

"She'll be just fine," advised Dr. Zhou happily. The wisdom on her face and in her eyes calmed Elliott as she stated, "Ms. Lillian's a little fighter. She's made great strides and she'll be ready to go home later today or tomorrow."

Elliott exhaled dramatically as he contemplated leaving the hospital with a newborn. Overwhelmed by the thought, he distracted himself with the dry erase board reporting Lillian's weight and length: "Wt. 5 lbs 6 oz. L 19 in."

"Still under six pounds, huh?" Elliott said with a wry smile and watery eyes. He told his daughter, "We're gonna hafta put some meat on those bones, kid."

Elliott gripped Dr. Zhou's arm and turned them both away from Lillian as if the infant would understand his words. The doctor, knowing the question on his tongue, permitted the contact.

"How'd Macayla die?" Elliott inquired bluntly. Dr. Zhou offered him a grave expression and measured her response. Closing his eyes, exhaling to again calm himself, and then reopening them, Elliott said bluntly, "I know about the coke."

"She was, in fact, using during her pregnancy," began Dr. Zhou. Elliott grabbed his face in exasperation.

"*Damn it, Cay*," Elliott muttered. Dr. Zhou moved him further away from the incubator.

"Most likely, that's what caused the premature birth," continued Dr. Zhou softly. She released Elliott's arm, placed her hands in the front pockets of her lab coat and explained, "It *is* what caused her death. She had a heart attack shortly after the delivery, and her condition declined from there. The damage to her heart, combined with the strain of labor . . . it was just too much for her body, and today, it gave out."

Elliott felt sick and his face went pale. Dr. Zhou gave him a moment before speaking.

"Fortunately, she told us about you before she passed," Dr. Zhou said. She added hopefully, "Ms. Barnes wanted her to be with her father, Mr. Warden."

Elliott clenched his teeth and contorted his face to ward against angry tears. The attempt was successful and he nodded over his shoulder at Lillian.

"How much damage did Cay do?" Elliott asked with rising ire. He gestured with both hands and queried, "I mean, is the kid addicted to coke now, too?"

"No," answered Dr. Zhou matter-of-factly. Both doctor and father turned back to the child as she expounded, "From what I can tell, Ms. Barnes at least attempted to stop using as she neared term and that, combined with Lillian being exposed for a lesser amount of time, likely kept her from becoming addicted. Additionally, in the case of stimulants like cocaine, babies more often suffer from the direct effects of the drug and not withdrawal. Your daughter is simply not showing any withdrawal symptoms."

Elliott pondered the information provided by Dr. Zhou. The future gradually came into focus.

"Well, Doctor, thanks for saving my munchkin," Elliott stated with a glance at Lillian. Returning his attention to Dr. Zhou, he stated flatly, "I wanna see Macayla."

"I'm afraid that's not possible because-," began the doctor. She stopped speaking when Elliott glanced at her with an intensity in his eyes surpassing even Emma's determined gaze.

"Look, some day that kid's gonna ask me about her mother, and I'm gonna tell her the wonderful story of how I said goodbye for her and promised to take care of her for the rest of whatever," Elliott declared. Dr. Zhou considered the request. She finally acquiesced with an affirmative nod.

"I'll see if we can make an exception," replied Dr. Zhou.

• • • •

CHILDREN'S HOSPITAL'S morgue possessed the grim ambiance one would expect of a chamber that temporarily housed the dead yet neither the presence of the deceased nor the chilly, antiseptic environment bothered Elliott. Lillian's birth and Macayla's death dominated his present and nothing short of Macayla returning to life would distract him from the matter at hand.

"I thought we said our goodbyes in your bedroom eight months ago," Elliott said flippantly. He sat on a high stool next to the gurney on which Macayla's ashen corpse lay with his feet on its crossbars, his forearms on his knees and his hands clasped before him. Speaking as if she would answer, he queried with a troubled countenance, "Why didn't you tell me?"

A scrub-clad morgue attendant entered the room wheeling another unlucky patient on a gurney, dutifully rolled it into position on the far side of the room and swiftly departed. Elliott waited for him to complete his task.

"I mean, that woulda' changed a lot, Cay, at least I think it woulda'," Elliott said when the doors swung closed. He straightened his body and folded his arms, continuing, "Maybe I coulda' helped ya' out, kept this from happening. I don't know if you and I, well, ya' know, woulda' been together, but, hey, for the sake of the kid . . . of *Lillian* . . . ."

Elliott smiled at Macayla. His eyes watered.

"I can't believe you named her after my mom," Elliott said. He stared at the floor, conjured memories of his beloved mother and explained, "I mean you never even met her. If you had, she'd've taken you under her wing, though. Shielded you from Em, helped you figure out bein' a mom. That's just who she was. I wish she was here to help *me* figure it out, now that I gottta be a mom and a dad."

Elliott became quiet and contemplated that he and Lillian both lost their mothers unexpectedly, tragically and far too early in their lives. He wriggled free of the unpleasant thought and sighed.

"I guess what I'm saying is," Elliott said with burgeoning gratitude, "*thanks.*"

Dr. Zhou's face appeared through one of the windows embedded in the doors. Elliott took the hint and responded with a raised index finger.

"I ain't got much time – we're kinda breakin' the rules here – but . . . ," Elliott said before trailing off and squirming uncomfortably. He struggled with his sorrow for thirty seconds before stating, "I wanna say goodbye, not really for me, but for Lil."

Elliott paused. The nicknaming of his daughter warmed his heart. The moment passed.

"I want her to know I did this because, someday, I'll tell her about you," Elliott told Macayla. He forced himself to touch her cold, lifeless arm and said, "While she's young, just the good stuff, but, when she gets older, I'm gonna tell her everything."

Elliott frowned. He squeezed Macayla's arm and then released it.

"I don't know, I guess I feel like it's the right thing to do," Elliott muttered. Rising to his feet, he stifled his sadness, steeled his will and announced, "But I'll tell you this. I've got her, Cay. I promise you that. *I've got her.*"

Elliott could say no more. Without looking at Macayla again, he walked purposefully to the morgue's entry doors, paused before them and then left the mother of his child behind forever.

· · · ·

"HERE WE ARE," SAID Dr. Zhou in a kindly tone as she and Emma arrived at the entrance to Lillian's room.

"Thanks," Emma replied uncertainly. She added under her breath, "I think."

Utilizing the emerging concept of "kangaroo care", Elliott held Lillian underneath his t-shirt so father and daughter could bond with skin-to-skin contact. He stood with his back to Emma, however, so his sibling could not see what he held in his arms. Dr. Zhou disappeared.

"Elliott, that's a baby you're holding, isn't it?" Emma inquired with nervous irritation.

"There's been a really big change in my life, Emma Renee," said Elliott while using her full first and middle names just as their mother once did.

"Whose baby is that?" Emma demanded. She reviewed Elliott's paramours and timelines in her head but could not determine the child's parentage.

"Not so loud," Elliott scolded his sister as he turned to face her. Emma covered her mouth to stifle a gasp when her eyes fell upon a sleeping Lillian and then went cold and pale. She stared at the child before letting her hand slowly slide from her chin.

"Whose baby is that?" Emma repeated sternly yet quietly. Given Elliott's loving attention to Lillian she suspected she knew, at least for one parent. Emma trembled.

"They're doin' a test to be sure, but I already know . . . *she's mine*, Em," answered Elliott proudly. Utter shock overcame Emma and she stood dumbfounded. When she failed to move, Elliott asked, "Wanna meet your niece, Lillian?"

"*How?*" Emma queried in astonishment. She felt very much as if she lingered in a dream.

"You've got two of 'em, you should know," quipped Elliott. Snapping out of her stupor, she wound up to smack Elliott's shoulder but then froze. The baby stirred.

"Oh my god," Emma cooed as her heart melted for her niece and her arm fell. Her eyes flashed to Elliott, her mien became serious and she asked sardonically, "So daddy, who's mommy?"

"Macayla," admitted a stoic Elliott.

"*Elliott*," Emma whined pejoratively with slumping shoulders.

"Don't worry, Em, she won't be coming to any Easter dinners," said Elliott flintily. His grimness became sadness as he uttered, "She's gone."

Emma offered Elliott a befuddled expression. He patiently waited for her to take his meaning.

"*No*," Emma lamented in disbelief. She gazed on the baby in pity. Deeming the moment inappropriate to further address Lillian's motherless future, Emma said with a muted grin, "Your nieces are gonna *freak* when they see her."

The siblings shared a quiet laugh, each one regulating their volume to avoid disturbing young Lillian. Their mirth evaporated and they went silent for over a minute as they both pondered the little one.

"Whadda I do with this, Em?" asked Elliott pensively. He began carefully pacing, and, feeling overwhelmed, said, "I mean, I can figure out the basics. Feed her, clothe her, change diapers, take care of her . . . but this changes *everything*. Everything I've come to believe about what I do with the next fortysomething years of my life. All of it."

A half-smile slowly came to Emma's face as she appraised the change in Elliott. He stopped in front of her.

"I know, I've done it twice, remember," Emma replied knowingly. Pride welled within her, and, indulging in Elliott's affectionate care of his child, she assured him, "And I think you'll be okay."

"She doesn't have a mother," said Elliott forlornly. Emma moved to her brother and took him by the arm.

"Maybe," Emma said as they watched Lilian sleeping, "but she has you. And me, and Dave, and the girls. *She has a family*."

Emma chuckled.

"And you watch," Emma added, "Rose and Tom'll attach to that kid like a third grandchild."

Elliott's eyes glazed as he wondered if the extended family could adequately compensate for Macayla's absence. Emma caressed Lillian's tiny head with a gentle finger.

"We'll all be a loving family," Emma announced with the utmost confidence, "and we'll all be okay."

"All the shit I've been through," Elliott said with a shiver, "it finally makes sense. Terrified as I am, I know. I know it's finally all worth it."

"I always knew you needed a her," Emma mused. She gazed on the baby lovingly and added, "But I never thought it'd be *a her*."

. . . .

"I *hate* leaving her," Elliott stated with angst, "but she gets overstimulated really easy, and I gotta be careful with that."

Elliott and Emma sat at an out-of-the-way table in the hospital's cafeteria and had breakfast together. It was sporadically populated, even for a Monday morning, and only the sounds of the busy kitchen workers filled the air.

"You'll need to come stay with us for a while," Emma stated as if the matter were settled. She took a bite of her toast and sipped her coffee.

"I don't think so, Em," Elliott declined. His meal consumed and his mug empty, he sat with his elbows on the table, his hands clasped together and the lower half of his face resting against them.

"You're gonna need all the help you can get, *single dad*, and it'll be easier if you two're with us," Emma explained as she pondered the matter. Her mind roiled with plans and she said, "I'm sure Rose'll watch her when one of us isn't around. And probably put her in a new outfit every day."

"Don't worry, I'll be leaning on the Hastings clan *a lot*," said Elliott. He fixed his eyes on his sister and expounded, "But the munchkin and I are gonna have our own place, our own home. I'm gonna take a leave from work and get us settled. And make damn sure she's good and strong before I go back."

"You can't raise her in an apartment, Elliott," Emma objected. She mimicked his posture, gazed over her hands and inquired sharply, "And how're you gonna support you and my niece without working?"

"The life of a bachelor has its advantages," replied Elliott with a smirk, his sister's ignorance of his financial status amusing him. He placed his hands on top of hers, the move causing her to withdraw them beneath the table and sit back. Laughing at Emma's fieriness and ignoring her glare, Elliott reassured her, "Relax. Between what Mom and Dad left us, and what I've saved up, I got a nice nest egg for Lillian, Jr."

"Don't call her that," Emma snapped, her face expressing her dissatisfaction with Elliott's plan. She sensed something different from his usual stubbornness, however; a resoluteness was taking root in him.

"What I'm saying, dear sister," Elliott stated, "is I've had all morning to think about that part of it and I got it figured out."

"How're mommy's vices gonna affect her?" Emma inquired with distaste. She decided to table Elliott's living arrangements.

"Doc says she's okay, other than all the stuff that comes with being born a month-and-a-half early," answered Elliott. His face glowed as he said, "Lil's doin' great, though, and the nurses all say she's a trooper. Dr. Zhou's cleared her to go home today."

"That's the Warden in her," Emma declared proudly.

"Yeah, I guess so," replied Elliott. The siblings took a moment to fondly remember their parents though, by the end of Elliott's reminiscing, Emma was scheming.

"Ya' know, Donna was such a big help for you after Nor- . . . this last month, and I think you'll be able to lean on her, too," Emma suggested. Her designs included her best friend's status as a homeowner.

"I know who I can lean on, Em," responded Elliott cryptically. Intentionally interrupting Emma's plotting, he stood up with his cafeteria tray in hand and said cheerfully, "C'mon. I wanna get back to my kid."

. . . .

ELLIOTT CRADLED A CRYING Lillian and gently bounced her in an attempt to soothe her. His first week with his newborn was both rewarding and exhausting and he spent it bonding with his daughter but isolated from the outside world.

Heeding Dr. Zhou's advice, he restricted visitors; only Emma entered his apartment and only David, his nieces and his well-meaning but nosy neighbor, Mrs. Franklin, were permitted short visits through the glass storm door. Elliott effusively praised his sister during each visit as her role as provisioner of supplies for the baby and respite care for Elliott proved to be his saving grace.

"You're just gonna owe me forever," Emma joked each time though she craved time with Lillian. She also considered it her duty to care for Elliott and his child in the absence of a wife and mother.

"Oh, what's the matter, Lil?" asked Elliott as he paced in the living room. A light knock at the door caused him to stop and say, "That must be Auntie Em."

Elliott paused. Lillian's crying continued.

"Insert *Wizard of Oz* line here," Elliott quipped, his brain being too tired to conjure one. Weary and prickled by Lillian's crankiness, he peeked through the peephole of his front door. Donna awaited him, her unannounced arrival prompting him to tell his daughter, "I may've mentioned this before but, sometimes, Auntie Em acts like the Wicked Witch."

Elliott opened the main door. Donna beamed at him through the glass.

"Oh my goodness!" gushed Donna. She adored Lillian and declared, "She's absolutely precious, Elliott!"

"Bad timing, Donna, I'm really up to my ass right now," Elliott pleaded. Intrigued by a new voice, Lillian's protests settled into mere fussiness.

"Look at that," said Donna about her effect on the infant. She yanked on the locked storm door handle and insisted excitedly, "Let me in."

Elliott turned his body perpendicular to the door, unlocked it and then quickly sidestepped away. Donna burst into the apartment while closing the main door behind her and then advancing. Elliott turned and shielded the infant from her reach.

"Ya' gotta wash your hands first," Elliott stated firmly.

"Oh, yeah, sorry. I'm totally healthy, promise," replied Donna apologetically as she circumvented Elliott and scurried into the kitchen. She quickly washed and dried her hands, blubbering in a soft tone, "This is just so incredible, Elliott. You're a daddy!"

"You do some meth before you came over?" Elliott inquired. He intentionally avoided the words "cocaine" and "coke".

"I'm on Elliott and Lillian duty for a while," advised Donna matter-of-factly. She returned to the living room and continued, "Em's gotta get back to the club full time so I took some time off to help out my Wardens."

Elliott cringed when Donna spoke the words "my Wardens" and the look she gave conveyed an intention to stay indefinitely. She again reached for Lillian who now dozed on Elliott's shoulder.

"So gimme," ordered Donna playfully, the demand prompting Elliott to reluctantly and cautiously hand over Lillian. Deftly swaddling the child against her body, Donna commenced a slow, swaying walk around the first floor of the apartment. She passed Elliott at the beginning of her second circuit and said sympathetically, "You look so burnt."

"Eh, I'm fine," Elliott deflected. He kept his attention on Lillian, the presence of his child in another person's arms making him anxious. He blinked the entire time and yawned twice, however, and sleep deprivation blunted his concern.

"I can handle her for a few hours, super dad," jabbed Donna, "so go get a little shuteye."

"Wake me up in an hour," Elliott instructed her sternly with a pointed finger. She reached him for a third time on her route and stopped.

"I promise," Donna said. Elliott kissed Lillian on the forehead.

"See ya' in a few, sweetheart," Elliott said in a weak voice.

"Lookin' forward to it," said Donna as if Elliott was speaking to her. He gave her a dubious look.

"One hour," Elliott demanded on his way to the stairs. Donna used Lillian's tiny arm to wave at her father.

"Nightie-night, Daddy," said Donna in baby-talk.

• • • •

ONE HOUR MELTED INTO four before Elliott awoke. His first thought was of Lillian's whereabouts and, with his daughter absent from her crib, he panicked.

"Relax," Elliott said to himself as his mind reacclimated to consciousness. Recovering from his initial anxiety, he sighed and added, "Donna's got her."

Elliott descended the stairs in his apartment thousands of times but was not prepared for what awaited him that night. Donna, herself nestled in Elliott's recliner, cradled Lillian in her arms and fed her a bottle.

"You were supposed to wake me up," Elliott scolded Donna gently. He walked to the chair.

"You needed the sleep," replied an undaunted Donna. Elliott knelt before her and lovingly caressed his child's head.

"How's she doing?" Elliott inquired with the usual discomfort he experienced whenever Lillian was in someone else's care.

"We're both fine, thank you," said Donna with mock offense. She extended her leg in a pretend kick at Elliott and continued with only an occasional glance, "She slept as soundly as you did then decided she was hungry. Don't worry, Em drilled the feeding *procedures* into my head. Oh, and there a was diaper change in there, too."

Donna kept her focus on the task at hand as Elliott studied her. She seemed a natural in her care of Lillian from her perfect swaddling to the way she adjusted the angle of the bottle. The trio maintained their positions until Lillian finished her meal.

"I'll burp her," Elliott said. He threw a cloth diaper over his shoulder and eagerly took Lillian. Laying her head on his shoulder, he held her closely and gently tapped her back. Donna leaned into the recliner, set her arms on its armrests and tilted her head.

"You're gonna be such a good dad," said Donna with a starry-eyed grin.

"As good as I can be," Elliott replied as he kissed Lillian. She emitted a little burp, its cuteness bringing smiles to their lips. Elliott encouraged her, "There ya' go, Lil."

"She was supposed to be *ours*, Elliott," said Donna sadly. Elliott pretended to miss the assertion as he discarded the cloth diaper and readjusted Lillian's baby blanket. Donna's eyes followed him around the room and, when he descended onto the couch, she stated, "I know you heard me."

Facing Donna, Elliott leaned against the far arm of the couch with Lillian cuddled against his chest. He stretched out his legs across its cushions and looked at his ex-girlfriend.

"Donna, she wasn't supposed to *be*," Elliott asserted. Deciding against a more detailed explanation, he stated simply, "This was *not* planned."

"She still could be ours," floated Donna with a serious yet hopeful countenance. An adorable yawn from Lillian softened Elliott's heart and, as much as he still mourned for Nora, he knew he desperately desired a family for Lillian.

"All right, Donna," Elliott relented, "let's hear whatever you and Em cooked up."

Content with Elliott's acquiescence, Donna rose from the recliner and sat on the floor next to him. She took his left hand and massaged it affectionately.

"I've loved you for a long time, Elliott," said Donna with watery eyes, "and Lillian for the short time I've known her. If we got married this year . . . "

A tingle hurtled down Elliott's spine. His shiver caused Lillian to stir.

" . . . we'd immediately be a two-income couple," continued Donna with increasing confidence, "with a house in a good neighborhood full of kids. We'd be within ten minutes of Em's house."

"C'mon, Donna," objected Elliott.

"You can't tell me that doesn't sound good," countered Donna emphatically. When Elliott averted his eyes and failed to respond, she resumed her argument by saying, "With Macayla gone, Lillian's lost a whole side of her family. But with me as her mother, she'll get that back. Mark and Crystal'll be a great uncle and aunt and, my parents, well, let's just say Tom and Rose'll make up for whatever they lack."

"You as her mother?" Elliott inquired doubtfully. He resented Donna's aggressiveness but could not gainsay the benefits of her proposal.

"This little angel needs a mother, Elliott," reasoned Donna passionately, "and I'm willing to, no, *I want to* be that for her."

"This is a lot to swallow, Donna," Elliott replied.

"*I'll adopt her*," declared Donna while squeezing Elliott's hand. Unleashing carefully crafted arguments, she maintained her grip and explained, "And with us married, we'll all have the same name, and maybe we can think about a brother or sister sooner rather than later. The only thing she'll be missing is a biological relationship with me, which she won't even suspect for years. And by the time she does, she'll feel *I'm* really her mom."

"I want her to know who her mother is," interjected Elliott. Telling Lillian the truth about her mother was his plan from minute one and he had no intention of abandoning it.

"So do I, and of course we'll tell her," agreed Donna without pause, "when she's ready. And she'll also need to know about her grandparents, about your mom and dad. And – this is really awesome for her – *I knew them.* They were like a second set of parents to me, Elliott, and I'll be able to tell her all about them."

Donna's line of reasoning dumbfounded Elliott. There was no denying that, after he and Emma, Donna knew John and Lillian Warden best and that Lillian would benefit from her wealth of knowledge.

"Elliott, I know you don't love me," said Donna bluntly with a dimming demeanor. Her hopefulness swiftly returned, however, and she reasoned, "But I know, at the very least, you care a lot about me, and you'll come to love me like you once did."

The gravity of the moment froze Elliott. Donna's path was laid before him like a lit runway.

"I know all about Em and Dave, and their story can be ours, too," Donna said as her final salvo.

The gears of Elliott's mind spun at blinding speed. He knew Emma was the primary architect of Donna's case but struggled to defy its logic.

"Whaddaya say, Elliott?" asked Donna as she rose to her feet. Planting a kiss on Lillian's head and then Elliott's lips, she said alluringly, "A fresh start for you and I and a ready-made family for Lillian."

"Sound too good to be true," Elliott said.

Toni burst into Elliott's apartment the second he unlocked the door. She drove him backward several steps and shook a finger in his face.

"You're in trouble, Mister," Toni admonished Elliott. She appraised his condition and caressed his cheek, saying with pity, "You look exhausted What's wrong?"

"Trust me, I am," agreed Elliott with a weak grin, "but everything's okay. *Better* than okay."

"I've been tryin' to get a hold of you for a week," Toni said loudly. She scolded Elliott, "You're lucky I had a busy stretch at work or I'd've been here sooner."

"Not so loud," urged Elliott while gesturing for her to bring down her volume. He grasped her shoulders and explained, "Let's just say it's been a little crazy around here. I was gonna call you, I swear it."

Toni noticed a t-shirt of Donna's that she had used to swaddle Lillian lying on the couch. Her heart sank like a stone and she broke free of Elliott's grasp.

"A little crazy, huh?" asked Toni. She felt foolish and her face warmed. Toni asked accusatorily, "That's not your t-shirt, is it?"

"No, it's not," Elliott replied guiltily. Overwhelmed by the thought of losing Elliott to another woman, Toni looked at the door and took a hesitant step towards it. Elliott read her mind and stepped into her path, saying, "Just hold up a minute."

"I shouldn't even ask this, but is it Donna," inquired Toni with a pained expression, "or someone else?"

"Someone else," Elliott said while battling a smirk, the admission shocking Toni. He freed his smile and suggested, "Wanna meet her?"

"She's here!?" exclaimed a mortified Toni. She teetered on the verge of tears.

"Shhhhh," Elliott rebuked her gently with a finger held to his lips. He again took Toni by the shoulders and guided her towards the couch, saying, "I'll go get her, but you have to promise not to leave."

"Gee, Elliott, I dunno," waffled Toni while refusing to look at him. He lifted her chin with a finger.

"Please, for me," Elliott pleaded. The earnestness of Elliott's request melted her resistance and the last traces of it were brushed aside when he added, "Oh, and you gotta wash your hands."

"Alright," pouted a bamboozled Toni as she slung her purse onto the couch. Elliott, certain that she would keep her word, bounded up the steps. Moving to the kitchen, Toni washed her hands in the sink. She asked herself in embarrassed annoyance, "Wait, why am I washing my hands? And why am I putting myself through this?"

"What're you doing awake, little one?" Elliott asked as he took Lillian in his arms. Toni heard his question through a vent as she lathered her hands. She scrunched her face.

"That's a weird thing to say to your girlfriend," Toni muttered, the word "girlfriend" tweaking her ego. She wanted to flee Elliott's apartment but, true to her promise, she finished washing her hands. Toni heard only one person descending the stairs and said aloud, "What, is he carrying her?"

"Actually, I am," Elliott responded as he appeared on the landing. Toni turned her attention to him and then gasped when she saw the tiny bundle in his arms.

"*That's* the someone else?" asked an astonished Toni. Rooted in place by the weight of the moment, she queried clumsily, "Is it yours?"

"Yes on both accounts," Elliott said with a shake of his head. He shifted Lillian to his opposite shoulder and approached Toni. She met him halfway and Elliott said, "Toni, meet my daughter, Lillian."

The baby cooed, the sound shattering the tension between Elliott and Toni. She smiled gently.

"After your mom," said Toni. A single desire arose in her heart and she asked, "Can I hold her?"

"Really?" Elliott queried. Lillian began to whine.

"Well, yeah," insisted Toni. Lillian began fussing more emphatically.

"Somebody's ready to eat," stated Elliott as he carefully passed Lillian to Toni. He entered the kitchen and asked, "Wanna feed her?"

"Can't keep that widdle hungwy bellwy waiting," a beaming Toni said in baby talk. Focused on the baby, she missed the look on Elliott's face as he watched them with an admiring yet serious mien.

"That's the most beautiful thing I've ever seen," thought Elliott.

• • • •

TONI SAT IN ELLIOTT'S recliner and fed Lillian. From his vantage point on the couch, he carefully watched every move she made and sensed her discomfort despite her attempt to hide it.

"She makes you uncomfortable, doesn't she?" Elliott asked shrewdly.

"*No*," objected Toni. She flipped her eyes to him and then back to Lillian, confessing, "Well, maybe a little. She's just so, so . . . *tiny*, and fragile. I feel like one false move and I'll break her. Lanie and Tessa are a lot easier."

Toni again noticed Donna's t-shirt on the couch. Elliott mentally scolded himself for failing to dispose of it.

"Donna's been helping out with her, hasn't she?' queried Toni while struggling to speak with an even tone. Elliott grabbed the shirt and tossed it out of view.

"Super sister got us through the first week," Elliott explained, "but she had ta' go back to the club so she recruited Donna for this week. I gotta admit, she's been a huge help."

"Em's somethin' else," replied Toni. She offered Elliott and unconfident expression and said, "And I bet Donna wasn't nervous like I am."

"You're doin' just fine," Elliott said with a reassuring grin. He and Toni sat quietly as Lillian finished her bottle, neither one wanting to proceed past the moment for fear of what lay beyond it. After Lillian was burped and tucked into his arms, Elliott took up the same position on the couch as when he spoke with Donna about their future. Toni pulled her legs into the chair and sat with them folded beneath her.

"Donna wants Lil' and I to move in with her right away, and us to get married soon after that," Elliott stated bluntly. Hoping the information would goad Toni to commit to a position, he continued, "She and Em think they've got the whole thing figured out. Dee even said she'd adopt Lil'."

Toni stifled a grimace, her sorrow over the revelation throttling her. She bit the inside of her cheek and composed herself.

"That'd be really great for Lillian," commented Toni. Refusing to look at Elliott, she conceded, "And it wouldn't be terrible for you, either."

"Maybe," Elliott replied while meticulously studying Toni. Wishing to broach the subject of her relationship with Lillian, he said, "But whether she adopts Lil' or not, Donna's a mom the second we get married. Hell, the second we move in with her."

Toni looked to Elliott. She knew where the conversation was leading but, like Elliott, utilized an oblique approach.

"Anyone I want to marry would have to go through six months of marriage counseling with me and my priest *before* the wedding," stated Toni in a veiled warning. She changed positions by resting her back against one of the recliner's arms and throwing her legs over the other one. Toni added, "And cohabitation's a no-no in the Catholic Church and, well, so are *other things*."

"Yeah, I've heard," Elliott uttered. He nodded to the infant sleeping on his chest and said, "Good thing I'm not a Catholic or I'd be in alotta trouble."

Toni failed to restrain an unhappy face. The story of Lillian's conception had been a bitter pill to swallow.

"Catholics get married in their church," Toni explicated, "during a Catholic ceremony."

"And not by a fountain at the zoo," answered Elliott with distaste. Toni felt nauseous; she did not like the tenor of their conversation.

"Then there's the issue of children," said Toni as if conducting a presentation on the Church's position on the subject. She paused, glanced at Lillian and then resumed her reasoning: "I want my children to be baptized and raised in the Church with all of the Sacraments."

Elliott shifted Lillian and furrowed his brow as he contemplated the issue. He knew little about Catholic theology and practice.

"I never really thought much about religion," said Elliott. Moving to more practical matters, Toni cocked an eye at him.

"A family – the entire family – goes to church together," Toni responded. She relented and said, "At least on holidays. And there'll be baptisms, communions and confirmations."

"You know how much I love church," said Elliott with a goofy grin and dripping sarcasm. The proximity to a discussion of their own marriage discomfited them both and he sought to break the tension. He took a deep breath, felt the weight of Lillian on his chest and added, "And how much it loves me."

Toni averted her eyes and bit her lip. She remembered Father Maurice.

"Before I make the decision to marry again," began Toni, "there's someone I *will* be talking to."

"Katherine?" Elliott asked.

"Actually, no," replied Toni, "because she might be a little biased."

"Then you *should* talk to her," Elliott quipped. His mirth faded and he asked with a hint of jealousy, "Not Bobby, though, right?"

"Of course not Bobby," objected Toni, the volume of her response disturbing Lillian. She gushed in a voice barely above a whisper, "Oh, sorry. I'm sorry."

"Who then?" asked a puzzled Elliott. The baby stirred for another few seconds and then settled back into slumber.

"There's this priest who's been counseling me on, well . . . *my romantic life*," Toni confessed. She hugged herself and said, "Keeping me from making any rash decisions, and making sure that, whatever I do, I do it God's way, and don't make the same mistakes I made with Bobby."

The degree of Toni's dedication to Catholicism and the high expectations it created made Elliott uneasy. He punted.

"Then I guess you should talk to the priest," Elliott advised Toni. His self-doubt rising, he remarked, "Who knows? Maybe he makes the decision easy for you."

"Before *you* made a marriage decision again," said Toni, "I'm sure there'd be someone you should talk to."

"It'd be a debate," Elliott muttered bitterly, "not a conversation."

"But you'd still do it . . . ," stated Toni determinedly, " . . . *if* you were considering getting married."

"Yeah," Elliott said with an exhale of resignation and several affirmative nods, "I'd still do it."

· · · ·

"THERE HE IS!" EXCLAIMED Toni when she spotted Father Maurice leading a group of walkers along a long, curving trail within Willow Metropark. She immediately swung her car into a parking space and shifted into "Park", the sudden maneuver causing Katherine to lurch in her seat.

"Toni Amanda!" Katherine rebuked her daughter to no avail. Toni jumped out of the vehicle and, leaving the door wide open, dashed across the parking lot towards him.

"Father Maurice!" beckoned Toni as she sprinted across the green field on her long legs, the twenty-eight-year-old occasionally weaving among intermittent trees.

"She's on a mission now," Katherine uttered with a sigh. She nonchalantly reached over the center console, turned the key to stop the engine and removed it from the ignition. Disembarking from the car, she closed her door and rounded the front of the vehicle.

"Father Maurice!" shouted Toni again as she closed on the group. Katherine, meanwhile, walked to the driver side of the car, pushed the door shut and then followed in her daughter's wake. Father Maurice and his companions – a gaggle of neatly-dressed and high-spirited black women in their sixties and seventies – stopped to gawk at Toni as she ran towards them.

"What the hell?" uttered the old priest as he shielded his eyes and watched Toni bound towards him. The women watched her approach warily.

"Why's a skinny white girl chasin' us, Father?" asked one of women incredulously when Toni arrived before the group. She felt the heat of their disapproval.

"I'm . . . s-sorry," replied Toni amid gasps for air. She leaned over and grabbed her knees as she attempted to regain her breath, saying, "Whew! That was . . . farther . . . than I thought."

"Ms. Toni, what're you *doin'* out here?" asked Father Maurice. He placed his hands on his hips and said, "You can't be chasin' old people around like that."

"I *really* need your advice," answered Toni in desperation as she straightened her body. Realizing her overzealousness, she composed herself and addressed the group, saying, "But I can wait until you're all finished. Sorry to barge in like that."

Taking pity on his mentee, Father Maurice waved off her apology. The women's disapprobation cooled.

"It's just our weekly Bible walk," explained Father Maurice as he patted the book he held. The women began studying Toni with interest as he continued, "It's good for the physical *and* the spiritual self. But we were wrappin' up."

"I'd ask whether you've lost your mind," Katherine told her daughter as she strode up to the group, "but it's quite clear you have."

"Where're all these white women comin' from?" asked another one of the women with a Bible in one hand and a cane in the other.

"An older version of you," remarked Father Maurice with approval when he saw Katherine. Sizing her up, he smirked and added, "That's more my speed."

Father Maurice's comments garnered looks of reproach from his flock. Katherine folded her arms.

"And you must be the fountain of wisdom my daughter's always chattering about," Katherine replied with the slightest hint of jealousy.

"Father Maurice, this is my mom, Katherine," stated Toni. Becoming antsy, she explained, "And I'm really sorry I interrupted, it's just that, well, things have *really* changed, and I don't know how much time I have, and the secretary at the Church said you were here and-."

"All right, ladies, how 'bout we wrap this up and meet again next Saturday?" queried Father Maurice with his hands raised.

"Oh, no," said one of the women. Nods of agreement followed as she turned to Toni and asked, "Now what's goin' on with you, young lady?"

Toni hesitated. Speaking to Father Maurice was one thing but addressing the entire group was another. Toni looked to Katherine for support.

"Let's hear it," Katherine said with a sly smile. Prodded onward by the curious countenances of the group, Toni clasped her hands behind her back like a teenager and gave them the truncated version of her history with Elliott.

"So what made you track me down here?" asked Father Maurice.

"There's a baby in the picture now and his old girlfriend's thrown down the marriage gauntlet," Katherine interjected impatiently. The Bible group emitted a collective gasp.

"Now that boy's *gotta* marry you," insisted one of the women to the affirmative nods of the others. Toni grabbed her stomach with both hands.

"Oh, no, it's not like that," blurted Toni with wide eyes. She expounded sadly, "The baby's his, not mine, and the mother, she's . . . she's *gone*."

A moment of quiet settled over the group with only the sounds of birds and distant parkgoers heard in the distance. Father Maurice ended it by clearing his throat.

"None a' that matters, Toni, and really, nothin's changed," said Father Maurice sternly. He spoke as if delivering a homily, stating, "This time you do the marriage counseling, *all of it*, and, if it's God's will for you to get hitched, you do it as the Sacrament in a Church with a proper Catholic ceremony. He's gotta agree to all of that, baby or no baby."

"I know," whimpered Toni as a melancholy descended on her. She fully expected Elliott to balk at the rigorousness of Catholic marriage requirements and felt him slipping away. The group sympathized with her and offered her caring looks and understanding nods. Even Katherine's mood dimmed.

"Maybe it's for the best," posited Toni forlornly. She saw Elliott and Lillian in her mind's eye and continued, "Lil's so precious, and I love her already, but I'm not sure I'm ready for that. Who knows what type of Mom I'd be."

"I think I can help with that," Katherine said. She opened her purse and retrieved two old photographs, one of an infant Toni in her christening dress and another of her during her first communion. She handed them to Toni who gazed at them before passing them to Father Maurice.

"I take it this darling child is our Toni," said Father Maurice. He passed the photograph to the group and each woman responded with expressions of adoration.

"Cute as a button," remarked the woman with the cane.

"Geez, Mom," said Toni with a tinge of embarrassment. Despite suspecting she knew the answer, she pressed Katherine, "What do those have to do with anything?"

"Do you love that man?" Katherine inquired bluntly. The women of the Bible study group hung on every word.

"Mom, it's not that simple," objected Toni. Father Maurice opened his mouth to speak but Katherine beat him to the punch.

"Answer the question," Katherine countered with a penetrating gaze.

"You know I do," replied Toni staunchly. Katherine's countenance softened.

"Then imagine his little girl in these photos, dressed just like you were," Katherine instructed her daughter wisely, "and think about how they make you feel."

Father Maurice chuckled. The women of the Bible study grinned and nodded warmly and approvingly.

"You're good," Father Maurice lauded Katherine.

. . . .

FROM ACROSS THE BACKYARD patio table, Emma bored holes into Elliott with her stunning yet wrathful eyes. Her brother uncharacteristically returned fire by glaring at his sister in unrelenting fashion. Neither sibling spoke.

Safe from the domestic dispute, Lillian was nestled in Rose's arms and worked on a bottle. The unofficial grandmother sat in between her men on Emma's couch as David and Tom watched the Tigers play the California Angels. Lanie and Tessa disappeared into their rooms, each with a five-dollar bribe from Uncle Elliott to abandon the swimming pool.

"All right," grumbled Emma. Prickled by Elliott's sudden backbone, she decided to break the stalemate and said, "I promised *my best friend* I wouldn't let you and Toni happen."

Elliott folded his arms in defiance. Emma squelched a scowl.

"But you're *demanding* I hear you out," continued Emma tersely, "so I'll suspend my promise for as long as this conversation lasts. But you'd better have one helluva reason for me to change my mind, Elliott."

"I'd like a drink first," Elliott said, his desire for alcohol less about courage and more about clearing his wits.

"Oh, no," objected Emma. She freed her scowl and sneered, "If you love her so much, this oughta be easy."

"Em, I'm an adult," Elliott snarled, "and if I want a drink, I'll have a damn drink."

"You're this close, Warden," replied Emma while holding her thumb and forefinger mere millimeters from each other.

"Now you sound like Brandy," Elliott jabbed. Emma pointed to the house.

"Get off my patio," said Emma through clenched teeth.

"Give it a rest, Em," Elliott demanded. To his great surprise, she reluctantly complied and her anger lessened.

"Look, you two're comin' off *a lot* of turmoil," Emma said. She leaned back in her chair and continued, "Hell, you're still in it. You just lost Nora, and found Lillian, and Toni was almost married just a few months ago. That's a lot for both of you to deal with *and* she still has a lurking ex. Donna's had *zero* turmoil, Elliott. Zero. She didn't leave some guy at the altar *and* she has a long history with you, which is something Toni doesn't."

Elliott rose to his feet, thrust his hands in his front pockets and walked several paces away. He stared into the gentle undulations of the pool water.

"You and Donna, you can be married by October, and tucked into a nice little house with Lil' just like that," Emma reasoned with a snap of her fingers. She leaned forward and continued emphatically, "It just makes *so* much sense. Are you really gonna wait six months, *or more*, and go through all that bullshit counseling to be with Toni? Do you really wanna make your daughter wait that long? And if it doesn't work out, all that time'll be gone, and maybe Donna will be, too."

Elliott groaned. He punched the air.

"Damn it, Em!" Elliott barked.

"Damn it, Elliott!" Emma mocked her brother. Tom soon appeared behind the screen door.

"Rose wants me to remind you two that Lillian is trying to eat in here," Tom rebuked the siblings. Their moods became immediately but temporarily apologetic.

"Daddy's sorry, sweetheart," called Elliott to his daughter.

"Auntie Em is, too, Lil," Emma added sweetly. Tom tilted his head forward, gave them both a dubious look and then disappeared into the house.

"Em, if I can help it, Lil's gonna have a great life with or without a Toni, or a Donna," Elliott reasoned, "or an anyone for that matter."

"It took a lot for her to do it, but Donna got up on a stage and *sang* for you," said Emma. She stood up, moved to Elliott and grasped his arm, saying, "All a' that 'independent woman' stuff's gone by the wayside, and she'll be happy just to have you and a home and family. I really think it'll be like the old times."

"I don't want her to be something *she's* not," insisted Elliott as he pulled away from Emma. He remembered his arguments with John Warden on the topic of Donna and, seeking to repress those memories, he walked along the west side of the pool and said, "I just don't want her tryin' to make me something *I'm* not."

His hands still in his pockets, Elliott turned towards his sister. She stood motionlessly at the edge of the pool.

"And then there's the fact that I don't love Donna," said Elliott bluntly. He shrugged his shoulders and stated simply, "*I love Toni.*"

The declaration brought a smile to Elliott's face. Emma quickly closed the distance between them but he backpedaled to avoid her approach. Elliott's grin vanished.

"I'm not going along with it," Emma warned Elliott. Frustrated by his sister's stubbornness, he went nose-to-nose with her as she insisted, "I mean it, Elliott. Toni's a mistake you're making on your own."

Elliott turned away from his sister and fumed. Sensing an advantage, she struck.

"I'll boot Morning Cloak from Johnny Dubs if I have to," Emma threatened Elliott. Her gambit failed, however, and his frustration morphed into ire. Spinning around, Elliott swooped up his astonished sister and hurled her into the deep end of the pool. Emma squealed and hit the water with a resounding splash.

"Elliott!" Emma screamed as she surfaced. Still stunned, she clumsily swam to the side of the pool and grasped the edge, shouting, "Elliott, you asshole!"

David slid open the screen door and stepped onto the patio. Elliott nonchalantly walked to him.

"I just threw your wife in the pool," Elliott stated matter-of-factly.

"Yeah, I see that," replied David without emotion. He patted Elliott on the shoulder with his large hand and advised, "I'll hold her off as long as I can but you'd better split."

"Thanks, man," Elliott said with Emma's angered squawking following him into the house.

. . . .

"HERE SHE IS," ROSE said as she handed the baby carrier to Elliott. A sleeping Lillian was tucked inside it.

"Thanks for munchkin wranglin'," said Elliott as he took the carrier.

"That's what grandmas do," Rose replied pointedly. Though Emma had predicted it, her unofficial adoption of Lillian as her third grandchild amazed Elliott. She pecked him on the cheek and stated, "I need Toni's telephone number."

"You do?" asked Elliott suspiciously. He eyed her closely and asked, "Uh, why's that?"

"Nothing you need to worry about, trust me," Rose answered with a sly, muted smile. Emma's griping came closer and she advised, "Now, Davie may be the best at it, but even he can only hold off an enraged Emma for a little while. I'd get going."

"Right," agreed Elliott. He descended from the porch and onto the sidewalk with his daughter and said, "I'll call ya."

"Elliott," Rose added. Elliott stopped and looked at her over his shoulder.

"Yeah, Rose," replied Elliott. She winked at him.

"*Be ready*," Rose said with a knowing look.

. . . .

ELLIOTT WALKED AROUND his bedroom and bounced Lillian gently, the motion diffusing her fussiness and sending her into the land of sleep. Once she was safely ensconced in slumber, he laid her in her crib and gazed on her with tired eyes.

"How 'bout you give Daddy a solid four hours tonight?" Elliott asked his daughter in a whisper. She did not answer, her silence prompting him to respond, "Well, at least consider it, kiddo."

Reaching down into the crib, he affectionately brushed Lillian's foot. He then shuffled to his bed, fell into it and drifted away with Rose's voice echoing in his head.

"*Be ready*," Elliott heard her say repeatedly. His last waking memory was of his digital alarm clock. It read "10:04 pm".

Though he walked many different paths in the dreamworld that night, Elliott's most vivid one occurred at the Rackham Fountain on an orange-tinted evening where the sun set amidst threatening clouds in the west. Only the darkening sky betrayed the oncoming storm, however, as there was no thunder or lightning. The noise of water gurgling from the fountain steadily increased and interrupted the stillness.

Elliott saw Nora sitting on the ground by its railing in the very spot they planned their wedding and dressed in the exact manner as on that day. She smiled at him in happy recognition but then she became sad as if she remembered her fate. Elliott attempted to call for her but could not speak, to approach her but could not walk.

Nora held out her hand and looked at the engagement ring on her finger. It shined with an abnormal brightness but, to Elliott's surprise, she stood up, removed it and set it on the fountain railing. Walking away, Nora did not look at Elliott again and faded into the mists of the dream. His focus fell to the ring, its shine dulled, and he could do nothing but gape at it.

Lillian's shrill cry tore Elliott from his dream. He opened his eyes and looked at the clock. It now read "1:37 am".

"Almost four," Elliott muttered as he rolled out of bed. Shuffling the well-worn trail to Lillian's crib, he forgot his dream and added, "I'll take it."

Nobody Wants To Be Alone

Anxiety rippled through Elliott. For the first time in many weeks, he settled onto his reserved barstool at Johnny Dubs. The experience proved surreal; his home-away-from-home seemed like his past as Lillian had become his present and future. That, however, was the least of his concerns.

"Somethin's about to go down," Elliot said to himself. Rose, with constant admonitions to "trust me", convinced Elliott to leave Lillian in her care and venture to Johnny Dubs for a night of "adult time".

"Well, look who's here," Emma greeted her brother, the tone conveying her foreknowledge of his visit. She deposited a fresh Grumpy Old Man before him.

"Please tell me Rose isn't part of this bullshit, too," a bitter Elliott thought.

"It's been a while since you plopped down on that seat," said an oddly bubbly Emma. She grinned at him with energetic eyes and asked, "Eatin' tonight?"

"No, I'm good," Elliott replied. Keeping his suspicions to himself, he pretended to survey the crowd as he searched the club for Donna. He noticed One Shot Rifle warming up on stage, this time with a keyboard player, and said to himself, "Real subtle, Sis."

"How's my niece?" asked Emma. Elliott turned his full attention to his sister.

"Eatin' like a little piggie and growin' like a big weed," answered Elliott fondly. He wanted to assert his knowledge of Emma's plot but managed to bite his tongue. The background music flowing through the club's sound system abruptly ceased and the hairs on the back of Elliott's neck stood up. He breathed deeply and thought, "All right, here we go."

Donna peeked her head from the stairwell door, ensured that Emma had Elliott distracted and then quickly slipped through the crowd.

"Lanie and Tess' want a sleepover with Baby Lil," advised Emma quickly when she saw Donna. She grasped the bar with both hands and leaned forward, saying, "So as soon as she's ready, plan on it."

"That's still a little ways off," Elliott replied before sampling his cocktail. Oblivious to her movements, he missed Donna slither onto the stage and speak softly and hurriedly with the band. Elliott took another small sip, savored it briefly, then admitted with a chuckle, "Though it might be more me than her. Either way, you can tell the monsters there'll be lots of sleepovers *next* year."

"How's it goin' tonight, Johnny Dubs?" asked Donna buoyantly. Some cheers erupted from the crowd as conversations waned and gazes moved to the stage. Elliott and Emma stared at one another with irked expressions.

"Tryin' to make her Toni ain't gonna work, Em," Elliott implored his sister. He rotated his barstool towards the stage where Donna stood with a microphone in her hand and adoration in her eyes. She was dressed in a spaghetti-strapped yellow top, country blue jeans and cowboy boots. Elliott laughed and said, "Geez, you even dressed her like Toni. The bottom half, anyway."

Spurred by Elliott's flippant attitude, Donna swiftly signaled to the band. The keyboard player began Crystal Gayle's *A Long and Lasting Love* and soon thereafter Donna sang the title and launched into the first verse. She fixed her attention on Elliott.

"Wow, she's pouring it on thick," Elliott muttered to himself. Donna, who had honed her voice since her last performance, infused every word with her desperate desire for Elliott. Some members of the audience lost interest as the song meandered onward, its melody and lyrics too flowery for their tastes.

"She's pretty good, huh?" Toni asked Elliott. While Donna drew Elliott and Emma's attention, she and her Morning Cloak bandmates had entered Johnny Dubs and nonchalantly strolled up to him. When Elliott turned to her, Toni tilted her head to the side, feigned a look of disapprobation and queried, "Here to see your girlfriend?"

"No, I, I, uh, I," stammered Elliott. Toni, whose self-assurance discombobulated him, placed a finger on his lips.

"Relax, Elliott," Toni said with a smirk, "you're *supposed* to be here."

Toni's presence caused Donna to stumble over a line of the song. Refocusing herself, she ignored Toni and again centered her vision on Elliott. She repeated "a long and lasting love" several times as the song coasted to its end. Applause ensued but it lacked the usual raucousness Johnny Dubs afforded Toni.

"My turn," Toni announced. Morning Cloak headed to the stage while Donna stymied the urge to confront Toni and bowed with her bandmates.

"No, it's not!" barked Emma after Toni. Elliott turned to her with a glower.

"For once, stay the hell out of it, Warden," Elliott chastised his sister.

• • • •

MORNING CLOAK TOOK the stage to the resounding approval of its fans. Tempted to make a scene but unwilling to risk the ire of the crowd, Donna forced a grin and held out the microphone. Emma glanced at Elliott, his sister uncharacteristically befuddled by the situation. He did not notice her attention, however, as his own was glued to Toni.

"He's mine," declared Donna with veiled vitriol.

"No," Toni countered as she swiped the microphone from Donna, "he's not."

Toni instantly whirled towards the crowd. Donna slowly melted away.

"You guys don't mind if we play a few songs, do ya'?" Toni asked happily. The crowd erupted in affirmative cheers, their approval causing her to beam and say, "I didn't think so. Just give us a few to get ready, okay?"

Applause, cheers and shouts filled the club. Emma sneered.

"Oh, no, sister," snapped Emma as she marched down the bar. When she reached the halfway point, the portrait of her father caught her eye. She stopped cold, endured a sudden wave of emotion and then studied the picture. Elliott's words echoed in her head.

For once, stay the hell out of it, Warden.

"I don't wanna fight with him anymore, Daddy," confessed Emma in a rush of relief. The sounds of Morning Cloak warming up filled the club but seemed distant as she thought, "We tried, damn it we tried, but we just can't make him do what we want him to do. We never could."

Emma laughed. All the pressure of stewarding her brother's life left her.

"And Mom always knew why . . . because he's just like us," said Emma warmly. She held together her index and middle fingers, kissed their tips and placed them on her father's cheek. Tuning to view the stage, she saw the radiant image that was Toni and said to herself, "I'd better get Donna outta here. This's gonna be rough."

"Okay, Johnny Dubs, let's get started!" Toni exclaimed. Donna met Emma at the entrance to the bar.

"Em, stop her!" insisted Donna, her eyes beginning to water.

"Not this time, Dee," replied Emma with an expression of pity.

"That song that Donna just sang, *A Long and Lasting Love*, was on an album with the same title," explained Toni. Donna attempted to rush the stage but Emma wrapped her arms around her and held her in place as Toni added, "And you'd think that'd be the song I'd sing about *my* man. *Because I love him.*"

Toni and Elliott exchanged amorous glances. Donna struggled against Emma to no avail.

"I don't know, it's just too fairytale, though, and doesn't reflect what we went through to get here," continued Toni, "but there was another song on that album, and, well, *that one . . . .*"

Toni paused to smile a vibrant smile that dazzled the crowd. She looked directly at Elliott.

" . . . that one is *us*," said Toni with an overriding confidence foreign to her character. The word "us" was the perfect cue as Eddie played the initial chords of *Nobody Wants To Be Alone* on the keyboard. Toni's singing of the opening verses sent chilling ripples down every spine in the club.

"*Be ready*," said Elliott as he quoted Rose's sage words and began fumbling in the front pocket of his jeans. Toni's gaze fell upon him and, enraptured by her melodious voice, he stood up and returned it. Pulling his hand from his pocket, he produced the engagement ring he bought for Donna and once placed on Nora's finger.

"Oh, my god, Elliott," gasped Emma though no one heard her over Toni's performance. The diversion allowed Donna to break free from Emma's grip but, instead of running to the stage, she burst into tears and disappeared into the stairwell leading to Emma's office. Emma watched her sibling approach the band and said, "How did he know?"

Arriving at the stage, Elliott raised the ring and, instead of sinking to one knee, he simply held it aloft and presented it to Toni. The stage lights glinted on its diamond, a tiny star in the smoky sultriness of the club. Tears rolled down Toni's cheeks and, as she sang about their luck in finding one another, she nodded her assent.

When the last lyric passed her lips, Toni hopped off the stage and bounded into Elliott's arms. The Johnny Dubs crowd erupted into a boisterous celebration as Toni and Elliott shared a loving kiss. When the clamor ceased, Elliott lifted her finger and slid the ring onto it.

"Those two're in a movie of their own and no one's stopping 'em," Emma said. Happy for her brother but saddened for her best friend, she left the loving couple behind and vanished into the stairwell.

· · · ·

MORNING CLOAK COMPLETED its set while Elliott watched his newly minted fiancé from his barstool and nursed a second drink. The band performed all its high-energy favorites and drove the crowd into a frenzy. Once the last note was played and the ovations ceased, the club settled into its late-night atmosphere. The radio station Z 95.5 flowed from the sound system and plodded through a string of slower songs.

"It's a miracle that woman loves me," Elliott thought when Toni entered his field of vision. She playfully sauntered to Elliott but halted three feet from him.

"Is it safe?" inquired Toni with a silly grin.

"Yeah, it's safe," Elliott replied, the declaration feeling correct for the first time in years. Toni slid onto the stool next to Elliott as he expounded, "Em put Sean at the wheel and took Donna home. She was takin' it pretty hard."

The pair kept their distance from one another like high schoolers in a budding romance. Luke made a quick appearance, delivered a capless Bud Light to Toni and then retreated.

"I feel bad," said a frowning Toni. She took a sip of her beer and then lamented, "I didn't do it to hurt her."

"All's fair in love and war, and I think we went through both tonight," Elliott said. He offered his glass for a toast but received only a doubtful look in response. Elliott continued to hold up his cocktail and stated, "Hey, you and Rose beat Em and Dee at their own game."

Elliott laughed. Toni furrowed her brow.

"And this is your prize," Elliott announced like a gameshow host as he gestured to himself. Toni shook her head and set her beer aside. The country vibe created by Morning Cloak had ended and the radio ballads inspired other couples to move to the dance floor.

"C'mon, funny guy, dance with me," said Toni with an extended hand. Elliott hated dancing but, unable to resist his wife-to-be, he took her hand and let her pull him to his feet. Leading Elliott to the crowded dance floor, Toni asked, "When do you wanna get back to Lil'?"

"Your co-conspirator told me to stay out as late as I wanted," Elliott answered. Toni blushed and chortled. Arriving at the dance floor, Elliott pulled her close and said, "But, to be honest, I'm already feelin' the pull. I really wish my girls lived under the same roof."

"By this time next year, I promise," said Toni. Drumbeats commenced ZZ Top's *Rough Boy* and its guitar opening rumbled through the club's speakers, the rock ballad in stark contrast to Toni's beloved country songs. She pulled her left arm to her chest so she could admire her ring. Elliott became uneasy.

"We can get you another ring if you want," said Elliott as they swayed together.

"Why would we do that?" Toni asked. The pair moved with the coordination of long-time lovers.

"Everything happened so fast, I didn't think about all the history behind it," Elliott answered. He stared at the ring and reminisced, saying, "I bought it for Donna, and gave it to Nora, and, well . . . ."

Elliott struggled. Nora wore the ring the night she died and he worried the memories attached to the ring would haunt him.

"Let's just say you deserve better than that old ring," Elliott said as he shook free of the past. He chuckled oddly and added, "But then again, you deserve better than this old guy, too."

"Don't say that again," Toni admonished Elliott. She moved her arm back to its original position and stated, "First of all, the ring is perfect."

"How's that?" a confused Elliott inquired. Toni's countenance became grave.

"Because it's a reminder to never take you for granted again," replied Toni stoically. Elliott lost himself in her big, beautiful eyes as she explained, "That ring could've been mine, and only mine, but I made the wrong choice, and I almost lost you. But, from now on, every time I see it, I'll know how lucky I am."

"Really? *You're* the lucky one?" Elliott asked with a smirk.

"I know where you're getting that from," scolded Toni.

"It wasn't just Em," Elliott advised. Mimicking Brandy's voice and brashness, he said, "'She's outta your league, Warden.'"

"That's bullshit," asserted Toni, her rare resort to profanity amusing Elliott. Frustration oozed from her and she griped, "All your people think I'm some weird, sophisticated, church-going party girl."

"You're not?" Elliott asked sarcastically.

"Hey, I love a good nap as much as you do," Toni said with a sly smile. *Rough Boy*'s guitar solo ushered the song to its end.

"I just hope I can keep you happy," said Elliott. They continued to dance as *Stuck With You* by Huey Lewis and the News began and the other couples vacated the dance floor.

"Yay! I love this song!" Toni exclaimed. Her effervescence was unquenchable and she said, "It was number one this week on Casey Kasem."

"So I take it we're gonna keep dancing?" Elliott inquired.

"You gotta keep me happy," teased Toni. His wounded response prompted her to assure him, "I'm a simple girl, Elliott. Take me to the movies, or to Mackinac Island for a long weekend, or to a new restaurant, or to a Tigers game. That's not so bad."

"Nah," agreed Elliott, "that's not so bad."

"Oh, and you have to sit in the audience and watch me sing," Toni insisted. Elliott grinned. He loved the way Toni glowed when she spoke of singing.

"That one's easy," replied Elliott with conviction. He spun her unexpectedly and then said, "Now we just gotta see if I can pass Catholicism 101."

"It's not a class, silly," said Toni. More than a few patrons watched the happy couple exist in their own private world as Toni explicated, "It's just meant to help us have a better marriage, and to make sure I maintain my relationship with God, even if you don't ever become Catholic."

Elliott stopped them just as Toni grabbed both of his cheeks. She paused and then laid a passionate kiss on his lips.

"Am I worth it all?" Toni asked.

"How the hell should I know?" replied Elliott. He shrugged and said, "I haven't gone through it yet."

Toni tightened her grasp on Elliott's cheeks and shook his head. The lovers looked upon one another longingly.

"I thought Hawaii was the right place, and Bobby was the right guy," Toni said, "but I was just wrong. The right place was my ordinary little church in Taylor, Michigan, and the right guy was the cable installer. Everything was here, in the right place. *Home.*"

The word "home" broke Toni's concentration and interrupted her smile. Elliott sensed her disquiet but let the moment pass without scrutiny. Hand-in-hand, they returned to their seats and talked of Lillian, their wedding and their dramatic history.

• • • •

ELLIOTT RETURNED HOME to find Rose sitting on the living room floor. Laying on a plush, pastel yellow blanket with cartoon ducks was an alert Lillian. The last segment of *The Tonight Show* played on the television.

"Wheeeerrrre's Johnny?" Elliott quipped when he noticed Bill Cosby was guest hosting for Johnny Carson. He set his keys on the end table near the couch and the noise caught Lillian's attention.

"I don't know where you get your sense of humor," said an unamused and serious Rose. She kept her gaze on Elliott and continued, "It certainly wasn't your parents, and your sister's not like that either. Strange."

"Strange, indeed," Elliott deadpanned. He turned his attention to his daughter and grinned, asking, "How'd my munchkin do tonight?"

"She was fussier than normal," Rose said with mild surprise. She lightly touched Lillian's nose and commented, "It seems she likes *The Tonight Show*, though. She's been wide awake and quiet since it started."

"Think you could hang out for about ten minutes?" Elliott asked as the reek of cigarette smoke became apparent. He removed his jacket and said, "I'd like to get a shower and change my clothes. I forgot how smokey the club gets."

"Are you forgetting something?" inquired Rose impatiently. She stood up and folded her arms, suggesting coyly, "Maybe someone you know received a gift, maybe some jewelry?"

"Either Toni or Emma or both called you and told you what happened, I'm sure," Elliott replied. His eyes watered and, after he and Rose shared knowingly grins, he said earnestly, "Thanks, Rose."

"You're welcome," said Rose. The wafting scent of cigarettes caused her to grimace and she instructed Elliott, "Now go take that shower before you give your daughter a nicotine high."

· · · ·

SITTING IN HIS RECLINER, Elliott fed Lillian her early-morning bottle by the bluish light of the television and pondered the previous evening's events. His whirlwind proposal to Toni amid the battle between she and Donna proved rewarding but exhausting. Elliott's eyes flickered like the television screen.

"I sure hope you're ready to go back to sleep after breakfast, kid," Elliott said. He yawned and then sighed, "Today will *not* be a productive day."

Thoughts of Toni gave him an unexpected burst of energy, however. The mere prospect of a future with her filled him with hope for both he and Lillian.

"Looks like Toni's gonna be your mom, or stepmom, or whatever," Elliott told his daughter. Speaking his mind as if an adult was in the room, he explained, "She might be a little unsure at first, so give her a little time to get used to it. But there's a lotta room in that big heart a' hers, Lil. She's gonna be really good for you. *Really good for us.* You'll see."

Elliott thought of Macayla. His conviction to eventually tell Lillian the truth about her parentage had not waned since her birth.

"Don't worry, though, I'll tell ya' about your real mom when the time's right," Elliott said. Lillian consumed her formula without acknowledging her father's words but he continued, "I've got some pictures, and I managed to get some of her stuff outta her house before the bank took it. Your mommy was terrible with money. Eh, I might leave that part out. I might leave a few parts out."

Elliott studied Lillian's tiny face in the wavering light of the television. He knew Macayla, at least in appearance, would live on through her daughter.

"You sure do look like her," Elliott remarked. He chortled softly and said, "Don't you dare get a tattoo, though."

Lillian drained the last of her bottle so Elliott set it on the end table. Shifting the infant onto his diaper-protected left shoulder, he patted her back gently and looked around the apartment.

"I don't see any need to leave here before we move into Toni's house," Elliott reasoned, "so we'll just stay put. Who knows? Maybe the three of us will get a new place."

A thought struck Elliott and he shook his head in the affirmative. Lillian was already asleep.

"Yeah, I'll get some pictures of you and I here," Elliott stated with a strengthening voice, "so I can show you when it was just you and me. *Your first home.* I like that."

Lillian stirred, burped and then went motionless again. The task complete, Elliott eased himself to his feet and glanced at his slumbering child.

"Good idea," Elliott whispered as he ascended the stairs with only deep sleep on his mind.

. . . .

CLOUDS SHIELDED THE October sky as a steady breeze herded them to the northeast. It had been a warm day but the temperatures now descended into the low sixties as the daylight faded and disappeared. Emerging from his apartment with the necks of two beers clutched in the fingers of one hand, Elliott stepped off the porch and moved towards the patio table.

"Operation sleeping baby was a success," Elliott announced as he leaned down to Toni. She sat in a chair and, after receiving a kiss on the cheek, she accepted one of the bottles.

"Thanks, sweetheart," said Toni, the use of endearing terms for Elliott still feeling somewhat odd. He sat in a chair across the table from her and sipped his beer. Toni did likewise before commenting, "Seems like she's starting to sleep more at night."

Elliott did not answer but instead closed his eyes, leaned his head back and indulged in the warm evening air. His radio, taking up its usual position on the table, moved from commercials to the disc jockey's banter to the song *Human* by The Human League. The neighborhood noises were louder than normal as everyone enjoyed the weather but, even so, they remained outside the bubble of the music.

"I want to talk to you about something," Toni said slowly and cautiously. She wore a jean jacket to ward off the breeze and her long legs were stretched out before her. Toni took a drink and then another before setting her beer on the table and adding ominously, "Something big."

"Uh-oh," Elliott replied with a smirk and twinge of anxiety. The song's vocals commenced.

"You gotta promise to let me say everything I have to say first, though," Toni insisted. She made a sweeping, right-to-left gesture and said, "Let me get the whole thing out before you say anything, and then we can talk about it all you want."

"Are you dying?" asked Elliott in jest. He outwardly projected humor though he panicked on the inside, querying, "Wait, am I dying?"

"*Elliott, stop*," Toni rebuked him.

"Okay," relented Elliott, "sorry."

"Promise you'll let me get it all out?" inquired Toni anxiously.

"Yeah, sure, hon," agreed Elliott. He sat up, reached across the table and grasped her right hand reassuringly, saying, "Hey, whatever it is, I'm here no matter what."

"*I know*," Toni said as her heart melted in the heat of Elliott's devotion. She squeezed his hand and then released it. Elliott settled back into his chair.

"Okay," Toni said with a dramatic exhale. Standing up like a grade schooler giving a classroom speech, she began, "Now, understand, I've been

257

thinking about this on and off, long before you, or even Bobby. And when Emma pulled her little stunt, and I sang *Meet Me in Montana* – *with* Bobby but *to* you – it really brought those thoughts back."

Elliott winced at the mention of Toni's ex-fiancée. He did not like the direction of the conversation and, reading his face, Toni decided to rip the bandage from the wound.

"I'll just say it," Toni said as she steeled her will. She braced for a negative reaction and stated, "I want to move back to Montana."

Toni paused and bit her lip. The declaration puzzled Elliott.

"Which obviously means you and Lillian come with me," Toni quickly added. Elliott's gaze momentarily dropped to the ground and he pondered her request. He raised his eyes to Toni and watched her with a serious mien, his countenance causing her to say, "What I mean is, I want us, *our family*, to move to Montana."

"Okay," said Elliott with a nonchalant shrug. His body relaxed.

"What?" Toni queried in astonishment.

"Okay," repeated Elliott. He took two gulps of his drink and stated without the least bit of reluctance, "Let's move to Montana."

"I haven't even told you why, or how, or when," replied a flabbergasted Toni.

"Ya' don't need to," Elliott said. Setting down his bottle, he crossed his legs, leaned back in his chair and folded his hands on his stomach. He stated calmly, "I just wanna be with you and Lil'. I don't care where that is and, if we're gonna make a big move, let's do it now and get her settled in whatever place she's gonna call home."

"You grew up here, though," said Toni, "and Em's *not* gonna take it well."

"Michigan's always been home for me," expounded Elliott wistfully. His nostalgia became sadness as he continued, "But unfortunately for Lil' and I, we both lost our moms here. Tragically and unexpectedly. And she'll never know John or Lillian Warden. Hell, all her grandparents are gone."

Elliott did not continue his thought: Nora, too, died in Michigan. He tamped down the memory.

"And, actually, I think Em'll get it," Elliott said. His contemplations shifted to their careers and he asked with goofy grin, "They got hospitals and cable companies out in the Wild, Wild West?"

"Yes," answered Toni with burgeoning excitement. She plopped onto Elliott's lap and wrapped her arms around his neck, explaining, "They opened a new hospital in Bozeman this year, which is about ninety miles from Butte. I've done a little checking, just to see if this was even possible, and I think I can get a job there when we're ready."

"What about your mom?" asked Elliott.

"She and I haven't talked about it lately," Toni began with uncertainty in her tone, "but she said she'd come with me the last time we did. She'd be a big help with Lillian . . . . and her brothers and sisters."

"Geez, how many do you want?" asked Elliott.

"Enough to keep you busy and outta trouble," joked Toni. The couple laughed, and kissed, and talked deep into the night about their journey west.

• • • •

"OH, I MISS WHEN THE girls were little," lamented Emma as she looked at Lillian and fondly recalled Halloweens past. Tucked into her baby carrier, which sat between Emma and Elliott on the living room couch, Lillian napped in a pink onesie made to resemble a unicorn complete with a small fabric horn. She caressed the child's forehead and said, "Now Dave and me're becoming chauffeurs to their friends' houses. I shoulda' just went to work."

"Yeah, I gotta buy their attention with cash now," Elliott said while shaking his head.

"This costume is absolutely adorable, Elliott," remarked Emma. She fiddled with it and asked, "Where'd Toni get it?"

"*I* bought it, thank you very much," Elliott replied with a trace of indignance.

"Well, then, I'm impressed," said Emma. She retrieved her mug from the coffee table, took a drink and pulled her legs onto the couch. The siblings sat in silence for a few moments, Elliott uncertain of how to break the news.

"I got something to tell you, Em," Elliott announced. The doorbell rang and several children yelled "trick or treat".

"Hold on," said Emma as she set down her coffee and headed for the front door. She griped, "Nothing like Halloween on a Friday. I gotta turn that porch light off. It's almost ten."

Elliott both loved and loathed the temporary reprieve. He worked up his courage as his sister dispatched with the straggling trick-or-treaters. With Toni working the late shift, he was on his own.

"Okay," said a returning Emma. She reacquired her mug, snuggled onto the couch and asked, "What's up?"

"Toni and I've been talking a lot about the future lately," began Elliott while keeping his gaze on his sleeping daughter.

"I bet," interjected Emma.

"And, well," Elliott continued cautiously, "we've decided that, after the wedding . . . we're gonna move to Montana."

Emma's face went pale and neutral. Her eyes, however, scintillated in a telltale sign of her angst. Emma also remained mute, her silence prickling Elliott.

"Em, I'll tell you the same thing I told Toni," said Elliott when Emma failed to respond.

"What? That you can't wait to get away from your meddling, domineering little sister," Emma snapped, the hurt evident in her voice despite the snarky smirk on her face.

"That Lillian and I have something tragic in common," Elliott replied. He expounded with the utmost seriousness, "That while Michigan might be our home, both our moms died here, and way too soon at that."

"Oh, my god, Elliott," Emma whimpered as several tears rolled down her cheeks.

"And that maybe she and I need to make a new home," continued Elliott somberly, "someplace where that isn't hanging over us."

Emma stood up and Elliott, expecting a sharp rebuke, joined her. Instead, she returned her mug to the coffee table and embraced Elliott tightly. Surprised but encouraged by the response, he wrapped Emma in his arms and kissed her on the top of her head as she wept.

"I thought I was doing the right thing," Emma whimpered, "but I just kept getting it wrong."

"I know ya' did, Em," Elliott answered sympathetically, "I know."

"I had all three of 'em in the club the day Donna came back," Emma mewled. She wiped her eyes and added, "*All three of 'em.* And I still picked the wrong one . . . *twice.*"

"But it all worked out, so it's all good," Elliott reasoned. Emma lifted her gaze to her brother.

"Go to Montana, be happy, be a family," urged Emma, her blessing a complete shock to Elliott.

"Are you serious?" Elliott queried in disbelief.

"I wanted someone to take responsibility for you and now that's Toni," Emma said. The siblings' embrace became a half-hug as they turned to view Lillian. Ceding the role she filled for over a decade, Emma sighed and stated, "It's her call, and I'll just have to accept that."

S oon to wed, Elliott and Toni sat together at the front of St. Alfred's Church as Father Maurice delivered his lively and amusing homily. Toni focused intently on her beloved mentor's spiritual insights on marriage but Elliott's attention drifted. Lillian voiced her displeasure at the long ceremony so Rose, charged with caring for the child during the mass, carried her to the rear of the Church.

"Smart kid," Elliott whispered to Toni. She quickly scolded him with a finger held to her lips. Elliott stifled a smirk and thought, "Thanks, Lil', now *I* can't get away with it."

A marriage within the Catholic mass, which meant the world to Toni, required one Catholic and one baptized Christian. An unexpected twist of fate that occurred over thirty years ago helped Elliott fulfill Toni's wish. Reestablishing the tradition in which she was raised, his mother joined the Allen Park Presbyterian church and had both Elliott and Emma baptized. That baptism permitted the couple to wed as part of the Catholic mass.

"Coming to my rescue yet again," Elliott said in his mind. Thoughts of his parents were bittersweet, particularly on such a joyous occasion, and he thought, "Damn I wish you and Dad could be here."

The ceremony differed from the weddings Elliott had attended; he and Toni sat on the altar's dais with their backs to the congregation and no bridal party. Its ritualistic nature made him uncomfortable.

"So weird," Elliott thought. However, when he glanced at a glowing Toni, her dream of a Catholic wedding unfolding, love welled within his chest and he said to himself, "But anything for her."

Father Maurice signaled Elliott and Toni to rise. Elliott felt jittery but another glance at Toni calmed him.

"Shinin' like she's on stage," Elliott said to himself. Toni chose a simple, elegant wedding dress with subtle floral patterns; long, lace sleeves; and a flyaway veil. She opted against a train and, given the up-and-down nature of a Catholic wedding, the decision proved wise. Elliott exhaled and thought, "Here we go."

"Dearly beloved," began Father Maurice. The remainder of the nuptials became a blur for Elliott and, whenever he reminisced about it later in life, he recalled only pieces of the marriage rite. Toni's beaming, contrasted with her happy tears, stood out in his mind but he also remembered phrases such as the traditional "for richer or poorer" vow and the Catholic line "receive this ring as a sign of my love and fidelity". He would never forget her trembling hand and the single tear that fell upon it when he placed the ring on her finger.

Once the marriage rite was concluded, Father Maurice proceeded to Holy Communion. Too esoteric and spiritual for Elliott's tastes, he focused on Toni and watched her pious participation in the Sacrament. He, when able, looked to the congregation and saw his family: Emma cradling Lillian, David sitting in between their daughters with his arms around them, Rose and Tom with hands clasped and Katherine with a satisfied expression. Behind them friends and acquaintances filled the front half of the large church.

"I now pronounce you Husband and Wife. You may kiss the bride," announced Father Maurice. Elliott breathed a sigh of relief to be free of the lengthy ceremony and, in an unforgettable moment, kissed his bride. The couple unexpectedly and affectionately touched foreheads.

"We did it," Elliott told his new wife, "we finally did it."

• • • •

DESPITE EMMA'S GENEROUS offer to forgo a reception at Johnny Dubs, Toni insisted it take place there. Her reasoning made Emma cry, a response becoming more common as her brother's life trended upward.

"It'll be like your mom and dad are there with us," Toni declared. She remembered speaking the words, watched the reception unfold around her and waited for the right moment. When it came, Toni raised a microphone to her lips.

"Can I have everyone's attention, please?" Toni requested when all the guests took their seats and the caterers, hired to allow Emma's staff to attend the ceremony, began delivering salads and drinks. Toni deftly ascended onto the stage with the microphone in her hand, saying, "Since there won't be any best man or maid of honor speeches, I arranged for a little pre-dinner entertainment."

The guests cheered as Toni's Morning Cloak bandmates took the stage, each one greeted with a big hug and a kiss on the cheek from their lead singer. Elliott expected and hoped his bride would sing but had no idea what awaited him.

"I have a special wedding present for Elliott," Toni said, the newlywed barely able to contain her excitement. She placed the microphone in its stand.

"Uh, oh, she's goin' off script," thought a suspicious Elliott. He wondered if she would reprise *Nobody Wants to Be Alone* or perhaps, given their impending move, *Meet Me In Montana*.

"Now *my* wedding gift is Lil," Toni said to a round of "awwws" and a wave to Lillian. Everyone turned their attention to the infant as Elliott bounced her on one knee and she gnawed on a rattle. Toni smiled brilliantly at her family and continued, "And I can't top that, so I'm not even gonna try."

"You are one lucky bastard," said David as leaned across the table to address his brother-in-law. He made a silly face at Lillian and she giggled with the rattle still in her mouth.

"Swear jar," interjected Lanie with a pointed finger.

"As you probably all expect, it's a song," Toni began. She explained ardently with every eye in the club upon her, "It's a song that means a lot to him, but, as I practiced it, day after day, it came to mean a lot to me, too. When Elliott and I were apart, and I thought I couldn't have him back, this song kept me going. I'd start playing it, and think about what it meant to him, and it was like we were sharing it, even though we weren't together. And that comforted me. But I think what's most important is it gives me a connection to a very special person in his life who, unfortunately, I'll never get to meet."

Delighting the audience with the way she slung her guitar over her shoulder while wearing a wedding dress, Toni sat down on a stool Eddie positioned behind her. When she lifted her leg to set her foot on one of its crossbars, she revealed her cowboy boots and the wedding guests cheered and applauded like a standard Johnny Dubs crowd. Toni's eyes sparkled and she laughed. Her mood then became serious and she took Elliott in her gaze.

"This is for you, Mr. Warden," Toni stated adoringly. She winked at her husband and said, "Love, Mrs. Warden."

"Dave, lucky ain't the half of it," said Elliott finally. He helped Lillian blow a kiss to Toni.

Toni suddenly plucked the guitar and launched into *The Gambler* by Kenny Rogers. Her dulcet tones gave a special nuance to the first verse and the audience approvingly applauded. The cacophony soon faded as everyone absorbed Toni's performance. Emma battled tears.

"Damn, she's good," thought Emma, her compliment referring to more than just Toni's musical talents. She looked to Elliott and discovered that, while everyone else watched Toni, he gazed at the portrait of his father. A few tears bested Emma and she sighed to herself, "I think he's figured it out, Daddy."

Elliott finally understood John Warden's love for his family and how it spurred his stern and sometimes forceful efforts to motivate his son. With a final glance, Elliott left the past behind and indulged in the present by kissing his child on the head and bouncing her in time with the tune. Lillian cackled with delight as Lanie and Tessa danced for her.

Turning his attention to Toni, Elliott joined the crowd in its enjoyment of Morning Cloak's performance. She focused on him when she sang the lyric about the good fortune of dying in one's sleep. A wave of emotion washed over Elliott and he exhaled deeply to center himself.

Toni hit the second chorus and, intending to raise her husband's spirits, dropped her foot onto the stage and began tapping it. The crowd responded by clapping in rhythm with the song and some even joined in singing it. The abrupt end of *The Gambler* brought the wedding guests to their feet but Elliott remained sitting and watched his wife take her bows and gesture towards her bandmates.

"Montana, here we come," Elliott said aloud though no one heard it.

• • • •

ELLIOTT AND TONI ESCORTED Rose and Tom to their Lincoln Continental. Toni carried her soon-to-be adopted daughter in her arms. The little one was alert yet calm.

"Thanks for packing it in early for us," Elliott lauded his in-laws.

"And giving us a little bit of a honeymoon," added Toni appreciatively. True to her word, she was content with their short getaway to Mackinaw Island.

"This little sweetheart is welcome at our house any time," said Tom as he tickled Lillian. She squealed happily and reached for Rose.

"Somebody wants grandma," said Rose proudly while accepting the child into her arms. Resting the child on her hip, she asked, "We have big plans while mommy and daddy are gone, don't we?"

Lillian made a waving motion towards Elliott and then a kissing gesture, the baby waiting for her father. He obliged and leaned his cheek towards her lips. His reward was a loving peck from his child.

"You're the only person she does that to," said Toni in a slightly jealous tone.

"And it never gets old," Elliott said. He and Toni doted over their daughter as Rose tucked her into her car seat. After another round of kisses and waves, the couple stepped away from the car.

"She was in such a good mood today," commented Toni as the Lincoln pulled onto Goddard Road and accelerated into the night. Elliott hugged his wife from behind and she wallowed in his arms.

"She was just helpin' me rope you in," Elliott replied.

"Oh, stop," said Toni with a giggle.

"Hey, Elliott. Hi, Toni," Donna said as she appeared from a dark area of the parking lot. Her sudden arrival caused Toni to start. Addressing Elliott, she asked, "Got a second for an old flame?"

"C'mon, Donna, really?" Elliott replied as he stepped in front of Toni.

"*Please*, just for a minute," begged Donna. Toni grasped Elliott's arm and he glanced over his shoulder at her.

"It's okay," Toni said with an affirmative nod. Lowering her voice, she whispered into his ear, "Maybe she just needs to say goodbye."

"It's *not* okay," rejoined Elliott in agitation, "and she damn well knows it."

"It is," Toni urged Elliott.

"Fine," conceded Elliott reluctantly, "but whatever you hafta say, you say it in front of both of us."

Donna nodded in agreement. A wary Elliott stepped backward so that he stood next to his bride and glared at Donna. She lowered her eyes to the ground and hesitated.

"Well, let's hear it," demanded Elliott. He wrapped an arm around Toni's shoulders.

"I wanted to tell you," Donna began. A pregnant pause followed before she continued, "I wanted to tell you . . . *I lied*."

"Huh?" asked a confused Elliott.

"When I said it was my idea to hide from you at your parents' funerals," Donna replied. Toni watched her closely but remained patient and still. Donna faltered and whimpered, "I lied."

"So it *was* Em's idea," said Elliott. Unimpressed with the news, Elliott gave Donna a dubious look and stated, "Look, Dee, it doesn't matter anymore. Just forget about it."

Donna shook her head in the negative. Elliott felt his blood boil but restrained his anger for Toni's sake.

"It wasn't," Donna confessed. She felt numb and no tears fell as she said hoarsely, "It was your mom's idea."

"Oh, bullshit," objected Elliott. Donna's intrusion on his wedding day irritated him and his patience waned.

"It was," Donna said. She approached Elliott but his renewed glower froze her in her tracks. Hugging herself as if suffering from a stomachache, Donna explained, "She called me before the funeral. Said that Emma needed me, but you didn't, and that I shouldn't see you while I was in Michigan."

"I don't get it," said Elliott while plagued by a kaleidoscope of emotions. He stuck one hand in his pants pocket and gestured with the other, inquiring, "Why would she do that?"

"Because she knew," Donna answered, the admission stinging her. Her demeanor became grave as she continued, "She knew if I came back, when you were hurting and vulnerable, that you might make a huge mistake. And she knew Toni was waiting for you out there, and that, no matter what everyone else thought about you and I, she was the one for you. I didn't like it, but I did it for your dad's funeral. And, when she died, I decided to honor her wishes again."

Uncertain how Elliott would react to the revelation, Toni grasped his hand tightly. He, to her surprise, became pensive.

"Does Emma know?" asked Elliott. He squeezed Toni's hand and then wriggled from her grasp.

"No," Donna said, "because I wasn't gonna lay that on her with everything she was going through back then, and I just never told her."

"But you're telling me now because?" inquired Elliott. Donna's decision was baffling unless she was trying to reclaim his heart.

"Because it's time for me to move on," Donna said, the declaration shattering Elliott's expectation. She moved closer to him and asserted, "And time for me to let you go, for your sake and mine. And coming clean with all this is part of it."

Donna quickly but, before Elliott or Toni could react, pecked him on the cheek and released him. Placing a finger on his lips, she squelched the words he was about to speak. Donna then turned on a dime and walked to her car.

"You know Em's still gonna try to marry you off, right?" called out Elliott. Donna turned to face him and walked backwards.

"Goodbye, Elliott," Donna said resignedly. There was a freedom in her smile, a freedom that Elliott had never seen before on her face. She turned around again and departed.

"Well, that was bizarre," said Elliott with an unsettled mien.

"I wonder sometimes," Toni said.

"What's that?" asked Elliott.

"Emma thought you were the one for Donna," Toni stated flatly, "for a long time."

"She was right," Elliott replied.

"What?!" Toni exclaimed.

"She was right," repeated Elliott. He grinned weakly and said, "Until the day I met you."

Leaving thoughts of Donna behind, Elliott swept his new wife into his arms. She wallowed in his affection.

"C'mon," Toni said. Disentangling herself from his embrace but keeping hold of his arm, she pulled him towards the club and said, "Let's get back, *my* funny guy."

· · · ·

"OH MY GOD," GASPED Emma in surprise and delight, "*Lillian*."

Three-year old Lillian walked hand-in-hand with Elliott and Toni as they exited the boarding bridge and entered the terminal. She wore an adorable, light blue dress that highlighted her eyes. Though Lillian shared her grandmother's name, there was no doubt as to whose daughter she was.

"Who's that, Lil'?" asked Toni as she squatted beside Lillian. Emma ran at first but then, realizing the child's apprehension, slowed to a fast walk.

"I dunno," replied a shy Lillian with a quick turn of her head. Emma kneeled in front of her.

"Yes, you do," Toni encouraged her. Elliott watched their interactions with amusement as she encouraged their daughter, "Remember, when we looked at the pictures? Remember what you said about her?"

"Aunt Em has priddy eyes," said Lillian as she kept her own eyes glued to Toni. The proud aunt melted.

"Awww," gushed Emma. Elliott shook his head.

"That's right," Toni replied, "Aunt Em has very pretty eyes."

Lillian scrambled into Toni's arms. Toni stood up and lifted the child with her.

"Hey, Big Bro," a bubbly Emma greeted her brother with a strong embrace. He kissed her on the cheek and she griped, "Six months is too long."

"I know," Elliott agreed with a discontented expression and affirmative nods. Emma shifted gears.

"How was the flight?" asked Emma as she and Toni shared a half-hug. Avoiding the swarming travelers, they moved to an out-of-the-way spot. Emma attempted to engage Lillian but she refused to look at her aunt.

"Not bad," Toni answered. She shifted Lillian to her other arm and said, "Little Missy slept for most of it so she's gonna be wired tonight."

"Good, because Lanie and Tessa are *psyched* to see their cousin and they've been drivin' Dave and I crazy for a week," replied Emma with an eyeroll. She leaned against Elliott and said, "They can wear each other out."

"I gotta go potty, Mumma," Lillian said quietly in Toni's ear with her hand held up to shield her words.

"She is so cute!" exclaimed Emma, her volume cowing Lillian. Her gaze flashed to Elliott and she said in a sing-song voice, "She needs a sis-ter."

"Bun's in the oven," replied Elliott as he patted Toni's stomach. Lillian laughed at her father's silliness and gently kicked her feet at his hand.

"*Elliott*," Toni scolded him. She bit her lip to contain her guilty grin.

"Really?" Emma excitedly asked. Toni paused and sighed. She then placed a hand on her stomach.

"Really," Toni confessed. She tilted her head and, slightly embarrassed, added, "Baby Warden, June 17, 1990."

Emma squealed and again hugged her brother. She then took Toni's free hand and squeezed it affectionately.

"You're gonna tell everyone on Thursday, right?" inquired Emma as if the matter were settled.

"Yeah, yeah," answered Elliott, "it'll be a Thanksgiving Day surprise, just for you."

Lillian gazed at her aunt until the gaze was goofily returned and then hid her face. The child laughed.

"Do you want a little brother or *a little sister*?" Emma inquired. She desperately wanted Elliott to have two daughters like she did though she would not admit it.

"A kiddy!" shouted Lillian with her arms in the air.

"She *loves* cats," Toni said adoringly, "and Mommy wants to get her one next year."

"But Daddy doesn't," interjected Elliott. Noticing that Lillian began to squirm, Toni searched for a women's restroom.

"Lil' and I are going to the ladies' room, so if you'll excuse us for a minute," Toni advised when she located one. She set Lillian on the floor.

"Bye-bye!" shouted Lillian with a wave to Emma. The siblings stood shoulder to shoulder and watched Toni depart. Once she and Lillian disappeared into the restroom, they began to stroll towards it.

"*Wow*, Elliott," Emma remarked with raised eyebrows.

"Yeah," said Elliott softly. Recalling the face of his old girlfriend, he sighed, "She's a midget Macayla."

"How's Toni handling that?" Emma asked with a wrinkled nose.

"Like the amazing woman she is," replied Elliott. When they arrived near the restroom entrance, they stopped and waited. Lillian's chattering could be heard from where they stood as Elliott continued, "Never having actually met Macayla probably helps. She's seen the pictures, though, so she knows how obvious it is."

"How are *you* handling it?" Emma queried.

"Thankfully," Elliott said while wrapping an arm around Emma's shoulders, "she only *looks* like her mother."

. . . .

ELLIOTT WELCOMED THE warm, smoky air of North End Bar after stepping out of the chilly, rainy Wednesday weather. Despite the sun's absence and the threatening clouds, it still took his eyes several seconds to adjust to its perpetual darkness.

"Like a bad penny, Warden," Brandy greeted him from across the bar. Allowing herself to beam with adoration, she sauntered to Elliott and embraced him. Brandy released him after a kiss on the cheek and asked, "Where's the country queen and the little princess?"

Elliott stifled a grimace: Brandy often called Nora "princess". He quickly sidestepped the emotion as she pulled out a pack of cigarettes.

"Back at Em's," advised Elliott. Forcing a neutral expression, Elliott explained, "There's no way the nurse is letting either munchkin near a place like this, mostly because of the smoke."

"*Either* munchkin?" Brandy queried while she nonchalantly returned the pack to her front pocket.

"Yep, there's one on the way," answered Elliott with pride. He and Brandy seated themselves at a nearby table and he continued, "It's supposed to be a secret but I don't know why. She's two months along."

"You drinkin'?" Brandy asked. Elliott studied her; in the two years since he last saw her, she aged considerably with developing crow's feet and new wrinkles. Her hair, however, remained black as coal.

"Nah, this is just a quick visit," declined Elliott. He began to speak, paused, and then asked, "You seen Em at all?"

"Whaddaya *you* think?" Brandy responded with an incredulous sneer.

"How's the family?" Elliott inquired. He leaned back in his chair, set his arms on the armrests and folded his hands on his stomach.

"Same shit, different day," Brandy answered. The pair did not speak for over a minute, Elliott examining the frozen-in-time bar and Brandy fidgeting as she craved a cigarette.

"We don't have much to talk about anymore, do we?" said Elliott.

"It's just not as much fun when I can't give you shit and you're not drunk," Brandy said with a shrug. She mimicked Elliott's pose and added, "You're just not a screwup anymore."

"You make it sound like a bad thing," said Elliott with a chortle.

"It's not," Brandy conceded with a disappointed mien, "but you were more interesting as a screwup."

"Yeah, I guess I was," admitted Elliott. He grinned and said, "But I'll take Toni and Lil' and baby over interesting any day."

"I rooted against that chick for a long time," Brandy advised Elliott with a scowl. Unable to maintain the act, she chuckled and said, "Hell, even I get one wrong once in a while."

"I think I'll take that drink," said Elliott as Brandy reacquired her cigarettes. He sat up and declared, "One ain't gonna hurt."

"My thought exactly," Brandy replied. She made no effort to get Elliott's cocktail and instead lit a cigarette.

"The last of old times," thought Elliott.

· · · ·

WHEN THE COMMOTION of Thanksgiving settled down, and Elliott and Emma finished their tradition of washing the dinner dishes, they and their families departed Rose's and Tom's house and returned to the Hastings' abode. Everyone but the siblings retired by eleven o'clock, sister and brother sitting on the couch, drinking beer and talking well into the night.

"Why didn't the mother-in-law tag along again?" Emma asked with a furrowed brow. Elliott held his beer bottle to his lips but paused before drinking.

"Believe it or not, Katherine's got a boyfriend," answered Elliott. He took a long pull of his beer.

"I can't imagine dating at that age," Emma said. She shivered in disgust and uttered, "I can't imagine doing it now."

Emma commenced a winding story about one of Rose's widowed friends dating and the perils of looking for love as a senior citizen. Elliott, lost in thought, let his attention wane until all he heard was her voice as a droning sound.

"Earth to Elliott," Emma called snidely when she noticed his inattention. Elliott blinked and subtly shook his head as he returned to the present.

"Sorry, I was just, eh, never mind," Elliott replied.

"You've been spacing out a lot today," Emma said. When Elliott made no attempt to explain himself, Emma insisted, "Spill it, Warden."

"It's nothin'," countered Elliott.

"I'm waiting," Emma stated in annoyance. Elliott finished his beer as a stall tactic but his sister remained undaunted.

"My life's about as good as it can get right now," began Elliott after a twenty second delay. Setting his empty bottle on the coffee table, he confessed, "But there's just one little piece, one little annoying splinter that I just can't get dig outta my skin."

"Go on," Emma urged. She pulled her legs onto the couch and set her feet flat on the cushion.

"It's Nora," said Elliott with an uneasy expression. Emma's countenance became drawn as he continued, "I mean, don't get me wrong, Toni's my girl and always will be."

"That's good," Emma said curtly, "because you married her and she's carrying your child."

"It's not like that," snapped Elliott. Regaining his composure, he explained with angst, "But, she *was* my fiancée, for a little while anyway, and it's like I just kinda forgot her in all this. It's been crazy since she died. First of all, *she died*, and then Lillian was born, Macayla died, Toni and I got back together, got married, and then moved to *Montana*. Now there's another baby on the way. I don't know. I guess I just feel guilty about it."

Emma hesitated and Elliott could discern his sister was debating whether to make a revelation. He waited with bated breath.

"I might be able to help you there," Emma said.

"Really? How's that?" asked a befuddled Elliott.

"First of all, Nora had a family, and I know they visit her," Emma said. An unimpressed Elliott waited for the second part, his expression prompting her to say, "She also had a boss who was her friend and almost her sister-in-law – and who loved her – and two little girls who did, too . . . although they're not so little anymore."

"What're you sayin', Em?" queried Elliott.

"Keep up, Elliott," Emma scolded him. The harshness of her gaze softened and she said, "Me and the girls, we still go see her a few times a year."

"You're kidding," said Elliott in disbelief.

"Nope," Emma said bluntly. She smiled a muted smile and expounded, "We take a morning, or an afternoon, have breakfast or lunch, and go visit Aunt Nora. The girls like pickin' out pretty flowers for her grave. So, she hasn't been forgotten. Quite the opposite, actually."

"Wow," replied Elliott as his eyes glazed. His mood improved and he said, "That was the last loose end."

"Glad I could help," Emma said. She playfully kicked her brother and added, "I don't get to do that too much anymore."

"Must be a relief," joked Elliott as Emma sipped her beer. She ran her hand through her hair.

"It is, but probably not how you think," Emma said. With her blue-green eyes scintillating, she stated hopefully, "The 90s are coming, Elliott, and I think it's gonna be a great decade for us."

The siblings looked at each other with love, each one smiling softly and appreciating the other's presence. Falling into the silence that permeated the rest of the house, they realized that the wounds of the past had healed and they were happy and whole once again.

THE END

NOVELS BY JOSHUA R. FIELDS

The Millstone Crusade. *". . . but whoever causes one of these little ones who believe in Me to stumble, it would be better for him to have a heavy millstone hung around his neck, and to be drowned in the depth of the sea." The Gospel of Matthew 18:6.*

Shocking abductions of ones they hold dear unite Catholic teenagers Judas Trent and Ursula Baumé and thrust them into the evil world of human trafficking. Mentored by a whiskey-drinking, cigar-smoking priest, the headstrong psychokinetic and the disfigured healer lead their friends against a local sex-slave operation in Southeast Michigan and Northwest Ohio.

Together, Judas and Ursula take the fight to those who would harm and enslave children and score early victories against their enemies. Yet as the dangers of their Millstone Crusade against human trafficking increase and their feelings for one another are continually frustrated, they are forced to consider one simple question.

Can they stay together?

A Dog Among Thorns. Descending on the post-apocalyptic city of Kaiser in a flurry of vulgarity and vitriol, the towheaded demon Miriam hunts the weak in spirit and the unlucky in love. Men mired in turbulent romantic relationships lose more than their faith in God as she manipulates them into taking their own lives. None of Miriam's victims survive her wily ways. Her latest mark, the brooding and sinful Jacob Gottschalk, seems easy prey until she discovers the Holy Spirit wards him from her very touch. Miriam's devious webs fail to ensnare him and she, instead of causing his downfall, becomes his reluctant-yet-loving protector. That impassioned defense, however, raises the ire of the most powerful person in Kaiser: Elizabeth Nicks, Jacob's wife and the city's Constable. The resulting war between the two women threatens to destroy them all as Miriam's penchant for carnage flourishes and Elizabeth confronts the dangers of the demonic world. Hurtling towards their intertwined destinies, the three troubled lovers enter a tempest of gory violence, romantic intrigue, shifting political alliances and the evil schemes of conniving spiritual beings.

Girls Without Gods. Emerging from the fog of her war with Elizabeth for Jacob's heart, a victorious Miriam departs Kaiser with her prize. The demon and her unlikely paramour travel to the fantastical skyscraper of Chinese Peak, an opulent casino that flourishes in the post-apocalyptic world. Miriam's evil nature and savage jealousy, however, clash with Jacob's spiritual growth and reluctance to abandon his marriage. The resultant emotional conflict threatens to tear their fledgling relationship apart at the seams. Elizabeth, meanwhile, remains in Kaiser, the Constable refusing to pursue her husband and his "demon whore." Yet the spiritual world forces her hand when Miriam's former handler, the demon Marcion, possesses her teenage daughter and absconds with her. Desperate to rescue her oldest child, Elizabeth travels to Chinese Peak seeking the aid of Jacob and Miriam in hunting down her child's abductor. Thrust together once again in a sea of unbridled decadence, Jacob, Elizabeth and Miriam encounter a constantly evolving kaleidoscope of nefarious schemes, political intrigues, old lovers, new threats and alluring temptations. The deadly demonic gauntlet through which they tread promises but one simple truth: loss is inevitable.

A Dog Returns To Its Own. Months after banishing his demonic lover, Miriam, to the Abyss, Jacob Gottschalk travels into the frigid Canadian wilderness to rescue the corpses of his possessed stepdaughters and properly lay them to rest. The violent and insatiable Sophie lures him from the narrow way, however, and, blinded by his waning faith, he fails to detect the terrible secret she hides. His fortunes seemingly improve upon his arrival at New Oneida, an esoteric Christian settlement located in a pristine river valley. Its leader, Dr. Irinushka Zhukova, tempts Jacob with many beautiful vessels of spiritual purity and seeks to create in him a wellspring of the Holy

Spirit. Unbeknownst to them all, a greater spiritual storm stains the skies of their future and threatens all those who dwell upon the face of the earth. Facing a terrible new evil and the destruction of everyone he loves, a stoic Jacob holds on desperately to the words of Christ: "But the one who endures to the end, he shall be saved."